Berkley Sensation titles by Joanna Bourne

THE SPYMASTER'S LADY
MY LORD AND SPYMASTER
THE FORBIDDEN ROSE
THE BLACK HAWK
ROGUE SPY
BEAUTY LIKE THE NIGHT

Beauty Like the Night

JOANNA BOURNE

BERKLEY SENSATION
New York

BERKLEY SENSATION
Published by Berkley
An imprint of Penguin Random House LLC
375 Hudson Street, New York, New York 10014

Copyright © 2017 by Joanna Watkins Bourne
Penguin Random House supports copyright. Copyright fuels creativity, encourages
diverse voices, promotes free speech, and creates a vibrant culture. Thank you for buying
an authorized edition of this book and for complying with copyright laws by not
reproducing, scanning, or distributing any part of it in any form without permission.
You are supporting writers and allowing Penguin Random House to continue to
publish books for every reader.

BERKLEY and BERKLEY SENSATION are registered trademarks and the B colophon
is a trademark of Penguin Random House LLC.

ISBN: 9780425260838

First Edition: August 2017

Printed in the United States of America
1   3   5   7   9   10   8   6   4   2

Cover art by Jon Paul
Cover design by Katie Anderson

To Rosemary

Acknowledgments

Beauty Like the Night was written with the generosity of so many kindly folks.

Writing buddies Madeline Iva and Adriana Anders stuck around week after week, being patient with me, helping me over the rough patches in the story and in real life. Margaret Staeben, Courtney Milan, Vicki Parsons, Isobel Carr, Kate Worth, and Ashley McConnell all took time from their own work to read, comment, and be knowledgeable and wise in my direction. I cannot thank them enough. Mary Ann Clark has been endlessly helpful, tactfully pointing out problems great and small. Supereditor Deniz Bevan gave her weekends to my panicked pleas for up-to-the-last-minute copyediting. My sister Rosemary has been a warm constant in my life, always, through this story and so many others.

Thanks y'all.

One

SHE SLID OUT OF SLEEP AND KNEW THERE WAS A man in her room.

He stood between her and the faint square of night sky in the window. Just stood, which was threat enough for all practical purposes. Any man who wheedled his way so silently through a window on the second floor was no amateur in the craft of housebreaking.

This was the way death arrived. Uninvited. Unobtrusive. An almost trivial break in the expected.

Séverine de Cabrillac, orphan of the French Revolution, fashionable lady of the ton, sometime spy, drew herself together under the blankets, preparing to fight for her life. She was very afraid.

He must have heard her move. He came slowly, smoothly, quiet on his feet, toward her. He was a tall column of shadow, lit on one side with red light from the fire, pure darkness on the other. He carried a knife in his right hand, being competent about it. He said, "I'm not going to hurt you."

That's why you're pointing ten inches of steel at me. "What do you want?"

Her pistol was loaded and ready, neatly under her pillow. Even in Buckinghamshire, at the Shield and Staff, the familiar, friendly inn halfway between London and home, she took precautions. But she couldn't get to her gun before he used that knife. It was never about having the best weapon. It was always about being able to lay your hand on it.

"I want the girl," he said. "Keep the amulet. Just give me the girl."

Her mind opened all its cabinets and turned out all its drawers and none of them held anything about lost girls or stolen girls or any sort of girl whatsoever. "There's no one here. Look around." Maybe he'd broken into the wrong room. Maybe she could send him off to menace somebody else.

"You don't have her tied up under the bed, but you know where she is." In complete silence, he took the last step that brought him to her side. His knee touched the coverlet and the mattress made the smallest tremor.

The point of his knife waited quietly, an eloquent eighteen inches from her throat. He said, "I dislike violence. I abhor it. Let's see if we can get through this interview without resorting to force."

Some situations call for great cleverness. Some for lies. She settled on blunt honesty. "I have no idea what you're talking about."

"How forgetful of you," he said softly. "Her name is Pilar. She's a schoolgirl, twelve years old, living in London. Three months ago her mother died in their front parlor. No one's seen the girl since."

He was anonymous in the dark, but she thought she'd know him again, if she survived the night and went hunting for him. There would not be many men who carried such a silent and deliberate presence. Who moved like a cat. His voice sounded like a cat had decided to talk.

He wore his coat—black or some shade close to it—buttoned up to hide his shirt. No cravat. No hat. Dark hair. Skin that showed swarthy rather than pale where firelight lay on him. His eyes held a flicker of reflection.

She would have liked to see his face more clearly. Along

with not wanting to be stabbed, she did not want to be stabbed by a man she hadn't seen.

"I'm sorry for this schoolgirl," she said softly. "It's sad and terrible, but it's nothing to do with—"

"If she's still alive, she's alone and terrified, a prisoner at the mercy of strangers. Do you know how it feels to be trapped and alone in the hands of an enemy?" The knife inscribed a small circle in the air. "This is how it feels."

He was wrong to think she didn't know what it was like to be alone and afraid and trapped. Her earliest memories were exactly that. The Revolution had not spared children.

"London's a sink of crime," she said. "But it's not my crime. Not my brutality. I'm not in the business of killing."

"You gave orders for death in Spain."

Very few people knew what she'd been in Spain. This man was not here by accident. This was no mistaken identity. He knew who and what she was. She said, "That was far away and long ago. That was war."

"This is London, at peace, and you're still playing the same games. But the girl isn't part of it. She's useless to you. Let her go."

She was sadly familiar with threats and the knife and a man who crept through the dark. She'd been part of the Great Game of spies and lies once upon a time when she'd been young and a fool. Now Napoleon was in exile on St. Helena, the battlefields were empty, and the Great Game had not ended. Three years after the last charge at Waterloo, spies still delved for secrets and spun their plots. Only she had changed.

If this man had come for her, knowing who and what she'd been, he was desperate or a fool or very dangerous. Or all three. She said, "I retired a long time ago."

"Innocent as a nestling harpy," he murmured. "All soft down and razor claws."

"I see myself as a battlefield crow. Retired, with a perch and a cup of fruits and nuts in the salon and a covered cage in the schoolroom. Do you mind if I sit up?"

"Not at all. Take this." The shadow of his body rippled. Something glinted. A soft weight landed on the blankets. He stepped back and went still again.

She wriggled out from under the covers and took up the shape he'd tossed in her direction. It was the knife, a fairly heavy example of its kind, the blade cold to the touch. The hilt was bone or wood, smooth and very slightly damp, as if it had recently been washed.

"A knife," she said.

"Right you are. I thought it might reassure you."

She became slightly less terrified and considerably more angry. She gripped the hilt. "Strangely, it doesn't."

Smooth as poured cream, he sank to sit on the bed beside her. His weight tilted the mattress. His body fitted next to her with only the quibble of a sheet and blanket between them. He was a solid presence now, as he'd been a shadow before. He was also empty-handed, which made no sense at all.

No one surrenders an advantage so easily. Therefore, this knife is not an advantage.

She didn't like his thigh close to hers. Didn't like to feel his breath stirring on her face. A stranger in her bed was profoundly disturbing. A man this close to her should be a lover.

She pushed her way out from under the blanket, fitted her back to the bedstead, and brought the knife up between them. *I hate not understanding this.* She was dealing with a man who didn't consider a knife important. Either he thought she wasn't dangerous or he knew he was, himself, incomparably lethal.

A deep game indeed. She said, "You break in here at midnight and give me a knife. Why?"

"To stab me with, of course."

"Always a possibility."

"Or to keep your hands sufficiently busy that they don't go after your pistol. You are exactly the sort of woman who'd keep a gun under her pillow."

She turned the blade and watched a line of light slip along the sharp edge. "I'll take that as a compliment."

"I meant it as one." He shifted to make himself more comfortable on the bed. "Will you kill me or talk to me? That sweet choice has hung in the balance every moment since I entered your room."

"I'm still deciding." Every word they exchanged and many

more they didn't say out loud waited like land mines on the counterpane between them. He was not in the least worried the knife was now pointed toward him.

Those who played spy games were generally more cautious. Perhaps she was dealing with a madman. Not the most reassuring thought. Who wants to share a small bedchamber with a madman?

He said, "Let me change the situation and see what happens. Do not, I beg you, cut this pretty face of mine. I'm fond of it." Slow as smoke rising, he stretched his left hand toward her, past the knife she held, and touched her cheek. A shock— a spot of uneasy fire—sparked where his fingertip met her skin.

"Don't." She brought the knife up and set the point to his wrist, to the best spot for jabbing straight into the pulse.

"One question answered. Many more raised." He withdrew his hand, carefully. "I congratulate you. You're completely convincing as a woman who knows nothing about a stolen girl."

They paused, unevenly armed, both of them thinking hard. Under the silence, she heard the tick and rumble of the fire and the tiny noises of the night outside the window.

His eyes weren't as dark as she'd thought. They were green-brown or gray. She'd need better light to tell. She could see his eyes were attentive on her, cool, utterly self-possessed. He said, "The problem with beautiful spies—one of several problems with spies—is they lie so well there's no way of discerning the truth." He stood in one single, smooth, unexpected moment. The bed sagged and sprang back. "You aren't going to say anything useful tonight, are you? We'll meet again."

He retraced his steps to the window. The darkness parted soundlessly around him.

She wrapped her arms around her knees, knife carefully ready, and didn't follow him across the room. If he left without bloodshed, all to the good. She'd seen enough confused, useless battles in her life. "Why did you come here? Why not stop me on the street and ask the same question?"

"So I could hand you that knife and see if you'd kill me with it."

"And if I'd killed you?"

"Then I'd have my answer, wouldn't I?"

She'd held a number of conversations in the dark. Never one this odd. "You'd be dead."

"Sometimes that's the answer."

This man didn't expect to die. He stood in a fighter's easy stance, one so practiced he made it look casual. If she reached for the gun under her pillow, he'd be on top of her before she could shoot. Or gone out the window.

She supposed it revealed a good deal about her that she wasn't stupid enough or bloodthirsty enough to introduce firearms into the evening. "Why did you touch me?"

He stood in the square of the window, against the diffuse glow of moon and stars. "I apologize. The impulse to know the texture of your skin became irresistible."

He was gone, out the window. It was a fifteen-foot drop but she didn't hear any noise of landing.

She grabbed her pistol. When she got to the window there was no one below and no sound of running. The black was unbroken except by the faint suggestion of outlying buildings.

She'd chosen not to fight. Now she chose not to shoot blind into the night. In most situations she preferred negotiation to putting bullets into people. She had not the least doubt she'd see him again.

She pulled her head in from the window and went to sit cross-legged on the bed, her gun across her lap, the useless and misleading knife beside her, going over every word the man had left behind.

A schoolgirl had disappeared. An amulet of some sort was missing. He'd played that down. Said he didn't need it. Whenever anybody said something was unimportant she assumed exactly the opposite. What else? He'd talked of the war in Spain. Orders given—orders *she'd* given—for someone's death. She hadn't given that sort of order. A mistake on his part.

As she'd been trained to do, she considered what he hadn't said and what he hadn't done. Not a word about Bristol or the assassin O'Grady. No mention of Wellington. No search of her luggage for informative tidbits about the turbulent Irish. You'd think he'd never learned the rudiments of espionage.

In this tangle of puzzlement, that swift, single touch on her cheek was more disturbing than anything else. Why had he done that? She'd worked hard to become the quintessence of dull, well-born spinsterhood. Maybe she hadn't quite succeeded.

After half an hour of pointless speculation she got dressed and went out to the stable to yell MacDonald awake and get the horses saddled. They'd ride out at first light. Some nights are not made for sleeping.

HIS boots hit the cobbles. Raoul Deverney absorbed the impact, folded in on himself, rolled, and ran toward the straggling line of bushes behind the stable. He'd be invisible against the stone wall.

Séverine de Cabrillac appeared in the second-floor window, searching for him in the darkness, the linen of her night shift pale in the firelight behind her. He wondered what she was thinking.

The yard smelled of the horses sleeping in their stalls. No noise from them. The inn dogs were either asleep or taking a cynical view of folks who wandered to and fro among the bedchambers in the deep of night, and remained silent. The stable cats were more wakeful. One came to twine about his boots, purring. He went down on one knee to scratch behind its ears.

After a minute the de Cabrillac woman pulled the curtains closed and went away.

He'd watched her from the day he'd found her name written at the scene of Sanchia's death. More than a week now. The name had meant nothing to him, but he'd recognized her at once, even after so many years. She was as beautiful as he'd remembered. In the same room with her, in her bed, the self-contained force of the woman struck like a hammer blow. It had been impossible to leave her without that one touch.

She'd been a legend in Spain a decade ago—the woman who took many names, who wore many disguises, who was always frighteningly effective. They said she'd given up spying. That she was a private person now, investigating private crimes. It looked as if the British Service still called her back to work.

Maybe the rage and helplessness he'd felt when they hauled him in front of her ten years ago colored his judgment, but he didn't believe she'd "retired long ago." Spies never retire. She was, at heart, the same as she'd always been. He had no trouble believing she could be involved in Sanchia's death.

One question remained. Would she kidnap a child?

Tomorrow, we continue. Tomorrow, another dangerous approach. Another hazardous move forward in this game.

He collected his hat from the tree branch where he'd left it and went over the low wall around the inn, out to the field where he'd left the horse. He knew more about her now, but not what he needed to know. Was she friend or enemy? If the latter, she'd be a formidable opponent.

Two

"SMALLER THAN YOU," SÉVERINE SAID.

"Everybody's smaller than me." Papa ambled along beside her.

"Taller than Hawker."

"Most men are taller than Hawker." She led last night's memories through her mind one by one. Pictured the man standing over her, holding a knife. Mentally measured him against the window frame where he'd paused an instant before he slid away over the sill in a smooth, practiced twist of his body. "He's midway between you and Hawker."

Papa—William Doyle in the spy world, Viscount Markham to the ton—was not her father by blood. That had been the Comte de Cabrillac, dead in the Terror of the Revolution. She barely remembered the horror of his death and her mother's. The months afterward when she and her sister Justine struggled to survive were a nightmare of pain and fear. Then a huge, gentle stranger had said, "She is my daughter," and carried her in his arms out of the gates of Paris. She'd never doubted for a moment that he'd spoken the truth. He was Papa.

"Fat? Thin?" Papa said.

"Thin and his muscles lie down flat to his body. He's not"—she grinned at Papa, who would appreciate the joke—"muscled like a fairground boxer."

"We can't all be great hunks of muscle," Papa said tranquilly. "You say he's thin. Thin and puny? Thin and stretched out long? Thin and nervous?"

"Lean. He does something that stretches his muscles out. He might be a fencer." The open street was a good place to discuss private matters. No one could overhear more than a half-dozen words in a row without making it very obvious they were following. She'd chatted secrets on the boulevards of all the great cities of Europe and felt reasonably safe about it.

She walked along beside Papa, neither of them hurrying on this fine cold morning. The hackney had dropped them at Cheapside, so they had a goodish walk through sleepy back streets to her office near the docks. The cloak she wore kept her warm in the chilly wind. Papa didn't so much ignore the cold as just not notice.

"He had a trained body." She could pick that certainty out of all the impressions crowded into her head. "When he came stalking across the room I could almost see a sabre in his hands. He's studied as a fighter."

"You are not reassuring me, lass."

"I didn't feel reassured, myself, at the time. Thinking back, I am. If he'd wanted to kill me, he could have done it when I was under the blanket."

"Where your admirable fighting skills are irrelevant." Papa hooked a thumb into the pocket of his waistcoat. "You think he knew you could fight?"

"Oh, yes."

"That's not widely scattered information. He knows too much about you, Sévie."

"Seems to. I'll find out how, eventually." They passed Londoners on their way to work, as she was. Papa looked them over as if they were sheep and he was waiting for one of them to bolt out of the flock and do something stupid or dangerous. There was a bit of the vigilant sheepdog about Papa.

Having shared what she could about unexpected midnight

encounters, she went on to what she'd learned in Bristol, being discreet as usual and not naming names.

Eight years ago, in Spain, she'd fallen from a horse, broken her ankle, and been set to watch the Irish of the British Army while that healed. Typical of Military Intelligence that they were just as happy to spy on British subjects as on the enemy.

The Irish had known all about her, which was also typical, since Military Intelligence didn't keep secrets well. For one long, hot, dusty summer she and the Irish had amused themselves fooling one another not at all. They became friends of an odd sort.

Sometimes, even now, the Irish sent her information. A month ago her Eyes and Ears, the old women who collected rumors for her, heard whispers of a plot in London. An Irishman was boasting through the taverns that he'd kill Wellington "right under the long noses of the English nobs." She'd sent out word to old friends here and there, asking for help, and Sean Reilly in Bristol gave her the name O'Grady.

The threat to Wellington made it political and a matter for the British Service.

O'Grady, Sean said, was a back-alley bully from Dublin. A criminal. No friend of Ireland. Not one of them. She could pass his threats along to the British Service with a pound of tea and their compliments.

"Could your visitor be this O'Grady?" Papa scratched at his chin a little, the way he did when he was thinking. He never shaved closely when he was being a colorful London workingman. He'd taught a generation of young male agents the same tricks. All those British Service agents wandered around with a bit of scruffy beard. "You've sent your Eyes and Ears looking for him. He might have heard."

"My Irish say O'Grady's a hulking, red-faced bully. A bruiser and a brawler. Dublin born, with a Dublin accent. Former army. All of that makes him the opposite of the man who paid a call on me at the midnight hour."

"A useful description of O'Grady though."

"I hope so. That's all I brought back from three days back and forth to Bristol."

"More than we had before," Papa said easily.

She hadn't talked to Papa about this at breakfast. It was impossible to get a word in edgewise with the little kids squabbling and Bartholomew—Bart—invalided home from Eton, mostly free of measles now, and edgy with boredom. Besides, she didn't bring work home. Papa had taught her that by example. Hawker, friend from her first days in England, married to her sister Justine, had too. She didn't let the ugliness of her work come near the family.

"That's the meat of it." She kept an eye behind them and around them. No one was tagging along, listening. "Whoever's after Wellington, it's not my Irish and not anyone they know of. I have what we call a negative result."

"Was your man with the knife Irish?"

She shook her head. "He spoke Mayfair English. Educated, upper-crust, London English."

"Born to it? Could there be Irish underneath?"

"You're determined to make him part of the Wellington business, aren't you?"

"Is he?"

She picked apart that drawling, deep voice she could hear so clearly in her head. "Not Irish, if he is. He's French, I think. Or he might be Italian or Spanish. You hear it in his *r*'s. And he moves like a Frenchman." She gave an impatient shrug, using her own Frenchness to indicate all the habits of body and movement that made a man French.

"So we could be dealing with one of the late enemy." Papa took some long slow steps. "All else being equal and considering tonight's business, I'd rather the French weren't involved. Is he a spy, Sévie?"

She thought that over. "He said, '*You're* still playing the same games.' He said, 'You.'"

"And thereby claims he's not in the Game. A retired spy? The woods are thick with retired spies."

"I'm one," she pointed out.

"He seems to know that," Papa said.

"Not precisely a secret. What Military Intelligence knows, the world knows."

Their reflections paced beside them in the shop windows. Nobody was taking an undue interest in them. Good.

Papa dressed as a laborer today in leather trousers and vest, thick brown coat, gray wool socks. He wore his fake scar, as he did when he was working.

She looked small beside Papa in those reflections, a straight-backed woman matching steps with the big brute. There was no real resemblance between them, of course. They were not related by blood, only by iron-strong ties of affection. Papa had stood near the gates of Paris and said she would be his daughter, always and completely, just as if she'd been born his daughter.

To her own eyes she looked thin and grumpy and tired. The stranger in her room had found her interesting. Nothing she saw in the dim images in the shop window explained why that man had casually tossed "beautiful" into the conversation.

She knew what it was like to be beautiful. Gaëtan, her gentle soldier, had called her that with all the passion of first love. She'd felt beautiful when she'd been with him. They'd both been so very young. He was long dead on a battlefield in Spain. It still hurt to remember him.

Robin Carlington—she would be in his house this evening—had lavished extravagant compliments upon her more recently, written witty poems to her arched eyebrows and red lips. With his hand on his heart, on bended knee, he'd called her a stern and lovely goddess. But he'd turned out to be no friend at all and certainly no lover. It spoke well of her common sense that in all the months he'd courted her she'd never believed him for a minute.

She said, "Sometimes there really are coincidences. I'm beginning to think this amulet and missing girl and a man who tosses his spare knife in my lap have nothing to do with Wellington. What if it's just an ordinary crime? London's littered with the murdered, kidnapped, blackmailed, robbed, and just plain knocked over the head."

"True," Papa conceded handsomely. "I like to think we have the most active criminal class in Europe."

"A matter of national pride."

"But there's still a fine selection of spies on offer."

They crossed Cannon Street, busy with delivery wagons and carts. It was not the most fashionable area of London, and the neighborhood deteriorated a bit from here to the Thames. But it suited her clients, who were generally not fashionable themselves.

She took a different path to work every day. Old habits. Old bits of caution that clung to her long after she should have become a mild and respectable investigator. Today she chose to turn down a narrow alley, nameless so far as she knew, and not on any of the maps. "I collected enigmatic remarks and a knife instead of questions about Bristol and Wellington and O'Grady. He's a lackadaisical spy if he is one."

"Not everybody has the concentration and deadliness to shine in this profession."

At the corner of Turnwheel Lane, within sight of the ordinary brick building where she kept offices, a woman with a thousand wrinkles sold hot cross buns. Papa gave thr'pence for a ha'penny bun, as he always did, and they walked on.

She picked away at the bun and went back to the salient point of her midnight encounter. "He didn't try to kill me."

"A model of decorum."

"I think so."

Papa walked with his hands clasped at his back. Eventually he said, "I'm not trying to protect you, Sévie. You don't need that. But my thumbs are pricking."

"I don't have your educated thumbs. But I'm uneasy."

"Deep currents."

Currents indeed. She felt herself being swept along, back into the spying life. Thinking like a spy. Acting like one. When you're good at something and you do it for a while, there's always a string pulling you back in. Probably bakers, retired to Hampstead village, kneaded dough in their sleep the way Muffin the dog yipped and ran while he dreamed.

They stopped across the street from her office. Papa said, "You don't have to go to the Carlingtons' tonight. This isn't your work. I have enough agents."

That was Papa trying to keep her out of the Wellington business. Too late, really.

"You never have enough agents." Before Papa could say more she added, "I can't avoid Robin Carlington forever. I'll look like a fool if I try."

Papa gave her an instant of calm study. Shrewdest eyes in England. "I could encourage Robin Carlington to visit Serbia for a while. Or China. Lots of ships at dock." Papa always knew exactly what to say.

"It's a kindly thought, but not necessary. I'll be aloof and ever so slightly puzzled at the fuss. He should behave himself in his brother's house."

The morning air filled up with comments Papa wasn't making. He only said, "We'll meet at Meeks Street this afternoon to go over plans for tonight. If you see your visitor, take care."

"I always do."

"If I believed that, I'd be a fool."

She didn't kiss Papa as they parted. They were not dressed as two people who would kiss affectionately on the street. They both knew better than to break a disguise.

SHE felt no eyes upon her as she crossed Turnwheel Lane. Forty windows in the buildings up and down the street had a clear line of sight on her, but they felt empty. That didn't convince her she was safe. It made her worry she was losing her old skills.

Ten years ago, when she'd been tired of everyone treating her like a child, she'd run away to war. She'd joined, not Papa's British Service, but the less competent and extensively more problematic Military Intelligence. In markets and city squares of Portugal and Spain, across Pyrenees mountain passes, and through scrublands and ravines, she'd walked with every sense extended, every nerve quivering, knowing she might be in enemy sights. Today she was reminded of those days.

The man who'd come to her bedchamber was somewhere in London, obsessed with amulets and a lost girl and Miss Séverine de Cabrillac. She had the absurd notion she'd know if his eyes were on her.

At the front door to her office building a brass plaque read

Fielding and Sons Imports; *Cyril Malone, Solicitor*; and *Horace Famble*. Famble was a sculptor with a studio and rooms on the first floor back. Finally, at the bottom of the list was *De Cabrillac Consulting*.

She walked past the stairs to the front door and on to the right, to the wide doors that led into the loading yard of Fielding's Imports. She was hit, as always, by the noise penned up in here. Wheelbarrows bumped up and down the ridges of the ramp. Ironclad wagon wheels clanked on cobbles. Men swore and shouted. Only the horses went about their business quietly.

She wove between wagons and horses, keeping her feet out from under hooves and wheels. Warehouse laborers unloaded barrels from the wagons and rolled them up the ramp onto the warehouse floor. They touched caps to her if their hands were free. They were used to Miss de Cabrillac being eccentric and taking the back stairs.

Young Peter was there, being useful among them, rocking barrels down the length of the wagons so men could unload them. He was too scrawny to be of much use otherwise.

It was early enough that the night guard was still on duty on the warehouse floor of Fielding's. That was Holloway, a former soldier with one arm and two sharp eyes. A crack shot. He only needed one arm for that. He gave her a casual salute when he saw her looking his way.

She climbed the bare, businesslike back stairs of the place, picking the currants out of her bun and eating them as she went. The floor above smelled of sweet smoke, ale, and marble dust. In Famble's studio, men were arguing about a boxing match in Essex. Those gentlemen weren't up early in the day. They'd been at it all night. Famble and his friends lived what might be called an irregular life.

Her office was above. She took the whole top floor. Everything up here was a shade more closely dusted, more freshly painted, better lighted, and better swept.

This was where she'd put Peter, here at the landing in the triangle-shaped space under the attic stair in what used to be a storage cupboard. It was warm and dry. The lantern on the hook burned day and night to light the steps. She'd found a straw-stuffed mat and blankets for the boy.

Peter had been sleeping in the alley behind the loading yard, taking any odd job he could find and not quite freezing to death. So she'd put him in this empty space she happened to have, just till the weather warmed up.

Then MacDonald started sharing breakfast with the boy. She'd associated with enough stray dogs and cats to know Peter was now a permanent resident.

She broke off a bite of hot cross bun and ate it, standing in her hall. Behind the first door on the left, MacDonald was frying sausages in his room.

MacDonald was somebody else she hadn't precisely intended to install here. He was an inheritance of sorts. A sixteenth-century MacDonald bride had brought a dozen retainers with her to France. They'd never gone home again. A line of MacDonalds had attended de Cabrillacs through the halls of Versailles and across the battlefields of Europe, guarding de Cabrillacs and falling beside them. The older brother of her particular MacDonald had died beside her father in the courtyard of the Abbaye Prison in Paris. The French Revolution and resulting chaos left this last MacDonald almost without de Cabrillacs to serve. He'd decided on her, rather than her sister, Justine, for some reason. He'd left France, tracked her to London, then across the mountains and pine forests of Spain, and stuck.

He was still with her, a short man, broad in the shoulder, strong as a mule, and weathered to leathery stubbornness. He showed no signs of taking up her offer to buy him a tavern or a stable or an inn in the country. His current great love was an actor at Drury Lane, but he spent his nights with the sculptor downstairs, Horace Famble.

MacDonald was company in her work, a reliable right arm, and an extra set of eyes to watch the trail behind. He brought her meals when she forgot to go out for them and handed her a cloak when it was cold. The night guards liked having another armed man on the business premises after hours, even if they didn't understand just how much of a defense they were getting.

She and MacDonald maintained the fiction that MacDonald was a servant, but they both knew better.

She walked past the door of his room, not being especially quiet about it because that would just make him nervous. On her right was a storage room with the water cistern, wash-basin, and shelves to hold everything under the sun. To the left, facing the street, was the room she'd fitted up as a bed-room. She slept there sometimes when she didn't want to wake up Papa's household, coming in at three in the morning. Sometimes she housed one of her clients there to keep them safe. Sometimes Papa asked her to invite in somebody who needed sanctuary.

Her office was on the right. A light was lit inside and the door was open an inch.

Three

SHE TOSSED THE CURRANT BUN SKITTERING DOWN the hall behind her. Drew her pistol. She set the muzzle against the door panel and pushed.

Chaos.

Her case boxes were emptied out across the floor. Her books grabbed off the shelf, tossed down. File folders dumped, the papers higgledy-piggledy across the rug. Every couch and chair in the room had been slashed open. The stuffing was loose in big fluffy piles.

A man sat cross-legged on the remains of the sofa, a case box open in his lap. He was tall, thin, dark-haired, calm and in command of the situation.

He said, "You keep an untidy office, Miss de Cabrillac." The flick of his fingers took in the overturned chairs, the ransacked bookshelves, the rack and ruin of her files.

Cold reverberated through her flesh. Not fear. She was not in the least afraid of him. This was the old, familiar readiness to fight. She said, "What do you want?"

"To continue our conversation." He glanced around austerely. "This carnage was in place when I walked in. Not my work. I'm neater than this when I rummage about."

If he'd attacked, his purposes would have been more clear. He remained ambiguous. Perhaps on the harmless side of ambiguous. He'd chosen a position that made it impossible for him to leap at her suddenly. She was supposed to feel safe.

She decided to act like a potato in a field, passive and mysterious, and not call for help. Meanwhile they both considered mayhem and performed none. It was reassuring, in its way.

She was more curious than angry, anyway. "Who the devil are you?"

He inclined his head. "Raoul Deverney."

That settled one small question. The trace of accent she'd caught in his voice was French. It came out clearly when he said his name.

The better light of morning revealed a face long and subtly predatory, with a high-bridged nose and slashed, straight brows. His eyes turned out to be a dark green. Malachite green, flecked with brown and amber.

Those eyebrows conveyed his opinion that her display of armament was gauche as well as unnecessary. Since she had no desire to kill him before he revealed his intentions, she put her gun away. She could take it out again if she needed to.

Silently, keeping an eye on all his bland innocence, she went to attend to the profoundly depressing landscape of her office.

At her desk, every drawer had been pulled out and upended on the floor, the contents kicked in every direction. Ink splattered her letters and papers. They'd broken her little blue vase. If she'd been alone she would have kicked the still-standing furniture or torn ruined papers apart or done something else angry and useless. But she wasn't alone.

Maybe she could kick Raoul Deverney. He was handy.

She turned to the windows, sick with anger and sadness and a sense of violation she didn't want to show him. "How did you get in?"

"I walked in the front door, unchallenged, to the accompaniment of horns and fiddles, drumming on the table, and clapping. And a flute. I was gathered into a scene of mild debauchery in the rooms of a man on the first floor. There were expensive liquors, which I drank, and opium of which I did not partake. A woman took her clothes off and danced. The conversation was interesting. I was there till almost dawn and regretted leaving."

"Horace Famble, sculptor. Sometimes his friends show up and hold a party. It enlivens an otherwise dull establishment." MacDonald would have been there, pouring drinks and seeing that Famble didn't get too drunk.

Deverney watched her under deceptively sleepy eyelids. "I came upstairs when the party began to wind down just before dawn and discovered your door unlocked. This"—a sweep of the hand—"was already in place. I almost walked out again to disassociate myself from the destruction, but it wouldn't have done any good. You'd have suspected me anyway."

"I would have, certainly." She stripped off her gloves and laid them in the only clear space on the desk. "In your favor— a fox massacres the chickens in the henhouse and runs. He doesn't settle down among the feathers and wait for the farmer."

"A clever man might think of that," he said. "He might do the opposite of what you expect."

"A clever and devious man."

"Like me." Deverney set aside the case box he was snooping into and went to resurrect the hat rack to an upright position by the door. He crossed to where she stood, held out his hand. "Your cloak."

The eyes of a clever man considered her. Saw every expression that crossed her face.

We're pretending to be civilized, are we? She handed over the cloak—the gun in a pocket on the left side was no secret, after all—and untied her bonnet and gave that to him too.

He propped it on his fingertips and turned it slowly back and forth. "This is a remarkably ugly hat. Do you wear this to hide the fact you're pretty?"

Such an offhand, indirect compliment. Perhaps it was intended to sneak under her defenses. It did not.

Vanity was a weakness well and truly burned out of her. In the years in Spain she'd used her prettiness to flirt with French officers and lure indiscretions from them. She'd teased out battle plans and troop locations and sent them in coded notes to her superiors in the British Military Intelligence. French soldiers, sometimes those same young French officers, had fallen in battle for injudicious words. She'd done her work and been charming and men had died. Gaëtan had died, taking with him all joy in being *pretty*.

She said, "It's just a bonnet. It keeps the rain off. It makes me invisible."

"And you're still pretty."

"You have a handsome face, Monsieur Deverney. Do you enjoy that? Employ it for your own ends? What do you think of men who trade on their looks?"

"I see what you mean," he said dryly.

Their eyes met. A little frisson of mutual assessment buzzed between them. Was it sensual awareness? Anger? Some odd feeling of connection? She wasn't even sure.

She was the one who looked away first. Whatever this tugging between them might be, it was a complication she would not allow.

Stop feeling. Start thinking. This is just another puzzle, even if it's set down in your own office. She circled her desk, letting her fingers run along the edge, till she came to the glass on the floor at her feet. Swirling blue glinted among the crushed green leaves and indigo petals of hothouse iris. Her fragile little Venetian vase, ground to bits under a boot heel.

Deverney said softly, "A favorite of yours?"

"Yes." It had been one tiny connection with her parents of birth, the de Cabrillacs. A lovely object, gone. Small things hurt and one is never prepared. Whoever had done this knew that.

She knelt and retrieved a curve of blown glass that was a piece of the rim. Picked up the thick pontil mark from the bottom. She set the pieces on the corner of her desk. Light from the window shone through it in a line of piercing sapphire blue across the wood. The vase had been made in Renaissance Venice. Its fragility had survived the journey from Italy and the sack of her father's chateau. Justine had found it and carried it across France to England in the middle of the war. She'd filled the vase with red-striped peppermint sweets and given it to her when she was seven. For her birthday. "Do you remember this, Sévie?" she'd said. "It sat on a table in the White Salon when you were a baby."

The men who'd searched her office had allowed themselves an extra minute to spoil a thing she might value.

A thing of value. Uneasiness struck her. She knelt on the floor in the scatter of destruction, bunching her skirts under her knees against edges of glass. Pencils, uncut quills, wiping cloths, ink-spoiled paper, a ruler, and a dozen small tools lay tumbled across the rug.

Her purse of coins and the expensive, accurate compass she'd bought in Paris were missing. Not important. But . . .

She turned everything over, all the rubble of her desk, till she was entirely sure. Her medal of St. Christopher was gone.

Maybe it took their fancy. Maybe they took it because it was silver. Maybe they guessed she cared about it. She hated to think they knew her well enough to know it was dear to her.

Damn them. Damn them, damn them, damn them to hell. She took a deep breath and made herself unclench her fists. Pain and bitterness ached behind her eyes, but she would not cry. *Think what this says about those men, not how much it hurts. Don't give them the satisfaction of hurting you.*

Experienced bastards had searched her office. At least two men. That was obvious from all the little signs. They'd gone clockwise around the room, from the edges to the middle, covering every square foot in turn, the way she'd been taught to search, both by Papa and by Military Intelligence. Somebody had received at least a portion of the solid training she'd had. No ordinary thieves had been in here.

But these hyenas were not the stuff of skilled spies. They were careless, greedy men. There was nothing more unprofessional than stealing during a search. She could eliminate the great spies of Europe. Training or not, these bastards were amateurs.

This wasn't Deverney's work. Deverney would not be stupid.

She kept her face turned downward toward the carpet, hiding her eyes, which, despite good intentions, would not stay entirely dry. "They appear to have stolen the gun from my desk."

It was a Brunon L'Aine, the most accurate pistol of its size ever made. It had been exactly fitted to her hand.

"You have another gun with which to shoot me," Deverney said mildly. "Shall I fetch it?"

"Not now. This one was a gift," she said. From her sister. There was a goat engraved on the handle. *Cabri* for goat. *Cabri* for de Cabrillac. That was Justine's little joke. "You're safe. I haven't killed anyone recently." She called one incident to mind. "Except once. Or twice if you want to be technical about it. Most of the people who hire me got into trouble by applying weaponry to a situation that called for running."

"Yet here I am and you're not running."

"I may yet." She got to her feet. Water and ink beaded in a spray across her desk told the story of a single vicious backhand that had hit the vase, a silver paperweight, and the ink pot. She ran her fingers across the wood. "That's the first thing they did when they got to my desk. They knocked the vase off and stomped it to bits. They did that instead of dumping the flowers out and looking inside. That reflects a certain crude brutality of outlook. You'd be more subtle."

"Unless I chose to be crude to throw you off the scent."

"The ultimate subtlety." She had to admire the way his mind worked. He saw the same things she did. Drew the same conclusions. "Doing this says, 'See what I can do. Be afraid of me.' I don't think you'd make that kind of threat."

"It doesn't seem to work, for one thing."

"You'd drop a sharp knife in my lap."

"I do believe I would."

"Or you'd tear the place apart and wait for me to come in and run to check my secret hiding places."

"A clever touch."

"Or you'd search invisibly. Then you'd leave a fresh quill pen upright in my vase to show you'd been here. Now that's frightening."

"Chilling," he agreed.

She touched the surface of her desk lightly. "This says . . . anger, impatience, arrogance. It may also say desperation. I don't know yet."

"But stupidity rules them all. They wasted time doing this. You wouldn't hide valuables in the seat cushions or your desk drawer. You'd put them in your safe."

He didn't glance at the bookshelf that hid the safe. He didn't avoid looking at it either. He was greatly skilled. She could picture him making his discreet exploration of the wreck of her office while raucous music played below. See him poking and prying, stepping lightly over broken things, finding the safe. She knew three people who could open a Magaud de Charf safe. It was unlikely this man was a fourth, but not impossible.

"If you aren't one of the burglars, you just missed them." Her ink bottle had splattered across the blotter and a half-dozen letters on its way to the rug. She touched along the line where ink lay in streaks and spots. "It's still tacky in the puddles. This was done less than two hours ago." No useful reaction came from him. Voice, eyes, face, and body gave nothing away. She was playing this game with an expert. Under other circumstances she would have enjoyed this.

"He spilled the ink early on," she said. "Then he went through the drawers and read my letters." Crumpled, ink-stained paper littered the rug. "His hands were messy over everything. Then he wiped them on a stack of my notepaper and threw it on the floor."

"Untidy of him."

Deverney had come to stand beside her and look over her shoulder. He didn't resist when she grabbed his wrists and turned his hands palm up and pushed them down on the desk. She said, "No ink."

"Not a speck." He didn't try to break her hold.

"If you'd rifled the desk, there'd be ink on you. Cuffs, sleeves, possibly your vest. The creases of your palms. Fingernails. There are inky fingerprints everywhere."

A slow smile eased across his mouth. "Unless I deliberately set a scene for you to find." He was baiting her.

"The man who climbed through a window and dropped a knife in my lap doesn't lay out crude, overelaborate schemes. This—" She rolled a shoulder to take in the ugliness of the room. "This is a boar pig rooting in the parlor. Grunting threats. Soiling everything. Stealing what he wants. Destroying what he can't use. You're not a pig. You're a fox."

"Fox meets vixen." The twitch of his lips was gone before

she was sure she'd seen it. He contemplated the grip she still
held on his wrists. This was the first time she'd touched him.

She became fiercely aware of every detail of the man. The
dark coat was fine wool, tight-woven, fashionably tailored. His
flesh was full of insistence. His forearm was the most stringent
muscle. His skin, surprisingly warm to the touch. The linen of
his shirt cuffs lay against the back of her fingers, smooth and
soft, expensive, crisply starched.

She'd called him fox for his twisty thinking. Touching him,
she felt the disquieting strength of a wild animal. He did
something regularly that demanded great strength. She wondered what it was. She knew he spent at least some small portion of his time climbing rough stone walls, like the walls of
an inn, hand over hand, sucked close to the stones, his toes
finding crevices. At least sometimes, he was a housebreaker.

He opened his hands in her hold, offering . . . what? A
question? Reassurance? A promise of complex delights? *Follow me*, those hands seem to say, *and I will show you Paradise*.

In that instant, he became unabashedly male to her, a
sexual and sensual being. Because she was no inexperienced
girl, her body reacted before she could stop it. Anger trans-
formed to something else. Her skin prickled. Little thrills
poked into every cranny of her and left her excited and dismayed. She didn't meet his eyes, preferring to pursue her acquaintance with the lines drawn in his palm.

The stubbornness she'd carried with her from childhood
returned in full force. She did not want this. She would not
have it.

She dropped his wrists and took a step away and another,
not caring that it looked like retreat. It *was* a retreat and she
felt no shame in it. He was more than she could deal with.
However curious she was—and he'd managed to hook her
curiosity as few men ever had—she would not be fascinated
by him. She was no child to be lured by mysteries. She wanted
him out of her office. "You might as well leave. Whatever it is
you want—"

"A missing child."

"—look elsewhere."

"But you're the key, Séverine de Cabrillac. I've seen proof.

You're at the center of this, somehow. I don't know why, but it's you. No one else. Help me."

"Those who ask for my help walk up two flights of stairs and knock on the door. Why the devil you'd climb into my bedchamber with a knife and expect—"

"Maybe that's the proper introduction to you, woman of the de Cabrillacs, army spy, investigator, daughter of William Doyle of the British Service. The strange thing is, I might have come here in any case. People keep sending me to you. They say you're a terrier at a rat hole when you investigate. That you see what nobody else sees. That you uncover the truth."

"There's less truth in London than you'd expect."

"They say you can't be bribed or frightened away. You defend a streetwalker one week and the tender daughter of a baron the next, but when you interest yourself, they're as good as saved. Will you take a new case?"

"Not from a man who waylays me in my night shift. You stand in the middle of this serving of malice and speak in riddles. You distrust me. You accuse me of kidnapping that girl. You lie to me."

"I distrust you, yes." He studied her, full of detachment. "I have my reasons, mademoiselle."

"What reasons?"

"I may tell you someday, since you don't seem to remember. And I haven't lied to you. Yet." He'd become sober, the thread of irony gone from his speech. "For your own safety, consider this. If I didn't despoil your office—and I didn't—someone else did. Find the girl and you'll find the authors of this." He gestured.

"I don't respond well to threats."

"It's not my threat."

"You ride on the wings of it. You use it to badger me. That makes it your threat."

"If I walked away this minute, you'd still have to deal with them." His index finger made a circle, taking in the disorder of the office. "They're looking for the amulet and they think you have it. They'll keep coming after you till they get it. After you, after your man and the boy who works for you, after the laborers downstairs, after your family."

Another pause settled down between them, being longer this time and somehow more complex as silences went. An angry pause, in which they considered one another with no great friendliness.

He said, "Besides, you owe me a debt."

"What debt?"

"You might remember if you think about it. You can't have condemned that many men to death."

He lied. She had condemned no one to death.

But her hands were not clean. In those years of war in Spain, the information she'd gathered had changed the outcome of battles. Frenchmen died instead of Englishmen. She'd been responsible. Accountable as a soldier is accountable. She'd learned to live with that. She wasn't the only veteran of the war who had bad dreams.

One nightmare in particular. The far circles of her mind held an old and bitter grief. Gaëtan, dead on the field of battle. Because of her. Because of the inescapable duty she'd chosen. The vivid pictures still overwhelmed her whenever she let her guard down. They'd been right, the women who told her not to go out on the battlefield to find his body.

With the skill of long practice, she closed the door on that part of herself. She was no longer the wild girl who'd loved Gaëtan. Who'd been so foolish. Who could be hurt so deeply. She would never be that girl again.

She drew in a deep breath. Why was she thinking of Gaëtan now? Deverney was nothing like him and Spain was long ago. She said, "Pilar is a Spanish name."

"Her mother was Spanish. If you won't help me, help the girl. She's twelve years old and she's been lost for three months. Find her."

She wouldn't let herself think of what happened to an unprotected girl on the streets of London. "I solve puzzles, Monsieur Deverney. I do not find human needles in the haystack of London. Hire a Bow Street Runner. Go to the newspapers and offer a stupendous reward. Talk to the magistrates. However much I pity that girl, I'm not the instrument you need."

But now she could see Pilar. Inescapably, she could see her—dark-haired, pale from the English climate, halfway between child and woman, with her father's odd green eyes. It was hard to turn her back on someone she could see in her imagination.

Deverney considered her calmly, assessing her reaction and seeing far more than she wanted him to. "Somewhere in London, she's trapped in God knows what pain and terror. She's afraid, wherever she is."

Doing whatever she must to stay alive.

She knew about fear. In Paris, in the Revolution, her sister had done terrible things so the two of them could survive. Everyone thought a three-year-old was too young to remember much. They were wrong.

Sometimes one cannot turn aside. Deverney had brought her to one of those times. She could easily dislike him for that.

"Tell me about this kidnapping of yours." She wasn't committing herself to anything by listening.

"I'll do better than that. I'll show you."

Four

HE MIGHT BE SHARING THE CARRIAGE WITH A MUR-
deress. Considering what she'd been in Spain, that was even
likely. Or he might have recruited an ally beyond price. One
or the other. Weighing the possibilities added a certain pi-
quancy to the journey across town.

Séverine de Cabrillac was inextricably linked to Pilar's
disappearance. Innocent or guilty, she'd involve herself in this
business sooner or later. He might as well keep an eye on her.

He hadn't precisely lied about how he got into her office
early this morning. He just hadn't mentioned it was his second
visit. Seven days ago he'd come over the roofs and down the
back stairs from the attic. His search of desk and file boxes
had been a work of art, silent, secret, and traceless as the passage of a ghost. Her safe was excellent. It had taken him an
hour to get into it.

He'd found much that was interesting, but no trace of Sanchia
or the amulet or Pilar's whereabouts. However, a letter in her
desk mentioned the Shield and Staff, an inn on the Bristol road,
as the place to forward messages. An unwary groom at her livery
stable revealed the rest. He'd gone to waylay this de Cabrillac.

He'd found a remarkable woman. Jerked from sleep, in her night shift, she'd betrayed no guilty knowledge. Not on her face, not in her voice, not by her words. Not in the naked courage she'd showed, facing him. He'd been impressed by her. He was pretty sure he'd come closer than he liked to getting killed.

Now, when a sensible woman would be shaking like a leaf in a high wind, she looked at the street going by with a calm, considering expression. She said, "You could just as easily talk to me as not. I'm not bored—the morning's been full of incident—but your secrets annoy me."

"You'll see everything for yourself in a few minutes."

She wore a working costume of practical wool dress and a dark cloak. Also that ugly bonnet. In those clothes a man would be forgiven for seeing her as irredeemably sober and brisk, a well-born meddler on her way to distribute largesse among the deserving poor. But he'd seen her dressed in fashionable printed muslin, shopping in Bond Street with her friends. More telling, he'd seen her in bed, in a bit of thin linen, exquisitely beautiful. Now he couldn't see her any other way.

The hackney rolled at a city pace, patient with the carts and wagons and foot traffic. The pack of street children who trailed them through the streets would find it easy to keep up.

Séverine—she was Séverine in his mind now—took an intelligent interest in the prosperous houses and little shops, the pleasant selection of London's worthy citizens, and that band of grubby followers they'd acquired at her office. That was an escort of sorts, provided by the chief of London's criminals, Lazarus, King Thief. Lazarus was an inquisitive man.

They turned into Gower Street. This was a genteel neighborhood in the West End on the fringes of Mayfair, a pleasant place where women didn't get murdered. Hayward, his man of business in London, had established Sanchia in snug rooms in Kepple Street, a little farther on. There was no allowance Sanchia couldn't squander and her lovers were unreliable about housing her, so he had Hayward pay the lease. There'd always be a roof over her head—hers and her daughter's—no matter how much debt she fell into.

Kepple Street, when they came to it, was dull, worthy, comfortable, and well-behaved. In the end, it hadn't kept her alive.

"Not far now," he said. It was more to have something to say than to give her this information.

Séverine had cinnamon-colored hair. In the right light, and this was the right light, it was full of gold streaks. That, and the fierce, intelligent eyes, made her look like the falcons he and his father used to trap on the cliffs of the Dordogne and carry home to gentle. He remembered carrying the half-tamed birds on his arm when he was small and they were almost too heavy for him to lift. He'd admired them for their beauty and approached them with caution and respect. He'd do the same with Séverine de Cabrillac.

Abrupt, impatient, she said, "If you're hoping to capture my interest with this secrecy—"

"I want you to see things for yourself and make your own judgment."

"Or you expect me to leap back in remorse and terror, confronted by the scene of my evildoing?"

"Perhaps."

She made a sarcastic little bow, sitting in the coach. "I will disappoint you."

She hadn't disappointed him so far. She intrigued him more than he wanted to admit. More than was wise. Only a stupid man let himself be attracted to a dangerous woman.

He undertook a risky game with her. Séverine de Cabrillac had been an agent of Military Intelligence. She was sister to a senior Police Secrète officer in France, foster daughter to one of England's top spies, and lifelong friend to Adrian Hawkhurst, Head of the British Intelligence Service. A selection of dangerous men and women protected her. She was deadly in her own right, as he'd learned in Spain a decade ago.

So far he'd played his hand correctly. He'd come to her office, faced her, and carried her off with him. He'd acquired no knife wounds or bullet holes in the process. He hadn't even been arrested. It was an auspicious beginning.

She ran a finger along the frame of the coach window. Not a nervous gesture, but as if she marked the thoughts going through her head. She said, "You might as well talk to me. I'll have nothing to do with this business unless you're honest."

"You'll find Pilar whether I'm honest or not, now that I've dragged her in front of you."

"That's one of several possibilities." She inspected the finger of her glove and made a little face. "Let's use this time for something besides staring into space. Tell me the things everyone knows. I'm useless to you if I know nothing at all."

"I'll tell you what was in the papers. Three months ago, Sanchia Deverney, my wife, was found dead in her front parlor. Dead without a mark on her. Pilar Deverney, aged twelve, was missing. No one's seen her since."

She thought that over for a while. "The amulet? The one you want, or don't want. Tell me about that."

"You can uncover that for yourself."

"I don't like mysteries."

"Then you've chosen the wrong profession, haven't you?"

One reason to say so little was to let Séverine de Cabrillac enter the *appartement* with an open mind. Another was to catch her revealing knowledge she shouldn't have. Yet another was because a hackney coachman and Séverine's short, ugly, well-muscled bodyguard sat on the driver's box, overhearing every word. Her errand boy, who clung to the top of the hackney like a monkey, was getting an earful too.

This part of Kepple Street was a line of houses and shops he recognized. Last week he'd methodically crisscrossed the neighborhood of Sanchia's house, street by street, asking questions. So many people and not one of them had seen a thing. In the end, he'd just walked, looking into the face of every young woman, though he would have passed Pilar without knowing her. He'd never met her and never wanted to.

The carriage slowed and stopped. Séverine hooked her fingers into the bow on that appalling bonnet and tightened it down. No chance she was going to lose that in the wind. Before he could open the door she'd tipped up the latch herself and pushed it open. Her errand boy clambered down to the pavement and unfolded the step. They had arrived.

If she recognized the house, if she'd done murder in the front room behind those lacy curtains, she gave no sign of it. But then, being what she was, she wouldn't make such a basic mistake. In Spain, she'd sent him off to die without a backward glance.

Five

SANCHIA'S FLAT WAS IN A HOUSE IDENTICAL TO THE ones on either side. The same red brick, the same four steps in front, this same drainpipe running down the right side of the building, the same tall windows. This door was on the left-hand side, with a fanlight above.

The ground-floor windows up and down this respectable street were unbarred and open to the day. Where Sanchia had lived, the curtains were pulled tight across the dark space inside.

Séverine stepped down to the pavement. She wore a curiously blank expression. She was . . . He sought for the right word. She was detached. Seeing and listening only, not coming to any conclusions, setting expectation and emotion aside. Where had she learned to do that?

The pack of street rats who'd followed the hackney claimed a stretch of pavement on the other side of the street and began a game with dice, throwing them against the steps of some honest householder.

Séverine ignored them. Without comment, she followed him up the steps, waited while he unlocked the front door, and went before him into the hallway. It smelled of fresh wax and breakfast recently cooked. Faint, intermittent noise from above said there were people upstairs.

He said, "The front appartement," and went to open it with the second key on the ring.

Séverine's errand boy, head down, tapped up the stairs after them and caught the street door before it closed. He held it open and followed, not leaving a dubious Raoul Deverney alone with Mademoiselle de Cabrillac. Her mastiff of a hired man paid off the driver, frowned at Lazarus's rats, and loped after his mistress. He wedged the street door open with a flat bit of wood he took from his pocket and leaned against the wall outside, arms folded. The way he took his place without orders, with assurance and authority, said ex-army. Said old colleague. This was not a servant.

There was a certain irony in the suspicion emanating from the boy and the bodyguard. Séverine de Cabrillac was utterly safe with him till she found Pilar or proved herself to be a villain.

He pushed back the door to Sanchia's appartement and held it open, patient while Séverine stopped in the doorway and took her first impression of the opulence and clutter.

They'd begin in the parlor, though some of what he wanted her to see was in the back. She'd believe that evidence better if she uncovered it herself.

He tried to see the room through her eyes. Brocade sofa, French bibelots, spindly chairs, ornate little tables. "Expensive things," she murmured. "Well-chosen, feminine, rare. This doesn't match the neighborhood. Always interesting when things don't match." She stepped across the threshold. "How did she pay for this?"

"She had an allowance from me, administered through my man of business, Thomas Hayward in Clement Lane. An allowance for her and the girl. And men gave her money."

Séverine untied her bonnet and dropped it on the table near the door. She laid her cloak, folded once, over the back of a chair. She continued to assess the room as she removed her gloves. "Generous men."

"She is—she was—generous in return." He'd had only one

brief encounter with her. Even now, many years later, he remembered Sanchia's skill in bed.

"This room's been searched."

Why did she say that? "Not by me or my agent. Not by the magistrate's men."

"Then maybe by whoever killed Sanchia." Séverine was already at work. Without touching, she minutely inspected the surface of a table. The frown between her eyes meant she'd found something interesting. She went to the next piece of furniture.

The messenger boy closed the door quietly behind him. Making no pretense of formality, he slid his back down the wall beside the doorframe, sat on the floor, and pulled his thin legs up to his chest. His shabby, overlarge coat tented around his knees. The big-brimmed hat, which he didn't bother to remove, swallowed his face in its shade. What could be seen of him looked sourly judgmental.

Séverine made her way around the room, utterly focused, unself-conscious, a magnifying glass in her hand, looking at everything but touching nothing. He and the boy, in their separate places with their separate attitudes, settled in to wait.

It took a while, all of it in silence. At last she stood from examining the bottom of the escritoire. "It's two men, working together, both right-handed."

"Is it?" He didn't hide his skepticism.

"You can see it here." She almost, but not quite, touched the shelf of the bookcase. "The books were taken out a handful at a time and slid back in place. They're pushed in, angling right to left. Right-handed. On this table"—she passed a gesture across it—"the magazines were laid back fanned left to right. Right-handed."

Formidable work, if she read that from lines in the dust. Or she might have been here when Sanchia died. Always that possibility. "Why two men?"

"They deal with the world differently. All the lamps were picked up and put back, which means they were looking for some piece of paper. See the marks in the dust." She touched the closest lamp, large, with a round, pink-flowered base. "On this side of the room, every lamp and candlestick was put back exactly in place. On that side, they're all off-center, one way or the other. Sometimes an inch off. Different men."

He'd spent three days searching these rooms and he hadn't seen any of that. The rumors were true. He confronted a remarkable mind in this woman. This was good news if she took on the task of finding Sanchia's child for him. Bad, if she was his enemy.

She began another slow, clockwise circuit of the room, this time delving deep, opening drawers, shifting the fussy decorations. From time to time she used the magnifying glass. Intense concentration closed seamlessly around her. He was now a mere distraction. He might have become invisible.

What was she thinking? What did she see that he didn't see? "Are these the same men who sacked your office?"

"I was wondering that. It's right-handed men in both places, one of them tall enough to reach the top shelf. You're involved here and in my office so I'm drawing all sorts of conclusions." She shifted her eyes to him. He could almost feel her picking clues and guesses off his face, however still he held it. "One of the men is your height."

"Or the height of any man or any woman, standing on a chair."

"Or that," she agreed. "I'm glad we're having this frank little chat." She unfolded the clever rosewood game table and studied it dispassionately. "I find myself wondering what do you do, Monsieur Deverney, when you're not sneaking into women's bedchambers."

"I grow the grape and make wine. Some of it I sell in England." The usual words came smoothly.

"You're a vintner? A trimmer of vines and a crusher of grapes?"

"I make very fine wine." It was amusing she doubted a story that was more or less true. "I have a few bottles in my hotel room. I'll send some to your office."

"Thank you, no. I will content myself with imagining you tromping about your fields, wearing a long blue smock and clogs, pruning your grapes."

She wasn't so very wrong. Deverneys had made wine as far back as there were records of the land. He walked the fields and knew his workers, as Deverneys always had. Every year since his return from the war he'd managed to be at the chateau for the vendage.

The Pinot Meunier grapes on the cool, west-facing slopes of the vineyard at Verney-le-Grand produced a full-flavored wine of intense bouquet. He could sell it for any price he liked, even in a poor year. A glass of it filled the senses. Two glasses and you were overwhelmed, drunk by the complexity.

When he was a boy, the families who'd cared for the vines time out of mind had taught him to respect the grape. "We care for them," they said. "That is our work. Then we stand back and let the vines do theirs."

It was a lesson with wide applicability. Today he would stand back and let Séverine de Cabrillac work. Séverine took a shallow dish of gaming pieces, pencils, dice, and three decks of cards from the drawer in the gaming table. She tossed dice across the green felt a few times. Rolled one interrogatively between her fingers. She flicked through one deck of cards and then another. It was a delight to watch the glinting intelligence in her face. "Marked cards," she said, "and loaded dice."

"It's a sad, dishonest world." Sanchia hadn't changed at all over the years.

"I wouldn't play cards with that mirror at my back anyway. My twelve-year-old brothers know better."

"It does remove the element of chance."

She ran her fingers inside and outside the empty drawers and knelt to explore the underside of the gaming table. He was gripped again by an awareness of the disciplined elegance of her body. Just lovely. Maybe a man got used to that if he spent a lot of time in her company. He hadn't. "There are men in London," she said, "nearly as smart as my little brothers. I'm surprised your wife didn't get caught. Unless she did."

"Get caught and killed?"

She stood up and dusted her hands. "It's one explanation. Cheating at cards is a dangerous profession." At the writing desk, she ran a finger in the dust. "You emptied this?" The desk lay open. The pigeonholes and drawers were vacant. The papier-mâché basket beside the desk was empty.

"My man of business took papers away the day after her

death. Letters, bills, her account books. I assume he has anything of interest. I can bring those to your office."

"Or I'll visit your Mr. Hayward myself and collect what he's carried off. If I decide to continue with this."

But she was already caught up. He saw that. She could no more step away from this puzzle than she could leave a chess game half finished. Maybe that was why she hadn't attacked him in the bedchamber of the inn on the Bristol road. She'd wanted to know who he was and why he'd come there more than she wanted to stay safe.

She completed the long spiral of her search to the center of the room, stepping carefully over boot marks left by the magistrate's men, the coroner, Hayward, the laborers who'd taken the body away on that rainy afternoon, and the men who'd killed Sanchia. Tracks led back and forth to where Sanchia's death had come to her. Séverine had saved that for last.

"The Watch found Sanchia on the floor. There." He pointed. "Beside the chair."

Séverine stood perfectly still, eyes intent, no expression on her face. The errand boy, who'd been watching him the whole time, tight lipped and frowning, turned resolutely away, not looking at where there'd been a dead woman. New at his job, apparently.

"No blood," Séverine said.

"No blood. There was no mark on her. The coroner called it apoplexy or a weakness of the heart."

"Did he now?" Séverine got down on her hands and knees, undignified and not caring about that, to look closely at the spot. Her lips were tight. Her eyes, angry. They'd finally reached a moment when she was no longer distant and cool. "Why do you think it's murder?"

He took out what he'd been carrying in his pocket, folded into a handkerchief. The piece of silk ribbon was about a foot long, creased and twisted, cut through, with a knot still intact. He handed it down to Séverine, wrapped inside the linen so she wouldn't have to touch it.

"They found this under her body," he said.

She took it from him to lay across the palm of her hand, her fingers delicate and careful. If she felt distaste, she didn't let it show. A strand of her hair, loose from the knot at her neck, slid across her cheek. She took no notice.

"If it was used to tie somebody, most of it was carried away." She frowned through the glass. "No obvious blood. Neatly cut ends. Nothing clinging to it but what might be a single hair." She wrapped the ribbon in the handkerchief again and slipped it into a pocket. "I'll look at it under the microscope in my office with a good light. Do you know, one thing I don't find in this room is any sign of your daughter. No painting of her. No schoolbook. No basket of handwork. Nothing. I would have expected—"

"We'll get along better if you stop calling her that."

"Calling her . . . ?"

"My daughter." He was annoyed every time he heard those words. "It's unlikely I had anything to do with Pilar's conception. When Sanchia finally wrote to tell me of the child, she didn't even pretend it was mine."

"A bastard?"

"Almost certainly. The wonder is Sanchia didn't have half a dozen."

Séverine wiped her hands on her skirt and said nothing. If she could read the history of a three-month-old crime in a smear of dust, she'd see the story of his ancient stupidity even more clearly.

"I was seventeen and drunk." *Very drunk.* "But I still should have known better. I accepted an invitation to Sanchia Gavarre's bed. In my defense, I was not the first man in that bed by any means and certainly not the last. At dawn I was awakened by her brothers, dragged in front of the priest, and offered a choice of castration or marriage. Wisely, I chose marriage."

"You think Pilar is another man's child."

"Who bears my name. My responsibility, but not my daughter."

"I see."

"I thought you would."

"It's not the child's fault," she said after a minute.

"I didn't say it was. She's not the first bastard with the Deverney name in the last six centuries. She'll be provided for. Will you find her for me?"

"I'll think about it." But her eyes said she was committed. "This is enough for today. If I agree to search for the girl, I'll need to come back tomorrow. Give the boy a key to this place."

If Séverine de Cabrillac was party to death and a kidnapping, he'd put her in charge of solving her own crime. If she was innocent, he'd just recruited the most useful woman in London. He'd see which one it turned out to be.

The errand boy accepted a key from him as if it were a small, venomous snake. He was probably another of the world's bastards, one who didn't have anyone responsible for him. Except Séverine. He could do worse.

Six

SÉVERINE DE CABRILLAC APPROACHED THE HEAD-
quarters of Britain's most feared and respected spy organization in a pensive mood.

Number Seven Meeks Street was as familiar to her as Papa's
London town house. She'd come with Maman to visit Papa—
the best spy in the world—in his office when she'd been so
small she'd had to stand on tiptoe to see the top of the table in
the front hall. It was an interesting table because it told her who
was in the house. Papa's battered slouch hat would be there or
Hawker's cane or Pax's gloves that she knew because they had
smudges of colored chalks in the seams.

In those days she'd check that table and skip ahead of Maman into the study or the dining room and find Pax sketching
or Hawker frowning at the report he was writing. She'd climb
into a lap, sure of welcome. Pax taught her to paint in water-
colors and Hawker gave her sips of his glass of gin or let her
play with his knife. Maman had been patient.

Then she'd run to Papa's office to be swung up for bristly
kisses and huge hugs. Papa kept sweets for her in the second

left-hand drawer of his desk, but sometimes they were all gone. The agents were always sneaking in and stealing them.

She'd had free run of the house. She disturbed no one at their work. Even at five years old she'd known how grave and desperate the life of an agent was. How lonely. So she hugged all of them and sat close to even the most grim and short-tempered of the agents, because no one else dared. But she'd come from that house of spies in Paris where women carried their lives lightly in their hands, knowing they had enemies, knowing disaster might come at any moment. No word spoken and no sight seen at Number Seven Meeks Street ever passed her lips.

She was passing Number Eleven now, a house painted and washed and polished within an inch of its life. The stuffy, self-important family that lived there possessed a small dog that stood on something—a sofa perhaps—and looked out the window all day and yipped importantly when anyone passed. The ancestor of this dog had yipped at her when she was five. This one yipped at her today. Things did not change much on Meeks Street.

When she was a child she'd wondered why the British Service set their headquarters in such a dull place. With more experience she realized the dangerous and unusual show up better against a bland background.

The big stone pots at Number Seven offered a collection of discouraged flowers, little purple crocus at this season. She'd never figured out why flowers in these pots never seemed to thrive. She walked up the stairs thinking she'd put her mind to that question one of these days.

Felicity opened the door almost at once and gave a brusque nod that might have been a greeting. She was the latest in the long line of doorkeepers and apprentice spies Sévie had known. Felicity went before her across the parlor of calculated hideousness and unlocked the door on the other side.

"They're upstairs." Felicity jerked her chin in the direction of the staircase and stalked off. Not one of the world's chatterers, Felicity. Papa and the others were meeting in the study upstairs as a delicate courtesy to her. If it had been only Service agents, they would have met in the library on the ground floor. This was Hawker reminding himself and everybody else that Sévie wasn't part of the Service. She was a civilian expert brought in for the day. They'd all pretend it was that straightforward.

She went up, her hand on the banister, another familiar object. Right from the first, she'd slid down this banister whenever the halls were empty and everyone in the house was occupied elsewhere. To this day she didn't know if they'd purposely let her get away with it.

At the top of the stairs she went to the front of the house and opened the door to the shabby, comfortable, familiar informality.

A place had been left for her at the big square table. Papa was drawing lines on the dark wood with a piece of chalk. Everyone else stood or sat to listen and watch, except Hawker, who was pacing the room while he did his listening and watching. Six men and a woman, the agents for this operation.

"I've put you here," Papa greeted her without looking up and tapped his finger on one corner of the floor plan he'd drawn. "First line of defense."

She recognized the floor plan of Carlington House, of course. She'd danced in this ballroom a dozen times over the years, as one danced in all the ballrooms of the ton. She'd been to dinner in the grand dining room four times. Sat in the parlor downstairs with Robin Carlington and laughingly avoided being kissed by him. She hadn't studied Carlington House as a venue for assassination any of those times, unfortunately. A failure of imagination on her part.

She leaned to inspect the map of Carlington House— ballroom, entrance foyer, first-floor parlor at the left side, dining room, the corridors leading in and out. She'd never looked at the whole from a tactical standpoint, but one couldn't help noticing. "There's a door to a staircase. About here. It's almost invisible because it's painted the same color as the walls. It goes down to the kitchen."

Papa took chalk and marked that and the other details she brought up. Hawker stopped to look, then resumed pacing.

"So." She spread her hand over her station, not touching the chalk lines. "I take this corner of the room and the top of the stairs."

"The orchestra's to your right." Pax—meticulous and truly deadly Pax—put his index finger on the spot. "Where you will see Ladislaus, violin in hand. He has the best view in the house."

An inclination of the head from Ladislaus.

"I'm here." Pax made a little circle with his index finger. "On the left. We split this part of the room between us. Everyone coming up the stairs has to pass you or me."

This was her contribution to the operation tonight. Séverine de Cabrillac, French aristocrat, knew every face in the ton. The guests she didn't know by sight she could still identify as genuine or pretender by the way they acted. There were many signs. Her training as a spy met her training as a lady of the haut monde and made her invaluable.

"Stillwater's here." Pax touched a spot halfway down the room. "She'll be somebody's dowdy country cousin. Fletcher's in as one of the hired waiters. MacAllister's in the mews behind the house, being a groom, watching the back."

The door to the study opened. Felicity came in carrying a tray with teapot and cups.

"Felicity," Pax looked up, "is a housemaid, hired for the night from an agency."

"One of you could come help with the tray." But Felicity muttered that without real heat. She was young and she was going on assignment, carrying a gun. She dearly wanted to shoot somebody. She set her tray on the sideboard and began to make tea.

Hawker had circled back to the table. He cupped his hands around the top of the ballroom. "Doyle and I keep Wellington here, at the far end. He's been told what's going on." Hawker worked his lips in and out, playing with possibilities. "This section will have the usual politicians and titles, but there'll also be a dozen old soldiers ready to throw themselves on the sword if they notice somebody trying to kill him. They'll be a damn nuisance, in fact. Is there a line of sight to those windows on the roof?"

That question was for her. She tried to picture it. "Yes."

"I'll send one of the Bow Street men to nail up the door to the roof." Hawker frowned. "O'Grady doesn't sound like a man to be acrobatic sixty feet above the ground, but you never know. It's impossible to keep a public man alive if somebody's determined to kill him."

"We might as well all stay home," Pax murmured.

Quiet amusement from everybody.

"That said," Hawker went on, "I don't want Wellington to die messily while I'm guarding him. Let us see if we can avoid it."

Papa was in charge of strategy for the operation tonight. Hawk would provide sarcastic comments.

This whole time, everybody in the room was thinking about Robin Carlington and wondering how she'd behave when she met him. They worried she'd be hurt or angry. Worried she'd be distracted by him. She wouldn't be.

Papa said, "Give me thoughts, everybody. When does O'Grady pick his moment? Early in the evening or late?"

The agents were in a tight group around the table now.

"Early." Felicity set a cup in front of Hawker. One sugar. No milk. "He won't take the chance Wellington leaves for another party."

Pax nodded. "Hit as soon as the target's in place. Your odds decrease every minute."

"It's inside the ballroom. Not on the curb outside. Not on the steps." MacAllister looked up at her. "Your Irish gave us that. O'Grady's words. 'Under the nose of the lordships.'"

"Many sizable noses," Felicity murmured. That got a grin passed around.

Papa said, "Will he come as guest or servant?"

"Guest," Fletcher said at once. "Somebody who can get close to Wellington. It's easy to forge an invitation."

"Servant," Pax said. "Invisible. They can go anywhere. He'll walk through the kitchen door and up the stairs. The waiters hired for the night don't know each other. A man like O'Grady can't pass as a guest."

From Fletcher, "For fifteen minutes he can. He's nondescript, apparently. Ordinary. I hear that again and again."

Fletcher and Pax argued amiably back and forth. She'd heard these exchanges around the dinner table all her life.

"He has to carry a gun or knife," Pax said. "Guests don't go banging about the ballroom with concealed armament. Servants can cart things around."

Fletcher said, "Doesn't have to be big for a single use and discard. Single-shot gun in a cane. A sword stick. A spring-loaded spike. Bottle of acid. Grenade."

Hawker looked skeptical. "You try sneaking around with a grenade in your pocket."

"It's possible. I've made one this big." Fletcher showed with his hands. "Thirty-second fuse and it'll blow a nice hole in anything you please. Not a grenade, technically, but—"

"Will this man work alone?" Papa asked.

Silence while they all thought about that.

"It's hard enough to smuggle one stranger into the house and close to Wellington." Pax was thinking out loud.

She could contribute. "O'Grady's always worked alone in the past. One of the few things my friends in Bristol know about him."

"Whoever hired O'Grady can hire another man as well. We could have two of them coming at Wellington the same night, not working together." Papa was matter-of-fact as always. He looked like he wanted to be fiddling with his pipe.

"Or more," Hawker said.

"Oh happy day," Papa murmured.

Hawker shrugged. "Two men won't be a problem. Wellington's used to whole armies after him."

Seven

RAOUL DEVERNEY DRESSED FOR WORK. HALF-NAKED, standing in front of the mirror, he took up braided silk rope, fine and thin, fantastically strong, and wrapped it around and around him from chest to waist. A surprising length of rope could fit round a man this way. Enough to assist in escape from an upper window or tie up an inconvenient guard. Useful stuff, rope.

He pulled his shirt over his head, tucked it in. Shrugged into his waistcoat and inspected himself in the mirror. Nothing showed.

He considered slipping a knife into the side of his waistcoat where there was a pocket sewed in for just that purpose. He decided against it. Walking around armed so often led to pointless confrontation. Better to sneak warily through the dark and avoid all chance of violence.

He left the top button of his waistcoat undone, as was the fashion among a certain set of young Whigs these days. The Tories who saw him arrive with the French delegation would note this and waste time speculating about a turn in French policy. Behind the dancing and fancy food, at bottom, this was a political evening.

He tied the simplest possible knot in his cravat. That might also be taken as political comment. In practice, a simple knot would hide completely beneath a turned-up jacket collar. He'd become invisible in the dark. He did some of his best work in the dark.

Robin. What grown man still calls himself by a boy's nickname? Who thinks of himself as "Robin" at thirty-five?

A fashionable English wastrel, obviously.

The lockpicks nestled into their pouches at the back of his trouser waistband. He carried both sets tonight. The large ones for getting through ordinary doors were on his left side. The more delicate picks for making entry to strongboxes were on the right. He slipped an ornate gold-encircled quizzing glass into his waistcoat watch pocket. *How did that man-boy lure a woman like Séverine de Cabrillac into indiscretion? Did he? Is it even true?*

He put on his jacket, twitching the shirtsleeves neat underneath. He wore English tailoring tonight since he intended to blend in among unimaginatively dressed Englishmen. His coat and trousers were sober black. His waistcoat, a gray dark enough to pass for black in poor light. His jacket sleeves were long enough to hide the white flash of his shirt cuffs. At one time, in Paris, during the Revolution, that would have been a declaration of Jacobin leanings. Tonight, it was a wholly practical choice, making it easy to hide in the dark. Soon he'd see Séverine in a ball dress, working for the family spy business. A nice change from the depressing outfit she chose to work in.

She wasn't impossible to follow. Just difficult. William Doyle's servants were impervious to bribery. The old man who swept out the livery stable, on the other hand, would gossip all day for the price of a glass of gin. William Doyle went to the Carlington ball tonight, the old man said. He'd take the big family coach.

That meant Séverine was going too. The British Service, Séverine, *and* the Carlingtons' safe. How could he resist?

Pilar was gone as if she'd vanished in a puff of smoke. The British Service would be good at supplying smoke.

The tools of his trade found their accustomed home in pockets sewed in the inside of his coat. An ivory-handled folding razor. A useful tool. It was a weapon at need, he supposed. He also carried a ball of string, a small file that glittered with diamond dust, a selection of iron hooks, and a handkerchief. That left many pockets empty. With luck, he'd fill them shortly after midnight.

He was looking forward to this robbery at the Carlingtons. He'd had it on his list for a few years. Pleasant to think he'd rob the place when the British were thick underfoot. He liked it when events converged this way.

Would a woman of Séverine de Cabrillac's caliber really be seduced by Carlington's looks? She seems too wise.

We're all fools for beauty.

For one moment in her office this morning she'd looked at him and he'd seen the beginnings of passion . . . before she denied it to herself and wiped it away.

She'd wanted him for that one small moment. Had she looked at Robin Carlington that way?

He selected an emerald signet ring from the box on the dresser and studied himself one last time in the mirror. The overall effect was restrained good taste and deliberate, expensive elegance. Nothing could be further from the Spanish mule driver Séverine de Cabrillac had met ten years ago in a dusty army camp in Spain.

What sort of man would say those things about a de Cabrillac? Who would insult her and her powerful family, bragging that he'd had her?

Eight

LIKE DIRT AND COLD, FALSE NAMES WERE PART OF this new world of being a servant boy. Peter was a good name. It sounded innocent and reliable. Peter the rock upon which I build. Peter with the keys of the kingdom. Peter Piper. Peter run fetch us a pitcher of ale here's-a-shilling-keep-the-change Peter.

A new name for a new life.

It was typical of this new life that it meant standing in the cold, satisfying curiosity in the only way possible, since nobody explained anything to the errand boy.

Carriages pulled up in front of Carlington House and spilled out men and women in beautiful clothes. Every window blazed with light. Upstairs they'd pulled the curtains back to show the ballroom. When the dancing started there'd be a whirl of black evening jackets, scarlet uniforms, and bright, fine dresses. For a few hours ordinary Londoners could watch their betters at play.

Miss Séverine arrived early, smiling pleasantly, pretending to be somebody who'd never dream of walking dangerous streets and being dangerous herself. The man beside her would be her father, William Doyle of the British Service. That was a new face, even after three months with Miss Séverine. He never came to Miss Sévie's offices. MacDonald said he was properly respectful of Miss Sévie's work and didn't intrude. William Doyle blinked out sleepily over the crowd that had gathered on the pavement and took his time getting out of the coach. Miss Séverine stepped down after him, one hand on his shoulder, the other picking up the hem of her cloak so it wouldn't get dirty.

She wore delicate, expensive clothes, like the fine lady she was. The sort of dresses that never came to the office in Turnwheel Lane. Her cloak was black velvet with a lining the same red silk as the dress. Blood-color red. It suited her. Her necklace of rubies glowed in the torchlight when she moved.

Her father offered his arm, being protective, as if she didn't hop up and down from hackneys all day long, spry as a sparrow. They stood on the pavement while Miss shook out her skirt and he straightened the knot in his cravat and they ran eyes over the populace the footmen were keeping back. And they watched the other guests preening themselves in front of an audience, making ready to go inside.

Times like this, those two showed what they were. Look once and you'd see father and daughter, harmless and fashionable. Look more carefully and you could see they were spying for all they were worth.

Miss was here on British Service business. She wouldn't go near the Carlingtons otherwise, not after the way Robin Carlington had talked about her. MacDonald had spent the afternoon muttering about "that limp rag of muck" and saying, "I don't like her going into that lickspittle's house without me." MacDonald had a colorful way of talking. MacDonald didn't like Miss doing work for the British Service at any time and told her so when he was feeling particularly grumpy. The Service, he pointed out, was full of family complications he couldn't even begin to list and why didn't she just hit herself over the head with a shovel if she wanted to be annoyed about something.

Maybe tonight they'd finish this Service business— something to do with Wellington apparently—and Miss would get back to her proper work. The British Service could meddle in French politics and decide the fate of Turkey and China. Miss Sévie could solve London crimes, starting with one woman dying in her parlor in Kepple Street.

Two pretty young ladies walked arm in arm past the admiring crowd and up the steps. Miss Séverine and her father followed, finding something to chat about as they went. They showed an invitation at the door and gave a last glance up and down the street before they went inside.

Neither of them would notice a drab coat and cap out in the dark, sheltering behind this plump grocer and his wife. There were advantages to being small and ordinary.

Inside, musicians began tuning instruments. A long steady note from the violin slid down to the street, clear and bright. The populace quieted, waiting.

Music was one more thing left behind with the old life, along with comfort and a name. There was plenty to do clsewhere tonight, but against the temptation of violins, flutes, and cello, temptation won.

Music began. Haydn. The shop assistants and draper's clerks stayed, shoulder to shoulder with the grocer and his wife. A pair of ragged children looked up with wide eyes and gaping mouths. An old woman rocked back and forth in time with the music. Everyone out on the street listened in silence or spoke only in a whisper. The clamor and clatter came from guests arriving.

A thin, artistic-looking fellow showed up and was admitted. That was one of the Service agents who came in twos and threes to sit in Miss Séverine's office, laugh, and talk about cases. He made sketches and drank red wine and talked in a soft voice. He had the sharpest eyes of them all. He was the only one who made her worried he'd see through her disguise.

They'd opened the windows a little. Laughter and talk spilled out, warm sounds on a night that was damp and chilly for everybody on the street, even packed together the way they were, sharing warmth. Monsieur Deverney arrived, hidden in the middle of a dozen loud, cheerful Frenchmen, at ease among them, just as elegant, equally highborn and expensive. To all appearances, equally French. He entered Carlington

House without challenge, buffered by companions on every side, them showing their invitations and making nothing of Deverney not having one. The footman at the door waved the whole group in together.

So Deverney was following Miss Séverine. That was good. He was a client. He'd keep her attention on Kepple Street.

"He knew where to find her." MacDonald's voice came from behind, inches away. "I'll start asking questions about how he does that." MacDonald had a habit of walking around the office, not making any noise at all. Now he was doing it on the street. It was annoying. He came forward till they were standing side by side. "He's interested in her. A wolf chasing after a fox."

"I suppose."

"I don't like it." MacDonald was wearing a kilt. In this weather. He should have been cold, but he probably wasn't, out of sheer stubbornness. No reason on earth MacDonald should run around London wearing a kilt. It wasn't as if he'd grown up roaming free as a deer in the highland mists. He'd probably never set foot in Scotland. "He wants something."

"He has a dead wife. He might be looking for justice. Who knows?"

The grocer and his wife were giving them sidelong glances. MacDonald noticed too. "This way," he pushed through the onlookers to a place at the curb. He was constructed entirely of gristle and elbows and nobody in their right mind was going to dispute with him over any square yard of pavement.

Then he stood glaring at Carlington House as if it were a stronghold of the enemy. As it was, in a way. After he'd brooded sufficiently he said, "She doesn't want me in there."

"I have no explanation for that."

"None of your lip, boy."

MacDonald had enlivened one of the dinners they shared on the stair to the attic by explaining the superiority of kilt over trousers in blunt anatomical terms. It turned out kilts were also good for concealing weapons, up to and including pistols. MacDonald looked like a man carrying a pistol.

"It's the kilt."

"They'd notice me," MacDonald said loftily, "whatever I wore."

"Sounds likely." Two paces behind Miss Sévie he looked almost natural. On his own, stalking the perimeter of a ballroom, he'd be a little startling, frankly.

"They wouldn't see you," MacDonald went on. Musing. Just musing.

"They would. Then they'd beat me for sneaking in to steal and toss my limp and battered body into the road. I have some experience in this field."

"The Service agents are watching whatever damn operation they're running. None of them is taking care of Miss Séverine." MacDonald's blue eyes had become quietly ruthless. "You're not much but you're better than nothing. If anyone asks, you're carrying a message. Messenger boys go anywhere."

"Maybe they go back home and get some sleep."

"I think not."

MacDonald turned out to be right, as he usually was. "Go," he said, and she did.

She couldn't imagine what she was supposed to do if someone actually did attack Miss Séverine. MacDonald seemed to think she'd rise to the occasion.

Peter the errand boy with no last name, who was also Pilar Deverney, bastard daughter of a murdered woman, fugitive, not the daughter—not any relation—to Raoul Deverney, took himself around to the back of Carlington House and into the kitchen, trying to look as if she were carrying a particularly significant message.

She was just the plaything of Fate, wasn't she? And why the Scots didn't rule all of Europe, she couldn't imagine, if MacDonald was a fair example of the breed.

"I'D rather kick Carlington's arse than shake his hand." Calmly stated, but when Papa said, "kick his arse," he meant breaking bones and knocking out teeth.

Papa was the most even-tempered of men. He made few threats. It warmed her heart, this evidence of fatherly affection.

They strolled across the grand foyer of Carlington House, beautifully dressed men and women of the ton on every side.

Marble tile and the great curved staircase echoed dozens of deep voices from men and the higher laughter of the women. Nobody would overhear Papa and no harm if they did. He sounded like any outraged father whose daughter was the subject of gossip. One had to have specialized knowledge to interpret what he meant.

People looked at him, saw a great placid bull of a man, and assumed he was stupid and slow. They were quite wrong.

Papa said, "I wish you didn't have to talk to that worm. I'm using you because I need you here. This is an apology." He frowned at the innocent marble railing of the staircase as they went up.

She shrugged. *"Il ne vaut que la puce de la puce."* He's less than the flea of a flea. Papa grinned.

Past Papa's bulk she saw harmless fashionables, ambitious young politicians, the old families of the kingdom being arrogant, and the recently rich minding their manners. Hard to believe a professional murderer could be hidden among them.

She said, "If we all avoided our former flirts, the ballrooms of London would be empty."

"Can't have that," Papa muttered, meaning exactly the opposite.

They came to the top of the stairs and the wide door to the ballroom and joined the receiving line.

Sir John Carlington, baron, was noncommittal, as if he didn't quite remember ever meeting her before. Lady Carlington was diamonds and an unpleasant smirk. Their gloved hands met for three seconds.

Sir John turned to become affable to Papa, who controlled six seats in the Commons and would someday vote in the House of Lords. It was time for her to offer her hand to Colonel Carlington. He was Robin's uncle and, like Robin, another spare relative living under the baron's roof. The colonel was a lieutenant colonel, strictly speaking, and even that by the bare skin of his teeth. She didn't remember ever meeting him in Spain. She'd been busy with Military Intelligence, the British Peninsular Army had been huge, and Carlington would have been infinitely unmemorable as a captain and quartermaster.

The colonel chose to be loud and hearty tonight and said

he'd missed seeing her sweet face lately and why didn't Robin bring her to dinner anymore? It would have embarrassed her when she was fifteen and capable of being embarrassed by fools. She extricated herself, took two steps to the left, and faced Robin.

She'd thought Robin would look different after his incomprehensible betrayal. More like a weasel. More shifty-eyed and unwholesome. But he was exactly the same.

He smiled warmly and held his hand out toward her as if nothing had ever happened between them.

Without expression she ignored his outstretched hand and made the smallest possible inclination of her head, exactly in the manner of an heiress possessing the bluest blood of France being approached by an encroaching mushroom of an Englishman. It was a complex and restrained slight enacted before many eyes that would recognize and appreciate it. Maman would have been proud of her.

She went immediately to the next Carlington in line. This was an elderly cousin, wearing a steel-gray gown and tight steel-gray curls, who did not approve of her. Two more minor Carlington relatives and she was free.

She didn't look back to see how Papa dealt with Robin, but she heard no shriek of agony and no breaking of small bones. Papa played a long game.

The gold-and-green ballroom opened before her. She set her shoulders straight, held her head high, took her pretty sandalwood-and-blond lace fan into a loose hold, and went to do her work. She would not concern herself with Robin Carlington and his coterie. The Carlingtons, root and branch, could be ignored.

She wandered across the room, pretending not to notice the people who caught her eye and beckoned. Friends mostly, but some were simply gossips she would not encourage.

At first glance, this was not a promising setting for assassination. The ballroom was as well lighted as any stage. Lamps glowed along the sides of the room. In the chandeliers, every candle was lit. A few alcoves were half concealed behind draped, pulled-back yellow brocade curtains, but no one in his right mind would lurk there. The marble pillars were narrow and the Carlingtons had refrained from dealing out a forest of potted greenery, convenient for launching an ambush.

O'Grady could hide in the crowd, one sheep among many. These harmless people were his defense, his camouflage, and his hostages. Part of her job tonight was protecting them.

The orchestra plucked strings and piped flutes in an experimental way. Ladislaus held a long note on his violin. An expectant pause from the musicians. They began a Haydn quartet, layering the music underneath conversations so the voices wouldn't fall into silence, but making it clear nobody was supposed to dance just yet.

For herself, she chose a spot to the side with a column behind her. She could keep an eye on the top of the stairs, the receiving line, and the faces of new guests as they arrived.

Papa finished his first sweep through the ballroom and came to join her.

"There's one clear shot from the balcony to the far end of the room," she told him, though he'd have seen that for himself.

"Felicity went up earlier and nailed the door shut."

"One less thing to worry about. But then he's in the crosshairs again when he walks along there." She slid one finger in the air, left to right. "From there to there."

"Hawk's bringing the man around the side, past the library."

Neither of them said Wellington's name. Harmless comments got lost in the general mutter. The one word you wanted to keep close fell into a lull in the noise and rolled out like trumpets and bells.

Guests entered in threes and fours, a flock of brilliant dresses and skillfully cut jackets. All of them easy faces for her to collect. In the ballroom, men crossed the floor to seek out partners, knowing the opening dance would begin soon. Comfortable little groups staked out the few chairs and settled in to talk.

That was another way she'd spot O'Grady. An outsider, he'd neither dance nor attach himself to any of those groups.

While she held this post of observation, she was, in her turn, meticulously watched. The ton rather hoped Robin would wander by and enact an interesting scene. Their boredom wanted tears and accusations, or at least raised voices and sarcasm. She was encircled by a languid spite waiting to feed. Even her friends wondered what she was thinking.

Eventually Papa would go away and she'd be on her own. If she had to stop O'Grady, violently, in front of so many eyes, she'd become notorious, not merely eccentric.

There are easier, less complicated battlefields than the ballrooms of the ton. Still, she'd weathered scandal before. She could do it again.

She silenced the clamor in her head. Pax had taught her to do that when he'd taught her precision with a rifle. She'd learned the lesson in full at Somosierra, in the mountains, waiting for the French, the butt of her rifle to her cheek.

Defensible terrain came in many forms. She estimated distances up and down the room and said, "Twenty feet."

What would have been obscure to most people, Papa understood at once. "Even with a pistol, he has to get closer than that. There'll be people going back and forth."

"Draw a line between the second columns. It'll happen inside that box. He takes his shot and scuttles out that far door, past the library, down the stairs."

"Where MacAllister catches him at the outside door."

"He goes through the card room and jumps out a window. Or the library window."

"Those Bow Street Runners."

"Always a problem. He shouldn't stage this here at all." She frowned and slapped her fan across her palm. "This house is complicated and unpredictable. People milling around. Footmen, maids, grooms, illicit lovers in the corners, men in the alley pissing against a wall. Bad escape routes. This is a stupid place to kill somebody. If it were me, I'd wait on the street and shoot him in his carriage. Anybody can be in a crowd. I have my errand boy and MacDonald outside right now."

"I'm glad the man doesn't have you to advise him," Papa said.

"I'd poison the lobster patties, if I were truly evil. It'd kill off a dozen guests, of course, which is excessive. And a dog." The Countess of Maybrey had brought an armful of fluffy yapmonger with her and was carrying it around, feeding it fancy tidbits from the platters.

"The old soldier's not going to eat or drink anything." Papa felt around inside his jacket, searching for the pipe he wasn't carrying, remembered where he was, and sighed. "I told him he might be in somebody's sights tonight. He wasn't impressed. Who's the brown-haired man, plump, about thirty, next to Faversham?"

She glanced that way, moving only her eyes. "That's one of the Norfolk Fortneys. Works at the Royal Observatory in Greenwich. Knowledgeable about the position of planets, if you ever want to know."

"I'll remember that, if the occasion arises."

At a moment when she should be wholly concerned with Wellington and bullets, other annoyances and worries bobbed to the surface of her mind, like bubbles in a boiling pot. "As long as we've got a minute, let me tell you what happened in my office early this morning. I didn't want to bring it up in front of everybody, but I've had a succession of visitors lately. My office was . . . rearranged. I'm annoyed."

"That was somebody's mistake," Papa said. "Tell me about it."

WITH the skill of long practice, Raoul Deverney made himself inconspicuous among the fashionable. He'd come to the ballroom not up the grand staircase and through the receiving line, but by ambiguous side paths, along the servants' corridors. Now he stood in the mouth of a hall leading to the ballroom, a plump attaché from the French delegation between himself and Séverine.

She hadn't noticed him yet. Her attention was elsewhere. Without being obvious about it she looked into every face that came upstairs into the ballroom. Even from this distance, he saw her as a sentry on guard, back straight, her whole being intent and vigilant.

Séverine's father lingered at her side, pretending to exchange pleasantries, looking harmless. Maybe he was giving last-minute orders. Maybe he was protecting her from the chitter-chatter infesting the room.

She wore a gown of deep ruby color that stood out even in the brilliance around her. Ten generations of de Cabrillac pride faced the slander of venomous tongues and did not hide. No slinking in corners for Séverine. Let the world chatter and be damned to them. She was magnificent.

The rubies at her throat were another declaration, one that spoke of her impressive fortune. That was power proclaimed insouciantly with very old, very famous rubies. She was well armored with every weapon the ton respected. She'd be armed in more brutal, straightforward ways as well.

Rumor in the small elite world in which he traveled said Séverine de Cabrillac held herself aloof from the British Service. But she was working for them now. Three Service agents he knew by sight were in the ballroom. There'd be others he didn't know. Something important was going on. Plots crossed and crisscrossed this room tonight. Everybody waited for something—the guests, the British Service, William Doyle, the small tribe of Carlingtons, Robin Carlington, and a cool-eyed Séverine de Cabrillac.

He should leave. The British Service, studded through the crowd, was a complication to burglary. Their business for the evening seemed unrelated to Sanchia's death. Nothing to do with Pilar. And yet . . .

He'd survived the last decade, lived and flourished and pursued his particular avocation, because he turned a cynical eye on life. Other men might fool themselves about who they were and what they wanted. He never did. Séverine glowed like a fire on the other side of the room and he couldn't look away. The sight of her, armored in her fine clothes and impressive calm, captured him utterly.

Ten years ago, he'd met her face-to-face in an army camp in Spain. He hadn't known her name. For a minute she'd held the Deverney Amulet in her hand, in the dark and shouting, in the confusion of his arrest. She'd casually passed it to one of the soldiers to give to the authorities, along with the other jewels he'd carried. He'd been dragged off to an appointment with the hangman. She'd ridden away, not looking back, obviously already thinking of other things.

Years later she was involved with the amulet again, with Sanchia's murder, and with Pilar's disappearance. One single clue, left in Pilar's bedroom, linked everything. But instead of studying her to see what villainy she might reveal, he ran his eyes around the room, looking for threats to her. That dangerous father of hers was doing the same, so unobtrusively. Tonight he made common cause with his natural enemy, William Doyle. Life was an infinite jest.

Something was going to happen here tonight. He tasted it in the air. Felt it in the blood. Instead of turning his back and walking out like a prudent man, he was foolishly, idiotically picking a good spot to wait, prepared to protect Séverine if the need arose.

He examined his feelings carefully and didn't like what he saw inside himself.

Nine

SÉVIE SAW THE REACTION TO WELLINGTON'S AR-
rival before she spotted the man himself. A stir spread through
the whole room. He was Carlington's great catch of the
Season, a true hero, a public man of genuine stature. The war
had been over for three years, but Wellington hadn't shrunk to
one more general, one more duke, one more important man in
a room glittering with power.

He was about to be appointed to the King's Cabinet as
Master-General of Ordnance. An ordinary-sounding title, but
basically it meant he'd run the army. He'd be formidable in
that position. She'd seen him chase Napoleon's Grande Armée
out of Spain, all brilliant strategy and tightly directed energy.
The British Army had best prepare. A new broom had arrived
to set right old mistakes and put order in place. He'd end up
Prime Minister if the Tories stayed in power.

"That's a fine figure of a man." Lucy looked Wellington
over. The military genius and steel-hard integrity were lost on
Lucy, but she did appreciate fine tailoring and a healthy body.

"Old for you," was the best answer to that. "And married."

"I want to paint him, not go to bed with him."

Lucinda Preston, sandy-haired and freckled, whippet thin, devastatingly frank, was an artist, which was why she thought that way. She was the daughter of a duke and said anything she wanted to. A loyal friend. Witness her here tonight, sticking like glue when Séverine was an object of spiteful gossip in some corners of the room.

Lucy said, "He has interesting bone structure."

"Look at a man and see a skeleton. Who would be an artist?"

Lucy grinned and called a waiter over to exchange an empty glass for a full one.

The elite who ruled England danced, flirted, and got drunk. Respectable, solid men collected in small groups under the colonnades to discuss horses, the health of the pheasant population, and, as an afterthought, the politics of empire. There was more than a scattering of men she knew from Spain, ensigns and lieutenants who'd been in the field tents while she delivered intelligence to their captain. Boys not much older than she'd been, who rode with her sometimes from camp to listen to what she had to say about the countryside they were about to march their men through. Solid army men, all grown up now.

As far as she could tell, nobody skulked about the perimeter of the ballroom, bent on assassination. But the night was young.

She'd expected an uncomfortable and lonely vigil waiting for O'Grady. Instead, a succession of socially powerful protectors came to hover over her and smile upon her and shape public opinion in her favor—a dowager countess, a general in the army, diplomats, grandes dames of the ton. Maman's friends and Papa's. Her own. People she'd helped with little problems, one time or another. You'd think they were taking turns so she'd never be left alone, naked to the spite of Robin's clique.

Friendship was unaccountable. She hadn't expected this.

Robin, freed from the receiving line, went about the room being charming. Sometimes he stared piercingly in her direction and looked worried. That shouldn't have been a distraction, but it was.

"We were saying—Gretchen and Emily and I—that we

should lure the Carlington pimple into the park and drown him in the Serpentine. Between us we have enough quarterings on the escutcheon to get away with it in plain daylight."

"I'm touched."

Gretchen, Gräfin von Gutzkow, danced, rather daringly, with her husband. Emily flirted like mad with an indolent dandy, both of them enjoying the game. And Hildebrand Garth, "Brandy," one of Robin's cronies, headed purposefully toward her.

She'd been waiting for a direct approach from Robin's set. They'd sent Brandy to deliver it. She preferred this, frankly, to slippery whispers in corners.

He brayed, "Evening, Sévie sweet. Evening, Lady Lucinda." When enough heads had turned in their direction, he added loudly, "Lovely dress, Sévie. Quite the scarlet woman, aren't you?"

Maman had taught her how to deal with presumption before she was seven. A de Cabrillac, one who had been a spy for years, who bore the marks of torture by Spanish *guerrilleros* and the scar of a French bullet, is not put out of countenance by a jumped-up fop strutting about in a ballroom.

She turned her back on him without reply. Beside her, Lucy said coolly, "We have not been introduced," and did the same. A duke's daughter can turn her back with a clang of disapproval heard from Soho to Suffolk.

Lucy linked arms with her and they strolled in the direction of the dancing. "Have you seen the Lawrence portrait of Wellington? Lovely brushwork. The real man looks surprisingly like his portrait."

Brandy was left gape-mouthed behind them. No cut was ever more direct.

"That happens sometimes." She drew Lucy to another spot with a good view of the room. She did not lose sight of Brandy Garth. One does not lose sight of an enemy.

Brandy should thank her for teaching him the rudiments of ambush. Next time, he'd bring a pack of his friends with him to surround his prey and snigger at the right moments. Next time, he'd know to approach her when she was alone.

Lucy gave him a sidelong glance. "Nasty little slug."

"Have you really never been introduced to him?"

"Who knows? Nobody's going to contradict a duke's daughter. I'm spoiled from the cradle. I'd be quite dreadful if I hadn't met you."

"My civilizing influence."

Lucy grinned. "You pushed me into the ornamental lily pond at Sommerworth. We were five. I've been terrified of you ever since."

"I have no memory of that encounter."

Twenty feet away, Brandy Garth fiddled with his watch fob and visibly decided he wouldn't be put in his place by a pair of uppity females. He started forward, composing his next brilliant comment.

Rescue came in an odd guise. Colonel Belford Carlington, bright in his red uniform, stamped toward them, harrumphing as he came. As he passed Brandy he muttered, "Go away, you jackanapes, before somebody puts a sword through you."

"What?" Brandy looked around. "Who? What?"

"You have the manners of a pig."

The colonel took a spot in front of her in exactly the place to block her view of everything she needed to keep an eye on. "Harrumph." The colonel was one of the few people she'd met who actually harrumphed. "In my day we didn't insult guests in our host's ballroom." He pursed his lips, considered the old days, and found them admirable. "We did it in the card room and then we fought duels. Insulting ladies got you killed in those days. Probably still does when it's a woman with relatives like yours."

As if Papa and Hawker would waste murder on a Brandy Garth. "Dueling is sadly out of fashion. I believe the Serpentine is available, though."

"Serpentine?" The colonel twitched his eyebrows together.

Lucy said in a choked voice, "I need wine. Lots of wine." Coward that she was, she fled.

There could be no more self-important old bore in the room than Colonel Carlington. He attached himself to the unwary like a limpet—if there were limpets with a limitless supply of anecdotes about the quartermaster corps. She'd been slower on her feet than Lucy and couldn't really leave her post, so she was buried under an endless story of Spanish muleteers. And Portuguese wagons. Or maybe Spanish wagons. Full of . . . something. It was not clear what. Something vital, anyway.

"There we were," the colonel said, "getting supplies to Obidos. Difficult countryside, that. Steep. Nothing you could call a road, don'tcha know. Foreign, uncivilized place. Wellington— Wellesley, as he was in those days—Wellesley said to me, 'We'll meet the French at Roliça, Carlington. I'm counting on you.'"

The orchestra struck up a lively Dutch Skipper and dancing began again. The rumble of voices rose, everyone making themselves heard over the music and the thump of feet. She could ignore the colonel almost completely. He wouldn't notice. No one would be surprised to see her glancing boredly around the room.

The colonel raised his voice. "Had to pick up the pace, you see, to get there on time. Not my fault about the mules."

She nodded. "Ummm."

Dancers bowed, took hands, circled, reversed. Servants slid through the crowd, carrying drinks, picking up glasses. Footmen followed the same path going and returning, patterns as predictable as the movements of the dance.

Guests were still arriving in twos and threes. She weighed them up as they passed.

Why would someone assassinate Wellington now, years after the war? What possible political purpose would that serve? Was it some old vengeance? A private quarrel?

The colonel had arrived on the plains of central Spain, victim of mule injuries and ambush, mysterious shortages in supplies, and barrels of gunpowder that did not blow up. "Fault of those navy fellows," he said. "They let everything get wet on the transports. Nothing I could do about it."

"Quite," she murmured.

At the other end of the ballroom, Papa flanked Wellington on the left, talking to a clever young MP from Cambridgeshire. Hawker was a few feet away, on Wellington's right, saying something that made Mrs. Kelling-Sherwood toss her head back in laughter. Papa and Hawker didn't have the look of men ready to throw their body between Wellington and a bullet, but that's what they were. That's why they stood so close to him.

"I told the chief muleteer—villain of a man—I told him, 'Your job is getting these wagons across those hills.'" Carlington gestured in the direction of some Spanish mountains. She'd probably crossed those mountains herself, one time or another. "I told him, 'There's no Frenchmen up there. Tell those thieving cowards of yours I'll hang any man who's not on the road in ten minutes.'"

She said, "Fascinating."

"Firmness. Good old British firmness. Only way to handle them. They speak English perfectly well, you know. They just pretend they don't, lazy bugg— That is to say, lazy badgers."

If they had any sense, they deserted.

The lines of the quadrille parted and she could see down the rows of dancers. Little tweaks of tension twisted like cold wires up and down her back. If she were a professional killer, this was the moment she'd pick. Now, in the middle of a dance, when the room was a confusion of noise, laughter, and spinning color.

The agents of the Service agreed with her. She saw it in the twitch of a finger, the infinitesimal lifting of a head. A pack of hunting wolves might exchange the same small signals when they caught the distant scent of prey.

If her fan had been genuine she would have opened it and moved some air across her face to give herself something to do. But the fan didn't open, it merely hung on its loop on her wrist, being deceptive, waiting to serve other purposes.

Carlington launched into excuses for the French ambush he'd sent his supply train into. Ambushes everywhere, apparently. Thick as plums on a tree. Not his fault.

"How remarkable," she said, considering and discarding faces. Papa and Hawk expected her to know O'Grady in whatever disguise he wore. Trusted her to stop him, whatever weapon he carried.

"Portuguese troops perfectly useless, of course. I told Wellington they couldn't be trusted to hold the center."

Wait. Wait.

A waiter had come from the hall, carrying a tray of drinks.

His eyes were fixed on the group far down the room. Nothing odd in that. Everyone was trying to get a glimpse of Wellington, even the waiters.

Something wrong about him.

The colonel's voice became the buzzing of a fly. The music and the noise of the ballroom disappeared.

This waiter wore black, not the blue-and-gold livery of the Carlingtons. He was one of the men hired from inns around the city to fill out the numbers for the party. But his suit was tight across the shoulders, long in the waist. His stockings weren't perfectly smooth. He was shorter than the others too. That was wrong. Inns sent their best, the tallest and handsomest.

Six glasses on his tray, laid out in two lines, instead of eight in a circle pattern. He didn't collect the empty glass on a table he passed. Didn't offer a drink to anyone. Just headed toward Wellington.

The left side of his jacket bulged over something tucked close to his ribs. How often had Papa stood up from the breakfast table and turned a slow circle, asking Maman, "Does my gun show?"

This man's gun showed. O'Grady.

She saw this in one round, ringing instant. She pushed past the colonel and went to do her job.

A dozen steps and she was in O'Grady's path. She gripped her fan and pressed the spring that released the thin hidden blade. Breathed deep and steady through her mouth and didn't look directly at O'Grady. *I'm a silly woman getting in his way. I don't even notice him.*

O'Grady didn't waste attention on her. He was blind to everything but his goal and she was just another highborn woman, harmless as a flower and stupid as a cow. His disguise as waiter might be flawed, but hers, as a lady of the ton, was perfect.

He changed course to avoid her. Excellent. She swung around and jabbed her left fist into his groin. The speed of it, the weight of her whole body behind her fist, the unexpectedness of it, folded him in half.

His tray crashed to the floor. Glasses shattered, crashed,

skipped and rolled everywhere. The silver tray rang like a gong.

She snaked her foot between his legs and tripped him. He went down face-first on the broken glass and she landed on him. He was taller than she was and much stronger, but he hadn't been prepared for an attack. His mind was still caught by his plan, not ready to deal with a knee on his back, his arm twisted behind him, and her weight holding him down.

She reached into his jacket, quick as a snake, jerked out his gun, and sent it skidding across the floor, out of reach, under a line of chairs. O'Grady elbowed her in the soft of her belly and knocked the breath out of her. Not enough to paralyze her, but it hurt like hell.

She jabbed her knife that disguised itself as a fan to his throat, hard enough to be felt by a man in the middle of fighting. Hard enough to draw a little blood. "Be still."

He didn't know death was at his throat, or he didn't care. He didn't stop fighting. Blood splattered the floor underneath them from the little cuts of her knife. From the sharp glass on the floor.

The closest onlookers were beginning to notice the struggle. "What? What? I say, what's happening?" from the colonel. A woman shrilled a question.

Then Pax was there, smooth and silent, coming to her at a dead run. He slammed O'Grady's head against the floor. Hard. Jerked him to his feet. Fletcher appeared a second later, scooping up the gun on his way. The two of them hustled O'Grady through the nearest door and out of sight down the servants' stair.

That was fast. Fast, quiet, and satisfying. She'd almost forgotten what it was to work with a pack of capable companions.

She rolled to her feet and began backing away, looking as if she were wholly bewildered by the broken glass and blood on the floor. Looking uninvolved. Looking, in fact, as if nothing had happened at all.

The orchestra played on, covering the patter of interest, Ladislaus and his violin setting an example of obliviousness. Dancers craned to see what was going on but stayed in their proper patterns and merely asked one another what the commotion might be. In most of the room, conversation never paused. It had happened so quickly, from her first punch to this final, decisive tidying away, that almost no one noticed.

She shook with reaction. It took both thumbs to slide the blade into the shaft of the fan. The tip of the knife was red and a few spots of blood had fallen on the fan's decorative trim of lace, but her dress hid any blood that had fallen on it, red onto red. A successful operation is half intelligent preparation.

Young Felicity, playing housemaid, slipped between guests, carrying dustpan and cloth to sweep the glass up and mop away the spilled wine. In three minutes, every sign of disorder would be gone. It would be as if this incident never happened. The Service erased the attack entirely. There would be no questions asked in the House of Lords about Irish unrest. No letters to the *Times* about radical challenges to the aristocracy.

And, obviously, Miss Séverine de Cabrillac had never held a knife at anyone's throat. The very thought was ridiculous. She dropped her fan into a tall Chinese vase as she went by. Her gloves had collected only a few pinpoints of red, almost invisible.

Nothing had happened. She repeated that to herself. Nothing whatsoever had occurred. She'd been nearby when that nothing had happened. If anyone asked, she'd seen it not happen.

The colonel found her, just exactly as if he were a good hound with his nose down on a scent. "There you are, my dear. It seems there's some problem . . ."

The colonel had seen nothing of what happened under his nose. No one quite so reliably dense as Colonel Belford Carlington. Regiments of British soldiers survived the war because he'd never led men into battle.

"I'm not quite sure . . ." The colonel considered among the many things he was not sure of and chose, "What happened?"

"He seems to have had a fit, poor man. The waiter, you know. I was quite close. He dropped his tray and then dropped to the floor himself."

"He had a *fit*?"

"He staggered about in a most peculiar fashion. Then he had a nosebleed." She shook her head. "I think he's drunk."

"Drunk?" The colonel opened and closed his mouth. "Good heavens!"

Thomas Stevenson, an honorable from the vast clan of York-shire Stevensons, came up and said, "What happened here?"

She held her breath. Could she count on the colonel?

"He was drunk," Colonel Carlington declared, no shadow of doubt in his voice. "Been tippling the wine. Not one of our servants. One of the hired lot."

"I'd have a stern word with his master," Stevenson said.

Behind Stevenson, one man explained to another, "Blind drunk. Tripped over his own feet."

"Knocked into a woman when he fell."

The colonel tut-tutted. "Broken glass everywhere. I'll take the cost of those glasses out of his pay."

"Shouldn't pay him at all."

"Hear. Hear."

"Disgraceful." Mrs. Wythestone pronounced judgment. She passed it along to the Misses Carstairs behind her. "A drunken servant. And on the good wine."

"What's the world coming to?"

The word *drunk* spread through the room like rings in a pool around a dropped stone. Mrs. Wythestone informed everyone that this was all the fault of Charles Fox and his followers in Parliament. The colonel held forth on drunkenness among muleteers in the late war. And the Honorable Mr. Stevenson appeared at Sévie's elbow to explain what had happened and advise her to avoid the glass on the floor.

She retreated, separating herself from events, becoming more and more a bystander with every step. By the time she'd made herself an unnoticed onlooker, there were three or four versions of what had happened circling the room. She could only hope her name wasn't attached to any of them. Here and there people looked at her with curiosity.

She caught Papa's eye and Hawk's approving nod. They didn't leave their post but signaled that she could. She had lost all usefulness. She'd been exposed for what she was to any hostile eye.

Determined gossips began slow approaches. She took a deep breath and selected which chatter from Maman's latest letter she would toss in their direction. Baby to be born. Snow in the passes of the Highlands. Drafty castles. She could be cheerful and informative about many aspects of Maman's adventures on the road. It was time for her to retreat into dull respectability.

She was so demure, in fact, her eyes so modestly lowered, that she didn't notice a perfectly tailored jacket and tasteful knotting of cravat till they appeared directly before her.

Deverney said, "My dance, I believe."

Ten

Deverney said, "It's a waltz. I do love a waltz, especially at an otherwise dull party."

She didn't let herself show surprise. Deverney probably saw it anyway.

How long had he been in the ballroom, watching her? She hadn't felt his eyes. She should have. She should have seen him before he got this close. She'd been too pleased with herself. Too complacent. And her instincts didn't seem to work when it came to this man. He waited while she decided on her next move.

"I hate it when someone sneaks up on me," she said.

"Does that happen to you often? What an exciting life you lead." His smile was mocking. "Do you know how many people are interested in you at this minute?"

"I have a fair estimate." The music seemed very clear, somehow. In deep notes under the melody, the cello repeated a six-note motif.

Deverney said, "They aren't all stupid and blind, you know. Some of the distinguished gentlefolk of London are asking each other what you did. Some are already fabricating tomorrow's gossip. The most ambitious are coming this way to pester you with questions. I suggest you dance."

"With you?"

"I'm closest." He held out his hand the way a man does when someone has just agreed to take the floor with him. "Let's give them something to gossip about besides your odd encounter with a drunken waiter. Come. It may not be obvious, but I'm rescuing you."

"You're annoying me." She set her hand in his and walked blithely to the dance floor with a housebreaker and possible wife killer and at the very least a man who should not be here. "How did you get in?"

"I know the French ambassador."

That had the ring of truth. "You sell wine to him?"

He consulted some inner accounting. "Oddly enough, I believe I do. He's a distant cousin."

"Why are you here, anyway?"

"I came for the pleasure of seeing you assault a waiter. That was nicely done, by the way. I am filled with fear and respect."

"You're filled with lies."

"That too."

They stood a little apart from the dancers, letting the music eddy around them for a while. "I'm glad it's a waltz," she said at last. "A complicated country dance is beyond my powers."

"We'll strive for simplicity."

"You offer many things, monsieur, but not simplicity." She said it amiably enough, playing a part for the room. She was used to this sort of playacting. To be a member of the ton was to be on stage at all times, dissected by a critical audience.

The chill that follows fighting crept damply along her skin. A hollow edginess filled her muscles. Deverney's eyes were thoughtful upon her and it came to her that he knew what she was feeling. Another proof he'd been in battle. She had no doubt of it.

"The waltz," he said softly. "Let me remind you how it's done. First you do this." He lifted her hand to rest on his shoulder. No bird ever sat more uneasily upon a shaky branch than her fingers perched on the finely woven wool of his jacket. "I, in turn, do this." He flattened his hand over the small of her back, lightly. The intimacy of the touch made her stiffen.

"Be at ease," he murmured. "Unique among your colleagues and family, I'm free of knives and guns."

His clothes were tailored to an exact fit that left little room for armament. That wouldn't deter a clever man. She said, "I reserve judgment."

"I will reassure you with my mild behavior. Now we hold hands. Come. Dance is a civilized art. It'll take the taste of fighting out of your mouth." His lips twitched. "You don't have to like me or trust me, mademoiselle. It's a dance, not a kiss."

She surrendered—with reservations—to Deverney's urging and let him lead her into the music, among the waltzers. His hand was light on her back, feeding tiny guidance to her body, warm and persuasive. This was not a bad vantage point to watch for a secondary attack. She could study every corner without being obvious about it. Deverney, damn him, knew what she was doing. He marked a slow and staid course around the room, a waltz of sufficient dignity to please the most starchy matron. He turned their steps to let her see what she needed to see. They could have been fellow agents, partnered together, working at the same operation. Deverney's understanding of what she was doing and what she needed, his awareness of what was in her mind, was disturbingly accurate. He knew, before she did, what path she wished to take through the dancers. He listened to her body even as he spoke to it. His awareness of her was as worrisome as whatever plans hid behind his face.

She would worry about this awareness and understanding later. For now, she sorted through the mosaic of faces. The butler, a man named Foster, set dignity aside and knelt to check that all the glass had been swept up. Colonel Carlington was boring one of the Jessup-Towelle girls. Robin took a glass of wine from one of the footmen and drank it in a couple of swallows, not talking to anyone. Not looking anywhere.

Hawker and Papa had stepped closer to Wellington. A phalanx of former officers—who'd alerted them?—some in uniform, some in stylish evening wear, gathered at that end of the ballroom and effectively blocked access.

Around her the men and women who ruled England engaged in the great sport of the ton. Gossip. She could pick out words on their lips. Enough to guess at the conversations.

Lady Penbrush's lorgnette followed her in the dance. "The de Cabrillac seems to have recovered from the shock, whatever it was."

"It would take more than a drunken waiter to shock her." That was elderly, clever Mr. Tuttsell at her side, as usual.

"Of course, she's French."

"One makes allowances."

"And she is a de Cabrillac."

"True."

On the other side of the room, plump Mrs. Summerton spoke into her sister's ear. "Such a pretty little fortune."

"*Not* for the Carlingtons, I think." Sly smiles exchanged. "I told Adele she wouldn't get the chit for Robin. A bit beyond his touch."

"Now he pouts about it in public and tells tales. So ill-bred of him."

"Say what you will of the de Cabrillacs, they're never vulgar."

Further on, a slender dandy murmured to Mrs. Frobisher, "She told me she wasn't dancing. She's changed her mind."

"Who's that with her?"

"The embassy people are calling him Comte Deverney."

"Deverney? I have heard of the Deverneys. An old title. One of her relatives, perhaps?"

"My dear, do I scent a family arrangement in the wind?"

"High time they settled that woman, if you ask me."

If she'd hoped to become invisible on the dance floor, she had not succeeded. On every side women whispered behind their fans and envied her the place in Deverney's arms. He was handsome and moved with the grace of an athlete, but the room was full of pleasant men who knew how to dance. He held himself with the pride of a man of ancient lineage, but the ballroom was stuffed with aristocrats.

Women saw that glint of reckless sensuality in him. The promise that he would not only please a woman in bed but make her laugh while he did it.

She didn't let herself imagine what Deverney would be like in bed. She wouldn't let her mind visit that country.

Deverney smiled down at her. "Have you defended England sufficiently for the night? Can we sleep easily in our beds?"

She was brushing her fingertips lightly along his shoulder. She stopped that. "Do you know, I have spent a long weary hour today convincing people Raoul Deverney had no interest in what was planned here tonight. Now I'm not sure."

"Be sure. I follow no causes that would lead me to harm that man." Deverney glanced toward Wellington.

"You know too much."

"I'd be a fool if I didn't guess what just happened. But it's nothing to do with me. I am the least political of creatures. When the great events of history knock at my door I send the butler to tell them I'm not at home."

"Yet here you are."

"Dancing with you, mademoiselle."

"Why?"

"Why not? These retired generals, these members of Parliament and lords of the realm don't interest me. You do. Did I compliment your gown?"

"Not yet," she said.

"It admirably hides the color of fresh blood. Good planning on your part. I also admire your quick and efficient way with a hidden knife. You are so very violent. I had no idea."

"The French continue to be masters of the flowery accolade."

"The English continue to bewilder me." His smile was genial as fine brandy, with the same bite underneath. "Your family"—his eyes flickered to where Papa stood—"set you in the path of a large man with a gun. You deal with that, alone. They remove the poor fellow but leave you to unravel the tedious social knot that results. Alone. Not one of these grim men scowling in my direction stomps across the room to rescue you from me."

"Perhaps they consider you harmless."

"I am cut to the quick."

"My intention, monsieur. My intention."

There. Wellington left his place and walked from the ballroom. The old soldier marked the end of action on this battlefield and released his troops. Papa disappeared with him. Pax melted into the edges of the crowd and followed. Felicity was nowhere in sight. She must have gone ahead. They'd see Wellington to the street and into his coach and away.

Hawker remained behind for a few minutes, searching faces in the crowd, watching for any last revealing expression. When he knew she was looking, he signaled, *Done here. Go home*, in the sign language of the London criminal underworld. He knew it because he'd been a criminal. She was fluent because he'd taught it to her when she was five.

Maybe Deverney felt the relaxation in her muscles. He knew the instant she was relieved from duty. He changed. She felt him let go of watchfulness and suspicion. Felt him become part of the music. His smile invited her to follow him into the waltz. And she did.

She plucked her own mind away from the worries of the evening as a woman disentangles her skirt from a thorn bush, point by clinging point, and gave herself to the dance. She let herself pretend she and Deverney danced alone under these bright chandeliers with no expectation crowding around them. Pretend there were no eyes watching her and no grave responsibilities to live up to.

One single waltz. Nothing important. Nothing she'd regret later. She could indulge herself for a short time. It was harmless. Harmless.

Or perhaps not. Their eyes met and locked.

Deverney was no longer urbane and amusing and French. He had become a hidalgo of the line of the knights of El Cid, descendant of Barbary corsairs, heir to the Romans and to the northern barbarians who drove the Romans out. He looked, to put it succinctly, proud as the devil.

He waltzed like the devil too. A particularly skilled devil who seduced honest wives and maidens with his dancing. Who was, perhaps, intent upon seducing her.

He succeeded somewhat. More than somewhat, if truth be told. Though she was neither wife nor maiden.

Suddenly and fiercely, she wanted him. What she felt was not the almost-innocent stirring any woman might feel for a handsome man. Not what young girls giggled about in the retiring room after a waltz, bright heads together, whispering of mysterious pleasures. Not what a chaste wife would feel for a passing stranger. More proof, if proof were needed, that she was not exactly a virtuous woman. Probably proof she was an idiot.

I know a mistake when I make it.

She was no stranger to this sort of wanting. When she was nineteen, on assignment among the French army, she'd fallen in love with a French officer she was spying upon. An enemy. Month after month, from battlefield to battlefield across Spain, she'd followed him and loved him to the edge of madness and reported on him for the British Military Intelligence and betrayed him.

When he died in battle, she'd thought she would die too.

The French battalion commander himself had come to their tent the day after Gaëtan's death when she sat staring out into the camp, doing nothing at all.

The battalion commander had said many words. She was without a protector, he said. Perhaps he offered himself. She didn't remember clearly. She knew she'd answered, "No," and "No," to everything. After the burial of the dead she'd taken her horse and ridden from camp, MacDonald a few dozen paces behind her, silent.

There were weeks after that she couldn't account for and didn't remember well. She had been in the mountains and the women of the small villages had been kind.

Eventually she'd gone back to her work for Military Intelligence. She traveled Spain, a dedicated spy, using many names, playing many roles. Eventually she'd come home to England, trailing little rumors of scandal and of heroics in the war, to take her place among the great families of the London ton. She'd made a life that was partly work that mattered and partly harmless play among the frivolous. She'd never loved another man.

With care, planning, and determination, she set about dwindling to a spinster. If madness and desire visited her, she could ignore them as she ignored any other weakness. She was in control of herself.

Feeling these foolish things while she danced with Raoul Deverney was an indulgence she might allow herself for the space of a waltz. Afterward, she'd pack away untidy emotions and get on with her life. As she always did.

Eleven

THE WALTZ REACHED ITS LAST NOTES AND ENDED
with a flourish. She held on to the warm feeling, not letting
herself think about anything in particular. Deverney still held
her, but the waltz was done.

Voices rose. The crowd rearranged itself. Musicians plucked
strings, tuning. She and Deverney had ended the dance near the
corridor that led to the library and card room. The library door
was open. A little privacy waited inside. He took her arm and was
encouraging in that direction, so she went with him. She was
curious what he'd say next. Not truth, necessarily, but almost certainly something fraught with interest.

The library was a masculine room with leather armchairs,
dark wood, and a globe. And books, of course. It was otherwise empty. He closed the door behind them. "I'll come to
your office early."

"Wait till I send for you. I'm busy and I don't have a chair to—"

He surprised her then. Carefully he set his index finger to
her lips. A startling, electric touch. A shock. He'd removed his
gloves and the skin of his hand was warm and rough. He
looked thoughtful, like a man studying a chessboard.

"I won't kiss you," he said. The tip of his finger slid to rest gently, just barely tugging on her bottom lip. "But damn, I want to."

"We will not indulge in that."

"No."

"We will not begin the lightest flirtation." She'd step away from him. In a minute. "I don't sneak into corners and kiss men at parties."

"Wise policy."

"I don't kiss men like you at all." But she ached warmly everywhere important when she said it. She ached significantly.

"You're wiser than I am," he said. "That's something else I admire." He went back to outlining her lips with his finger. "I've changed my mind about a kiss. Have you?"

"Yes." Only a whisper, but that was enough. She was about to do something moderately stupid. Stupid but harmless. It was all a piece with that foolish dance. How much trouble could she get into twenty feet from the ballroom when anyone could walk in?

Slowly, he leaned to take her mouth and give her a secret library kiss. A flirtatious kiss. Raoul Deverney gauged it nicely. He was offhand, knowledgeable, assured.

Pleasant. This is pleasant. I didn't have to worry—

Then she did have to worry. Because this was not flirtation.

Before she could list the many ways in which this was different from flirting, she stopped thinking altogether. Traitors opened the defenses of her body. Invaders poured across the barricades. Vandals took the portcullis and lowered the drawbridge. The barbarian horde surged through.

Kissing Raoul Deverney was invasion and maybe an earthquake or two wrapped up in fire. She was stunningly aware of his lips and her lips finding various ways to fit together. Maybe he was planning all this. She wasn't.

She stood on tiptoe to pull him toward her.

I'm safe. Foolish but safe. Nothing could happen between them here.

This was an exploration. A scouting party. A limited incursion into unknown territory. It didn't mean anything. She could do this because it didn't mean anything. It would be only this one time. Only . . .

She stopped listening to her own excuses. Then she stopped

making them. At some point, his tongue caressed her lips. His teeth nipped the outer shell of her ear and wandered off onto the sensitive skin at the nape of her neck, under her hair. At some point, she tongued across his face and tasted soap and clean skin and invisible stubble. That taste and texture let loose an elemental hot pang inside her that drove her body hungrily against him. In further dispatches from the field, his cock was fully aroused and rigid.

I will stop this before someone comes in.

"Enough," she whispered.

"One more kiss." He took his time with it. She did not keep count of the seconds. She just let herself enjoy them.

At the end he held her chin in his outstretched fingers. His eyes were complex jewels, fringed by long dark lashes.

He said, "That was unwise."

"Beyond unwise by several miles. We left unwise back at the crossroads."

"I had not expected my evening to end in such poor judgment. I have more control than this." His thumb barely touched the soft skin under her jaw before he said goodbye to touching her, altogether. He stepped back. "You're about to say something I won't like. I see it in your face."

"Don't come to my office tomorrow, Monsieur Deverney. I'll take Pilar's case. I'm working for her. Not you."

"I have some of the answers you're looking for. Don't let a harmless kiss be more important than murder and kidnapping."

"If I need you I'll send for you." *But I will not. You are chaos in my veins. You are madness. I will not disrupt my life for any man. Certainly not for you.*

"I'll be at your office early tomorrow. This isn't the place to discuss anything."

"Stay away."

"A feat beyond my skill, *querida*." He dropped his hand from its touch upon her. "Find one of your ferocious colleagues to see you home. The night is full of killers, you not the least among them." He pushed the door open. *"Au revoir."*

Au revoir. To meet again.

In his mouth it was in the nature of a challenge, rather than saying goodbye.

$\mathcal{T}$welve

A FOOTMAN OPENED THE DOOR ONTO THE STREET and Sévie went out into the cool night to stand in lamplight and torchlight on the steps of Carlington House. She wasn't the only one leaving the ball. Now that Wellington had departed, a dozen other guests were going onward to their second event of the evening.

She took her place among departing guests, more than a little unusual in that she was a woman alone. But she had a long-cultivated reputation for eccentricity and no one was really surprised.

Far down the street Papa's carriage pulled into the far end of the line. She'd have a little wait. It wasn't as if she had nothing to keep her mind busy.

A lost girl. Pilar. Only twelve, but she'd be treated as a woman if she'd landed in one of the brothels of this city. Sanchia Deverney—Sanchia Gavarre she'd be called in Spain—dead. Not an admirable woman. Deverney, an unfathomable man, deep in plots, who insisted they'd met once in Spain. Anyone that comfortable in a ransacked office was probably a criminal himself.

At the end of the first day of an investigation she usually had a neat flock of facts lined up in logical order. She'd be sorting truths from lies. Some insight about the dramatis personae would be emerging.

This time, she'd reached the twenty-four-hour mark and her hands were still empty. Worse than empty. She knew less than nothing because her judgment was entangled in emotion. She'd lost her detachment.

Deverney wrapped her in confusion. He seduced her with every word, look, and touch. He implied he was equally attracted and equally dismayed about it. She found that hard to believe.

She added Deverney's pretense of bemused fascination to her list of matters to consider.

Lively boys from stable and kitchen of Carlington House ran past her, looking for the next coaches and coachmen to motion into line. At the curb the assembled Symingtons— father, mother, aunt, two sons, one daughter, and a harried genteel companion—loaded themselves into two fashionable town carriages with more inefficiency than one would believe possible.

She'd put her office in order tomorrow. How could she think with everything in that state? MacDonald could send the furniture for repair. She'd meet Tweed for lunch and talk to him about the autopsy. She'd come back to search this place inch by inch. She'd—

Behind her, a man said, "Sévie."

She'd hoped to avoid this.

"You have to talk to me," Robin said.

She turned to face him. Raised an eyebrow. "No, I don't." It was easy to look as if she'd been interrupted in the middle of more important thoughts. That was true, after all. She created an expression of impatience, boredom, and haughty displeasure.

Why was Robin talking to her at all? Why had he come without a pack of sniggering friends?

He took her arm. Not gently. "Come back to the house. We have to talk." He glanced around pointedly. "Somewhere private."

"No."

"Listen to me. I'm—"

She took two of his fingers and twisted his hand from its grip on her sleeve.

He didn't yelp. Score one point for public school training. He cradled his hand and glared at her. "You don't have to break a man's wrist."

He'd feel that for a day or two. "It's not broken. It will be if you lay hands on me again. What do you want, Robin?"

His voice dropped to a hoarse whisper. "What the devil were you up to in there? What did you do?" That was genuine bewilderment and panic. Robin Carlington didn't have the depths to counterfeit them. Odd that Robin should be the Carlington to detect the undercurrents of the evening. He'd never struck her as particularly perceptive.

She'd known Robin for years, in a distant way. The ton was a small world or, more precisely, many small worlds. She and Robin didn't move in the same circles. He was a golden lad, a sportsman, a noted whip, the darling of a certain segment of the sporting world. She moved among scholars, writers, and artists. Visited back and forth in the great, noble families of England and France. Had a large acquaintance among the military and spies of every nationality. Consorted with rogues and criminals on a regular basis. Their paths simply didn't cross.

Then, a few months ago, Robin had begun what looked like a single-minded pursuit of her. It would have been courtship in another man, but she'd sensed no real attraction on his part. No heat. No desire. She hadn't taken him seriously. She'd laughed at him.

But she hadn't quite pushed him away, either. The winter had been a dark time for her. She'd lost a client—one of those rare innocent men—to jail fever. He was dead before she could get him to trial and free. His widow had blamed her, loudly and angrily. She'd blamed herself.

Robin had been there, playful, frivolous, light of mind and light of spirit, a gentleman entirely separate from the gritty world of her work. He was exactly what she needed. For a few long, cold, winter weeks she let herself enjoy his foolishness. If she went to a scandalous play in his company, if she rode in his high-perch phaeton racing at dawn in Green Park, if she kissed his cheek when they won the race, it meant nothing because they were playing a game.

That had ended abruptly when vicious stories began and she traced them back to Robin. How strange that she hadn't seen the spite inside him in all the hours they'd spent together. She'd seldom been so wrong in her judgment of anyone.

He was tightly furious now. "You shouldn't have come here tonight. You're making it worse. What did you do to that man?"

She tilted her head and looked blank. He didn't deserve more effort than that.

"The waiter wasn't drunk. I saw you trip him. I saw the gun."

Dozens of guests had seen that incident and been uncomprehending as sheep at a balloon ascension. Robin chose this night to see clearly.

She said, "The poor man had a fit. Everybody's saying that."

"Why was he hustled out of sight?"

"You'd best ask him, I should think."

"I can't. He's gone."

Three carriages to load before her own rolled up. Several people looked at her curiously. Major Gridley was obviously wondering if she would like an inconspicuous rescue or a punch delivered to Robin's guts. Gridley waited only for a signal to come over and provide one or the other. He was another man she'd worked with in Spain.

She said, "I'm not interested in your problems with staff. Go away, Mr. Carlington."

Robin glared off into the night, stiff and silent, resentful, not looking at her directly. "I didn't send that idiot Brandy to annoy you. That was his idea. Not mine."

"He had an idea. How nice for him."

"I apologize," Robin said loudly, and then, more quietly. "There. You have it from me. I apologize. Does that make you feel better? I was angry and said things I shouldn't have. I'm sorry."

More lies from Robin, pointless ones at that. Now that she thought of it, everything he'd done in the last months had the flavor of lies to it.

She knew the worst of his slanders. A pitilessly truthful account had been carried to her ears by both friends and the ton's reliable pack of busybodies. Robin had laid his poison in snide and sniggering jokes that never quite claimed he'd had her in bed. Never stated it openly, but implied it in every sentence. It had been a calculated campaign. A cold one, strangely without anger. She might have forgiven anger.

In the torchlight, his eyes were fixed on her. He licked his lips uneasily. Not a happy Robin Carlington. Not at all.

Something to think about when she wasn't working on something important.

Papa's carriage rolled up. Fletcher was on the box, hunched in a driving coat, being a driver, except more armed and dangerous. That was the Service seeing her home safely. Beside him on the box sat MacDonald in all his Scottish glory, arms folded over his chest, glowering and stubborn. There was just no point giving orders to MacDonald, was there?

She said, "The horses are waiting," and stepped past Robin.

Almost, Robin reached to stop her. At the last second he remembered why that wasn't a good idea. "We can't leave it like this. Meet me in Green Park tomorrow. We'll ride and talk this over."

"No."

He lowered his voice. "I know I said unforgivable things, Sévie. I make mistakes. But part of it's your fault." Robin's smile became boyish and hopeful. "You're a better person than I am. You can forgive me."

Robin Carlington was said to be the handsomest man of the ton. His fine, pale hair lay like a caress at his cheekbones. His features were almost uncannily perfect. He had the most mobile and tender mouth imaginable. Not that he was womanish. His body was smooth muscle on a strong frame, lean from driving his racing curricle and riding to the hounds.

"One more chance," he said. "That's all I ask."

Odd that she felt nothing for him. Had she ever? She could look upon Robin and see his great beauty and be moved to nothing but annoyance. He was no Raoul Deverney to ensnare a woman with a dozen words and a raised eyebrow.

"I could forgive you," she said. "But I don't think I will."

She shook out her skirts and swept past. She said the last words at a volume that would reach all the listening ears. "You were once amusing. You become tiresome."

She accepted a footman's arm into the carriage and ignored Robin's scowl. That, she thought, was that. Getting rid of Deverney would be considerably more problematic.

RAOUL propped a heavy chair under the doorknob. The library was his. An Englishman, finding the door locked, would go away. A Frenchman would peek through the keyhole and see nothing because Raoul had stuffed his handkerchief there. A Spaniard . . . But he was the only Spaniard or half-Spaniard here tonight, so he'd never know what a Spaniard would do.

The English library. Why were these always gloomy, masculine, and stuffed with the dullest books in creation?

He picked his way, both at ease and infinitely wary, across the room, barely making an impression on the carpet. Silent, because this was a secret business, after all. Confident, because this was his métier and his art. He was very, very skilled at it.

It was good to be the Comodin again. The wild card. The thief. The jester. The pilferer of other men's baubles. He saw more clearly, his hearing was keener, he was more alive when he was the Comodin. Everyone should have a second life to slip into.

The safe was concealed behind a mediocre Italian painting. Safes were always concealed behind mediocre paintings in this country. The well-bred Englishman was the most predictable animal on the planet.

Raoul found the catch and the painting swung away. *Ah*. His evening had been enjoyable on so many levels and was about to become even more so. Here was a Carron safe, made in Scotland thirty years ago and old-fashioned even then. It was a heavy, stupid turtle of a safe that would withstand about ten blows with a sledgehammer before the door popped loose. It opened—God help us—with a standard key that was probably hidden with incredible cunning in the top drawer of that desk over there.

It would yield to the most common of lockpicks. Raoul

extracted the one he needed from its place in his waistband and went to work.

He didn't dawdle. For the moment, the British Service was wholly concerned with returning their important politician to his home. Eventually they'd turn their attention from assassins to the suspicious foreigner in their midst. He would be wise to avoid meeting them when his pockets were full.

The safe opened so easily it was almost unsporting. Banknotes, legal papers, and similar trash filled the top. Jewelry took the shelf below, boxes and boxes of it.

He spilled everything out on a convenient table. The Carlingtons had made a collection of his family's goods. Here, a familiar piece. There, another. Six . . . Seven . . . He sorted out a dozen Deverney heirlooms, each with a centuries-long history in his bloodline. Many of them were famous.

He held a bracelet up into the lamplight. The Graciela bracelet, brought into the family by his several-times great-grandmother, an Andalusian princess. Emeralds set in yellow gold glowed back at him, the artistry of the Renaissance, the passion of Andalusia. The emeralds had come as spoil from Montezuma. They'd been sacked in cities all over Europe. They were used to being stolen.

It had decorated Lady Carlington's bony wrist. A London friend recognized it and sent him word. He'd added Carlington to his list of those who held stolen Deverney possessions. It was only a matter of time before he dropped by to collect them.

The Graciela bracelet went into the pouch that hung around his neck under his shirt. You'd think he'd have learned not to carry the most important pieces there, but he never had.

That was the last of his family's property. Fourteen pieces. These and a dozen others had been on him when he was captured by the British in Béjar. It looked like Colonel Carlington had helped himself to the spoils of war while he was in Spain.

Normally the Comodin would tumble quickly through the rest of the baubles and pick a dozen that caught his fancy. He never helped himself only to Deverney pieces. He didn't want the authorities connecting the Comodin to the Deverneys.

Tonight he scooped up the other trinkets and shoved them back on the shelf in the safe. He'd carry away only Deverney jewels. Colonel Carlington, hypocrite and dealer in looted goods, would know what these particular pieces had in common. He'd be afraid tomorrow. He'd quake in his boots, waiting for his old, dirty secret to be pulled into the light.

Softly, he closed the door of the safe and centered the picture back in place. They'd discover the theft when they went to put those vulgar Carlington diamonds away.

He'd left himself time to poke about the library, which he did just on general principle. He discovered three more places of clever concealment. Lord, but the British were fond of their globes that opened and clocks with false backs and secret panels in the walls. They had such admiration for the scheming Medici but no trace of their cunning.

He uncovered hidden decanters of brandy, letters of timeless fidelity addressed by the baron to a woman not his wife, and an impressive collection of pornography being shy behind a false front on the bottom shelf.

But enough amusement. Time to get on with the evening. He untucked his shirt, unwrapped the rope from around his chest, secured one end to the window frame, and let the rest dangle down the wall outside. The thief departed that way, obviously. The Comte Deverney would walk out the front door under the gaze of the many guards and guests.

He grazed his fingers along the picture frame as he left, saying a fond goodbye to another safe he'd burgled. It pleased him to rob the Carlingtons while British Service myrmidons swarmed about. How embarrassing for the Service.

Pornography, illicit love affairs, and war booty hid behind the façade of Carlington House. Like anyone who rummaged through his fellow man's possessions on a regular basis, he found the human race infinitely ridiculous. It was a pity Séverine couldn't be here to appreciate the humor with him.

$\mathcal{T}$hirteen

PILAR DEVERNEY Y GAVARRE LEANED AGAINST A damp wall and stood in darkness, patient as the bricks behind her. She knew how to wait.

Kepple Street was most perfectly silent. It was so late at night there were few carriages, even out on Gower Street. This was the hour the men who'd killed Mamá would come back to search the appartement. Now, when no one was awake. When there was no one to see.

She watched here most nights for an hour or two. They had to return, those evil men. They hadn't found what they wanted.

This stairwell, across the street from what had once been her home, was chillier than the air up on the street and it smelled of mold, but it was a fine hidden place. Even if someone passed and noticed her, no one, not even neighbors who'd known her for years, would recognize her in these clothes.

When she was young she'd hidden here, watching till Mamá's guests left. She'd been cold, hungry, and afraid in this familiar stairwell in the dark between streetlights. In those days she'd had nowhere else to go. This damp and chill was better than sitting inside on the stairs of the house, taking the chance one of Mamá's men would come searching for her. Even when she was a child, nine or ten, some of them had looked at her in a way that made her flesh creep.

Tonight she was no longer a helpless child. Tonight she followed a path of duty and great purpose. She was embarked upon revenge.

And there was another difference from the past. Tonight when she left this vigil there was a certainty of warmth waiting for her, a safe place to sleep, and a door that locked behind her when she crawled onto her mat. There'd be a plate of food left on the attic steps because no one who worked for Miss went to bed hungry. MacDonald cooked on the fire in the hearth in his room, French and Spanish and Scottish food. He was uncannily deft with those big, scarred, rough hands.

"I'll tell you what is important in this life, me lad," MacDonald said one time when they were eating dinner together and talking. "A full belly. If you can keep your master—or in this case your mistress—well fed, she will keep you alive no matter what trouble she leads you into." MacDonald had pulled the bread apart and given her half of it. "De Cabrillacs keep you alive, usually, which is more than most people do. And it's never dull."

The flat bread they shared was something MacDonald made himself, since he liked it and no bakery in its right mind would try to sell it in London. Havercake, MacDonald called it. Not so bad once you got used to it.

The Scot was right about this being an interesting life, she supposed, and a well-fed one and fairly warm. Tonight she wore a good thick wool jacket and sturdy shoes because no one in Miss's service went to work cold, even in the damp of late night, lurking in a cellar stairway.

She'd been cold to her bones the day Mamá died. She'd walked endlessly in freezing wind with nowhere to go. She had been so alone and so frightened.

The murderers had left the parlor and come down the hall toward her bedroom. She'd escaped through the window without her cloak, with only the money in her pockets and an ugly amulet. Mamá had hidden that among her daughter's shifts and stockings where no one would think of looking.

For reasons she did not understand the amulet was important. It had been Mamá's death. Perhaps it would be her own as well. She wore it around her neck now and it was heavy with the treason and blackmail. It did not look beautiful or valuable enough to cause death but, because she wore it, murderers were looking for her.

Two men had come to talk to Mamá in the parlor that day. One was a gentleman. A rich and powerful man from the way Mamá had answered him, very afraid. He had been contemptuous of her, as men were of women like Mamá. Afterward, he was unconcerned that he had killed her. On that horrible day, walking in the shuddering, knife-edged cold, she had known there was no one to help her. Her father's man of business—Deverney's man of business—inspired no trust. Mamá had told her he was not honest in his dealings and also a fool. Any magistrate she went to would think she was a hysterical child. She would be patted on the head and sent where anyone could find her and kill her for the amulet. If she went to a friend, she put them in danger. No one she knew could stand against men so powerful they could do murder and walk away laughing.

That first night she'd slept in the cellar of her school. There was an unlocked window all the girls knew about. The next day she'd used the money in her pocket to buy boys' clothing, and she'd set off to find safety and revenge.

The men who'd tormented Mamá had asked again and again if de Cabrillac was part of the blackmail. Did de Cabrillac know about the amulet? Where was it? What had Mamá told de Cabrillac? There was that in the gentleman's voice that said he was afraid of the name de Cabrillac.

Now, three months later, she understood why a man might be afraid of Miss Séverine.

Three months ago, Séverine de Cabrillac had not been hard to find. She'd seemed honest, but one does not trust a woman merely because murderers mention her name. One does not trust her with great secrets. But she'd settled into Miss's household and waited for her father to come for her and felt safe. If the killers showed up to bully and beat Miss with those same questions they'd asked Mamá, Miss would dispose of them neatly.

Her father would come from France. He'd find the message she'd left and walk into Miss Sévie's and know her at once, in boy's clothing. She would give him the information she'd collected and leave it all in his hands.

Then Deverney did arrive and he was nothing like she'd imagined. He did not give a fig for Mamá. He resented having a bastard thrust upon him. He spoke cynically about providing for his unwelcome responsibility. A number of childish dreams had died very quickly. She wished he hadn't come to England at all.

She would go to one of Mamá's men and sell herself—she knew exactly what that meant—before she would take the charity of Comte Deverney. She would avenge Mamá herself. When that was done, she would go to Spain and find her mother's people. She'd like them better than Deverney she was fairly sure.

A coach rolled down Kepple Street, the lamps lighting the way ahead. It didn't slow or stop or show interest in any of the houses. If they chanced to see her, they paid no attention to a bedraggled figure, grimy and ragged. The streets were full of her kind. Her camouflage was perfect.

She huddled into herself and rubbed her hands along her upper arms. *Mamá would approve of all that I have done. Mamá would—*

Her *madre* had not been an admirable mother, perhaps, but she had been someone to come home to. Now there was no one.

The pain of losing Mamá came less often now. Sometimes it still stabbed like a hot poker when she didn't expect it. Like now. There was another sort of pain that was long and slow and sour in her whole body and came to her when she lay in bed, trying to sleep. That was guilt, because she did not feel the sorrow a daughter should.

Two streets north, the crier raised his voice to say it was three of the clock on a clear, cold night.

It was time to end the vigil for tonight. She needed the hours of sleep left in this night and some food. It would involve potatoes. In a different and better world MacDonald would be her father or her uncle and she would be a young MacDonald in training to become the next generation to serve de Cabrillacs and follow them around the world on adventures. She wouldn't have to deal with Monsieur Deverney who had no use for her.

She put her hands inside her coat between her unimpressive breasts and held the amulet through her shirt. It was cold and heavy and ancient and she did not care that she had no right to it. She would defy them all. She would take what she wanted, as Mamá did.

She whispered, *"Madre de dios, me ayude a hacer mi trabajo. Trae a mis enemigo a mí para que yo pueda ser su muerte."*

Mother of God, bless my work. Bring my enemy to me so that I may be his death.

Fourteen

DAWN HAD NOT YET RATTLED ITS CHARIOT INTO
the streets of London when Doyle arrived at Meeks Street.
Wellington was home and relatively safe, with a squad of dra-
goons posted around the neighborhood.

Doyle had three hours' sleep under his belt, which wasn't
nearly enough. But there was work to do and his Maggie
wasn't in bed with him, which made sleeping there less attractive than it might otherwise have been.

Felicity came to open the door at Meeks Street, alert and
irritable. The front parlor had been emptied of most of its furniture. It looked better that way, frankly. Since he was a senior
officer of the British Service with years of experience, he
could figure out what had happened to it.

The lamps in the hall were turned high and bright. He could
hear muted voices upstairs. It looked like nobody had slept.

He walked to the Chinese dining room at the back of the
house looking for a strong cup of tea, which he'd neglected to
get at home for reasons involving his youngest children. There
were plenty of lamps lit here too. The wallpaper showed ladies
in kimonos carrying fans and parasols, crossing little half-

moon bridges or standing decorously under fringed trees. A nice restful room if you didn't know who met here and the sort of things they discussed.

They'd built the fire high. The curtains were drawn back to let in the light when it chose to arrive. Coffee and tea and food were spread out on the sideboard. More food on the table. The rangy, ragged-eared house cat—named Cat—sat squarely on a copy of the *Morning Herald*, eyeing the sliced ham, biding his time.

Hawker sat at the head of the table, his feet propped on one chair, evening coat and cravat thrown over another. His shirt was open at the collar, his cuffs rolled back, and his waistcoat unbuttoned. He drank French coffee from a small Étoilles cup. That was his drink of choice for late at night and the best clue that he hadn't slept.

Doyle counted empty cups and made an estimate of how many agents had been through here. Seven or eight, it looked like. He said, "Somebody's stolen that couch from the front room. A couple of chairs too."

"I sent them out for an airing."

"Time somebody did."

"They'll find their way home eventually," Hawker said. "Hideous chickens always come home to roost."

Doyle had chosen a West Country accent this morning, overlaid with Cockney. One of his favorite voices. *Speak as you dress*, he told young agents. "The Great Man's home and under guard. He'll spend the day at Whitehall. Nobody can get to him there."

"Sufficient unto the day."

Not so indulgent of the cat as Hawker, Doyle displaced it from the table as he passed and went to wrap his hand around the teapot on the sideboard. Not piping hot, but still acceptably warm.

A tray of bread and meat and a bowl of apples kept company with the tea service. On the long table, plates and cups alternated with copies of the morning papers. Stillwater's evening gloves languished on the mantel. Somebody's hat perched askew on the chiming clock. The agents themselves had scattered elsewhere.

"You haven't slept." Doyle poured milk, added tea to it and two lumps of sugar. He wore leather and rough wool today, looking like a short-haul carter working the North Road or a publican near the docks. He took his first slurp of tea still standing, like an honest tradesman at a tea stall in the market.

"Not yet," Hawker said. "We dealt with Sévie's office. All of us. The sad part is, she'll return that furniture."

"I raised an honest daughter. I could do the first work on O'Grady."

"No need. I find myself wide awake and moderately annoyed. I'll employ that usefully upon him."

Doyle nodded and drank tea. He held the delicate teacup in his great paw of a hand with a natural-looking awkwardness.

"We'll bring O'Grady down"—Hawker looked out the window—"soon. Felicity's heating pokers. Nothing like a hot poker to encourage reasoned discourse, I always say."

"So you do." Doyle selected sliced ham and cheese, folded bread around them, and ate standing at the sideboard. He'd sneaked out of the house without breakfast because Sévie, not to mention the rest of his pack of sharp-eared offspring, would have heard him in the kitchen and come down to keep him company. As it was, he'd had to send the youngest back to bed. "I've put two men at my own house. Bodyguards for the children."

"Good."

Doyle sat down, chewing. "What do we know about this Deverney?"

That was another reason he hadn't stayed to eat breakfast. He wasn't ready to chat with Sévie about her choice of dancing partners.

"The French embassy vouches for him." Hawker pulled at his lower lip. "It's a genuine title. Old aristocracy and full of military honors. Find a doomed charge in the history of France and it was led by a de Verney. Some of the embassy people know him by sight."

"Careless of him to let his wife get murdered, apart from losing a daughter. And his wife lived in England while he's in France." Doyle frowned. "Sévie's been jaunting around the city with him."

"Problematic."

"Ain't it, though?" Doyle finished his tea in a single long swallow. Small teacup. Large man. "When I pointed that out, she said to keep my nose out of her business, but more politely."

"That's what a good upbringing does for you. Lets you tell somebody to go to hell politely. Why was he at the Carlingtons'?"

"Good question."

"Why the devil did Sévie dance with a man who brings a knife to her bedroom? The world's not overcrowded with men who do that." Hawker put his cup in the saucer with a click. "Here's our guest coming along."

O'Grady's approach grew louder. The scuffle and bump on the staircase held curses twisting through it like snakes. Some of the curses were in Gaelic, which Doyle understood and Hawker could make an educated guess at.

"We'll see how talkative he becomes. I will attempt to be terrifying." Hawker went to look out the window where it was not noticeably more bright than it had been half an hour ago. He began collecting dirty cups and plates. "Deverney does not appear to have served in any of the varieties of French Army. Perhaps he is a fainthearted and cowardly civilian."

"He climbs stone walls, apparently."

"So he does. I will point out that dealing with murderers and thieves was supposed to keep Sévie out of trouble. I distinctly remember discussing this with all and sundry back when she set up in business."

"It seemed a good idea at the time." Doyle went to make himself another roll of ham and cheese and refill his teacup.

"'Let her chase murderers,' you said. 'It'll cheer her up. It'll give her an interest in life now that she can't spy on the French.'"

"I did say something of the sort," Doyle admitted.

"'A good steady profession' you called it. 'There will always be murderers,' you said."

"I was right about that last one."

"It wasn't enough." Hawker balanced crockery across the room. Sometimes, on assignment, he'd played a waiter. He'd learned the work in the kitchen of British Service headquarters in Paris. "Murderers aren't keeping her sufficiently busy. I watched her with Deverney. Tell me there's nothing going on there. Tell me I'm wrong."

"Can't do that."

"I've waited five years for her to be stupid with somebody the way she was stupid with that Frenchman who went and got himself killed."

"I doubt he did it on purpose."

"She meets ten thousand Englishmen—street sweepers to royal dukes—and she has to take up with another questionable Frenchman."

"That sums it up."

"You'd think she did it on purpose." Hawker clattered cups into the dumbwaiter. "At least she's armed."

"A cogent summation of the women of my family."

Hawker took up pacing, quartering the room. The dining room wasn't really large enough to pace in, which annoyed him, and Cat curled around his ankles, getting in his way. "I suppose he could be Police Secrète."

"Not that I know of." Doyle knew most of the French spy service.

"Stillwater says he left Carlington House singing obscene songs, leaning on a drunken *secrétaire* from their embassy. I admire the art of an exit like that."

"Of course."

"I'll talk to him."

"Sévie won't like it."

"I said, 'Talk to him,' not break his bones."

"Go ahead. I'm not that stupid, but maybe you are." Doyle chewed and swallowed. "He says he's a wine merchant."

"And I'm a seller of jellied eels." Having collected the used china, Hawker started pacing again. "Sévie has to see he's not what he says he is. He's not harmless."

"I don't think she'd be interested in somebody harmless."

"Why can't she fall in love with a banker? Pax knows some splendid bankers." Hawker picked an apple from the bowl and began tossing it and catching it. "Yes?"

Felicity came through from the study into the dining room and closed the door behind her, shutting off a string of colorful complaints. "Are we going to start with O'Grady anytime soon? The pokers are hot."

Fifteen

SÉVIE WOKE IN HER BEDROOM, KNOWING SHE WAS not alone.

Somebody—two somebodies—had climbed into bed with her. She opened one eye. A gray object dangled in her line of sight, suspended by its long tail, swinging slightly. It had two ears, little paws, and whiskers. A mouse. A thoroughly dead mouse.

"I took it away from Shadrack-the-Cat," Anson said.

Anna clambered up on her other side. "I did."

"Did not."

"Did."

Anson was five, Anna three. They could keep this up for hours.

"And you brought it to me," Sévie said. "How kind."

"Maman isn't here," Anna explained.

For which Maman was no doubt grateful. A chilly castle in Scotland and Sylvie's impending baby would be skittles and beer compared to the joys of home life.

"She's helping Sylvie have the baby," Anson said.

"It takes a long time." Anna frowned. "Till Trinity Term. Then Maman comes home."

She grinned to think of Sylvie's baby arriving promptly with the new school term in April. But that sounded about right. Three weeks till the baby was due. Maman would stay to help out. Then Maman and Justine would make the long trip home from the Highlands.

A low growl came from under her bed. More company. She rolled over and looked down in time to see a gray paw snake out to bat at the bedding. Shadrack. The whole gang assembled.

"Papa's gone," Anna said. "He left in the dark." She began to bounce gently on the bed.

"Before morning," Anson said. "'In the belly of the night,' he called it."

"He was wearing his scar. He said it was time for rebskeletons to be in bed."

"He meant us," Anson said.

Rapscallions, she translated. "Did he now?"

"Then Shadrack caught a mouse," Anna said. "Behind the curtains in the front room."

"This one," Anson said, showing her.

"Shadrack was going to eat it. Do people eat mice? Are they good?" Anna wrinkled her forehead and considered this one.

"Not unless you are very, very hungry." She'd been that hungry when she was Anna's age, in Paris, during the Revolution. Her brothers and sisters never would be.

Anson had been found, newborn, in a gully near the Customs Wharf. Anna, barely toddling, in an alley in Wapping. They were the youngest of the family.

Dawn was some little distance away, but it looked like her time allotted to sleep was ended. She'd take Anna and Anson, collect their aging monster of a dog, Muffin, and head for the kitchen. The kids would get under the feet of the kitchenmaids and she'd drink tea and eat toast and possibly decide what to do about Monsieur Deverney. She'd read the *Morning Chronicle* when it arrived.

She did not like to wake up and immediately think about Monsieur Deverney. She didn't like finding the man so firmly settled inside her head.

She said, "Let's give the mouse—it's a very fine mouse—back to Shadrack and go find some breakfast."

"I'll give it to him," Anson said.

"No. I will."

"Me."

"Both of us," Anna compromised.

They ducked under the bed with an offering of dead mouse. The bed shook for a bit and Shadrack, with mouse, sprinted from the room.

"Now . . ." She pulled herself from under the covers and rose slowly from the mattress. "I am Shadrack the Mighty and you are my helpless victims. I will show you how I deal with little mousies."

Shrieks. She cornered them on the hearthrug and threw herself upon the pair of them, tickling.

Sometimes she considered setting up housekeeping on her own. There'd be no one to poke into her business or ask awkward questions about who she danced with. It would be nice to sleep late once in a while.

But then she wouldn't come home in the evening to her noisy, welcoming pack of brothers and sisters. To Papa and a scattering of Service agents gathered at the dinner table, discussing cases. To Max, home from Cambridge, full of Greek philosophers and politics. To the ingenious mischief of the twins, Bart and Turner, twelve, and the terror of Eton's schoolmasters. To this pair of demons who woke her at the crack of dawn with dead rodents. To Maman, who made them a family.

There were many reasons she'd never marry. She'd never found a man she wanted to be that close to, not since Gaëtan. She'd never again fallen into that madness of desire and longing. She'd been spared that.

Anson and Anna ran ahead of her down the stairs, making a wholly unnecessary clatter. Worrisome thoughts also accompanied her. It was time to admit to herself that Deverney disturbed her on some deep level. She desired him. She would admit that and push it away because it was not important. She would not be ruled by her body. Not by cold or hunger. Not by fear. Not by the pleasure a man offered. She found Deverney intriguing, but she would also not be lured by mystery.

She shouldn't feel anything for him. He might need arresting at some point.

But beneath all the common sense, around it and behind it and under it, was the knowledge that she'd loved and destroyed one good man. That was enough for any lifetime. She wouldn't take that risk again.

She did not need a lover. She'd arranged her life exactly as she wanted it. He offered nothing she wanted. Nothing she should want.

Sixteen

It was nearly dawn when Pilar crawled into bed. She wouldn't get much sleep. In a few hours, MacDonald would climb the stairs from Famble's rooms. He'd bang on the wood of the cupboard under the stair as he went by and mention the benefits of a good morning scrub at the pump. In return for that good advice MacDonald would expect two dozen buckets of water carried up from the pump outside to fill the cistern.

The mattress underneath her was stuffed with straw. The rough ticking and scratchy woven blanket kept most of the straw from sticking into her flesh. The blanket on top of her was warm as anyone could wish, and clean. No warmth was to be despised, of course, but she did remember now and then that it had started life as a horse blanket.

This triangular space under the attic stairs, dark and airless when the door was closed, lit by the stub of a candle, with space for nothing but the mat and a wood box, was the prize of a desperate gamble. She'd come to this after three weeks living in the frigid cold, sleeping in doorways and stairwells, starving, haunting this building. Three weeks, crouching in Turnwheel Lane. She'd watched the warehouse, rushing forward to hold horses or sweep the yard, and when a certain tolerance grew among the laborers, to run errands and fetch beer at dinnertime.

Finally came the sleeting night Miss Séverine tossed over the reins of her horse and ran upstairs to gather up papers and a gun. It had been twenty long minutes, holding Miss Séverine's horse, walking it conscientiously to keep the mare's muscles limber, finding a bit of shelter for it in the entryway to the yard. When Miss came out and stepped into cupped hands to vault into the saddle, she'd said, "Go into the warehouse and sleep beside the stove. I've arranged it with the foreman."

There was a man killed that night. Miss Séverine had shot the fellow, who apparently needed it. The warehousemen knew all about it by dawn, somehow. They spent the day bragging, proud and possessive of their eccentric lady.

That morning, Miss had emptied out this closet and found a blanket. MacDonald had set the first of many meals on those stairs to the attic.

"You can stay here till it stops being so cold," she'd said.

Since then there'd been more blankets, this straw mat, a lock installed on the door, regular food, and the sound of Mac-Donald snoring away every night, guarding. There'd been the bustle every morning when Miss Séverine came in, leaned over her desk to frown at her working notes, and thanked whoever brought her tea.

It wasn't icy cold on the street anymore, but the meals and the safety continued. And the errand boy Peter made himself useful, learning the way around the magistrate's offices and the Inns of Court, through the prisons great and small, the records offices, the newspaper file rooms, and the cubicles of all the petty officials of London.

It was an interesting life and it suited her. She followed Miss Sévie into the rookeries of St. Giles and Seven Dials to look at corpses and comfort the weeping family. Everywhere, they walked past dangerous men who didn't touch Miss Séverine because she was protected by the most powerful people in London. Not just the British Service and her highborn French relatives. A surprising number of villains had reason to be grateful to her.

Besides, Miss carried a gun. She was teaching Pilar how to load and fire one.

For a long time she'd trusted Miss Sévie completely. It would have been easier to tell Miss everything and ask her help, but Miss had turned out to be a great meddler in everyone's life and stupidly protective. If she'd known her errand boy was a girl and in danger, that girl would have been whisked off to a boarding school in the provinces so fast her ears would flap.

Weeks passed. No evil men sought out Miss de Cabrillac asking what she knew about an amulet. No one hunted Mamá's daughter to her hiding place. No one showed any interest at all. Sometimes it felt as if Mamá had died and her memory had dropped like a stone into the sea. Raoul Deverney didn't come.

Then he did come and he was only a problem and a complication. He was not her father anyway. He was nothing.

A rolled-up jacket made a good pillow, once she got it in just the right position. At least Deverney was making Miss Sévie look at Mamá's death. That was useful, even if he said stupid things about his responsibilities and his honor and wasted time being suspicious of Miss. She was glad she wasn't a Deverney if they were that stupid.

Miss would track down the evil men responsible for Mamá's death. She was the best in London at finding the truth.

Then nothing more would be needed but to kill them.

Pilar turned over on her mat. There were hours of sleep left in the night. Three, maybe. When it was light she would help Miss Séverine find murderers. Everything was going well.

$\mathscr{S}$eventeen

NOTHING LIKE AN EARLY START TO THE DAY. WITH mice.

The coach Sévie took across London ran with its lanterns still lit. It might be dawn out there on the orders of the nautical almanac, but the sun was not yet on duty.

She made the trip with her pistol laid across her lap, as she did when she was working on a dangerous case, and she ordered a roundabout route to her office. She let the stolid and incurious hackney driver roll right to the door and asked him to wait till she let herself into the building. She took no chances.

She'd turned down Anna and Anson's offer of the dog Muffin to accompany her to work. That was not altogether childish fancy. Muffin was retired from years at Meeks Street. Ten stone of fighting dog, gray-muzzled and a little stiff, but with six-inch fangs, was protection not to be despised.

That was why she left him in the front hall, guarding her home.

This morning would be a morning of housecleaning. She'd sweep the corners of her office for broken things and put her files back in order. It would give her time to think.

One of the laborers from the loading docks stood outside the double doors, holding a lantern, waiting for the arrival of an early shipment. He waved at her as she went up the front steps and put her key in the lock.

When the light was better she'd go back to Sanchia's flat and continue searching. Deverney expected her to find something she hadn't laid eyes on yet.

She closed the door to the building behind her and locked it. The entryway was dim and empty. There were no lamps lit and the hall was silent. Nobody seemed to have arrived at the front office of Fielding and Sons.

She climbed the stairs, making mental lists. That was a comforting activity and perhaps even useful.

She'd start a case file on the death of Sanchia Deverney. She'd collect the papers Deverney's man of business had walked off with from the Kepple Street appartement. Collect all his Deverney records, really. She'd send Peter off to copy the coroner's report and the accounts from the newspapers. She'd better see the magistrate herself.

She had no neat item on her list for what she'd say to Deverney when he showed up. She hated being uncertain more than she hated being wrong.

Then she turned at the landing to the second floor and saw the door to her office stood a little open, letting out a line of light across the hall floor.

That could be MacDonald, up to greet the dawn, sweeping and sorting. It could be one of her many informers from the rougher parts of the city, come with useful information, picking the lock, and hiding in her office. It could be someone very nasty indeed. She was always meeting problematic and interesting people.

It was probably Deverney, however.

She had the pistol out, not even thinking about it. She held it level, close to her side, and entered the room.

Two shocks hit. One shock of complete amazement and one small, troubling shock that didn't actually come as a surprise.

The small shock was Deverney—and wouldn't he be annoyed to know she'd expected him? He sprawled, lean and sardonic, on a familiar and ugly red sofa. He'd picked a pile of her letters for his morning reading.

The larger shock was everything else.

She confronted a scene of strange normalcy. Her office was restored to . . . maybe not exactly order. The red chairs and the not-quite-matching sofa had grown wings and flown here from Meeks Street. They were familiar as her back teeth and utterly, bizarrely out of place.

The disorder was vanished away. The floor was clear of chair stuffing, of broken glass, of shredded cloth. Her desk had been straightened intelligently and knowledgeably. Ink-stained papers were gathered into flat stacks. Her books, her files, her case boxes were back on their proper shelves.

Deverney said, "Your colleagues have restored order and propriety to your world," as if she hadn't noticed. "You must be relieved."

Meeks Street was filled with men and women who'd known her since she was in pinafores. They knew—nobody knew better—how she'd slogged through battle and horror, killed when she had to, and now consorted with pimps and murderers on a regular basis. They didn't often take care of her.

"I wish they wouldn't do this sort of thing," she said, and knew that she lied.

Hawker had brought this ugly furniture from the front parlor at Meeks Street. The green blotting paper came from Stillwater's desk in her austere, neat, little house. The ordering of her papers and case files would be Pax's work. When he visited here he'd have casually noted the exact placement of everything on the shelves. It was the way his mind worked.

The kindness of old friends surrounded her. She might fight free of their protection, but it warmed her heart when it was offered, as it was today.

"I watched them carry furniture in and furniture out," Deverney said. "A little crowd of them, stumbling about in the dead of night. I did not feel impelled to assist and eventually they departed, quite in the manner of thieves. I felt free to enter and make myself comfortable since half of London had preceded me." He patted the sofa he sat on. "Using 'comfortable' in the loosest sense."

"They're meant to be lumpy. It discourages unwelcome visitors."

"As I am unwelcome?"

"Very."

She stalked past him and didn't look back, but she carried an acute consciousness of him across the room with her. It prickled along her shoulders and neck. It settled as a warmth in her belly.

Papers crinkled behind her. Did the man do nothing but help himself to her files? His boots scuffed on the floor as he rose and followed her across the room, the noise a deliberate communication. He told her exactly where in the room he was, when he could have been silent as a table. Her life was filled with people whose natural mode of action was silence and secrecy. She recognized it at once.

Here was the coup de grâce, this chair at her desk. They'd brought her the armchair from Hawker's office at Meeks Street till her own was repaired. Brought her a chair of gravitas and history, a witness to the unrolling of great events.

She walked around it and curved her hands over the back. Deverney stood at the other side of the desk, facing her, incalculable as flame that rose upward from a fire. She was not in the mood to be patient. "I have work to get through today, looking for your Pilar. Go away and let me do it. Alone."

"You need me." Deverney didn't sound patient himself.

"I doubt it. And I decide."

"A reminder, then." He said it low and his voice was perfectly serious. "The men who killed Sanchia came here, to the heart of your power, to deliver their threat."

"That's a dramatic way to put it."

"You lead a dramatic life, Séverine."

"I'm not Séverine to you, monsieur."

"You're Séverine, whether I say it out loud or think it. You've been that in my mind for a while now. Séverine, they know where you live."

"A fine selection of the most vicious criminals of London know where I live."

"There's a small army of men, craftsmen in death—none of them terribly law-abiding—who'd tear London apart looking for anybody who hurt you. But you're dealing with people who don't know that or they don't care. Or they have powerful protection."

"Or they're stupid as cows."

"Or desperate. In any case, you need somebody with you. I don't claim I can guard your back, but I can give you one minute's warning so you can guard your own."

"I have MacDonald."

"And your undersized errand boy. A formidable array. Bring me too." Deliberately he leaned across the desk toward her. His hands, fingers spread, took possession of a territory of wood. "Besides, I know things I haven't told you yet. That's your best reason to keep me close. You never know when I'll become talkative."

True. All that was true. She wrapped her arms around herself, holding in the annoyance that had taken up residence in her chest.

On every side, in file boxes and folders, her work surrounded her. She'd chosen to confront greed, violence, and stark ugliness. To face the occasional chance of death. To see the worst of mankind in its natural habitat. This life had matched her mood when she came home to England, battered, exhausted, disillusioned, and sick of spying. She'd come home more broken than even Maman realized.

In this shabby corner of London, in this office, slowly, she'd glued herself back together. She'd become someone who mattered. Each of these case boxes was a puzzle solved. Sometimes, a man or woman saved from hanging or transportation. Sometimes, the small triumph of justice. Sometimes, one or two lives made better.

She held that knowledge to her heart on the nights she woke and stared at the ceiling and life felt very empty. This was her work. This was one thing she'd done right.

Deverney's damned self-possession and tough, elegant turn of mind tore up the peace she'd built for herself. He made her want something more than the sensible, useful, careful life she'd created. He made her long for madness again. He did it just standing there and breathing.

She met his eyes and fell into them. She'd packed passion

and its train of attendant demons away and slammed the lid down hard. But she wanted this man. She wondered if it showed on her face, in her eyes, in the way she held her body. He was the sort of man who would see such things.

"You need me," he repeated.

It was an echo of her own thoughts. She hoped he meant something more innocent by the words.

He said, "Something I know or can discover is key to this puzzle. I am a treasury of secrets."

"I know men who could lighten you of those."

His lips quirked. "The British Service? Will you give me up to their curiosity?"

"I'm tempted."

"But you won't do it. You're a woman who will always commit her own mayhem."

Did the gods laugh when someone smug fell off the high scaffolding of good resolutions? Did they punish hubris by tumbling the culprit into an obsession with the most unsuitable person at hand? It had happened to her, anyway, and she did not like it.

"That's settled then," he said. "Unless you need to commune with your new furniture, we'll go see my man of business. You want those papers he took from Sanchia's rooms, and I want to see his face when he hands them over. I told him to be in his office."

"It's early." The first light was not yet leaking through the ragged dark line of buildings.

"On the contrary, we're three months late. Let's get started."

Eighteen

PILAR GRIPPED THE BRASS RAILING THAT RAN around the roof of the hackney coach. MacDonald took the best spot, next to the driver, and left the slippery, tilting top for anyone else who might be on this expedition. The errand boy was left clinging on where the luggage traveled. The best that could be said for it was there was an excellent view.

It wasn't raining. It also wasn't not raining. This season of the year, London offered a choice of a dozen states between bone dry and actually underwater. It tried them out, one after another, all day long. This made life slippery and cold for those who weren't tucked up inside the coach with a lap robe over them.

Better not to think about being warm and comfortable. That wasn't going to happen anytime soon. There was much to be said for the life of an errand boy, but it was marvelously uncomfortable.

On the other hand, perched up on top of the coach one could hear most of what was being said inside the hackney.

". . . your supercilious Mr. Hayward who sneers at me and does not meet my eyes." That was Miss Séverine.

"I don't hire my man of business because he's likable. I hire him to collect rents and repair my London property."

"You need not patronize me, monsieur. I own extensive properties in three countries. My mother set me to managing them when I was fifteen."

The hackney rattled over a course of noisy cobbles and the voices inside the hackney became indecipherable.

". . . know the difference between integrity and a pleasant nature. Your man did not give you all the records of the trust he administered for your wife and daughter. There should be account books for—"

"My wife's daughter," Deverney said. "Not mine." Cold words that sounded as if they had been repeated many times before. Truth could be very cold.

"You have an exact and meticulous nature," Miss Sévie said. "I'm not sure I admire it. And that does not change the number of account books I expect to find."

The coach arrived in Kepple Street and pulled up to Number Twenty-nine. Revelations ended. MacDonald counted out coins for the driver and growled that some boys needed to stir their stumps and get down to see Miss out of the coach.

There were three or four ways to get to the ground from the top of a coach. Simplest was to ignore those rungs on the side and scramble over the boot, setting foot in the spokes of the big back wheel and jumping to the ground. This was when you hoped the coachman had the brake set tight so you didn't accidentally get your toes cut off when the wheel moved. The life of an errand boy was one of continual nimbleness.

There was no need to rush. Deverney provided all the help Miss Séverine needed in getting down from the coach, and then some. His hands were polite and impersonal, but his eyes were sharp on her when she wasn't looking at him directly.

Miss did more than her usual glance up and down the neighborhood. She was sizing it up. It would have been interesting to know what she thought of it.

Miss Séverine improved the next few minutes going through a list of errands that had to be discharged all over London. That started with five letters to deliver, three of them to men at the Magistrate's Court, one to the coroner's surgeon,

Mr. Tweed. There'd be lunch with Mr. Tweed today. She did that every week or so because they were old friends. Then there was a letter to Annie, the chief of Miss's Eyes and Ears around town. A spoken message went to William Doyle, Miss Sévie's father. He'd be in one of half a dozen public houses, some of them unsavory. William Doyle was to be told that Deverney had showed up. Nothing was put on paper and the words were for William Doyle's ear only.

Then there was a grocery list. Working for Miss Sévie was an education in so many ways.

MacDonald wasn't given errands to run. He stumped across Kepple Street to stand at the door and guard Mademoiselle de Cabrillac from anything dangerous, including Monsieur Deverney.

BARTHOLOMEW Horatio Markham—Bart to his family and his friends at Eton, Bar to his twin brother, technically the Honorable Bartholomew Markham—jogged along Whipple Lane with Latin books knocking against his back. He turned the corner and paused, pretending to shrug the books easier on him, actually looking back over his shoulder.

A carriage turned the corner behind him and slowed. What he saw was an ordinary brown carriage without markings, a heavy chestnut horse, and a driver with his face half covered by a scarf.

He set off again, picking up the pace to see if they'd do the same. They did. He was almost sure now.

He wasn't scared yet, though he probably should be. What was it Sévie said? "Being afraid keeps you alive."

Hard to imagine Sévie was ever afraid, though.

He'd been making this trip to Mr. Landeta's house three times a week since he got well enough to walk a mile without getting black spots in front of his eyes. He didn't like Latin, but he liked Mr. Landeta, who'd talk about anything under the sun when the exercises were done, so long as it could be said in Latin. They had to make up words for things like alcohol lamp and grenade and sulfur, though they'd finally confirmed sulfur in a book by Francis Bacon. It was almost the same word. *Sulphure.*

Last time he'd walked to Landeta's he'd felt an odd uneasiness along his spine, an itch that made him want to spin around and catch somebody watching. He'd taken a narrow alley on the way, a shortcut, and the feeling was gone before he got to Landeta's tiny crooked house. So he ignored it. Sometimes he got dizzy when he walked a long way. He wasn't altogether past the measles.

This morning the itch was back. He was being followed. He was almost certain of it.

What would Sévie do? Or Hawker or any of the rest of them?

They'd find out who it was. And they wouldn't lead whoever it was to Mr. Landeta.

Frigate Bookseller lay thirty feet ahead on the right. It wasn't open for the day, but the shutters were off and the shop boys were carrying books out to the display tables in front. He ducked through the door as if he had business to conduct inside and waited, looking out the window.

The carriage rolled past. The passenger, a man-shaped outline inside, didn't turn to look at the shop. One glimpse and the coach was gone, clattering along the street.

He tossed his Latin books onto the counter, muttered, "I'll be back for these," and ran.

They'd already disappeared around the corner. For a minute he thought he'd lost them, then he saw the coach, almost anonymous. Almost getting away from him. He wove in and out of horses and carts and caught up with it five streets later.

No time like the present.

He sprinted till he was level with it, grabbed the frame of the window, pulled himself up, and hung there.

The coach was empty. If there'd been anyone inside, they were gone now. Not so much as a glove left behind. If this was even the right coach.

The driver twisted round. Holding the horses left-handed, he brought his whip down again and again, hitting face, shoulders, and hands, dislodging a human barnacle.

A final sharp crack on his knuckles and Bart lost his hold. He hit the cobbles of the street with the wind knocked out of him. Blackness slapped down across everything.

"Fool boy!" A passerby grabbed his arm and pulled him from under a set of oncoming hooves, up to the pavement. And dropped him there. Vigorously.

"Serves you right," the man said. That was London for you. Always somebody taking an interest.

He sat on the curb, elbows propped on his knees, forehead in hands. The coach disappeared into the traffic. The driver didn't look back. His rescuer stalked off, muttering. And Bart concentrated on not vomiting. That would be the final indignity.

Was he being followed or was it all his imagination? Had there even been somebody in that coach?

He'd tell Papa the next time he saw him. At supper tonight or breakfast tomorrow morning. He didn't relish the prospect. Any way you looked at it, he'd made a fool of himself.

Nineteen

DOYLE SAT IN THE CHINESE DINING ROOM IN MEEKS Street going through the clothes O'Grady had worn for his masquerade as a waiter, every item right down to the skin. The gleanings from the pockets rested in the blue-and-white bowl that usually held fruit. O'Grady's gun, unloaded, was on Doyle's left.

"Torture," Hawker was saying in the next room, "is not the art of pain. That's a layman's view. Torture is negotiation." He was repeating, almost word for word, something Doyle had said two decades ago when they were hiding in the basement of a house outside Paris. "Reasoned discourse is more persuasive than pain."

The door between dining room and front study was left a hand-width open. Closed, it was a firm barrier to sound. A little open and conversation traveled easily between the two rooms. Through the gap Doyle could see a slice of Hawker's back. He held his cup of coffee. He'd gone over to stare out the window and enjoy the gray dawn. Hawker would be in no particular hurry. Time is always on the side of the interrogators.

Out of sight, O'Grady, tied to a chair, was complaining.

Felicity made click-click sounds at the hearth, dealing with pokers.

O'Grady would have said the questioning hadn't begun yet, but Hawker, drinking coffee and ignoring him, was part of it.

Doyle went through the pockets of O'Grady's greatcoat and felt along the seams. O'Grady would hear the slither of cloth and the click of buttons against the wood of the table and know somebody was in the next room. Nothing more discouraging to a man being tortured than an unseen audience.

"Are we ready?" Hawker asked.

"Oh, yes," Felicity said. "See." Scrape. Click.

"Lean them there, against the andirons. It works better if you let iron cool a bit before you put it to use. Same way you use a dull knife instead of a sharp one."

"I'll remember that." Felicity's voice was perfectly serious.

O'Grady panted. "You can't just drag me in here. There's no charge against me. You can't get away with this. I have friends."

Nobody bothered to answer.

"You don't want to do too much damage, right at first," Hawker said. "You need unbroken skin to work on. I prefer the side of a hot knife, myself. Small burns. Precision and control."

"Precision and control," Felicity repeated.

Doyle hadn't expected to find anything in the greatcoat, and he didn't. He was doing the second or third search. The coat smelled of tobacco and beer. Less strongly of gunpowder. A little bit, of oranges.

Hawker said, "The key is taking your time and doing it right."

"Stop this," O'Grady snarled. "I'll tell you what you want to know."

Hawker, pleasantly, "Yes. You will."

This was not the first prisoner questioned at Meeks Street. There was a routine. Agents went through the house and picked up gunsmithing tools and intimidating kitchen implements. The cruel apple corer generally played a part, and the fiendish corkscrew. There was something of a competition to locate the most horrific machineries.

"Where are the thumbscrews? When I find out who keeps

running off with my thumbscrews, he's in trouble." Hawker murmured, "Felicity."

"Sir?" Surely the first time in memory Felicity had called Hawker that.

"I need a knife. A blade about so long. There'll be some in the kitchen. It doesn't have to be clean."

"Yes, sir."

The door banged behind her.

"It was a job. I did it fer a hundred pounds." O'Grady coughed and coughed again. "I'll tell you everything if you let me loose. Everything."

Hawker crossed the open slit of the door, into sight and out. "Who wants Wellington dead, Mr. O'Grady?"

In the dining room, Doyle turned to O'Grady's possessions, loose in the blue-and-white bowl. A handkerchief, cheaply made. Under it, a key suitable for getting into a house.

O'Grady said quickly, "I was ordered to wound the man, not kill him. As God is my witness, I didn't go in there to kill. Just hit him somewhere. Frighten him. Lay him up for a while."

"Who gave the order?"

"A nob. A foreigner, dressed fancy. I don't know his name. A man like that's not going to give his name to the likes of me."

"Then you have nothing to bargain with, do you?"

This was going predictably. Doyle laid a silver watch beside the handkerchief. It wasn't ticking, but it started when he wound it. A careful man, O'Grady. He carried no noise with him when he went to work.

"Listen to me. Listen." Fast words from O'Grady, but he wasn't panicked yet. "I met him twice. We were in the Olive Tree in Covent Garden."

"A good place for hiring a killer. It's dark and the immediate surroundings are not salubrious. Ah. That's our knife arriving."

Felicity's voice. "Will this do? Can I use it on him?"

Hawker, cheerful. "Of course. The first rule is, burn shallow and close-spaced. You can take off an amazing amount of skin and still keep the man alive. There's an art to it."

Hawker was convincing as a torturer, maybe because there'd been a time in his life he'd have done torture without a second thought. Maybe because he'd been intelligently and creatively tortured by the French a couple of times.

O'Grady said quickly, "I got a good look at him."

"I'm sure you're about to describe him to us," Hawker said.

"Short, brown-haired, stoop-shouldered. Spoke with a French accent. He has a scar on the back of his left hand. He said to call him Mr. Cooke, but that's not his name."

"No. I don't think it is. You forgot to say he walks with a limp."

"He— How did you know?"

"We'll move on to better lies as time goes by."

Doyle opened and set aside a thin wood box holding powder, shot, and the damping rod. Then a comb. Shirt studs. A two-pound note and a dozen small coins in a pouch. If O'Grady had been paid, he wasn't carrying the money around with him.

"There is a school of thought," Hawker pontificated in the other room, "that says to start with the bollocks. I respect that point of view and I've seen it done artistically. But overall, I disagree. I like to save the genitals till later."

All this time O'Grady had been talking. His voice was getting hoarse. "I can't tell you what I don't know."

"Then I'm wasting my time, aren't I?" Hawker said amiably. "Except for a chance to instruct the young."

"Can I start now?" Felicity sounded eager.

"I don't see why not." Hawker, indulgent. "We'll begin with the feet. They're sensitive, they have lots of little parts you can break, and the fellow's not screaming right in your ear when you do this. After you've burned a man's foot for a while he's unlikely to escape with any speed."

"It was a Frenchman," O'Grady said quickly. "LaForge. Jacques LaForge. It's something to do with Wellington when he was in Paris. Some woman."

"Liar." There was no anger in Hawk's voice. More quietly, to Felicity. "The first thing we do is double-check the ropes. You don't want to get kicked in the head by somebody you're working on. Remind me to tell you a funny story about that sometime. Check the ropes and then go ahead and heat up that knife."

"I won't talk," O'Grady said. "No matter what you do to me. I won't talk."

"Fine. I'll chat with my colleague here and you stay quiet," Hawker said. "We'll manage to amuse ourselves."

Doyle caught an eager murmur from Felicity. "I've never worked with hot knives before." It was acting, of course, but she was also letting her inner ruthlessness show through.

Something bright gleamed at the bottom of the blue-and-white bowl, there, among the coins. Doyle fished it out by its well-made silver chain.

He turned the medal face up, but he already knew what it was. A burly St. Christopher held his staff in one hand and cradled the Christ Child to his chest with the other. A roil of water curled at his knee.

Doyle studied it a minute, got up slowly, and crossed to knock on the door to the study. Within seconds, Hawker came through and closed the door behind him.

He looked down and saw the medal. He went death pale. "Justine."

"Not hers! Sorry. Sorry." Doyle held it out. "I should have warned you. It's not hers."

Clumsily, Hawk took the little silver medal into his hand. He was breathing hard and his voice wasn't entirely steady. "Right. Of course." Color took its time getting back into his face. "She's wearing hers in the wilds of the north." He ran his fingers across the silver. "It's not worn on the edges the way Justine's is. And it doesn't have that scratch on the back. Nothing like it, really. Mine's upstairs in the top drawer in my room. So this is—"

"This is Sévie's," Doyle said. When she was seven, Sévie had given one St. Christopher to her sister Justine, who spied for the French, and a matching one to Hawker, who spied for England, because they traveled into danger again and again and needed protection. The third she took for herself.

Doyle said, "She keeps it in her office, in her desk. She likes having it there while she works."

"So O'Grady's one of the men who broke into her office. Deverney was in her office that same night. There's a coincidence for you."

"Coincidence one."

Hawker closed his hand around the medal, held it an instant, then slipped it into a pocket in his jacket. "I'll get this back to Sévie. Let us go on to coincidence two. Deverney was in the Carlington ballroom when O'Grady came to kill Wellington." Hawker pulled at his lower lip. "Sévie disposes of O'Grady and immediately Deverney's dancing with her, being charming. Coincidence three."

"He's not the first man to be charming to her."

"He made her laugh, which is worse than being charming for a fortnight. Then she wandered off with him, out of the room, out of sight." Hawker frowned. "He'll show up at her office today." After a pause, "Damn him."

"She can protect herself."

Hawker—almost—smiled. "I've been teaching her the fine points of deadly since she was four years old and I handed her my knife for the first time. I still don't like this."

"We don't have to like it." Doyle scooped O'Grady's pile of small possessions back into the bowl. "I'll be at the Crocodile, consulting with my wide criminal acquaintance. One of them may know something about Deverney."

"I'll talk to the French." Hawker measured the light outside the window. "The attaché, I think. Tardieu's the greatest gossip to come out of the Loire Valley. He won't be in bed yet."

"Or he's in bed with company."

"I'll roust him out."

"And O'Grady?"

"I'll let him stew in his own juices for a while. With luck, I have ten or twelve hours before I have to turn him over to Bow Street." Hawker pushed open the study door. "Felicity, put Mr. O'Grady back in his cage. I'm going out."

Twenty

SÉVIE BACKED HER WAY OUT FROM UNDER PILAR'S bed and sank onto her heels.

"Will you need this again?" Deverney indicated the lamp he'd been holding for her at floor level while she scrambled about under the bed.

"You can douse it."

She'd learned a great deal about the girl Pilar in the last hour. She'd done some thinking on the matter of Raoul Deverney while she was at it. Facts and suppositions slopped over the brim of her brain.

This last discovery she'd made, lying on her belly under the bed, was disturbing for many reasons. She rubbed her face, which was dusty and beginning to itch. "So. I find my name and the word 'amulet.' I don't suppose you scratched that into the bedframe yourself?"

"No."

"Nobody noticed those interesting words till you showed up in London and made your own search? Everybody and his cousin tromped through these rooms and that wasn't found?"

"I said no." He was angry behind that well-controlled façade.

Good. Nothing was more revealing than anger. A man who didn't let himself get angry was hiding something. Of course, Deverney was hiding encyclopedias of things whether he got angry or not.

She sat on the rug and gave herself time to calm down. Her name. Here. She'd been at the center of murder and kidnapping for three months. She just hadn't known.

Raoul Deverney had studied her and made judgments. Even now, this minute, he stood over her and watched her reaction.

My name here and a dead body in the next room. It's damning.

"You should have told me this was here," she said.

"You'd have accused me of making those marks myself. You believe this better when you find it on your own."

"I don't like being manipulated."

"I don't like anything about this, mademoiselle."

Dislike it and be damned to you.

"Is there very much else you're lying about?"

"I'd call it concealment."

She thought about concealment while she studied the coverlet since it was a few inches from her face. She preferred dealing with what was right in front of her face when other questions were too large to answer. "It would be hard for somebody your size to fit under that bed and write at that angle. There are a dozen easier ways to leave a message."

"Any number."

"You saw 'Cabrillac' and tracked me down to my room at the inn. You tossed that word 'amulet' in my face, looking for a reaction." She tilted her head back and met his eyes. She was tired of this cat-and-mouse they played. "What is this amulet?"

He said, "You held it in your hand, in Spain."

"If I did, it was long ago and I've forgotten." *How long ago? Where?* Spain had been filled with things she'd tried to forget. "I don't have time to play stupid games, Monsieur Deverney."

"Neither do I. Neither does Sanchia's daughter." Without moving, he'd gone some great distance from her, hiding behind a level gaze. "Coincidences follow you, Séverine de Cabrillac. They circle you like vultures."

There was no friendliness in his face, none of the admiration she'd seen when they danced. When he'd kissed her. That was gone. They had become opponents in the ring, waiting for the fight to start.

She was dismayed on many levels. She'd thought her attraction to Deverney was straightforward and simple, the hunger natural to a woman who'd once loved joyfully and now slept in a lonely bed. She'd seen it as a weakness, but one she could ignore. Easy to explain. Easy to set aside. Trivial.

This though . . . She looked straight at Deverney's suspicion and hostility and she was still attracted to him. She hadn't expected this and didn't know how to fight it.

He was a hard, straight, well-knit man. His expensive clothing slid over an admirable strength. She saw herself touching him. Making love with him. His mind, too, attracted her. He was brilliant and irreverent, with a ruthless insight she respected. The man enticed her, body and soul. Any minute now she'd start making bad decisions because of it.

She drew her knees up close to her chest and decided not to look at him for a while.

In front of her was the coverlet—rough-woven cotton, white, and shabby from many washings. She picked off a tiny ball of gray that clung there and rolled it between her fingers. It spoke to her. Inanimate objects were always talkative.

She cleared her throat before she spoke. "I have a piece of good news. See this?"

"Dust."

"Not merely dust. This is what you find in corners when the maids have been lackadaisical." She picked a bit of fluff off her dull, anonymous skirt and set that wisp on the flat of her hand, next to the fluff she'd taken from the coverlet. "The great secret of dust is, if you look at it under a magnifying glass you can tell where it comes from. Even without my lens I can see these two dusts are the same. The fluff on the coverlet comes from under the bed."

She was proud of herself. She was engaging in a calm, reasoned discussion. The jumpy nervousness in her belly was entirely hidden. Soon she'd remove herself from Deverney's presence altogether and the feeling would stop.

Deverney looked down at her palm. At her. "I see."

"This tells me your Pilar wasn't taken out the front door by the men who searched the parlor. She hid under the bed and scratched that message, which makes it important. She knows me or something about me. I have to think she sent someone—you—to find me.

"All right."

"Then she crawled up across the coverlet—see how the bedclothes are rumpled—and escaped through this window, leaving this evidence of bad housekeeping behind. Your Pilar left the house, ran across the yard in back, and out into London. Clever girl."

She tucked her feet under her and stood up. Deverney offered a hand, but she didn't take it. She did not feel cordial toward him. Also, there was a difference between imagining the hard, warm strength in his hands and knowing it, skin to skin. She didn't want to cross that divide again.

Deverney took the rebuff so well you'd think it hadn't happened. Maybe he raised an eyebrow.

She said, "This must have happened while the men were in her parlor. She took the time to leave a message. She would have been very afraid, but she was thinking every minute. And she's no fool."

"No. I suppose not."

It would serve no purpose to imagine that time of hiding, alone in the cramped space of dust and dark. Pilar would have felt the vibration in the floorboards as those men walked around, searching the front room. Probably she'd known what happened to her mother.

"You're seeing it, aren't you?" Deverney said. "You look around and get a picture of what happened."

"Something like that." She didn't talk about the vivid ugliness that took shape in her mind at scenes of murder and violence.

His eyes, which saw too much, followed her as she crossed

the room. He said, "Seeing murder would be one of the less comfortable ways to go about your investigations."

"There are no comfortable ways." Part of her was still there, with the young girl, Pilar, in the stuffy darkness under the bed. "It took her a while to scratch those letters in the wood. Five or six minutes. We'll find a nail she worked loose somewhere under the bed."

"She left it behind on the floor. I have it."

"She knew she had to run. She worked up the courage to do it." Sévie crawled across the bed to open the window and look out. Not a loud window at all. It moved in a well-oiled sash.

She thought about Pilar, who'd lived in this bare bedchamber, furnished with the discards from the other rooms. She imagined the girl putting one leg out the window and then the other, letting herself hang down, full-length, faced against the cold brick till her feet could find that barrel and balance on it. Pilar had scrambled away, through the cluttered yard with dustbins and sheds, out the back gate, down the alley, and into the streets of London.

Where did you go, Pilar?

Sévie scrubbed her face, still feeling cobwebs on it, though they were gone. She wondered what window Pilar looked out of this morning. The story of a twelve-year-old on her own in London generally didn't have a happy ending. She'd hope the girl who'd grown up in this barren, dreary room had become tough enough to survive.

Pilar's clothes were piled on the floor. Wool dresses, poorly made. Calicos, washed too many times. On top was a shift, a dispirited and limp garment, shabby, perfunctorily ironed. She poked the pile with her boot. "My sisters would give this selection to the kitchenmaids. Your daughter wasn't pampered in this household."

"She's not my daughter," Deverney said automatically.

"She doesn't seem to have been anyone's daughter. This is a rich appartement, stuffed with pretty things. She lived in this bare room like an orphan."

Deverney's face was without expression. "I gave Sanchia a generous allowance."

"And you trusted her to take care of a child."

"I trusted my man of business."

"So you did." She started to pick up the box she'd filled with Pilar's schoolbooks and papers, but he was there before her. He lifted it with a nonchalant twist and stretch of muscles that caught at her mind and captured all her attention. So foolish of her. She couldn't even think he did it on purpose. She said, "I'm done here. Let's go." He carried the box and followed her down the hallway, past Sanchia's much larger bedroom and the little kitchen, into the front room. She didn't stop being aware of him for a minute. He lingered at the edge of her mind, a whisper and an enticement and a damned nuisance.

They came to the parlor and she stopped, looking the parlor over, taking in last impressions.

He said, "Where do we go next?"

She didn't say anything quickly, and when she did she didn't answer his question. "I am impressed by this. Pilar climbed from the window and ran across the yard, uninjured and free. She didn't yell for help. That's important. She didn't go to the Watch or the beadle or the magistrate. Didn't knock on doors up and down the street. She just ran."

He saw what she meant. He'd always see the subtlety. He said, "She ran from someone so powerful she didn't trust a magistrate to keep her safe."

"That's what I think. She has no relatives in England, I suppose. I wouldn't go to your business agent if I were bleeding to death and choking on a fishbone. You were in—"

"Vienna. Sanchia didn't know that though."

"So Pilar didn't know where to find you. The best possibility is, she went to a friend and she's still in hiding. That's what I'd do."

"So we discover her friends."

"I'll go to her school. The girls should know something. I'll send a note." Before he could speak, she shook her head. "I don't need you. You can wander off and do whatever it is you do. Sell wine."

He put the box he was carrying down on the desk and leaned his elbow on it, insolent and elegant and perfectly amiable. "I'm sure you have the influence to break down the door of any school in London, Séverine." There was that use of her name again. He went on, "But not today. On the other hand, no one can deny me the right to ask questions. My name will get you in faster."

He was right and they both knew it. She said, "Write the letter. We'll go there together."

He didn't gloat over his little victory. She watched him carefully not gloat, which was just as bad.

She added, "I'm thinking about one more thing. That girl who isn't your daughter left a message under her bed, staying to carve it into the wood when she must have been terrified."

"Yes."

"Who was the message for, Monsieur Deverney, if not you?"

She left him finding ink and a quill and went outside. Her Eyes and Ears had arrived. They gathered around the front steps, smiling and cozy to MacDonald, who was being monosyllabic back. They liked to tease him.

Her ladies. Her gossip gatherers and rumor collectors. She had a good number for such short notice, fifteen. Sarah, Jane, Emily, Susie, Anne and Annie, Laura, Rebecca, Motley Jean, Rose . . . all the regulars. A few more might turn up later. Her people were plump middle-aged women and gray-haired grannies, every one of them sharp as an Italian dagger, not a pretty one in the lot. They were shabby, ordinary and harmless, comfortable, with neatly pressed skirts and pleasant faces. Chattery women. Nosey, gossipy women, fluffy and fluttery as pheasants. They were invisible on the street. Put a basket over their arm and they could go anywhere.

She listened to good news and some bad. Sympathized and congratulated. A new grandchild. A husband out of work again. A son joining his ship tomorrow. She asked after the women who weren't there.

Then she brought them in close around her and described what she wanted. Find someone who'd seen Pilar Deverney on the day her mother died. Find her friends. Who did she know? Who did she trust, this slight, shabby small girl who was so disregarded under her own roof? What was she like and where did she spend her time? Come back with any whisper at all.

These women would catch rumors for her. They'd pick them right out of the air. She could send them off knowing that within a day Pilar would begin to take shape for her. They might even find someone who'd seen her run down the streets, alone and scared, without a cloak, on a cold day three months ago.

ROBIN Carlington didn't like this grimy mercantile building. Didn't like this whole section of town. It was the sort of place a man drove through on his way to somewhere more interesting—sordid, ugly, and crowded with the hoi polloi. He didn't like the people Séverine de Cabrillac met here or the damn hobby her family let her play at. He'd been polite about it when he was cultivating the chit. At least he didn't have to do that anymore.

He banged on the door again, loudly, and called. There was no sound inside, nothing stirring, so she wasn't there. Sévie wasn't the kind of woman to skulk behind closed doors. He only wished she had a little more feminine modesty.

Oddly, now that any chance of marrying Séverine de Cabrillac was at an end, the prospect had never seemed more attractive. They would have dealt well together, once she settled into being a wife. The first thing he'd have insisted on was an end to this idiocy of meddling in the affairs of the unwashed.

He went up and down the hall, trying knobs. Every door locked. Everything closed up tight as a drum.

There was no point leaving a note in her letterbox. He didn't want to leave anything behind him that might turn up in court. Besides, she'd tear it up and throw it away. He had to track her down.

Somebody in this grubby place would know where she'd gone. One of the stinking apes in the loading yard or a vacant-eyed clerk in the front office. Just a matter of laying down the right bribe.

Where was she?

Twenty-one

THE BELVEDERE ACADEMY FOR YOUNG LADIES OF Quality possessed no least sign of a belvedere or cupola or battlements or spire or any other architectural adornment. The school occupied an ordinary private house on a dull, quiet street not far from Sanchia's rooms. Sévie had to wonder how many Ladies of Quality had been attracted here.

She pulled the bell and listened to the faint ring in the distance. No one appeared. Deverney's message had been delivered an hour since, so they were expected. As minutes passed she tried to decide whether this was the most incompetent household in West London or if she was being offered a deliberate slight. She narrowed her eyes and considered possibilities.

Here was a whole host of objects telling her stories. The plaster façade was fresh, with a new coat of limewash. The brass plaque with the school's name was bright in the sun, as were the windows upstairs. The doorknob was spotlessly polished. All very well.

But the windows down on the kitchen level weren't clean. The stairwell that led below street level was cluttered with leaves and stray papers from the long winter months. Not just untidy, it was an invitation for some hapless maid to slip and break her neck.

This was a household of surface cleanliness and neglect anywhere it didn't show, of cheap cuts of meat with thick sauces, day-old bread from the baker's, of darned stockings in well-polished shoes. In the old days in Spain she would have been suspicious of the finances of a person that lived in such a house.

Did Deverney see what she did—an establishment of appearance and pretense?

He was looking around, just as she was. "My agent had money to give the child better than this." Anger didn't break the surface of Deverney's voice, but it swam underneath like a creature with sharp teeth. "I said to put her in a good school. Sanchia was a Gavarre. This is not the school of a Gavarre."

"Nor a Deverney," she said.

"Nor a child who bears the name of Deverney," he agreed. "She'll be better provided for in the future."

"She hasn't been a major expense so far, if this school is anything to go by."

Almost silently, Deverney ground his teeth.

In the front room of the school, someone moved behind the curtains. They were being watched. This delay was to establish that they were not important. That they had no power here. A wiser schoolmistress would have welcomed them in and made much of them and told lies. But then, a wiser schoolmistress would have washed the windows on the kitchen level.

Deverney raised his voice. "The bourgeois English school. A dispiriting place. *Non?*" He had suddenly acquired a strong French accent. "And careless of its students. I ask myself if they are perhaps culpable in her disappearance."

However annoyed she might be with Deverney, it was pleasant to work with a man who understood the art of the threat. "The magistrate will know. He is a good friend of Papa's."

She also spoke to be overheard.

"Then let us converse with him. Bah. I waste my time to speak to these silly schoolgirls who will know nothing at all. It is better to question the parents."

"I had hoped to avoid that. But it seems not. The patroness

is Lady Hadley, who knows me and will be frank. She will have a list of names."

"In any case, my patience is at an end," Deverney said. "Come."

Footsteps hurried toward the front door. A woman's deep voice called out, "Jane. Jane, you lazy girl! Where are you? There's someone at the door."

The door jerked open to reveal what must be the headmistress of the Belvedere School, a creature of dour face and wide, muscular body. A bulldog of a woman in black bombazine. Mrs. Bowker.

"Count Verney." She panted from the sudden effort of scurrying through the halls. "I am *so* sorry you've been kept waiting."

Deverney bowed, not low. He was now one of the old nobility acknowledging a shopkeeper. "Good morning, madame. We disrupt your routine, *peut-être*, despite the note I sent."

"Not at all, Count Verney. This is an unexpected—"

"You may address me as Monsieur Deverney. I do not use my title in England. I have come"—Deverney achieved all that was disdainful and aristocratic—"to discuss the disappearance of Mademoiselle María del Pilar Teresa Catarina Deverney y Gavarre, your pupil, who was last seen at your school." He extracted a silver note case from an inner pocket of his jacket. He clicked it open, one-handed. "My card."

"Count Verney, it is an honor to—"

"You may call me 'monsieur,' as I said. This is Lady Séverine de Cabrillac. You may address her as 'mademoiselle.' Do you intend to conduct this interview on the street?"

"No. Yes. Of course. My office is this way, Count. Please come with me."

Deverney removed his hat and carried it through the halls with him in preference to setting it upon one of the several tables in the hall. This was the behavior of a man in a low gaming club or some commercial establishment where the rules of civility did not hold. It was a very subtle insult and Mrs. Bowker probably did not recognize it.

The hall smelled of onions. Behind the open door of a classroom nine little girls wrote in their copybooks with pen and ink. A pair of older girls passed them, walking arm in arm, whispering.

She hadn't been in many girls' schools. They were dismal places if this was typical.

The headmistress's lair lay at the end of a gloomy corridor. Mrs. Bowker pushed ahead through the door and left them to follow. She sat at her desk. "Although I am not involved in the unfortunate disappearance of your daughter, I feel your concern, Count. I am sorry for your loss—"

"Pilar is not the umbrella misplaced in a shop, madame." Deverney sat without invitation and stretched out his legs and crossed them. "You and your . . . establishment are inescapably involved. I will speak to her friends and see what they know."

"That is not possible. I will not allow my students to be connected to this dreadful incident. It has nothing to do with the school. Miss Deverney's mother is undoubtedly the source of whatever horrible thing may have—"

"I will take tea." Sévie removed her glove, finger by finger. She was aware of Deverney beside her, filled with amusement. "Hyson, if you have it. Congo, if you do not. You will arrange for the older girls to speak to us, together in one of the classrooms. I may want to see a few of them afterward. Alone. This is not open for discussion."

Mrs. Bowker's jaw muscles tightened. "I will have you know—"

"My understanding is excellent, thank you." This Bowker woman reminded her of nothing so much as the keeper of a rough sort of brothel. Bullies were everywhere and it was always a delight to call their bluff. "But you are correct. It will be simpler to interview the girls in their homes with their parents. If it means your school becomes known as one that mislays its young women, that cannot be helped."

"I am responsible for these young—"

"You are free to be responsible for anything you wish. I am finished here." She began a leisurely gathering herself together to leave. That looked impressive but didn't involve actually standing up. "I will talk to Lady Hadley first. She is a great friend of my foster mother, Viscountess Markham."

Mrs. Bowker opened her mouth and closed it again. "Naturally I want to do everything I can to help find poor Miss Deverney."

"Excellent. I will drink tea while you assemble the girls." The issue had never been in doubt. It was only a matter of setting terms.

THEY met the students in the main schoolroom. The walls were hung with improving paintings. Bookcases held neatly matched, leather-bound volumes, the pages still uncut. Mrs. Bowker huffed away. No teachers lurked in the background, being censorious. Fifteen girls sat on sofas and in chairs around the room and denied all knowledge of where Pilar might be.

A blond, blue-eyed girl, about twelve, was typical. "I didn't have anything to do with her."

An older girl said, "*I* heard she ran away with a man. Not that *I* know anything about that sort of thing."

"Following in the footsteps of her mother." The sly whisper snaked from the far side of the room and everyone giggled.

"That's not kind, Edith."

"I wasn't her friend." Edith wore pink and was admiring the lace on her sleeves. "No one was. She wasn't much liked, if you want to know the truth."

"Suffered from a bad case of nose in the air, if you ask me."

"I don't know what she had to be so proud about."

"She wasn't even English."

Deverney had placed himself between a romantic landscape with shepherdesses and a classical landscape with maidens playing lyres and become all that was saturnine and cynical and disturbingly handsome. He didn't say anything. He didn't have to. Really, she couldn't blame silly girls for wriggling and posing.

She cleared her throat. "Did she talk about someone who frightened her? Something she was uneasy about?"

The room rustled as fifteen girls returned some of their attention to her.

"She talked about France. And politics." Edith, the one in

pink, sighed. "She'd go on and on about Bourbons and Talley-rand and Richelieu till I wanted to scream."

"She didn't understand half of that, I'm sure. I certainly don't."

"And her *clothes*. My dear, she wore the same dress till she positively grew *out* of it."

"Something smoky about being a Spaniard with a French name, if you ask me," a plump girl in white said. "I never understood that."

"She didn't explain."

"She didn't even *try* to talk to one. Not cordially." A red-head in pale green dimity simpered. "I have to say it was her own fault if nobody liked her. I cannot *count* the times I asked after her mother, meaning *nothing* but amiability. She never had a word to say."

"Cold and secretive, I call it."

"She never invited anyone to walk home with her."

"Not that I would have set a foot in her house if she'd asked me."

"My mother said that *her* mother was a little too friendly with men, if you know what I mean."

That called for giggling from all quarters.

Raoul Deverney shifted position slightly and every eye snapped in his direction. The young ladies of the school assumed attitudes of grace and femininity. Deverney gazed steadily out the window, looking bored.

A sallow example of young British womanhood said, "It's not Pilar's fault, of course, poor thing. With a mother like that . . . Well, we try to be charitable."

Just the sort of girl one wants to kick in the shins. She wondered if Pilar felt the same way.

Another girl said, "I was always pleasant to her, of course."

"Of course."

"When I said she was cold and secretive, I meant it in the kindest possible way."

An older girl, about sixteen, spoke for the first time. She sat in the largest, most comfortable chair, the one closest to the fire. With her first words, the titters died away. A power in this school, obviously. She said, "Pilar shouldn't have been here."

Many agreements came at once.

"Of course not, Catherine."

"That's exactly what I meant. This is not the school for Her Sort."

"My mother told me—"

Cutting through the chatter, Catherine said, "She deserved better."

Every voice died away.

"Pilar speaks five languages. She's finished the advanced mathematics book for seniors and is working ahead on her own. She has the best mind this school has ever seen."

The girls shifted uneasily. One said, "I'm sure I don't see what that has to—"

"Let me tell you what none of them are saying." Catherine shook her shoulders as if throwing off an annoying insect. "We're the daughters of ambitious shopkeepers and genteel merchants. We come here to learn a better accent and how to tinkle out a dozen easy tunes on the piano. We pretend to be well born, but we're not. My father made his tidy pile selling salt meat to the navy." She smiled scornfully, looking girl to girl. "Pilar was the real thing. An aristocrat. The envy here was so thick you could cut it with a knife."

In the silence, Catherine took a long look at Deverney, then at Séverine. "You took your time coming to ask about her. There's a street sweeper on the corner who'd get more attention if she vanished."

"I'm sorry," Sévie said. Explanations and excuses would sound frivolous. She didn't attempt them.

"I'm her friend, as much as she has a friend here, and she didn't come to me. She wouldn't have gone to anyone else here. Wherever she's been for three months, she's been alone."

When the other girls crept from the room, she and Deverney talked to Catherine for more than an hour. It was revealing and sobering, but it was hard to say if they learned anything useful.

Twenty-two

WILLIAM DOYLE SAT IN THE CROCODILE NEAR COVent Garden, playing with his pipe and thinking. On the other side of the glass panes, it was a bright, warm day, full of birds and the open carriages of the rich, headed for the park. A relief after the cold weather. Metaphorically speaking, he'd sent ferrets down an assortment of holes, seeking information about O'Grady and Deverney and any rumors touching on Wellington.

Reports were coming back to him. O'Grady had a woman in Seven Dials. He rented a room in Lemon Street in Whitechapel. He was a former army sergeant with an explosive temper and a liking for drink. He'd served in the Peninsula from Roliça till he got cashiered after Fuentes de Oçoro.

Of Deverney, he'd learned nothing. The most harmless man in France, apparently. His usual informants shrugged when confronted with that name.

He couldn't help thinking Deverney was a man considerably more dangerous than O'Grady. No tie between the two of them, so far.

Doyle tamped tobacco into the bowl of his clay pipe, taking

time about it. Pipe tamping and filling and scraping was a meditative activity. It gave him something to do with his hands and it scattered an authentic workingman's smell about his person. Eventually he might even light the pipe, though that was not strictly necessary.

Four laborers, familiar faces here, left the tavern together. A market woman, fat, hearty, and red-faced, came in to settle on a bench.

The Crocodile was a convenient meeting place. The dregs of humanity and the more or less respectable rubbed shoulders here. The tavern had collected a fine patina of age in its long history compounded from ale spills, the marks of knives drawn in anger, and clay pipes knocked clean on oak tables that were never scrubbed down to the wood. Old smoke lurked ghostlike in the plaster. Cracks in the floor held mud tromped in anytime in the last few decades. Regular patrons were especially fond of the grime on the windows. Daylight filtered in tactfully, keeping everybody dim and anonymous.

The door opened and a boy came in hesitantly. He stood blinking just inside the door and everybody in the Crocodile got a long look at him while he squinted into the darkness. That argued he was a lad without evil intentions or a green and innocent youth. Or stupid.

Somebody's messenger, most likely. The boy spotted his goal, being obvious about it, and picked his way between the tables.

Eventually the lad stood before him, body stiff as if he expected attack, eyes lowered. An unprepossessing specimen. He was small and thin, with a narrow pale face, wearing mismatched, oversized clothing. The word that came to mind was "flimsy." He took off his oversized hat and held it. "Mr. Doyle, I—"

"That's me. Sit."

That earned a blank stare. Fingers clutched the hat more tightly. "It's just a few words, sir."

"You're not the newest page reporting to the Lord Chancellor. You stand there and you're pulling every eye in the room in this direction, which I don't want." With his boot, Doyle skidded the closest chair in the boy's direction. "I said, 'Sit.'"

Slowly the lad lowered himself into the chair. His hat found shelter in his lap, clutched tight. "Miss de Cabrillac sent me with a message. I've been—"

"When did she give you the message?"

"Two hours ago. I've been looking for you off and on ever since. You weren't at Meeks Street."

"Sometimes I'm not at Meeks Street. I expect to get words delivered in good time anyway."

So this was Sévie's latest acquisition, Peter something. She'd found him sleeping on the streets, concluded he didn't belong there, and taken him in. She'd fed him, as one might feed a stray cat. Now she was stuck with him.

The boy's mouth set mulishly. "It wasn't urgent. She would have told me."

"Or maybe she thought you'd figure that out for yourself. What's the message? Softly now." There was enough space around them it wouldn't be overheard.

"She said, 'Tell him the man I danced with showed up at my office at dawn. My thumbs aren't pricking yet. Thanks for the loan of the red couch.'"

"What else?" he asked.

"Nothing."

"Where is she now?"

The boy considered that, apparently making finely honed decisions on how much information he could hand over. "I left her in Kepple Street."

"Deverney's with her?"

That called for more thought. "He was when I left."

When he left, but not necessarily now. Clever young Peter. Doyle had trained Service agents for years, some of them as young as this boy. That kind of hairsplitting generally meant someone was lying.

This boy wasn't a beggar's brat. By his accent, he'd fallen a long way to end up on the streets. He'd probably acquired a number of things to hide along the way. "That's precise."

"I am precise," Peter said. "It's my nature." A tic pulled at the corner of his eyelid but his voice stayed steady.

"What did they talk about, Sévie and Deverney?"

Opaque black eyes showed absolutely nothing. "They didn't talk in front of me."

"Where will she go next?" Before the boy could say he didn't know—being precise—he said, "Guess."

The boy looked down at the oak table, admiring the collection of rings left by glasses and mugs over the years. "She sent a note to the surgeon, Mr. Tweed. She's meeting him at the Sleeping Hound for lunch."

"She's not taking you with her. Why is that?" It was a bit of a prod, just to see what emerged.

"Because I'm delivering a message to you. Then I'm carrying letters back and forth across town. When I get through with that, I'll start copying three-month-old newspaper articles. Next I'll buy bacon, carrots, and a bottle of ale for MacDonald and cart it all upstairs." He stood abruptly and dropped his floppy, shapeless hat back on his head. "At that point, if nobody has more work for me, I'll get on with my true calling. I'll scrub the hall floor."

That was sarcasm for you. And a temper. Pride in the way the chin lifted. Education in every word he spilled out. There was more to the lad than showed at first glance.

What was he made of, this Peter with the educated voice and no last name? Doyle took out the pouch he carried and slipped the string, felt through banknotes—all of them folded differently so he'd know what they were by touch—and pulled out a pound note. He held it up between two fingers. "I need to know what Sévie's doing. Where she goes, who she sees, what they talk about. Report to me and I'll give you one of these every week."

"No."

Immediate and singular and the boy didn't feel impelled to explain his reasons. Wise, in the circumstances. He needed training in what to do with his face, though. It wasn't enough to keep it blank as a sheet of notepaper. He needed to write something there—a layer of fake interest, outrage, cupidity, puzzlement—something. Blank was an invitation to curiosity.

Doyle tapped the note on his sleeve. "You're sure?"

One nod. Obviously this was somebody who'd learned to hold his peace. That was useful in a henchman. Henchboy in this case.

He held the boy's eye a minute before he motioned dismissal and watched him out the door. Young Peter might do for the Service. He'd ask Sévie what she thought.

Doyle pushed himself to his feet and went to the hearth to lift a twisted paper spill of fire into his pipe, being calm and meditative about it. That was his practiced façade—a big, placid, reasonable man.

He sat back on the bench, sprawled his legs out under the table, and took a few puffs to get the pipe going well. He blew smoke out and watched it weave through a patch of light.

Years ago, he'd promised himself he wasn't going to be an interfering father. Or rather, Sévie'd told him he wasn't going to interfere with her life. Then she'd taken off for Portugal and Spain and the war to do work he hated to see his daughter do.

He was ridiculously proud of her. She'd become a major source of French strategic information. Done it with no help from him or anyone in the Service. Military Intelligence hadn't even known who she was till she'd made herself too useful to send away.

He'd had to watch Military Intelligence waste her talents. They'd never used her as well as they could have. And they kept putting her in danger.

The tavern cat leaped up to sit in the window. The barmaid, making rounds, glanced at his mug, saw it was still full, and passed onward. Doyle let the worry that lodged in his belly unravel and looked at it.

She was a wise and canny woman, his Sévie. Tough. Uniquely perceptive. She'd be a top agent in the Service, if she ever wanted. There was no one better at fitting complex puzzles together.

She was also the little girl he'd carried out of Paris in his arms when she'd weighed about as much as a bird. He'd sat by her bed, up all night, when she had fever. He'd come to poke through all the shadows in her room when she lay awake with nightmares. He'd swung her up on her first pony. Taken her to feed ducks on the Serpentine. Taught her to clean her first pistol.

He'd never stopped being her father.

Now she was part of this Wellington business. She was also

hunting a murderer and a missing girl. Two dangerous bits of business, possibly related.

She was interested in a man he didn't trust. Deverney. If that man hurt Sévie in the smallest degree, he'd pound him into a pulpy mass. And enjoy it. Fatherhood did that to you.

Because he was dwelling wistfully on violence, it seemed perfectly natural to see Hawker walk into the Crocodile, slinking like a feral cat and sober as a bank clerk in black trousers and coat and a gray vest.

Doyle offered him the chair Peter had just vacated. "You're wearing a lot of black."

"I am mourning my reputation." Hawker motioned for his usual glass of gin. "Last night, I was the man who saved Wellington. A model for the ambitious. A hero adored by the multitudes— Thank you, Polly." He picked the glass from the barmaid's hand. When she'd sauntered away, he went on, "Or at least heroic to a select group of Service agents."

"A credit to the corps, in short. I gather that is no longer the case."

"Today I am in disgrace with Fortune and men's eyes." Hawker drank gin. "I had the pleasure of a visit from Lord Carlington an hour ago. He is not leaking bonhomie from every pore. He reports a burglary at Carlington House. Stolen jewels. Many of them."

"He reports it to the Service rather than Bow Street?"

"He's been there too. But the thievery went forward while the Service was posted in every corner of the ballroom and slinking through his halls and kitchen. We were there. He pointed that out to me at length."

"We were watching Wellington, not his lordship's trinkets."

"A distinction lost on the Carlingtons. Unfortunately, Bow Street told him about O'Grady. Carlington demanded we turn O'Grady over to the magistrate, having convinced himself O'Grady is part of a gang of desperate thieves. He cannot be moved from this belief."

"Inconvenient," Doyle said.

"Very. He brought his solicitor and a Bow Street Runner. There's some niggling legal point . . ."

"Habeas corpus."

"That. I gave O'Grady up to the Runner, reluctantly. He has popped our criminal into Newgate prison with his fellow miscreants. I should have barricaded the door."

"We are servants of the Crown. We yield to the might and majesty of the law. And the squawking of a Tory baron."

Hawker said, "Damn the law."

"Always a good choice."

Sitting side by side they watched people pass on the street for a while.

At last Hawker leaned back and stretched his feet out. "It could be worse. I've made sure he'll stick in Newgate. Stillwater has O'Grady matched to that nasty bludgeoning death in Hampstead in November. We have witnesses. And while he enjoys His Majesty's hospitality I can drop by to discuss hanging versus transportation. He may part with useful information." Hawker turned his drink lightly in the circle of his hands. "The theft is interesting."

"The timing wouldn't be coincidental."

"Almost certainly not. But listen." Hawker was laughing inside. Not just amused. Relieved. "This is what Carlington had to say. It's half the jewels."

"Half?"

"Not all of them or some of them or most or just the sparkly red ones. Half."

"Tadpoles"—Doyle scratched the fake scar on his cheek—"on tenterhooks."

"Carlington was coy about details, but half were left behind. A graded and careful half, including some of the most valuable pieces. Our thief wasn't interrupted. He set half back into the safe before he fled into the night."

"The Comodin."

Hawker took his glass between his forefingers and slid it six inches to the right. "So it would appear. Just when I thought matters were sufficiently complicated, the Comodin shows up, collecting baubles. Is this a good sign?"

"And what the devil it has to do with Wellington, God knows."

"While I do not." Hawker moved his glass back to its original location. "The Comodin is not a spy. Not political. Not an assassin. He is, according to all accounts, a well-regarded professional thief."

"We're wondering the same thing," Doyle said. "Is Deverney the Comodin?"

"Somebody has to be. We know Deverney climbs into upper-story windows for amusement," Hawker said.

"Why was he at the Carlingtons'?"

"Why the devil was anyone at the Carlingtons'? What does he want with Sévie?"

"That, at least, makes sense. Hard to see reason in the rest of this." Doyle wasn't disagreeing, just pointing it out.

The Comodin had appeared in Spain—*comodin* was Spanish for "jester"—and become notorious among those who enforced the law in Europe. For a decade he'd robbed safes of every nationality and political persuasion with a fine neutrality. He was a master of theft, followed no pattern, and left nothing behind except . . . half the jewels.

He never touched secrets, even when they were lying naked under his hand. The Service wasn't officially interested in him, but more than one young agent studied his technique with a sneaking admiration.

Doyle rubbed his thumb up and down the stem of his pipe. "I've discussed the Comodin's skill with Sévie a time or two. Being a bit approving, maybe."

"Awkward."

"I didn't anticipate her ever meeting the man."

"No."

"And now he's in London, if we're right about it. It's been a while since the Comodin stole in London."

"One year, three months, seven days. I pulled that out of the files. We'll find Deverney was visiting London then. We'll find him in Vienna or Edinburgh or Amsterdam when the Comodin was working there."

"I won't bet against it."

Hawker sipped gin and set his glass back on the table. "Let me get through the rest of this. Deverney is also a perfectly genuine French aristocrat. Old aristocracy. I pulled Tardieu out of bed. He was in bed with somebody inappropriate, of course. According to Tardieu, the family was wiped out in the Revolution, contributing heroic corpses to both sides. An aunt took the last surviving heir—Raoul Deverney—off to Spain, fleeing before the usual howling mob. A few years later the Comodin began stealing. In Spain."

"That's tidy," Doyle said.

"Isn't it? Flip forward a few pages and the young Deverney returns to France and buys back the family estate. He sets up a number of dull, respectable businesses, which he makes profitable. He also revives the family wine trade, which is even more profitable, making himself popular in the village. I stopped at Bunyon's, Wine Merchant, on the way here and he tells me they sell all the Deverney Mont Trousel label they get their hands on."

"I like a man with a trade."

"I suspect we're dealing with two trades here," Hawker said. "He can crawl up the side of an inn to get to Sévie. Once there, he can offer her a distinguished red wine."

"Or toss a knife in her lap. Has the Comodin ever hurt anybody that we know of?"

"Not once. It's one of his signatures."

"Then he's unlikely to take up killing just to deal with Sévie." Doyle drew in smoke, puffed it out. "I don't like him roosting in her office."

"I don't like him having a dead wife. Or some tenuous connection with O'Grady and the Wellington matter. Or a missing daughter."

Another puff of smoke. "Why steal from the Carlingtons? Why do it last night in particular?"

"And why did he dance with Sévie? That is exactly what I asked myself in the Carlingtons' ballroom." Hawker finished his glass. "I said to myself, 'Who is he and what is he up to?'"

"Preparing for a robbery."

"Not impossible." Hawker gave one of his more pleasant smiles. "I will ask him. I can finally use those implements of torture I have handy."

"You and your implements of torture." Doyle got up and carried his pipe to the hearth to tap it empty on the andiron. He went to consider the scene outside.

Hawker joined him at the window. "She's not safe with him."

Doyle sucked on his pipe, remembered it was empty, and stopped. "She hasn't been safe for a long time. Not since she first went to Spain. Not now, doing what she does for work. We should be used to it."

"I'm not. Where is she?"

"With Tweed, talking about death and eating lunch at the Sleeping Hound."

"I'll share this with her. Let us find some worthy citizen to carry a few cryptic words across town. Then she can deal with Deverney, which should be interesting for all concerned. Maybe she'll employ the instruments of torture."

"She won't. You saw her face."

Hawker snorted and strode toward the door. Doyle picked his hat up from the table and followed, looking at peace with the world, as always. The tavern cat, black as a shadow on the windowsill, magnificently indifferent, watched them go.

Twenty-three

❦

AT THE SLEEPING HOUND, RAOUL CRADLED HIS CUP between his hands. The food smelled good, but he wasn't here to eat or drink. Ten ounces of ale was enough to establish his right to a table in this crowded tavern.

Across from him Charles Tweed, surgeon for the Coroner's Inquiry of Central London, spooned a carrot from his stew. He was a plump little man with sharp eyes and a bulbous nose. His scalp gleamed even in the dimness of the public house. Tweed was a noted surgeon when he wasn't looking at dead people for the magistrate. Séverine said a questionable corpse couldn't do better than Mr. Tweed when it came to investigating the circumstances of its demise.

Tweed was Sévie's old friend, obviously, and ready to be frank about the inquest as a favor to her. He said, between bites, ". . . hyperinflated to fill the entire thoracic cavity . . . petechia beneath the visceral pleura . . . other signs indicative of advanced asthma."

Sévie's eyes slid away from Tweed, toward him. "Did you know she had asthma?"

"We were not well acquainted."

"You weren't well acquainted with your wife?" Tweed narrowed eyes at him.

"It was an arranged match." The grim humor of that struck him. He remembered the poke of a pistol in his back. The cold of the chapel. He'd been swaying on his feet, half conscious at that point, thanks to an imaginative beating. One of the Gavarres grabbed his hair and made him nod a proper response.

"The aristocracy continues to amaze me," Tweed said dryly.

He brought the conversation back to the inquest. "You're saying she died of asthma?"

"Long-established and severe asthma was the proximal cause of death. I eliminated involvement of the . . ." Tweed lapsed into technicalities.

At the end, Séverine tapped her pencil on the notebook that lay flat on the table beside her. "I don't understand half of that."

"Then don't ask me complicated questions. If it's a skull bashed in, I say that. Stab wound in the belly, I call it that." Tweed chased a vegetable around his stew. "With this one there's no simple answer."

The barmaid came to refill mugs and look disapproving that no one but Tweed was eating. She was more pleased with the table across the room, where Séverine's Scots manservant was working on his second bowl of stew.

Only one question was important. He said to Tweed, "Are you telling me it was a natural death?"

Sévie looked up from her notes. "You saw that she'd been tied up?"

Tweed chewed for a while. "It wasn't murder," he said. "Or I would have called it that."

Damn this juggling words. "She chose that moment to fall over dead? Pure coincidence?"

"Pretty much." Tweed crumbled bread into his bowl. "This is why I never talk to families. It's pointless."

"Do it as a favor to me," Séverine said.

"For you, then," Tweed said, "and your father, who's one of the few sensible men I meet in the way of doing business." He scraped his spoon around the bowl. "She died of asthma, Mr. Deverney. That's a disease and can't be accused of murder."

"You called the death natural." Séverine slid her untouched strawberry tart toward Tweed, making the gesture both impatient and graceful. She just couldn't help riveting the eye. "Do you want this?"

"I do and I thank you, Sévie."

"Sanchia Gavarre is dead because she was tied up, gagged, and beaten," Deverney said tightly. "Medical quibbling doesn't change that."

"Those are the proximal and contributing factors to her death." Tweed cut a bite of tart off with his spoon. "The legal question is, did that kill her? None of that tying and beating would have caused her death without the asthma. That would have got round to ending her sooner or later. Sooner, by the looks of it."

He'd had no liking for Sanchia. Probably no one did. But— "She was choking behind the gag. They saw that. They could have helped her and they didn't. That makes it murder."

"Don't argue the law with me, sir." Tweed tapped his spoon on the table for emphasis. "Putting it simply, you won't get a conviction of murder, even if you find the man. No intent. Any judge is going to say that's a damned stupid way to kill somebody on purpose. If it goes to a jury, you might not even get a conviction of manslaughter."

"Your juries can deal with English law. First, I'll find the man," he said.

"You probably will, with Sévie working on the problem." Tweed tucked into the tart and finished it in six bites. "I'll send you the report I gave the inquest, but that's the gist of it. Sorry not to have better news." He pushed the plate away. "I'm off to the hospital to check on a Mrs. Murphy I sewed together this morning. She was alive after breakfast. We'll see if that happy state continues. Then I have a double murder to cut into, courtesy of your lively acquaintances in Seven Dials." He picked up his hat from the far side of the table and nodded to Sévie. "I'll leave you to pay for my meal in return for the lesson in the prognosis of asthma. You can afford a bowl of stew, God knows. Regards to your father."

Tweed tipped his hat and left silence behind at the table. Sévie's face had become complex. Most people would have seen it as a frown. She was turning over the medical evidence that had just spilled into her lap, holding a hundred details in her mind, breaking patterns apart and fitting them together new. Her thumb slipped back and forth against her index finger as she thought, a habit she probably didn't know she had.

At a table next to the wall MacDonald finished his stew and called for another ale. The barmaid pointedly paused in front of Sévie, obviously hoping somebody would pass over a tip. No reaction, so she flounced on her way. And a young man, thin featured, pale, looking like a shop clerk, came in the door. He headed for Séverine.

She looked up without surprise. She knew why he'd come. You could see she was a woman who received messages at any hour, in any place, some of them important.

"Miss Séverine de Cabrillac?" He pronounced the French painstakingly. Almost correctly. And, "I'm sorry. I have to look at your left hand."

She held it out at once, palm down. This was something else she was used to doing. The curved scar across the third knuckle would be an identifying mark. She said, "Can you see? I'll go over into the sun."

"I see it fine, ma'am. I'm supposed to say the words to you when you're alone." This was a conscientious, careful young fellow. "And I was promised a shilling."

Sévie already had a coin out of her pocket.

Pity this interesting message seemed to be private. No help for it. He said, "I'll wait over there," and left her to it.

MacDonald pulled his legs in to make room at his table. The two of them found temporary common cause in watching Séverine without looking like they were doing it. It would take impossibly sharp ears to hear what someone was saying from here.

Séverine took the precaution of turning the man to face her when he spoke. The message was short, whatever was said, and soon delivered. She asked a question and received a few words back. At the end she passed the coin over. The man departed without a curious look behind. The words must have seemed ordinary.

The message mattered to Sévie, though. Minutes ticked

past and she sat unmoving. Once she glanced up and ran her eyes across him and looked away again. Her face had a stiff, frozen quality.

"Something she doesn't like is going on," MacDonald remarked.

"Looks that way."

"Best to leave her alone till she stops being mad," MacDonald said. "What they call being canny back in the Highlands."

"Do they?"

Séverine stood up abruptly and strode toward them. To MacDonald she said, "Get the wagon for tonight, please. We'll leave after dark. And put out tea for the Eyes and Ears. They'll be coming in all afternoon. Get some cakes from the bakery and ask them to wait for me, will you, if I'm late. Feed the boy when you see him." But all the while her eyes were on him, not MacDonald. "I'll talk to you tomorrow, Monsieur Deverney. At my office. Ten o'clock." She stomped away before he could answer.

When the tavern door had closed behind her with a nice solid thump, MacDonald said, "A sensible man wouldn't follow her."

"He certainly wouldn't." Sévie'd forgotten to pay the barmaid, so he laid down money for it. That would annoy her when she found out about it.

MacDonald meditated over his ale. "You aren't a sensible man."

"You aren't either or you wouldn't have been following her around Europe these last few years."

The Scotsman showed white teeth in a reddened, weather-beaten face. "It's never dull, Mr. Deverney. Never dull."

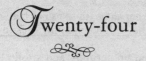Twenty-four

SÉVIE WALKED AWAY FROM THE SLEEPING HOUND, thinking about thievery in general and Deverney in particular. MacDonald didn't follow her out of the tavern. He was pretending to be a man with the piercing curiosity of a moss-encrusted rock. Raoul Deverney did follow. She had no idea what he was pretending to be.

She mulled matters over for the dozen steps it took Deverney to catch up with her. An experienced and careful campaigner—she was experienced and very careful—would hold on to this newest information a while. There'd be advantages to knowing the truth while Deverney was still lying to her.

"You're the Comodin," she said, striking right to the soft heart of the pudding.

The air between them became thin and empty, as if it had been pulled down off a mountain of great height.

"You know about that." Deverney's expression raised non-committal to an art form. "You were bound to find out sooner or later. I'd hoped it would be considerably later."

She felt like a pitcher filling up with a thin dribble of water, except it was anger coming in. "You make your living stealing."

"Among other things."

She pushed past him and he followed. A pleasant day lay around her, sunny, with a little breeze. The cobbles cupped warmth like generous hands. London at its most gentle. There was no press of noisy traffic. No boisterous voices. This shabby narrow road held nothing but the tiny drama between them. A quiet street altogether. One that minded its own business.

She tried to picture Deverney as a greedy man driven by the desire for money. An amoral man who stole without conscience. It didn't fit.

He kept pace with her, walking at her shoulder, glancing casually sideways. Amused, she thought.

"You're a thief," she said, tasting that on her tongue.

"An accomplished and significant thief. A legend in my chosen profession. It's not as if I steal apples from a cart."

"A jewel thief."

"Jewels are considerably better guarded than apples. More of a challenge. Not everyone can collect major jewels. You could, if you wanted to. I'm sure you picked locks before you mastered Latin declensions."

"What would I do with Latin? What does that have to do with anything?" Hawker had taught her to defeat her first easy locks when she was five. He'd called it "something to do on a rainy afternoon."

A gang of boys, not overly clean, charged past then, deliberately knocking into her as they went by, trying to get at the lumps they felt in the pockets inside her cloak. Deverney pulled away the handiest pair, knocked them into each other, and left them stumbling behind him. London. It was a city you had to love.

Without breaking stride, he said, "Do you plan to turn me over to the nearest magistrate?"

It was tempting to let him see the inside of the lockup at Bow Street. Probably it wouldn't be the first jail he'd been in. She said, "I don't like thieves."

"I'm not fond of spies."

Damn him, anyway. "I was raised by spies."

She'd played spillikin with the agents who guarded

England as much as any troop of soldiers in uniform. They didn't make a fuss about it. Not Papa, when he put on his slouchy hat and his scar and left for another trip to France. Not Fletcher, crafting his unpredictable, ingenious, explosive devices. Not, God forbid, Hawker, who would have laughed himself silly if she'd talked about ideals.

"You spent a childhood learning to lie, cheat, steal, shoot harmless strangers, and read other people's mail. A rich and satisfying education, in short."

"I don't think much of men who turn the same skills to their own profit." She looked sideways, to meet cool eyes in return.

"But then," he went on evenly, "I didn't sack towns or burn houses in that bloody endless war in Spain. I didn't chop down olive trees and ride horses across the standing grain. How many soldiers can say that, Séverine?"

"I told you not to call me that."

"So you did." He paced off step after step at her side, tall, proud, and enigmatic. Arrogant. "The jewels I collect—"

"Steal."

"Steal . . . have been looted back and forth in every war for centuries. I'm the latest in a series of thieves. I pick jewels the current owners have the least moral claim to. I repay theft for theft."

"A virtuous thief."

He smiled. "Something like that."

Hyatt Street broke into manic activity around them. A plump woman with a basket turned to lock the door behind her before she set off to do some shopping. A dog barked inside one of the houses. Sparrows hopped along the center of the road, taking their luncheon.

She strode through swathes of anger, pushing them aside as she might make a path through stinging nettles. She should hold her tongue. But she didn't have sense enough to do that, did she? She was determined to poke at all the particularly sore points. "You went to the Carlingtons' to steal."

"I've been planning that burglary for a long time."

"You danced with me to make it look as if you'd come there to see me. I wondered about it at the time." She kept her voice emotionless. "That was very clever."

"I was stupid as an owl. I haven't begun to explore the edges of my poor judgment."

She'd waltzed with him, deploring her own weaknesses and indulging herself in them. She'd let herself be flattered by his interest. He'd fooled her finely.

Humiliation wasn't fatal, or she'd have been dead long since. But it was painful. She said, "Even kissing me had its uses, I suppose. You—"

"Never doubt this." He stopped her. His hand closed around her elbow, gentle as wind and unyielding as carved oak. "I was thinking about your breasts the whole time, Séverine. Your beautiful little breasts that were just showing over the bodice of your dress." His voice stayed steely calm but his eyes kindled to fire. "That's why I kissed you. Your male colleagues can explain it to you if it's not obvious."

"I can see the obvious from time to time. I also recognize lies." She sounded, in her own ears, like a sour old spinster.

There, stopped in the middle of the pavement, Deverney spoke softly. "You swim in a sea of liars among the criminals of London, the spies of Europe, and the nest of glittering vipers you call the ton. That egregious plum pudding of self-satisfaction, Robin Carlington."

"I won't talk about him."

"Wise of you. By comparison, my kisses are wholesome as new milk. I am—let me be immodest for a moment—a sophisticated lover, a much-sought-after partner for dalliance. I failed myself and you. In the middle of what should have been a pleasant waltz, all I could think about was carrying you off to an empty bedchamber."

"And theft."

"I planned that for later in the evening. Larceny didn't distract me from you for an instant. For that hour I was entirely a rutting oaf. I was greedy, when I should have been all consideration. I offered fumbling kisses behind the arras instead of flowers to match your beauty. Clumsy of me. An insult to you. Last night you saw me at my least calculating."

"Perhaps."

"Someday I'll show you my cynical, manipulative side and you can compare the two."

Hers was not the face that launched a thousand ships. She had not lured this cool, ironic man to indiscretion. Even for a jewel thief, Deverney was turning out to be a man of many dishonesties.

How did the Comodin fit into assassination plots and the death of that woman? A kidnapped girl? Jewels? The Carlingtons? Everything had to be part of one weaving with one purpose, but when she pulled loop by loop, thread by thread, the knots only tightened. Fifty paces from the Sleeping Hound wasn't nearly long enough to delve into these complications. Fifty miles wouldn't be.

She continued down Hyatt Street. Deverney ambled along at her side, looking harmless. He was undeniably a slinker in the night. A hider in shadows. A thief. A dangerous, devious, deplorable man. She could picture him going hand-over-hand up the side of a building. See him pry open a window, delicately, silently. A lesser man would be staggering under the load of lies and evasions he carried.

She wished she disapproved of him more.

"I know very little about the Comodin," she said. "I haven't paid attention."

"I'm crushed."

"No one's ever asked me to recover loot from you. I glanced through your file once at Meeks Street and I couldn't find a pattern. Mansion and rented room, countryside spa, small town, great capital, nobility, merchant, military man, young fop, wizened old woman, old money and new. Nothing in common. No predictability."

"That's because you don't know what I'm looking for. Once I robbed the Bishop of Mainz. I was particularly proud of the madness of that. He was, unfortunately, a man of many good deeds and few jewels. Do you know how hard it is to fence portable religious objects in Mainz?"

"I have no idea."

"Very difficult. And they're heavy. In the end I left them in St. Stephen's Cathedral, under a bench." He glanced over his shoulder, then far ahead, calmly assessing. "This is a useful street, long, straight, and boring. A fine street to separate oneself from followers."

"You're not the first dubious character I've met at the Sleeping Hound."

"I wish you wouldn't call me a dubious character." But his eyes laughed at her. "Remind yourself I'm an honest merchant most of the time, a man of account books and demurrage, enemy of export duties. Also a noble of France. I manage vineyards and the wine pressing and sit on the city council. I spend very little time stealing jewels. Must we discuss this in the open air?"

"Better here than in a tavern room."

Well behind them, with considerable fuss and clatter, a private town coach arrived at the door of the Sleeping Hound. The steps rattled down. An impatient voice complained the coach was too far from the curb. It was not drawn level with the door of the tavern. It was not standing stock-still. Apply the brake more firmly. It was a familiar impatient voice. Robin Carlington achieved the pavement with athletic ease. He reached behind him to pluck up his cane from the seat of the coach. Not looking left or right he strode across to push open the door to the Sleeping Hound. Obviously a man with a mission, planning to annoy somebody before the day got any older.

For twelve hours she hadn't thought of Robin. She wouldn't start now. She had better things to be annoyed about.

Deverney evidently agreed with her. The narrow lane to their left, a mews, led out of Hyatt Street into shadows and sliced light. Big stable doors were propped open to let the air in. Other huge doors, barred and locked, protected the coaches. The coachmen's living quarters were above that, behind small, neat, blue-painted shutters.

"In here." Deftly, Deverney took her with him out of Hyatt Street, out of the hard sunlight, into the coolness and silence of the mews.

Twenty-five

A DOZEN YARDS AHEAD OF THEM, DOWN THE MEWS, a stable door stood open. Nobody came to object when they stepped inside and pulled the shadows in after them. The stable boy might be taking his dinner in one of the snug rooms upstairs. In any case, he wasn't here. There was no sign of life except a sturdy, inquisitive chestnut in his stall.

Deverney said, "This is good. Private."

"Nothing about this is good. Not you. Not your wine making. Not being the Comodin. Not death or destruction or missing girls or jewel thieves. Not Robin Carlington showing up. Nothing."

"I'll admit there are complications."

She let herself slump back against the whitewashed wall, which was cool and solid and offered no counsel. She faced Raoul Deverney. Aristocrat. The Comodin. He'd come close enough that she could count his every individual eyelash and see the fine lines that marked the corners of his eyes. His mouth was supple but not self-indulgent. This was a clever, lived-in face. Not a dandy, not a creature of card rooms and parlors, not a courtier. Men came back from war with faces that had become like this. When she searched a crowd for the dangerous men, this was what she looked for.

He was a thief by custom and inclination and had been for years. He was a tremendously skilled and famous thief. That shouldn't matter, of course.

She said, "Go away. I need to be alone for a while and think. I'll track you down when I want you."

"No reason you can't think and talk to me at the same time." Deverney's words dropped upon her wrapped in their individual breaths. "Stay. I'll tell you about the amulet."

He held it out as a bribe to placate her. As a temptation to her curiosity.

It worked. "No more silence and half-truths and lies?" Not that she would necessarily believe him, whatever he said.

"I haven't told you lies."

"Evasions that might as well be lies. I want an end to cleverness from you, especially today when I have this stinging annoyance of a Carlington buzzing about."

"Someday you must tell me why you put up with him. Now pay attention. I will tell you a story that contains many revelations."

The flat of his hand took possession of a piece of wall beside her shoulder. It was a traditional, strategic, right-flanking position any general would admire. He was not blocking her path if she decided to leave. A courtesy that meant he intended to do things she might want to escape. That was unsettling.

He said, "This story begins, 'Once upon a time.'"

"The best stories do."

"Shush. Long, long ago, in a faraway land . . . To be exact, in Spain, about a decade ago."

"I was in Spain then," she said.

"I know. You're part of the story. Let me continue. In a city in this faraway land—we will call the city Córdoba—there was a great battle."

Córdoba had been sacked by the French. The French troops were allowed four days and nights of pillaging.

"I was in Zaragoza then," she said, "scrubbing floors in the house of a Spanish general, learning much about complicated Spanish political intentions. But I know what happened in Córdoba."

"Of course you do. An old woman lived in Córdoba, a great lady of the nobility of both France and Spain. She was robbed in the looting after the battle."

"I'm sorry."

"Others fared worse. She was armed, determined, and mean as a sack of snakes. She kept herself and her servants in safety, but the jewels she protected were stolen."

"I begin to see."

"Of course. It is a straightforward matter, after all. The hero of this story left school and came to take his aunt to what sanctuary there was in that land at that time. Then he set out on a quest to recover the treasures of his ancient house. It was all very quixotic."

"You became the Comodin."

"I was young. I'd handle matters differently now. Let us pause for a discursion." He touched the side of her mouth with two fingers, deliberate as if he were adding one of the smaller punctuation marks to a sentence. "We stopped too soon last night."

"No, we didn't. Let's talk about the amulet."

"We'll get to that." With those two fingers, shock leading to shock, he outlined her lips. "I did this poorly before. Let me be more skillful. Kisses can be an enjoyable game. Harmless, lighthearted, friendly."

"Not for me, monsieur."

"But then, you live a useful, busy life, filled with grim purpose, while I'm a thief and frivolous. Did you never find the right man to play these games with?"

In Spain, once, long ago. "For some women, there is no right man."

"Certainly it's not that bastard Robin Carlington, the weasel with the handsome face. He's enough to put a woman off the whole race of men, if you ask me. Given your cohort of murderous friends and relations, why does he still walk the earth?"

"I told them to leave him alone."

"Benevolent of you." Lightly he set lips to her temple. Then to her eyelids.

Raoul Deverney's kisses were not reassuring and ordinary.

The drawling stroke of his hand at the curve of her ear disturbed her profoundly. Robin Carlington, in all his attempts at seduction, had never created one tenth the magic Deverney achieved with one finger arrested in its tracing down her cheek.

The green-hay smell of the stable filled her senses. Thick walls kept the city's noise at bay. The plaster was cool at her back even in the heat of the day. The floor, rough and gritty beneath her feet. So ordinary a stable to enfold her so completely.

They engaged in a few more kisses. The chestnut—surely the worst duenna in history—scraped hooves in the straw. Nobody came into the stable to make certain they were not stealing sacks of grain, or horse tackle. Or horses, for that matter.

At last she said, "I don't like this."

"You don't like stables? Horses? The second Tuesday of the month? Me?" He looked down at her seriously as he spoke. "You don't like kissing?"

"Exactly."

"I do. That's one of those British understatements, by the way."

All day she'd turned her mind away from his face and his body. Now she could think of nothing else. The wide forehead with straight black hair fallen across it, the sensual lips, the heavy-lidded eyes fascinated her till she couldn't look away.

She knew what he intended. Every fiber of him was aimed at her like a drawn bow. Tight. Throbbing. A beautiful tension inside her answered him and agreed. She would never be able to pretend to herself she'd been taken by surprise by what he would do.

He whispered, "You are desirable beyond belief," and they kissed.

$\mathcal{T}$wenty-six

SHE CLOSED HER EYES AND FELL INTO THE SENSA-
tion of Raoul Deverney. It filled her like leaves shaking in the
wind. Like music. Like sand pulled upward and falling in
ocean surf. She did not resist in the least.

He drew away, looked down at her, and brought one
knuckle to rest against the side of her face, appreciative about
it. "It's a poor life that doesn't have room for a few kisses."

"My life has no such spaces."

"A pity." They engaged in another kiss, not a brief one.
Then another. She didn't try to find excuses anywhere inside
her. She just kissed him back.

He stopped. "This is . . . I'm looking for an English word
that means very, very unwise."

"At this moment the word is Séverine de Cabrillac."

"Or my own name," he said.

"This . . . this little indulgence is not important. You said
so yourself. I take your word as an expert." She was no blush-
ing debutante, but a woman who had loved and been loved in
return. A man's touch was familiar. She'd felt the warmth and
hardness of a man's body pressed against her before. Had she

been so overwhelmed when she was a foolish girl in love, mad for her Gaëtan? Had she been plunged so deeply into unreason? She did not think so.

He shook his head. "I have been one of life's trivialities. Trifling, in all the word's meanings. You, on the other hand . . ." He took a strand of her hair and slid it between thumb and index finger, savoring. "You're not trivial. You are solemn as an olive tree, Séverine de Cabrillac. Not afraid—I don't know what would make you afraid—but wary. You watch every second between us as if it might turn and bite you. Were you betrayed so badly?"

One recovers from being betrayed. Never, never from betraying someone else. "My disloyalties are complicated. They are also none of your concern."

When she was young she'd run away to be a spy, that being the life she knew best. She'd gone to Spain, to Military Intelligence and men who did not know she was Papa's daughter. They'd set her to spy upon the French officers. That had gone well enough till she met and fell in love with Gaëtan and they became lovers.

It is tragedy enough to be young and enmeshed in a hopeless love. The greater tragedy is when both lovers do not die of it. When one of them lives.

She'd done her duty. Coming from the family she did, she did not know how to do otherwise. She'd carried French battle plans to the British Command and stood on the heights of La Puebla, above the battlefield of Vitoria, and watched the Light Division plow into the French line. After dark when the fighting was over, she found Gaëtan among the French dead.

In the circle of Monsieur Deverney's arms, she was overwhelmed by emotions she had not expected to feel again.

She said. "This is probably a disaster in the making. I would much prefer to be flirting with you and not giving a damn."

"I know. I couldn't hold you like this and not know."

She bowed her head to breathe against the palm of his hand. The moment was intimate beyond bearing. They were both shaking. They were very annoyed with each other.

Resolutely, she straightened away from him. "Wanting you makes me stupid. I will stop now."

"We'll both stop." He paused in stroking the skin behind her ear, his place marked with his fingertips. "It's hard to think of you being less than wise."

"This moment is the rare example. Let's discuss the amulet instead."

"I am obedient to the commands of a woman as well armed as I suspect you to be. We continue, then, with my little story." He took his finger from her skin. "Have you remembered meeting me?"

"Not in the least. No."

"Then I will remember for both of us, *querida*. Our young hero—have I told you yet he was a fool?—set out on his quest to retrieve the treasure of his family. They had been scattered far and wide among the French and the English, gambled away, tossed to whores, traded for a plump chicken." Deverney motioned an unmistakable trade in chickens, doing it so skillfully she could almost hear them squawking. "Every army was awash in stolen goods. No one knew their value."

"I suppose a skilled thief could make himself rich on secondhand loot."

"I was and I did. You were the first and last ever to catch me. A salutary experience for a young thief." He paused. "We were near Béjar."

Béjar. The air had been dry and dusty there, smelling of pine. Wind blew down from the mountains in the north, cold at night, blisteringly hot in the day. Donkin's Brigade was encamped on the river in a long bivouac of tents outside the village. She'd delivered her messages to Colonel Donkin, one of the men she regularly passed reports to. A friend.

He'd grilled her about French troops and given her a meal and a tent to sleep in with guards outside. Her best sleep in weeks. Five hours of it. "Someone was stealing from the officers' tents." It was coming back to her. "They took jewels, only jewels, and left the money behind. It made everybody nervous."

"My work." Light streamed through the open door of the stable. All the light she needed to watch the complex interworking of amusement and irony in his face.

"The jewels were illegal loot, of course. Donkin didn't

want them brought to his attention because he'd have to confiscate the lot and discipline everybody when they were headed into battle. He asked me to make the problem go away. So I did. I owed him favors."

"You arranged a loud and drunken dice game with the winnings tossed into somebody's trunk. They locked it with a big shiny padlock. Nicely done."

"Thank you."

"They caught me picking that padlock. They dragged me in front of you on the way to hanging me."

"You were a thief," she pointed out.

"I'm still a thief, but I still don't want to be hanged." Absentmindedly he rested his hands on her shoulders. "They dropped me in the dirt in front of you. I looked up and saw you on that ugly horse, high above me, riding astride like a farm girl, dressed in shabby black, with your hair tucked under a man's tricorne."

"That ugly mare could travel two days straight on a hatful of meal. I liked her better than most of the men I served with. And she had more sense."

"I'm sure she was all that is admirable in a horse. You bent down to one of the soldiers, asking questions, and I saw your face in the lantern light. Your skin was very white, you sat in the saddle like an Amazon, and you looked tired unto the death. I thought you were the most beautiful woman I'd ever seen."

He'd been thinking that? She hadn't known.

"But then," he went on calmly, "I didn't expect to lay eyes on very many more women. That may have influenced me."

She was catching vivid glimpses of that little interval, long ago. She hadn't wanted to look at the thief they'd caught. It was hard enough to do the work she did without looking into men's eyes. "I didn't get a good look at you."

"Obviously not," he said lightly. "If you'd seen me, you wouldn't have forgotten."

"There was a crowd of men around you and they didn't bring you close. It was dark."

But she remembered a skinny boy, dark-haired, half-naked,

covered with dust and blood, his rib cage a stretched bellows gasping for air. He'd been exhausted and beaten and no longer fighting, but his eyes were sharp on everything around him, desperate and alive. He had been so beautiful and so tough. Doomed. She'd thought, *He's no older than me.*

The whitewashed walls of the stable enclosed a quiet space and the past visited, picture by picture. She said, "You were carrying small leather bags in your clothes, each full of jewels."

"The fruit of several robberies. You had me dead to rights that night. I liked the way you barely glanced at a fortune and waved it off to a sergeant. You said, 'Take it to the quartermaster. It's his problem.'"

"It wasn't mine, anyway," she said.

She'd been impatient to leave. The moon was an hour from setting and she had a long way to go. The hills were full of armed men, most of them casually murderous. MacDonald waited for her with the Spanish partisans. The French and the English were on the move. Everything in her life was more important than the fate of a young Spanish thief.

Who'd turned out to be Deverney.

"That's when you saved my life," Deverney said. "You told them to turn me over to the mayor of Béjar. You said, 'He's a Spanish thief. Let the Spanish hang him.' Did you know the mayor could be bribed and that he wasn't fond of the British?"

"No one is fond of the army occupying their land. You have to be in that army to think otherwise." She remembered sending him to the mayor. Yes. She'd been trying, again, to save one life in the middle of so many horrible deaths. Sometimes she succeeded. "I didn't think you'd have anything left to bribe with."

"A gold ring, sewed into the seam of my breeches."

"So you lived."

"No one was more pleased than I." He might have been taking the most gentle inventory of the bones of her shoulder, touch by touch. She didn't object. She was lured so easily, so thoroughly, by this unsuitable man.

He said, "We come to the Deverney Amulet."

"You wore something around your neck, a dark cylinder the size and shape of a man's thumb."

"Perfectly remembered. You win."

"I thought it was lead. Base metal. Valueless. That was the amulet?"

"It's silver, with a couple centuries of tarnish. In the family it's considered bad luck to polish it." He left one hand on her shoulder. With the other he gestured an impression of something intricate. "There are symbols cut up and down the sides that no one can read. The stone in the bottom is a cabochon ruby."

"I didn't see the symbols in the dark. Or the stone."

"It is the oldest treasure of my house, brought back from the Crusades and already old then. A reliquary. They say it held something important once upon a time. Nobody knows what."

"You wore it, instead of carrying it in your clothes with the other jewelry."

"They were just jewels, not the amulet. You said, 'What's that?' and they pulled it from around my neck and walked over to hand it up to you. You said, 'Put it with the rest. Give it to the quartermaster.' When I was assisted in the direction of the mayor's house, you were just handing it down to the sergeant. It turned up in an antiquary shop in Madrid a year later, then went bouncing around Europe from there, changing hands as a curiosity."

"Until Sanchia."

"Six months ago a London jeweler recognized the amulet and returned it to the Deverneys. To Sanchia." Deverney touched the base of her throat, on her heartbeat there in the notch of her collarbone. "Most of the baubles you took from me in Béjar ended up with your friend from Spain, Colonel Carlington."

The accusation came offhandedly, in the best tradition of interrogation. She was no stranger to those methods.

"The Carlingtons are no friends of mine," she said, coolly. "Not Robin Carlington, who tells lies about me. Not Lord Carlington, who could have stopped Robin's lies with a single word. Not Colonel Carlington, Robin's uncle, with his endless boring stories about Spain. I never met him there, you know. Not once."

"There were many English soldiers in Spain."

"A quarter of a million. I was with the French, anyway, or the guerrilleros or Military Intelligence or English officers of the line, none of which describes that old fool. Is that why you came to Carlington House? To retrieve those jewels?"

Gravely, as if he were telling an important truth, he said, "I came to dance with you."

"You came to spy on me. And play the Comodin. And pursue schemes of your own I can't even imagine."

"All of that. But before everything else and more important, I danced with you." His mouth tucked up at one side in what might have been amusement or might have been anything else. "I didn't go there planning to kiss you, but I enjoyed it immensely."

She disbelieved most of what he said. "It's more complicated than that. In Pilar's room, two weeks ago, you found my name written beside the word 'amulet.' Everything you've done since then is to find out if I'm a killer and kidnapper."

"I thought you might be."

She had been—she was—a woman of some ruthlessness. That knowledge lay between them, almost toothed in its intensity. She put her fists, the tight knuckles of them, to his chest and pushed. He stepped back at once.

She said, "I'm not an innocent white lamb. Distrust me if you want, but don't kiss me again." Robin Carlington had begun the job of humiliating her. Raoul Deverney had finished it, and his work was infinitely more skilled. "You didn't have to make a fool of me."

She shouldered past him and started toward the door of the stable.

"Nothing we've done makes a fool of you," he said.

She just kept walking.

He said, "One thing more."

She turned back. She wasn't the only angry person in the stable this afternoon. "Do you know how dangerous you are to me? Do you think I'd toy with someone protected by the British Service if I were sane? Do you imagine I sat down one morning over coffee and decided to walk into a den of lions?"

"I think you came to Carlington House to stir up the hornets' nest and see what would fly out. A waltz with me was a good way to do that."

"You give me undeserved credit. I'm not nearly that cunning."

She said, "I think you are. The last time we met you almost got yourself hanged. Take it as a warning."

Twenty-seven

HAWKER ON HER RIGHT SIDE, PAPA ON THE LEFT, Sévie walked down one of the low-ceilinged, unlit, and smelly corridors with which Newgate was plentifully supplied. The guard went ahead, carrying a lantern, making excuses. Newgate was not a pleasant place but it was a familiar one. She'd been here any number of times, mostly trying to get men and women out.

She said, not referring to Newgate but continuing with what they were talking about, "I'm not a political person."

"Wellington asked for you in particular," Papa said. "Apparently you briefed some of his officers before the battle of Salamanca, talking about the ground they'd have to cover."

"You were, of course, impressive," Hawker said.

"That reputation of yours," Papa said. "It haunts you still."

There were uglier buildings than Newgate prison. Buildings more dour. Any workhouse or tenement held a generous helping of human misery. But Newgate was bad enough.

They went through the huge iron gate that locked off the yard from the interior, iron bars thick as her thumb, suitable for stopping riot and invasion or leading to a deeper section of hell. Oh, she was feeling cheerful today.

"Wellington's not short of political advisors," Hawker said. "They're stacked up around him like ship lumber. You'll be a refreshing change."

"When he's talking to you about army transport problems in the Peninsular Campaign," Papa said, "he's not riding in Green Park, being a target."

"The army calls me in and asks questions because I'm a woman. They're amazed I know anything at all."

"World's full of fools," Papa said comfortably. "Wellington isn't one of them, though."

Papa was right. She had friends in the army who were alive because he'd been the man in charge of battle. "Then send me over if you need a raree-show to entertain the Great Man. We all do what we can."

Inside the stone walls, the quality of chill changed. The cold slithered like water under her clothing. Maybe it was actually warmer in here, but it didn't feel like it.

For someone moderately honest, she'd spent a remarkable amount of time behind bars, including a few weeks as a prisoner in Madrid as a guest of the British Army when they decided she was a French spy rather than Military Intelligence. One couldn't blame them for that, she supposed, since her French was suspiciously fluent and Madrid was full of French sympathizers. She was lucky not to have been shot.

That was the story of her life. It mostly boiled down to she was lucky not to have been shot.

They were here because O'Grady had not been so lucky in his prison stay. Shortly after arrival he'd been stabbed in the back, just grazing the kidney. The "just grazing" part was why O'Grady was still alive.

"If he were in Meeks Street he wouldn't be flirting with death," Hawker said. "He'd be locked up, suffering as much mortal terror as I could inflict, but not bleeding internally."

The guard called back over his shoulder that they'd kept O'Grady from escaping. That was what they did at Newgate. They locked people up. Nobody expected them to stop prisoners from killing each other if they took it in their head to do that.

"A lesson to us all," she said, holding her skirts up out of the mud and so on because Newgate was not just pristine clean at the best of times.

"If he's going to die anyway, I could have arranged it with less muss and bother," Hawker said. "After I talked to him."

They'd come to a hall with a row of ten closely spaced doors, all of sturdy wood and all with a slot to pull back and look in at a prisoner. These were cells for prisoners who could afford a little luxury, oases of privacy from the crowded hell-holes downstairs. It was even fairly quiet up here. Stone walls muffled all the noise from the general cells.

At the next-to-the-last door a man sat on a wood stool, doubled over to play a game of solitaire laid out on the stone floor in front of him. This was Dick Soames from Bow Street, a tough and conscientious Runner. He'd hung a lantern on a hook on the wall above him.

"Still alive, I take it?" Papa said.

"Last I checked." Soames heaved himself up. He didn't bother to peek through the bracket on the door. His key rattled in the lock and he pushed his way in.

O'Grady lay on a decent enough bed with a blanket over him. His eyes were closed and his face gray as the dead, but for the moment he clung precariously to life. He breathed in a damp wheezing way she didn't like.

"Alive," she said, "but just barely." O'Grady might yet live to die on the gallows or discover a new and useful life in Australia. The rookeries of Dublin bred durable felons.

"He's not going to talk to us anytime soon." Hawker frowned around the cell and went over to look out the window that opened on the exercise yard twenty feet below. "I could get in through here."

"Let's hope no one else decides to." Papa put his hand flat on O'Grady's forehead. "I'll order wood brought up." To Soames, he said, "Keep a fire lit as long as he lives to need it."

She said, "Somebody thinks he's worth killing. He must know something."

"Let's keep him alive, just in case," Hawker said.

"No reason not to," Papa said equitably.

She checked the pitcher, which turned out to be empty. "He's not going to last long at this rate. I'll send up a woman to nurse him. There'll be someone down in the general cells who knows how. Don't let her get drunk."

Down the corridor. Down the stairs. Out into the yard under a gray sky. She said, "I don't like the timing of this."

On one side and the other Papa and Hawker exchanged looks.

"Neither do I," Papa said.

They'd all reached the same conclusion. She'd be the one to say it. "The attack on O'Grady was arranged before he walked into Carlington House. Whoever's behind this meant for him to die."

Papa said, "Somebody's thorough."

"And stone cold," she agreed.

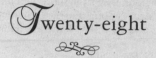Twenty-eight

PILAR DEVERNEY Y GAVARRE HAD BECOME COMPE-
tent, if not expert, in the art of following someone around
London. Her employer had never ordered her into outright
danger, exactly, but Miss Séverine had a pliable view of what
was dangerous. She also assumed anyone who worked for her
would have or acquire certain questionable skills. It seemed
spiritless to do otherwise.

This afternoon, she spied upon Miss Séverine with her new
skills. The irony of this situation did not escape her. She also
followed Monsieur Deverney, the man who was not her father
and wanted no part of her. There was more satisfaction in that.

She wore the worst of her boy's clothing, Peter's clothing,
which put her a hair's breadth from ragged. It made her just
another among the swarms of street urchins of London. She'd
clapped a new and concealing cap on her head and she kept
some distance between herself and the objects of her interest.
So far, she hadn't been noticed.

She knew Miss Séverine's plans for today, up to the doorstep of the Sleeping Hound. After that, anything might happen. She loitered about Hyatt Street, keeping an eye on the

tavern and waiting to see what came next. To conceal her presence, she played tuppence brag with a pair of well-dressed schoolboys who used the marked cards widely sold in stationery shops. They must have thought themselves very clever. She amused herself taking their pocket money. Who could grow up Mamá's daughter and not be skilled at cheating?

She was not the only one watching Miss Séverine this fine afternoon. A changing crew of street children did that duty, three or four of them in place at any time. They were rather better at the work than she was. They belonged to Lazarus, King Thief of London. The British Service and Lazarus usually kept a politic distance from one another, but they did a great deal of watching back and forth.

Time passed. Another lot of watchers replaced the current street rats and began lounging about the place. A messenger entered the tavern and could be seen approaching Miss Séverine's table and talking to her. When Miss came out a few minutes later she walked away with brisk, annoyed steps. She and Deverney then had a less-than-cordial exchange, one that left anyone who spied upon them wanting to turn invisible and get closer. They seemed to be saying interesting things to each other.

They walked off, more or less together, headed north, not speaking to each other and not acting affable. Probably one or the other of them would end up doing something intriguing.

That left her with a dilemma of sorts. Hyatt Street wasn't a place she could hide in the bustle and follow them discreetly. It was, in fact, an excellent place for stropping off unwanted interest, like her own. A good reason to conduct business at the Sleeping Hound.

She crouched with her head down over the cards till Miss Séverine was some way off. Then she scooped up her winnings and bid farewell to the budding card sharps—she'd had more skill at palming cards when she was eight—and nipped off in subtle and indirect pursuit. She knew the streets here. Knew most of London, in daylight and in darkness. She'd been five or six when Mamá started turning her out of doors while she entertained men. Mamá had neither known nor cared that her daughter was out in any weather at any time of the day or night, walking aimlessly in streets where she could have been attacked to steal the shoes from her feet.

That was another legacy of her mother, a knowledge of the streets and a certain toughness. Both were useful now that she was Peter. Life with Miss Séverine was filling the gaps in her education at a great rate.

As soon as Miss Séverine and Deverney disappeared from sight it was time for her to go and be clever. She pulled her hat down firmly, held her big, flappy coat tight, and ran. She took Tacker Lane away from Hyatt, slipping in and out between women on their kitchen errands and men gossiping in tight groups. A left and another left. She sprinted full out down an alley and she was on Hyatt again, panting.

She was ahead of Miss Séverine and Deverney, in time to see them turn in to a little mews. It was a dead end. What the devil did they want down there?

She picked a vantage point in an untidy innyard and settled down to loiter with no visible purpose. Nobody'd be surprised if a servant boy was left to cool his heels here. So long as she didn't cadge tips that belonged to the inn servants, no one would bother her.

She sat down on her heels by some stacked trunks and took an apple out of her shirt, the one she'd picked up earlier from a barrow. Stolen from a barrow, to be frank about it. Looking at the apple, it struck her that Miss Séverine wouldn't like her stealing. She got struck by all sorts of new ideas working for Séverine de Cabrillac.

She polished the small, red and brown, wizened apple on the sleeve of her coat, thinking about theft. She liked stealing and did it fairly well, just for the fun of it. An undersized, deft, innocent-looking child made a good thief.

She bit into the apple and found it hard and sweet. She'd been hungry when she was small. The maids didn't stay long. Mamá would take opium and forget she even had a child. Or she'd go away for days and leave no money. She cheated at cards and blackmailed young idiots for their indiscretions and took money from the men who shared her bed. Mamá was no sterling example of honesty. Pilar followed in her footsteps.

A coach pulled into the innyard and she was treated to the

excitement of a country parson unloading an extensive collection of baggage. Hyatt Street remained quiet. No one entered the mews and no one came out. She sat and practiced patience, which was one of the virtues she was cultivating. If her father and Miss Séverine parted ways when they came out she'd have to pick which one to follow—

Not my father. He is not my father. Mamá had lied about that, as she lied so easily about everything. Liar, blackmailer, thief, traitor, and whore . . . her mother.

The stolen fruit had stopped tasting sweet. She tossed the apple into the street and sat back on her haunches and waited. She wondered what Raoul Deverney thought about stealing. He probably disapproved of it.

In the fullness of time Miss Séverine came stalking out alone into Hyatt Street, looking unhappy and angry. She headed toward the Thames, walking fast.

Deverney followed a minute later. *He is nothing to me.* He watched after Miss Séverine till she turned the corner. He didn't look happy, either.

It was sexual desire, of course, that made them so unhappy. The sort of thing Mamá sold so profitably. It seemed to her a stupid thing to engage in. She would not be so stupid herself, when she was older.

Miss Sévie was probably headed for the office. Deverney would be the interesting one to follow. She pulled her cap low to hide her face and followed him, keeping just in sight. When he got into a hackney, she tucked the amulet securely between her breasts and ran down the street behind the coach, keeping up. This wasn't a problem. In London, in the afternoon, the traffic of the town moved slowly, and she was used to running long distances. She was dressed for it.

Twenty-nine

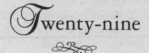

FOUR HOURS LATER, AFTER A CHAT WITH HIS BANKER and a wine dealer, Raoul Deverney stepped from the hackney a hundred yards from Covent Garden. He'd walk the rest of the way. A wise man approached the sort of rendezvous he'd arranged with deliberation and decorum. This wasn't his first meeting with dangerous men.

Covent Garden was a microcosm of London—busy, vulgar, talkative, and just a little brutal. It got dark early this time of year. The façades of the theaters were lit by tens and dozens of lanterns. They'd begin the night's performance in an hour. The market stalls lined up across the vast square had their lanterns lit too. Some of them did their briskest business after sunset.

He made his way past knots of strolling fashionables, nodded to flower girls and pasty vendors, touched his hat to the pretty whores, and searched for the outer ring of Lazarus's guards.

If he were walking beside Séverine he'd have coaxed comments out of her about these people. She'd see more than he did, know more than he knew, pick a hundred significances out of this ebb and flow of chaos. Just strolling through, she'd have made the colors brighter and every detail more precise.

It wouldn't be easy to talk his way back into her good graces. He'd offer his report on this meeting—assuming he survived it—and get her opinion of Lazarus. That would be somebody else she'd be well acquainted with.

Lazarus, King of Thieves, ruled the pickpockets, beggars, hired killers, prostitutes, and pimps of this city. A succession of men called Lazarus had performed that office for three centuries. Probably the Celtic village here before the Romans founded Londinium had hosted some skin-clad predecessor. The current Lazarus was thirty years in his office. He was ruthless, brilliant, and one of the most powerful men in London.

Most of the men and women who dealt with Lazarus never met him face-to-face. His lieutenants conducted the lion's share of his everyday business with a brisk and brutal efficiency. They were sufficiently intimidating for most people. Raoul trafficked with lieutenants after his London burglaries, which suited him just fine. Tonight, he'd talk to Lazarus directly.

He crossed the south corner of Covent Garden. A selection of rogues and villains assessed him as he passed before they moved on to easier prey. Rationally he knew London was no more dangerous than Paris or Vienna, but its hazards were less well known. Habit is everything. Being attacked in the alleys of Faubourg St. Antoine would have the comfort of familiarity.

Twenty feet ahead a man leaned against the bricks, playing with a watch fob that hung in his waistcoat pocket and studying everyone who passed. He saw Raoul. A gesture from him and a little girl selling flowers scampered off in the direction of the Cobbler's Last.

He didn't like being recognized by King Thief's men. The cracks in his anonymity had widened since his last visit to London. Even if he didn't get killed, it might be time to retire from London theft.

He crossed the road and pushed open the door of the Cobbler's Last. The tavern was new to him, but its cousins stood on back streets in every city in Europe. This one smelled better than some.

He stopped on the threshold and considered the inhabitants of the haze of smoke. Twenty people lazed about the taproom, eating, drinking, smoking, talking. One of Lazarus's senior lieutenants sat at the table next to the fire in the warmest place in the room, looking so permanent he might have sat with his back to that hearth since Tudor times, collecting the tax Lazarus demanded of the thieves of town and river.

The man called himself Mr. Monday. He was tall, thin, polite, precise, and knowledgeable about jewels. They'd dealt amicably in the past. This evening Monday looked uncharacteristically annoyed. He glanced up, dismissed the barmaid who was giving her left breast a little rest on his shoulder, and beckoned.

Raoul had dealt stolen property in many cities. London's criminal establishment was less dangerous than some. Here, the lesser hyenas of the pack did not claw and bite with impunity. Customs were respected. Bargains were kept. Theft was very much a business in this town.

It was easy to know who belonged to Lazarus. Mark the ones whose eyes followed him as he walked through the taproom. Those who ignored him were sheep. The men who watched him—and that old woman sitting alone with her half-empty glass—were the wolves of this world.

The wolves were intrigued. They knew he'd asked for a meeting with Lazarus and were hoping for a little violence.

They kept their eyes away from Monday, which was no surprise. As Raoul passed he saw there was another corner of this tavern they avoided looking at.

In the back a man sat alone, easy and relaxed on a bench, half hidden in shadow. He was a sturdy, respectable-looking man, past middle age, dressed in the rough worsted of a tradesman. Perfectly ordinary. He could have been anyone. Tonight, in this place, he could only be one man.

Monday said, "Verney." The chopping of his name wasn't ignorance on his part, but a deliberate de-aristocrating. Verney, not de Verney. "Take a seat." Monday pushed one of the chairs with his booted foot.

"Monday." He didn't sit. He didn't like sitting with empty space behind him and he didn't take orders from underlings

like Monday, no matter how powerful they were. Some of the
men in this room would see the message he was sending. One
in particular.

Monday said, "You owe the pence, apparently."

"From last night. I'll pay it to Lazarus."

"That's not your decision." Monday had to look up to glare.
He obviously didn't like it. "If you have a request, pass it
through me."

Demanding an audience with Lazarus, demanding anything from Lazarus, was the act of a man weary of life. In the
decade or so he'd been dealing with the London gang he'd
been pleased enough to avoid meeting King Thief.

"I'll see Lazarus." What he had to say didn't get said in
front of this many ears. What he wanted to buy, Monday
couldn't sell.

Monday said, "We've dealt together a long time, you and I.
You've been an honest man and I appreciate that. You know
how things are done here. I suggest you change your mind."

"No."

A sigh. "On your head be it, then." Monday looked re-
gretful. His shrug was a signal.

In his dark corner a dozen feet away a man stood up easily,
put his hat on, and walked toward them. He was light on his
feet for such a large man, calm, cold-eyed as an executioner,
and in no hurry. He didn't leave coin for the drink. He crossed
the tavern with the calmness of absolute power, a shark swim-
ming through minnows, a naval frigate among dories. As he
passed, the ordinary patrons of the Cobbler's Last switched
their gaze to the floor, to the ceiling, to ales unfinished on the
table, to their harmless boots. His pack went alert, awaiting
instruction.

At Monday's table the man said, "Mr. Deverney. You insist
on talking to me." He sounded mildly annoyed. "You shall.
Not here, though. Let's walk."

Thirty

THEY LEFT THE TAVERN QUIET BEHIND THEM. SOME few of the usual patrons of the Cobbler's Last would recognize Lazarus. Some would be stupid drunk or just witless by nature. But every one of those customers would know something dangerous had passed close by. They'd hunkered down with their drinks, glad to be overlooked.

Lazarus was accompanied from that tavern by his entourage. Members of his pack sidled through the door one after another and spread out, moving to the sides, going ahead, or lagging along the pavement and street. One man took a place three paces behind. That would be Black John, known even to a stranger to London as bodyguard and close associate of Lazarus. Nobody but Black John got close enough to overhear. For jackals, they were well organized and discreet.

And he—he walked beside Lazarus into the crowded evening of Covent Garden, between fruit hawkers and bun sellers and rich men on their way to an evening of vice, trailed by men ready to kill him at a nod from Lazarus.

For the moment he was safe enough. Lazarus wouldn't kill a master thief who paid a hefty fee for the privilege of stealing in this town. It was time to remind him of that. "I owe you money," he said.

"You're good for it."

Every pickpocket in London, every beggar and whore, paid for the privilege of doing business in London. A weekly farthing from a street thief. Tuppence from a beggar. A shilling from a brothel keeper. And up and down the streets of the city, honest tradesmen paid the pence for protection from those same thieves. It made for a tidy system.

If Lazarus looked over Covent Garden with the proprietary air of a farmer measuring his crop, he had reason.

His own particular payment was set in gold. Fifty guineas for a major jewel theft committed in London. He took the leather sack from an inner pocket of his coat and dropped it into Lazarus's outstretched hand.

Lazarus juggled it in his palm. "Paid full and on time, as always, Monsieur Deverney. A profitable night for both of us. I like dealing with honest men." He whistled softly, and thirty feet away a boy about ten years old separated himself from the background of idlers and peddlers. He came running and skidding to a stop. Lazarus tossed the purse. "Put this away someplace."

The boy slipped it into the front of his shirt and departed, running.

"Who did you rob?" Lazarus asked.

"Carlington."

"That's been kept quiet." A flatness of voice said Lazarus—the man who knew all of London's secrets—hadn't heard about the robbery and didn't like that bit of ignorance. "He was your host last night."

"The very one."

"You eat his food and drink his wine and then rob him. The treachery of the upper classes never fails to amaze me."

"It wasn't particularly good wine."

He'd amused Lazarus. It wouldn't keep the man from killing him, but it might prolong the conversation.

They took a random, crooked path through market stands, past substantial housewives buying kidney pies, past sellers of melons and lettuces, past schoolboys peeling oranges and dropping peels behind them. Ahead, a little imbroglio unrolled, a matter of pushing and shoving and raised voices. Three young gentlemen, well dressed and comprehensively drunk, arms over each other's shoulders, staggered between the rows of stalls, pushing folks out of their path.

The black bodyguard lengthened his stride and went around Lazarus to stand in the path of those idiots, treelike and unperturbed. They broke on the rock of his solidity in confusion. Without comment, he heaved one to the left, into baskets of cabbages, one to the melons opposite, and sent the third to roll across the dirty cobbles to the feet of a cake seller. He dusted his hands and stepped back to take up guard again.

Without pausing, Lazarus walked forward through outrage from the fallen and laughter from the bystanders. A dozen paces onward, he remarked, "Men don't seek me out unless they're fools or desperate. What do you want, Mr. Deverney, and why do you think I'd bargain with you for it?"

Not a good way to begin. "I want to know if there's any connection between the British Service and the disappearance of a young girl, Pilar Deverney, from her mother's appartement, three months ago."

"You don't ask much, do you?" He'd amused Lazarus again.

"It's not an ordinary service, but it's not impossible. They'll have left evidence if they're poking in that direction. Your man Monday said no."

"On my orders."

"Reconsider." This was rash and he knew it. "I'm not buying felonies and assault, just information. I'm not asking for anything that brings you into conflict with the Service. They won't even know. And I pay well."

"I stopped needing money when you were in short coats. Why should I touch your job?"

"Why shouldn't you?"

They covered another dozen paces. Lazarus said, "Do you think the Service killed your wife and took your daughter? Odd behavior for them somehow."

That answered one question. Lazarus knew about Pilar's disappearance. If the Service wasn't responsible, there was no man in London more likely to be involved. "Or you might have her."

"You think that?" Lazarus raised his eyebrows. Amused? Mildly surprised? Probably very few men accused him to his face.

"If she's not in government hands and not dead, the odds are she got pulled into the undertow of your world. You have a great collection of young women, Lazarus."

"Not, I think, that one. My taste don't run to children. My pimps are less particular. I can ask, but look there."

They'd reached an open space in the middle of Covent Garden, relatively free of vegetable sellers and evening strollers. Lazarus pointed to one of the streets running out of the square, lined with restaurants, taverns, and shops. Brightly dressed women stood in the circles of light under the lampposts. "There's a flock of doxies, a good many of them working for my pimps. Pretty chicks. They're good sturdy scullery maids and farm girls, Irish lasses, runaway wives who got beaten at home, and brats from the rookeries. You see any chains keeping them there?"

"No."

"That's because, not being fools, they'd rather do this work than scrub floors and carry slops and get poked by their employers for free. Covent Garden pays better if they're going to get poked anyway. Most of 'em have family to support. If one of them leaves, there's barely a ripple. The streets are full of pretty girls ready to take their place. There's less of this kidnapping of delicate aristocrats than you'd think."

"I'm looking for one girl, not a lecture on modern whoring."

For a minute he thought he'd gone too far. Then Lazarus chose to be amused. "Fair enough."

Ahead, where one lane of booths crossed another, a vendor sold tea from a giant urn. The market folk had lit a brazier there to warm their hands when the night got cold toward dawn. To one side, a narrow passage opened down the backs of the booths. Some of the stalls stayed open all night. A good number were closed and quiet. Young boys, ten or twelve, slept inside, guarding melons and cherries and the very slats that held the merchandise.

Lazarus plucked a lighted lantern from the nearest stall. Nobody stopped him. They looked away and kept on drinking tea. He jerked his head to the walkway. "In here."

This space between booths was filled with muffled voices and the smell of rotten vegetables, urine, and burned sugar. No air stirred. Every edge and corner was full of darkness.

"An unpleasant meeting place," he murmured.

"Private," Lazarus said. The shadow that had followed them into the passageway was Black John, keeping close, equally prepared to defend Lazarus or kill somebody who annoyed him.

Every night was an adventure when you dealt in stolen jewels. One of these days he'd stick to the wine trade.

Lazarus said, "Stop here." In the flicker of lantern light Lazarus's eyes were dense and hard as stone. "Are you a spy, Mr. Deverney?" He didn't raise his voice. He didn't need to. There was no lack of menace. "An employee of some government here or abroad? Be careful what you say next. Men don't lie to me more than once."

"I haven't worked for any government since the war ended. I never spied." He was, at this instant, in some impressive amount of danger.

"You come to me reeking of spy plots."

"A robust scent, but not mine. Thieving keeps me busy enough."

"The British Service and I have an agreement," Lazarus said. "The Service don't pimp, pick pockets, or housebreak. I don't spy. I don't let my people spy."

"And I avoid politics altogether. It's the wisest course for a Frenchman these last few years. A girl's missing and I'm going to find her. That's not politics."

"Your wife dabbled in secrets, they say. Bought and sold them. Blackmailed men with them."

"I didn't live with the woman. I have no idea how she amused herself."

"You should have." Lazarus was illuminated from below by the lantern he held. It made him look sinister. Not that he needed help in that. "This is what I see, Deverney. The senior British Service was stacked three deep at the Carlington ball last night. Practically a reunion of spies. You were there."

"Not working for or against the Service. My interest is Pilar Deverney. If the Service doesn't have her stashed somewhere, they're not my concern."

"You arrived with a French attaché who spies for the Bourbons."

"He used to spy for Napoleon. Before that, it was the Directoire Exécutif. Before that, the Republic, more or less. And before that, Louis' police. His true passion is collecting snuffboxes."

"You waltzed with William Doyle's daughter."

"She was the most beautiful woman in the room."

Lazarus showed his teeth briefly. "So she is. But you went looking for her on your first day in London, before you knew she was pretty."

"I found her. She's tracking down Pilar for me. We have a business arrangement."

A shrug from Lazarus and he seemed to relax. "Good enough. I'd hire her myself if I was looking for somebody."

"The British Service is her blind spot. She won't look at them."

"Neither will I." Lazarus glanced toward the bodyguard, exchanging silent comment. "I think you lie, Deverney."

The sense of threat became profound. The bustle of Covent Garden receded. The thin walkway between booths filled with arctic chill. The bodyguard edged closer. Lazarus said, "I think you're playing a game against Meeks Street. I won't be dragged into the middle of it."

"You already are." This was a time to make no sudden moves and show no fear. "You became part of this when you took a commission to follow Séverine de Cabrillac around town. Sending a few people to interest themselves in whether the Service has a young girl in custody won't make it any worse."

Lazarus was expressionless. "If the Service has your daughter, it's unlikely any harm will come to her. But it makes this business political. And important. They don't interfere unless it's important."

"I don't care how important it is to the British government. Why should I?"

"Why indeed? And if the Service has taken her, what then?" He sounded genuinely interested.

"I'll get her back." He surprised himself by how certain he was of that.

"Ambitious of you. We'll see." Lazarus gestured to Black John. "Fetch him here," and got a nod.

That argued some tenure on life.

"I have a"—Lazarus considered his words—"respect for Séverine de Cabrillac. She's done me favors from time to time and won't touch my money. I'll repay her by returning you to her in one piece."

"That's good."

"She might take it amiss if I break your neck. So I won't." Lazarus turned. "Here's a present to take with you when you leave."

A shuffle and drag approached. Two men jostled a boy into the alley between them, an undersized boy with his black hair hacked off raggedly, his cap missing, and his face bloody. They let go and he dropped to his knees.

"He's been trailing you a while," Lazarus said. "Almost well enough to be one of mine. He was admirably silent when questioned. Tell Miss de Cabrillac I'll be happy to take him into my organization if she gets tired of him."

The boy raised his head, panting. It was Séverine's lad-of-all-work, Peter. He looked more stunned than defiant.

No. There in his eyes. Wells of resentment and stubbornness. Defiance enough to set rocks on fire when he was older.

Looked like the boy was his responsibility for a while. He pulled Peter to his feet, then kept an arm under his shoulder so he didn't fall again. "I need a hackney. Do you have anybody else lying about the place, injured?"

"Not yet." Lazarus sent a villainous fellow off, either to get a hackney or to commit mayhem in some distant place. "You're wrong about a commission to follow Miss de Cabrillac, by the way."

"I saw your rats."

One of the men who'd been beating Peter sniggered. Another grinned.

"I have no client in this matter, except my own curiosity. Someone—besides you—was asking questions about her and following her. It started months ago. I want to know who." Lazarus said, "That concludes our business. Come see me next time you rob in London," and to his jackals, "Escort them out of here."

Thirty-one

⁂

IT WAS AN UNCOMFORTABLE HACKNEY, RAOUL
thought. An old, poorly sprung, lumbering carriage that
smelled of unsavory assignations between people who didn't
wash much. Lazarus's men must have chosen it carefully.

Peter sat on the seat across from him with his knees pulled
up to his chin and bled gently onto the seat cushions.

"Take this." He passed his handkerchief over. Sévie would
be less than pleased if her messenger boy had broken his nose.
Nothing to be done about it at present, though. It wasn't as if
he'd brought the fool with him.

He said, "Why did you follow me?"

"I was curious."

"That was a poor choice."

"Seems to have been." Peter held the cloth to his mouth,
which was also bleeding.

"Did somebody pay you to follow me?"

The boy's eyes flashed fifty emotions, impossible to sort or
identify. Fury. Contempt. Why would the boy be contemptuous of him? Pain. Impatience. Then he looked down and
everything was hidden. Peter said softly, "I don't bribe easily."

"Then why?"

Peter dabbed at his mouth for a while, dealing with the bleeding. When he'd ruined the handkerchief in a thorough way, he said, "I wanted to see what you were doing."

"Now you know. I'll take you back to Miss de Cabrillac and she can lecture you about the stupidity of following a man who visits Lazarus. Where is she?"

Not at once, but after some consideration, Peter said, "She might still be at the office. Might be breaking into your agent's by now, since you don't seem to be any good at getting hold of your papers." Peter sounded fed up. "I should be there in case she needs a lookout. You can drop me off at Clement Lane on the way to wherever you're going."

There were few women in London better prepared for housebreaking and pilferage than Séverine de Cabrillac. He didn't doubt she'd had a chance to hone these skills over the years. But he was the expert. And if they got caught, he had a reason to be in Hayward's office. She didn't.

He looked the boy over. "Are you hurt? Besides the nose?"

A headshake said no.

"Cracked ribs? Loose teeth?"

"Nothing like that." Peter leaned his head back on the seat and closed his eyes, pressing cloth to his face, waiting patiently for the bleeding to stop. "They knew what they were doing."

"An advantage of dealing with professionals." The boy would do well enough. He wasn't a street brawler, obviously, but there was some toughness to him. "I'll come with you, robbing Hayward. We'll give her a hand."

"Good. You can carry things for her." Peter wasn't even being sarcastic.

"So I can. My hotel first. It's on the way. Then on to Clement Lane." He stretched up to pound on the roof of the coach and shout directions to the driver.

$\mathcal{T}$hirty-two

SÉVIE SELECTED SMALL EMPTY CRATES FROM THE loading dock of the warehouse and carried them one by one and two by two over to where the wagon waited. She tossed them up into the bed of the wagon and straightened them into stacks. More than she needed, but the warehousemen had been generous. Who knew what interesting things she'd find in a solicitor's office?

The warehouse floor and the loading dock were empty at this time of night, except for Holloway. The night watchman walked with her, holding the lantern, lighting her way. Annie paced on the other side, continuing the report she'd started upstairs half an hour ago. A busy night.

Annie was the best of her Eyes and Ears, a big, comfortable, motherly woman, full of shrewdness. She'd arrived this late because she'd stayed to talk to men and women who were out on Kepple Street after dark, a wholly different cohort from the ones there at dawn or at noon.

"The woman who lives upstairs," Annie was saying, "that's Mrs. Bruno, says the girl would be out in the hall, sitting on the stairs in the dark for the whole night. Back when she was just a little snip of a thing. Mrs. Bruno would come out in the morning and find her there, half-frozen. Or the girl had been outside on the street somewhere all night. And all the time that mother of hers was making the beast with two backs with some so-called gentleman." Annie didn't try to keep scorn out of her voice. "No good talking to the mother, either. 'Mind your own business,' she'd say. Wicked, I call it. But the girl wouldn't hear a word against her mother. Not then and not ever."

Her Eyes and Ears were not just talkative women, they were good women. People didn't gossip with strangers unless they sensed genuine warmth under the nosiness. More than that, her women paid attention to what was really being said. They asked the right questions. They made that last leap of intuitive understanding. Annie, in particular, was always worth listening to.

This last crate brought to the wagon was larger than she'd need, really, and so heavy it was hard to carry. What was she going to use it for and how did she expect to cart the thing about when it was full? A job for MacDonald, obviously. He was the best possible man to assist at robbing offices and she was glad he'd be there. Though a man like Deverney was probably useful too.

She said, "Annie, when Pilar wasn't spending the night curled up on the building staircase, where did she go?"

Annie puffed up with scorn. "Nobody cared, if you ask my opinion. That big set of rooms on this fine street and the child lived no better than a beggar. My grandchildren are better off."

Annie went home every night to a big noisy household of grandchildren, cousins, aunts, and nephews. They'd share a hodgepodge of a collective meal, brought in by the whole family from whatever they found or earned or stole everywhere in the city. The kids tumbled over each other, fighting and laughing, and crawled six and eight into a big communal bed when the last lamp was blown out. She knew this because she visited and sat on one of the low stools and shared their tea every couple of months to see that all was well. De Cabrillacs took care of their people.

One of Annie's cheeky little grandsons would be waiting

outside in the street right now to walk his grandmum across London in the dark.

Annie said, "She was stealing food, Miss Séverine, when she was that little. The costermonger said she'd watch his cart and he knows what hungry looks like. She wouldn't take a gift. She was proud-like. But if he turned his back, she'd steal an apple. So he turned his back some."

"Does she sell herself?" Because, sadly, twelve was old enough to do that, especially if her mother set an example. It made a difference in where she'd look for her.

"Not yet," Annie said grimly. "Matter o' time, if you ask me."

Another virtue of her Eyes and Ears. She'd chosen women who knew the streets.

Annie left, still fuming. Sévie carried the last pair of small crates across the yard and asked herself questions about the ebb and flow of money in Sanchia's household. Where did it come from? Where did it go? Money was the first thing she looked at in any case. The second and third thing too. Those expensive *objets de vertu* and china shepherds collecting dust on Sanchia's shelves shared household with a child stealing to get enough to eat.

Ironic that Deverney was so certain Pilar was not his child. They seemed to share an interest in theft.

Holloway departed on his rounds. MacDonald came down the warehouse stairs carrying a black satchel. "I tossed in a crowbar," he said.

"Good. I'll probably end up smashing my way into something tonight. The man kept calling me Miss Cabby-yack." But mostly she was still angry with Deverney and she knew it, even if she was cleverly concealing it from MacDonald.

"Deserves whatever he gets, in my opinion." MacDonald fit her bag of criminal gear into the space behind the seat.

"He called me 'my dear,' and offered to go over the books with me and explain the numbers."

"Hanging's too good for him." MacDonald was expressionless as the dray horse in its harness.

She pulled canvas over the crates in the back of the wagon and began tying the sides down with slip knots that would let go easily.

MacDonald lifted his head. "Somebody's coming."

She heard it too. Outside the freight yard, in the street, a carriage slowed and stopped. In a minute a man approached, alone, walking with light, quick steps. In a hurry.

It wasn't Deverney. She knew that before the sound turned from the street into the yard. Deverney didn't click when he walked. He could teach cats a thing or two about going soft-footed.

Robin Carlington rounded the entry to the loading yard.

"The Mawworm." MacDonald felt that was comment enough and went around to make a fuss over the draft horse, Bluebell.

Robin passed through the circle of light from the lantern hung at the gate and came to her, frowning and impatient, through a stretch of darkness and into the light around the wagon.

He seemed diminished, somehow, though she knew he hadn't really changed. She was seeing him with new eyes tonight, knowing his uncle, the colonel, had taken looted Spanish jewels for himself. Had profited from the war. This was massive theft, illegal, unethical, and greedy. Robin had to know about it. He was, in essence, part of it.

He was still a very pretty man, easy and athletic. He wore excellent tailoring. But she was considerably less impressed than she'd once been. His easy self-confidence came from being handed authority as soon as he stretched out a languid hand to take it. His body and mind had been shaped by a life of doing exactly what he wanted.

Three months ago, she'd fallen a little into infatuation, not with him, but with the idea of him. It had been a heady experience to be accepted into the fashionable crowd he ran with. It had been such lighthearted fun to steal the hands off the church clock at Bobbingsworth. To balance a tall beaver hat on the statue of King Lud in Fleet Street. To race high-wheeled phaetons on the turnpike road. To do all the foolish things she hadn't done when she was seventeen. She'd been in Spain that year, dancing with life and death when other young women were wearing thin muslin and dancing at Almack's.

Maybe if she'd been young and silly in the proper season

for nonsense, she'd never have been fooled, even for a minute, by Robin.

Or perhaps she hadn't been quite fooled. In the weeks she'd played the games his set indulged in, it had never occurred to her to trust Robin with even one small secret or tell him any truth of significance. She'd never mentioned her family. Never spoken of her work. That, more than anything else, showed how little she'd cared about him.

When he was close enough to snarl down at her, he let himself do that. "You've been avoiding me."

"Well, yes," she said.

"This is important. Put your hurt feelings away and listen to me." He curled his fingers into the canvas cover she was securing to the wagon as if he wanted to peel it back and have a look underneath. He didn't try that, but he worried away at a corner, trying to loosen the rope tie and make it look like an accident. He was not endearing himself to her in any way.

He said, "What is all this? What are you doing here?"

"Waiting for you to say anything worth listening to. I'll spend as much as three or four minutes on it, then you leave."

"You've already wasted too much time. You." He tossed that at MacDonald. "Go away."

MacDonald stroked Bluebell's ears and ignored Robin Carlington.

Robin raised his voice. "Get out of here, McNeil, Fergusson, O'Hara . . . whoever you are. Make yourself scarce. I need to talk to Sévie. Alone."

With a small gesture she sent MacDonald off. Yesterday she would have sent Robin away instead. Yesterday he'd been just another of the caltrops that scattered the fashionable world. Today he was Colonel Carlington's nephew and Deverney had just robbed the Carlington household of what she suspected was a tidy fortune in jewels. That made the Carlingtons less dull, didn't it? She'd give Robin a few minutes even on what was turning out to be a busy evening.

Wordlessly, MacDonald slipped the reins loose from the hitching rail and led Bluebell away. He didn't bother to look back, which was a testament to how harmless he thought Robin was. If it had been Deverney next to her in this deserted yard, MacDonald would have followed her order just as quickly, but he'd have conveyed a silent opinion as he left and he'd have found some secret vantage point to watch the meeting.

Robin took MacDonald's departure as a symbolic victory. She could have told him she didn't deal in those.

"Did you even bother to read the notes I sent?" Robin passed his hand over his face and pushed his hair up and away from his forehead, being dramatic and beautiful. He'd have made a fine living on the stage. "It's probably already too late."

"That sounds ominous. What is this urgent matter? I have other things to do tonight." Her hands were dusty from loading boxes. She wiped them on her skirt. "If you've got yourself into trouble with your pack of lies, don't expect me to get you out of it."

"That's over. It's not important now."

"How nice for you." Two men had showed an interest in her recently and they were both full of lies.

She wanted to kick someone. Robin was closest but Deverney deserved it more. She packed her anger away to use on Deverney the next time she ran into him.

Out on the street, MacDonald yelled at Robin's fancy, well-dressed driver to pull the coach farther up, out of his way. A colorful conversation ensued. Words were exchanged concerning Bluebell's ancestry and the intelligence of Robin's matched chestnuts. A fine example of London invective. If it came to fisticuffs, she'd back MacDonald against Robin's driver at thirty-to-one in a free-for-all. Ten-to-one in an honest fight.

"You never listened to me," Robin said bitterly. "You're not listening now. You'd dance and play cards with me and go to gaming dens in places that made *me* nervous. But I was just an amusement. I envied you beyond belief."

She dragged her mind back to Robin. What was he nattering on about? "Envy?"

"You never saw that, did you? My friends and I played at being wild rogues. Off we'd go to the dangerous parts of town to pretend we were splendid brave fellows. And you were at home there. You knew every dark corner before we turned it.

We didn't get robbed because we were with you. We didn't even get cheated in the hells." A glimmer of the careless, clever Robin she'd known showed through. "Useful, since I'm in debt up to my ears. You knew all those thieves and beggars and whores. And soldiers, everywhere, officers and men, right up and down the ranks."

"I was four years in Spain. Of course I know soldiers."

"They'd come over to you in some tavern and it'd be 'Remember this' and 'Whatever happened to John or George or Old Athelstan the Sergeant Major?' Eventually they'd notice me and get around to, 'Carlington. Didn't see you there. How are you these days?'"

"I can see how that would have annoyed you." But she hadn't seen it at the time.

"They always wanted to talk to you—the duchesses and chimney sweeps and bankers from Florence. You were game as a fighting cock and generous and a heroine in the war. My friends and I hadn't gone to war and been heroic. We resented you to hell."

She'd known she was an outsider among that set. She hadn't known how much.

"We were an amusement to you, not as important as some army sergeant driving a hackney. I could lure you out with us because I made you laugh." He didn't meet her eyes. "I used to plan what I'd do. What I'd say. A challenge, really. I used to do things I knew were silly, because you'd like them. That time I hired a fiddler and we all danced a reel in the middle of Green Park in front of the starchy governesses. It made you laugh. That was the only use you had for me, you know. Your licensed fool. Your buffoon. And I wanted to be your lover."

She shouldn't have let him talk. She didn't want to hear this.

Because he was right. She'd used him as a holiday from common sense, a sweet cake, a glass of bubbly wine. She'd enjoyed him when she was with him and dismissed him from her mind when she wasn't. She hadn't tried to know him.

"I didn't plan it." He was talking to himself, not her. Justifying himself. "It wasn't my idea. It wasn't my fault."

She stopped feeling sorry for him. "Whose idea was it then?" One of his many laughing, cheerful, vicious friends, doubtless.

"You were supposed to leave town in disgrace, but you acted like I didn't matter. You ignored me and everyone else despised me. Whether they believed me or not, they were on your side."

"You did lie through your teeth," she pointed out.

"You walked through scandal like it didn't exist. Your reputation was as leathery tough as your maidenhead. I barely dented it." Robin looked peevish. Handsome, but peevish. "I barely dented your reputation. I didn't get near your maidenhead."

She could have told him that was long gone.

"If I had," he said, "you would have married me."

"There was never any chance of that." She'd never, not once, thought of him that way.

"It's not an unequal match. I'm well born. I'm English. And you're not exactly young, you know. Your reputation is questionable at best."

"More questionable than it used to be."

"I would have treated you like a queen." His hands curled into ineffectual fists at his sides. "But you didn't see me. Didn't care. Some women are like that—cold as ice, right to the heart. I loved you and you felt nothing for me."

Oh, nonsense. "Right now what I feel is disgust. Go away. I'm through talking to you." She turned her back on him. There was work to do, places to go, and offices to rob.

Robin called after her, "Wait. This is important."

Once, when the world had seemed very black, Robin had made her laugh. She owed him one minute. She looked back.

It wasn't just the dim light that made him look haggard. The gold had washed out of his hair. His skin was blotched and pasty. He looked wilted and old and desperate. "If you'd married me," he said, "I'd have taken you to Paris, to Rome, to Vienna. I'd have kept you away from England till it was safe to come back."

"Safe?"

"You never think about that, do you? You just go traipsing

around, digging into things you don't understand. Stirring up old crimes. Old mistakes." His voice got higher. "They can get you killed."

Dramatic enough for Drury Lane. Almost certainly nonsense. "Killed by whom and for what? Digging up what?" When he didn't answer, she said, "You've gone this far. You might as well finish."

He breathed heavily and shook his head.

He was a Carlington. This did not require complex deductions. "Crimes from the war? From Spain?"

"I didn't say that." But he might as well have. "You don't understand."

She could read every line of this story. Robin had panicked over threats he'd heard across the family breakfast table. She could imagine them at it. Haughty Lady Carlington pouring tea and sneering. His lordship planning to wield the political weight of a minor baron. That damned idiot Colonel Carlington, huffing and puffing.

"Your uncle had sticky fingers in Spain." The Deverney jewels were probably only part of it. "It's going to come out. Some cats can't be stuffed back in a bag." She gathered up her cloak from the loading dock.

Robin said, "I'm trying to—"

"Robin, go away. Stop writing me notes. Stop chasing me across London. Stop telling lies about me. If you want someone to leave London, you do it."

"You have to listen to me."

"No. You listen to me, Mr. Carlington. Go home and get drunk or go to the park and put a hat on some statue. Nobody cares about crimes in Spain, years ago, in a war everyone wants to forget. Nobody, frankly, cares about the Carlingtons. And nobody dies of scandal." She let herself be tart about it. "I know."

"I'm not responsible for that." Robin ran his hands up and down his jacket sleeves, as if he were scrubbing her away. "It's not my fault." She imagined him in the nursery, running to lay his head in Nanny's lap and deny breaking the lamp in the study.

"You've convinced me. Now go away." She swirled her

cloak around her. She'd be glad of it later in the night when it got cold. On a sudden impulse, she called to him, "Where is the amulet?"

"What?" He didn't look bewildered. He looked scared. "I don't know what you're talking about." He seemed on the verge of saying more, but he didn't. He hurried away from her. He was running by the time he reached the big doors and went out onto the street.

Thirty-three

❧

SÉVIE ENTERED THOMAS HAYWARD'S OFFICE IN A manner not precisely free of niggling legal problems. It was three rooms and a tiny hall. The front room was for visitors to wait in, uncomfortably. The first door off the hall was where a pair of clerks sat on high stools and copied papers on their slanted desktops. There was a row of file cabinets and tall windows, now covered with thick velvet curtains. Next came an awkwardly shaped space dedicated to making tea. At the end of the hall one came to the office of Mr. Thomas Hayward himself. It held a Turkey carpet, legal books behind glass doors, three leather chairs, and a big desk where Hayward could sit and impress clients. Also a large safe in the corner.

Sévie went through the clerks' room first and filled three of her smaller crates with papers from file cabinets there. Six minutes through the front door and she'd already proved her point. Hayward hadn't turned over Deverney's papers. She left the boxes filled with her first take beside the front door. The tea room contained no secret compartments that she could find. Nice brand of tea, though.

She carried the rest of the boxes back to Hayward's office

and piled them in the middle of the floor. This was where he'd be hiding his secrets, the ones too incriminating to keep in those files in the clerks' room. She'd find them.

She went around lighting lamps, then sat on the floor next to the desk, tailor fashion, and loosened her skirts up over her knees to make herself comfortable. The desk drawers were locked, every one of them. Hayward apparently took his desk keys home with him every night instead of leaving a set on the top of a bookcase or under the pot of ivy at the window. She was put to the trouble of picking the lock in each drawer.

A careful, honest man would lock these drawers to keep his clients' business private. A sneaky embezzler would be keeping his own secrets private. Before dawn, she'd know which Hayward was.

This was a solid, well-built desk but there was nothing special about these locks. They were more decorative than anything else. A matter of *click click* and she'd be in. The challenge lay in that safe in the corner behind her. If she'd been in a hurry, she'd be working over there. As it was, she left it for last.

A soft tap sounded on the street door, followed immediately by the sound of the door opening. She leaned to the side and looked around the desk, down the hall. Deverney was walking toward her, quite as if he belonged here. Deverney took a lot for granted.

She wasn't as angry at him as she'd thought she'd be. Perhaps she was learning wisdom. Or maybe she was just very busy. There could be other reasons she didn't want to look at closely.

She went back to doing what she'd come here to do, which was picking away at a lock, the next mundane task in finding Pilar. Breaking and entering was not nearly as exciting as it sounded to the uninitiated.

"I expected you earlier," she said when he'd walked the length of the hall. "Generally you're waiting for me at the scene of breaking and entering."

"My apologies. I was busy with machinations and plots elsewhere." He folded himself down on the carpet next to her. "Good evening, Miss de Cabrillac."

"I should tell you to go away and leave me in peace."

"You should. But I'd go join MacDonald in the wagon and pepper him with pointed questions. Who knows what he'll let slip?"

"MacDonald wouldn't let slip that water is wet or the sky is blue. A man of unfathomable mystery, MacDonald."

"Or I might chat with Peter. He'd be a fount of information and he's young enough to be indiscreet. But I'd rather sit by you."

"I wondered where Peter was."

"I have dropped him in the wagon beside the stolid Mac-Donald. Peter is very slightly damaged. No." He touched her arm, brief and light about it. "Not badly hurt. No worse than he'd get in a scuffle on the street. A bloody nose and some bruises. He won't thank you for running out to hover over him."

"What happened?"

"In brief, he followed me into a dangerous place. Bad judgment of mine to be there. Worse judgment on his part to follow me in."

"You have been busy." She rested her cheek on the upper drawer of the desk and fiddled away some more with her chosen lock. "Where were you being unwise?"

"Covent Garden. I went to see Lazarus."

The last pick turned and she pulled out the drawer. "Lazarus."

Deverney, wine grower and aristocrat, would have nothing to do with Lazarus. Deverney the thief, the Comodin, was part of that world. When he sat beside her in the midst of a burglary he was so very much not a wine merchant.

He said, "I had questions for King Thief. I didn't get answers."

"One doesn't." She laid the drawer—it was the bottom drawer—across Deverney's lap. "Since you're here anyway, you might as well make yourself useful by glancing through these papers."

"My pleasure."

"You were a fool to go to Lazarus."

"Thank you for pointing that out. There is complete accord between us."

"If you wanted something from him you should have asked me. That's why you hired me. For the expertise."

"Which you provide in abundance." Deverney took a silver

rod from an inner pocket, extended it, and ran it around the sides of the drawer and underneath the stack of letters. He was, in himself, an advanced seminar in the art of the search. The world was full of tiny, spring-driven knives and poisoned needles.

He said, "Why am I not surprised you know Lazarus?"

"We have a long and complex relationship."

"Really?" He seemed amused.

"I went to see him, which was foolish, but I was only eight. One of my friends didn't come home from a mission in the Low Countries. He was dead, but nobody would tell me straight out. So I ran away and went to hire Lazarus to find out what had happened to him."

"That must have been exciting for all concerned." Deverney took papers from the desk drawer and leafed through them.

"I was with Lazarus three days," she said. "There was a ransom involved. He fed me too many sweets and told me stories about Hawker when he was young. He let me help with a housebreaking. I didn't wash the whole time I was there and I got fleas in my clothing. I still see Lazarus from time to time."

"You live an eventful life, Séverine."

"Everyone tells me that."

At the bottom of the drawer was a pretty rosewood box, too large for keeping coins in, the wrong shape to hold a gun. Opened, it revealed a packet of letters. Deverney slipped the first one from the ribbon that held them.

She worked at the lock of the middle drawer and Deverney was silent for a while, opening letter after letter. At last he murmured, "Mr. Hayward, Mr. Hayward, you disappoint me. Having an affair, keeping the letters, hiding them so clumsily. Sanchia has behaved particularly badly, it seems. Disappointing on all fronts." His voice was perfectly noncommittal.

He stuffed everything back into the box, closed it, and reached around to drop it to the side.

"You were right about Mr. Hayward," he said. "He is unreliable. Did you know Lazarus is having you followed? That gang of street children I thought were trailing me is apparently for you. He won't say who hired him."

"Professional ethics." This lock went faster. She extracted the middle drawer and handed it over to him. "He's an honest King of Thieves."

"Admirable."

"He might be trailing me because you've taken an interest. He likes puzzles."

"Maybe."

She'd always worked alone. Yet here she was, comfortable as an orange pip in its orange, knee to knee with Deverney, splitting the work between them. There was a worrisome naturalness about it. Even the rustle Deverney made as he sorted papers was absurdly comforting. He was not merely a seducer of women and an ornament in the ballroom. He was as much an expert in the clandestine art of theft as British agents were in spying, all adepts in their specialized trades.

One becomes clumsy as passion creeps over the body. Distracted and clumsy and stupid. She sighed and set lockpicks into the lock of the top drawer. "You're patient, waiting for me to get through these locks."

He raised his eyes, briefly. "I've seen it done slower by men who called themselves professionals."

"You're tactful."

"You're modest." The next letter got a long inspection before he put it aside with the rosewood box. "Lockpicking is an art I practice because it's my profession. You're a practical woman. If you wanted that desk open fast, you'd make it happen."

"I'd waylay the clerk in an alleyway and bribe him to tell me where the second key is. There'll be one somewhere in here. It seemed to me the clerk looked discontented with Mr. Hayward, so it probably wouldn't cost much. Or if I were in a hurry I'd use my crowbar and pry the drawers out, though I'd hate to treat a nice piece of furniture like that."

"What else would you do?" His eyes turned up at the corners. He was enjoying this.

She gave the matter some thought. "With the four of us here, I'd put the whole desk in that wagon and take it back to the office to rummage through at leisure. Then I'd sell the desk. Practical and thrifty."

"Or you'd step outside and whistle up one of the street ur-chins following you. Send them to find somebody who picks locks."

"Or I'd make you do it. I will ask you to open that safe over there. It would take me the rest of the night." She frowned at her picks and chose one. The top drawer received more atten-tion. "I wouldn't pay the street rats. I'd just let them rob Hay-ward generally. It would cover my presence here and, again, it's thrifty."

"There. You see. No need to worry about picking slow or fast into the desk. You have a set of valuable and unique skills. Anyone can learn to pick locks."

A last turn of the pick and the top drawer was open. It was a repository of clean note paper, pencils, a pair of reading glasses in a leather case, quills, stamps, a penknife, two ink bottles, and one silver flask of brandy. She passed that last over to Deverney.

He pulled the cork out of that, sniffed, and was dismissive. Probably he made and sold brandy too. They both had a set of valuable and unique skills when it came down to it.

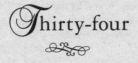Thirty-four

SHE STUDIED HER HANDS WHERE THEY RESTED ON her knees. They had old familiar marks on them, souvenirs of twenty-eight years of using them for many purposes. A scar on the side of her knuckle from the same fight that had left an unpretty slash on her ribs, a crescent-shaped burn mark from a gun barrel, a crack in her thumbnail from fighting with O'Grady. That hurt right now. A cut on her palm, almost healed, that she couldn't account for.

She said, "Do you think I'm cold?"

Deverney put aside a stack of papers and sat back on his heels and considered her. "Cold that can be cured with mittens? Or cold that a man calls a woman who won't go to bed with him?"

"You see too much." She let some time pass, but he didn't say anything. "Cold as a woman."

It took only a little rearrangement for him to shift close and put his arms around her and wrap her up in him. He was matter-of-fact about it, though they hadn't spent any time this close together. "I see that elegant bowl of porridge tracked you down. Robin Carlington."

"Outside my office, as I was coming here."

"A mistake on his part."

"I didn't hurt him. I didn't even cut him to ribbons with my sarcastic tongue. I let him say his piece."

"To find out if he knew anything about plots against Wellington, English politics, and other matters in which I do not interest myself. You shouldn't listen to that fribble about anything. Here. Wait a minute."

He took his jacket off and settled it around her shoulders. It was a comfort in many ways. Maybe she was chilly and hadn't noticed until she became warmer. They arranged themselves to sitting side by side, and there was no clumsiness of elbows and arms and clothing pulling awkwardly. Easily as shadows merging, his shape matched hers or hers matched his.

"This is better." Deverney set the back of one finger to her cheek where it rested, not doing anything.

"This means nothing, you know," she said. "It's just bodies finding something in common. Just pleasure. And we should finish burgling this place."

"We will. We will be sober and conscientious because you have two men outside who will eventually attract the attention of the Watch. Not that your MacDonald can't deal with all the minor public officials of London on his own." But he slid slow, nuzzling lips down her cheek, over the line of her jaw, onto the column of her neck. She was aware, as she had never been before, how sensitive her skin was.

He murmured, "I am always so tempted to touch you." His voice was another sort of stroking, like velvet all over her body. Across her breasts. Deep in her belly. She prickled with a dozen shocks of wanting.

"I see," she said.

"By the way, you're not in the least cold as a woman."

He curled his hand at the nape of her neck, warm and casual about it. That was all. No more than that. But rackety, mad sensations grew and twisted inside her everywhere. Her breasts ached. Between her legs, her body had become demanding.

He breathed and it was warm in her hair and on the skin of her face. "I expected to find you angry with me. When did that stop?"

"When I was coming here in the wagon, about halfway along Shoemaker Lane. I was thinking, you see. I do that when I'm plodding along in a wagon."

"Do you?"

"It's because I used to drive a wagon for the guerrilleros, back in Spain. I was with a little band, delivering arms. I'd dress as an old woman and go into the mountains with a wagonload of cabbages or parsnips and ammunition and guns underneath. That was frightening. Coming home empty was the restful trip. I'd think about lots of things, driving home."

He wrapped his arm around her more tightly, shifted position, and settled them comfortably together again. He was aroused, the size of him perfectly obvious if she cared to look. He neither hid it nor brought it to her attention. He was one of those men who managed to be magnificently unembarrassed about such things. She didn't need to be told he had enjoyed and been enjoyed by his fair share of women.

"In any case . . ." She closed her eyes and enjoyed every feeling inside her and outside her. "In any case, I was in the wagon on Shoemaker Lane and I became philosophical. I reached several conclusions that made me less angry with you."

"I'm pleased. You decided I shine by comparison with Carlington?"

"You do, but that's not exactly why I stopped being angry."

They rested softly, one body against the other. His utter concentration closed around her as if he were counting her breaths in and out. The one long, slow fascination of his finger on the side of her face continued and brought with it the dance between his appreciation and her response.

He didn't plunder or cajole. He showed no expectation. No demand. As far as he was concerned they could have sat there in silence till tomorrow when Hayward and his clerks walked in, or till next week. She relaxed a little more.

She said, "Robin wanted to marry me."

"The bastard." Deverney was amused.

"He mentioned love." When she shrugged, her body slid against him in so many ways she found enjoyable. She was so easily distracted.

"Not love," Deverney said, being certain about it.

"Not love, but he thinks love is an excuse for just about anything. In any case, I sat in the wagon, clopping along the cobbles on my way here, and thought about Robin. He takes the smoothest path, you see, like a trickle of water. What happened, I think, is he decided it was time for him to be settled in life and he looked about for a likely heiress."

"And saw you."

"An aging spinster who'd be grateful for any attention."

"You play that role with some skill," Deverney said.

"Thank you. You see that. He wouldn't. He ups and bestirs himself to pursue me, which he does very well because he is charming. Since I'm pretty enough, he decides that he desires me. It's an easy, pleasant way to be a fortune hunter. He can think well of himself if he's attracted."

"More than attracted. I saw him in the Carlington ballroom and he had all the signs of a well-born fortune hunter about him. I know the breed. But he was also gazing at you with perfectly genuine lust. He wanted your money but he also wanted you."

"I suppose that's flattering."

"And you terrified him right to the soles of his feet."

"Did I?" Robin had very nearly admitted that. "I suppose maybe I did."

Everything Robin had said that hurt her. Everything he'd done. His lies. His blunt, unflattering truths. The little pouf of a scandal he'd made. All that was suddenly ridiculous. She'd been a fool, and she frightened him. She leaned against Deverney and laughed out loud.

"You didn't know?"

"I had no idea. I was stupid as buttered toast the whole time." She was so warm, next to Deverney. Under her skin, little bubbles of excitement danced. "He did tell one truth. I never asked what he thought or wondered what he felt. If he'd mattered to me, I would have. He was harmless, you see."

"A trait I share with him, though I do it better. Tell me why you stopped being angry at me. I may need to use that trick again someday." He stroked her hair and with the caress turned her head so it rested on his shoulder. "Stay. I like feeling you breathe. Like that. Yes. You pull everything inside me along with you when you breathe."

When she spoke she didn't sound exactly like herself. "I stopped being angry because I know you want me. It isn't a sensible desire, the way Robin was sensible, picking me out to fall in love with because I'm rich. You want me against your better judgment. You'd rather not, but you do it anyway. We talked about that once or twice."

"Civilized of us."

She didn't turn in his arms and crush herself to him, kissing all the parts of him she could reach. She didn't push him underneath her down to the carpet and fall on top. She didn't say, "Let's lie on the floor naked." She only thought about it in a mature, reasoned way.

She said, "That's what I decided when I was riding the wagon. To you I am a damned inconvenience. That night at the Carlingtons'—" She had to stop because a pang held her whole body, tight as a fist. She was easily enflamed by Deverney. "At the Carlingtons', when we danced, you were annoyed at yourself. You'd come there to be inconspicuous and observe events. You didn't scheme to dance with me. It just happened somehow. You did it knowing you were drawing the interest of the most dangerous men in London."

He twitched his jacket to lie more comfortably across her shoulders. "I'll let you deal with them."

"Thank you. I think. But we're not convenient for each other. Not profitable. You are not the battleground I'd pick, and I'm not your strategic highlands. I'm a complication to you and you're a problem to me. We want each other in bed, but it's a nuisance."

"I wouldn't say that, exactly."

"A damned nuisance."

"That's closer. You're saying you stopped being angry at me because we annoy each other."

"You are exactly, precisely the opposite of Robin Carlington."

"That's a lovely compliment." He rested his forehead against her hair. His lips touched her temple, not in a kiss, but more as if he breathed her in. As if he consumed the warmth of her skin.

When his hand suggested she turn her face toward him, she did. His lips came to find hers, and they kissed. A warm, dark, all-hell-breaking-loose kiss. Readiness crashed over her. She clenched her fists into the linen of his shirt to hold him.

"I don't just want to kiss you," he whispered. "I want to lie with you, here and now, offering nothing but a madness of passion and a hard floor. No worship at the shrine of Eros. No restraint, no feather bed, no silk and rose petals, no fine vintage of wine. I have prided myself on being a good lover. Today, I fall this low."

In his trousers, hidden but perfectly obvious, his cock nudged toward her and argued silently in favor of shared pleasure.

"Well, then," she said. "Let's do that."

Thirty-five

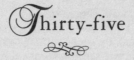

His hand covered hers, where she was hold-
ing on to him. Her skin was all fluttering desire inside, warm
and cold at the same time. She wanted to close her eyes and
sink into this feeling. "We have not chosen a wise place to be
foolish in, monsieur."

"I'm not a wise person."

"A little wise, a little foolish. Like me. You make fine wine,
which is not an easy thing to do. Stealing jewels is also difficult.
They are both arts. To do anything at all in this world is to yoke
the ox of wisdom to the ass of foolishness. If you will bring your
greatcoat over here and spread it down upon this rug, we'll do
well enough. This is not the season for rose petals."

"I'd find something. I'm ingenious."

"I know you are. I've never made love in a feather bed, as
it happens."

"I can give you that, at the very least. Tomorrow maybe."

She still held his clothing tight in her hands. The dry, warm
linen of his shirt. The slick, rich, heavy brocade of his waistcoat. Masculine clothing. As much as she wanted to kiss his

skin, she wanted to feel and taste and smell his clothing too. It took a force of will not to rub her face against him like a cat.

She was not seduced. Throw that word away altogether. She acted on the hunger coiled inside her. Desire that had been waiting and growing since she'd first seen him. "I don't want to wait till tomorrow."

"I don't want to wait, either," he said.

The calmness of her voice was a sort of small miracle. "I'd like to be romantical. I wish I had time to say 'No' and 'Yes' and 'Maybe' and slowly succumb to the complex joys you are skilled in. But—" She let her fingers speak of the papers scattered around them. "This is a dangerous enterprise and it may also be urgent. We do not have time for the pleasure of lengthy seductions."

"You are the most pessimistic woman. Let me kiss the tip of your nose." He proceeded to do that. "And see if that will lighten the mood." He kissed the thin, vulnerable skin of her eyelids, left and right. "I'd planned to take a while getting to know your body. I was going to explore the palm of your hand for an hour or two, suck on the inside of your wrist, kiss your earlobes."

When he said that, in every hidden place she ached for him. A silver ache that chimed through her like bells.

He said, "I wanted to call forth Eros with the heat and flame of our bodies. I wanted to torment us both into madness. I planned an exquisite seduction. You deserve nothing less."

"Let's try madness now and seduce each other afterward." She laughed.

He said, "Turn to me." With such simple words, it began.

His hands cupped her buttocks. Consideringly, gently, inquisitively. She put her hands on his shoulders while he lifted her and slid her downward upon him so her legs settled on either side of him. Between her legs she was soft and warm and trembling against him. Against the hardness of his cock, beneath his clothes. He held her rib cage, ran strong, long-fingered hands down her ribs, over the tense muscles that moved with her breathing.

"I am a descendant of the high chivalry of the land of France." He might have been speaking to her or, ironically, to himself. "With six centuries of courtly tradition in my veins. I know the love songs of the troubadours. I've studied the erotic arts of the East. I have been the lover of many women, given them intricate pleasures. But all of that vanishes when I touch you. You unlace the command I have over my body. You undo me, Séverine."

"Deverney—"

"Raoul." His voice was husky. "Use my name, for God's sake."

"Raoul." She could no more stop this loosening of her body, this tidal pouring of herself toward him, than she could fly away. She rubbed herself on him, tightening and throbbing. "You do the same to me."

His cock pressed upward, all on its own. His whole body tensed. He muttered, "That is some consolation."

He had loosened the ties at the back of her dress, so quickly and smoothly she had not felt him do it. His claim to be a skilled lover of women was not mere boasting. He lowered her bodice and caressed her breasts through the thin linen of her shift. Held them, opening and closing his hands, running his thumb over her painfully sensitive nipples. She twitched when he did that. Every time.

He said, "Kiss me." Command and plea and inevitability all at once.

She tasted him while he gasped underneath her. She felt . . . powerful. It was no small thing to have this man helpless beneath her. She sent her tongue to explore every detail of his mouth. She sucked at the stubble of beard on his jaw, the slanted muscles of his throat, warm and filled with pulse beats. "I like kissing you," she said. "I—"

The kiss that ate her words came hard across her mouth, impatient as if he'd been holding it back as a rider holds back an eager horse. Another kiss followed, holding a sound of deep satisfaction. Then kisses were everywhere across her face, stitched together, one to the next, pausing now and then at her lips.

"Listen to me," he said.

She opened her eyes. His face was inches away, very intent upon her.

"We're not lovers," he said. "Don't think it's that simple."

She had no idea what he meant. She had, in fact, no ideas inside her at all, only enchantment.

He seemed to look at the words carefully before he used them. "Twelve years ago I was married to a woman I didn't want to share a city with, let alone a bed. I expected to live my whole life with no true wife, no children of my own, no happy ending, no fulfilled passion."

She could only shake her head. She knew this.

"I created the shadow and pantomime of love," he said. "A game, but it was an honest game and I had no other. There's little enough warmth in this world. I gave some to women who needed it and took theirs in return. I've shared laughter and a few months of joy with many women, but I've bought none. Seduced no innocent. Touched no one unwilling. Lured no one who didn't understand the limits of what I could offer."

"I understand. I'm not an innocent."

"That's not what I'm saying, Séverine. Not what I'm asking. I want to explain that this isn't a game to me. I'm free. This is courtship." He leaned to set his lips to her breast, through the fabric of her shift. "I thought you should know."

His tongue curled around her nipple and he bit down so gently it was a caress. His fingers sought the cleft between her legs. He wrote pages and volumes of his intentions. She could have pushed him away at any time but she did not.

Thirty-six

SHE LET THE ROUGH DEPTHS OF HIS VOICE VIBRATE in her bones and didn't try to understand the words. He stroked her body through the barrier of dress and shift, finding the soft places that were hungry for him.

She said, "This isn't about marriage. Nothing I do is about marriage." Raoul Deverney courted her? Not possible.

"All right, then." His hands tunneled under her skirt, along her skin. Hands warm on her thigh. On her buttocks. Pushing her clothing aside. He burrowed between them to unbutton his trousers and free the hard column of his cock. It sprang upright, butting against her. He fit his cock into her. Inside her.

She wanted him. Oh, how she wanted. "I just want to lie with you." She was babbling. Saying too much. "I'm not going to marry anyone."

"Fine. Fine." He ran a hand across her forehead, across her eyes, and wiped away thought. Brought her with him into a darkness that held only the two of them. He said, "We'll make love. Good?"

"Yes." That was settled then. She nuzzled upward into the palm of his hand. "Now," she said.

"As my lady wishes." He thrust deep. Again. Again.

Her breath rasped loud and harsh. She matched him, thrust for thrust, with the same strength, the same madness. There was nothing in her mind except this feeling. No words, no thoughts, only this man.

He whispered, "Take this. What I can give you."

For an endless time his hands tightened into her skin. He held her upon him. Held her while the muscles inside her clutched his cock in a tight grip. While within herself, she dissolved away till she was nothing but fire and urgency.

Her breaths sucked inward in sobs. Came out in cries. She could not hold still. Would not. She gripped handfuls of his shirt and thrust herself down upon him again and again.

There was no surrender. This was the headlong rush across a battlefield, banners flying, heart pumping, utterly committed. It was hard to get breath in and out of her lungs. Every muscle in her body was strung tight as a wire.

Time slowed. Joy exploded within her. Filled every part of her being. The moment became vivid, wholly significant, poignant. Her skin contracted and shivered. Her breath was grabbed away as if she fell suddenly from some great height. Shocks thudded through her like the pounding of a great drum. She clutched his shoulders into the muscle and bone of him and cried out desperately and gasped for breath.

She felt him withdraw and spend himself against her thigh.

He took long, deep breaths. After a minute he set a long kiss to her forehead and put his forehead down to hers, where he'd kissed. They breathed into one another's faces. He pulled her against him and held her cuddled to him. It felt like being complete. The lover and his beloved. It was right.

Her body was a length of satisfaction. Perfectly relaxed in every nerve and blood vessel as well as the major bones and muscles.

"I can't think," she said.

"We don't have to. There will be better moments for foresight and logic and rationality. Now we hold on to another minute of enjoying each other."

"My common sense has gone to sit in a corner and sulk," she said.

"Mine also." He slid from the entanglement of their bodies and stood up. He smoothed the skirt of her dress into decency. Set damp strands of hair from her face to behind her ears. Quickly pulled together the ties at the back of her dress. Every touch while he did this was a caress.

He reached down to take her hand and brought it to his lips and kissed it. Kissed again on the palm. Then in a row of kisses down the knuckles. "I will eventually show you my skill and good manners as a lover," he said ruefully. "I will impress you with my sophistication and experience. Not today, evidently."

Her brain was limping along. Thinking somewhat. "You said, courtship?"

"It's not a fearsome threat. Between us, we'll figure out how it's done. As I said, it's new to me."

"It's not possible." She'd need to think for hours, or possibly days, before she knew what to say. "It's not necessary anyway."

"'Necessary' is a grim word. I was thinking delightful rather than strictly required, but you'll be the judge of that." He glanced to the corner where the safe stood. "I'll need ten or fifteen minutes to get the safe open. Maybe longer since my hands aren't steady."

"I'll carry the crates we've filled out to the wagon." The night air on her face would settle her head, though it was the rest of her body that needed settling.

Deverney—Raoul—had his lockpicks out. There was a similarity in all such tools, but his set seemed a little more elegant than the ones she used. The flat velvet pouch he kept them in was particularly tasteful and expensive looking. He ran fingers across the metal of the lock in a graceful movement, complex and possessive. That was how he'd touch her body when they came together again. Her naked places. How he'd make her hungry.

She wished she hadn't thought that. Really, she was easily distracted. She wanted him again, just as if they had not just made love.

"Be careful." Deverney immediately shook his head. "Sorry. I forgot who I was talking to. But don't trip on the steps going down. It's dark out there."

"I'm always careful." Her skin felt oddly as if he were still touching her. It was ready to be touched again. Anticipating it.

He inserted the first of the picks into the keyhole. She didn't stay to watch him pick the lock because Raoul picking a lock was a sensual and seductive thing that aroused her.

She arranged his jacket over the back of the desk chair where he would find it and carried her filled box down the hall, past the clerks' room, and out the front door. She'd been wrong about one thing. The cool night air and exercise did nothing to banish demons from her body.

Thirty-seven

THEY LEFT HAYWARD'S OFFICE QUITE OPENLY. SÉVIE sat at the back of the wagon beside Raoul, their legs dangling down over the edge, for all the world as if they were farmers coming home from the field with a fine crop of business records. MacDonald drove. Peter beside him. They made good time. The narrow back ways they traveled were empty. These streets might get a few deliveries in the hours near dawn, but for now all these streets were deserted.

The wagon had carried sand recently. Nice clean sand, fortunately. It was gritty under her hands on the boards. It clung to her cloak, but brushed away easily. Bluebell clopped along willingly enough. He probably preferred pulling boxes of paper and account books to carting sand. MacDonald had picked his wagon well.

Raoul—it was beginning to feel natural to call him that in her mind—said, "The letters from Sanchia's desk were in the bottom of the safe." He reached under the canvas to touch the closest crate. "Here."

"Hayward didn't turn those over to you. You'll have a worried man of business when he arrives at the office in a few hours."

"He has an angry employer right now." They rolled directly under a streetlamp and she could see his narrowed eyes and cool suspicion. She'd been treated to that expression a few times in their early acquaintance. "What I charge him with depends on what I find in those papers."

They sat close together. The wagon offered many fine choices of places to sit, but she chose this one. "You may not have the chance to charge him at all," she said. "He may leave for a pleasant villa in Italy the minute he walks in and sees the state of his desk."

"We'll look at the accounts when we get to your office." As they rolled forward lamplight drew a thin, shining line in his hair. "If the numbers are what I think they'll be, Italy isn't far enough."

"I'll help you. Peter can make tea. He's getting good at it."

In the front, Peter mumbled something.

They'd almost come to the corner of Turnwheel Lane where the bun seller made her living in the daylight hours, selling buns and information. The wagon made a wide leisurely turn.

Her office lay thirty yards ahead, but all was dark. The streetlamp was out. The one beyond that, also. She'd left a lantern hanging on the hook at the warehouse gate. That was out. Ahead, they confronted unbroken darkness that reached down the whole street.

Too late to turn back.

They were in plain view here at the corner, under the last working streetlamp. Whoever waited for them in that darkness would shoot the minute they tried to run.

MacDonald recognized ambush the instant she did. He made some light comment to Peter and kept Bluebell to a steady pace.

Her heart thumped in her chest so hard she shook with it. Steadily, the wagon was leaving this bubble of light. In the next dozen feet, somebody would shoot at them. At her. At Raoul. At MacDonald. Maybe even at Peter.

Beside her, Raoul continued to talk, his voice light and easy as ever. But now he said, "Your bowl of porridge was right. We have found that danger he mentioned. How prompt."

He was tense as an iron band beside her. He also recognized ambush.

She said, just loud enough to be heard by all of them. "We jump on the count. Ten . . . Nine . . ."

In the front MacDonald gave Peter a few words, barely audible. "You drop over the side and lie flat. Roll away and crawl. Wait . . ."

She said, ". . . Six . . . They can come from either side."

Years ago she'd walked the streets near her office, picking out the likely places for an enemy to lurk with intent. Sometimes people wanted to kill her clients. Sometimes her. One of the best spots for ambush was at her front door.

". . . Three . . ." She took a second to worry about those street children who were still following the wagon at a distance. She hoped they'd keep well back.

MacDonald whispered to Peter, "Wait for my word. I'll tell you when. Wait . . ."

They'd let the boy go first. She and MacDonald didn't have to discuss that. They both knew what to do.

Bluebell ambled his way across some invisible line, into the dark. MacDonald whispered, "Now, Peter," and there was a little thump as the boy hit the ground.

Ahead of them, a boot scraped on stone.

She said, "Go!"

Raoul's body slammed into her, hard. Shoved her to the floor of the wagon. A gun flashed in the dark. The crack of explosion slapped her ears. A bullet smacked into something nearby. Raoul grunted. They rolled off the wagon together with her wrapped in his arms. She hit the stones with her hip and her shoulder.

He barked in her ear, "Stay low, goddamn it," and levered himself off her and was away. She lost all sound of him. She'd expect that from the Comodin.

She flipped to her belly and crawled through the dirt and dried mud. She hoped she couldn't be seen. Since she was still alive, maybe she couldn't be.

Total darkness surrounded her. Streetlamps burned in the distance, keeping their light to themselves. Close by, boots hit the stones, striding and angry. The men trying to kill them yelled at each other in . . . Italian, she thought. Four of them? No. More than four. Through it all Bluebell bumped along, placid even with the reins dropped and nobody on the driver's seat. She could have used that horse in Spain. *Good choice, MacDonald.*

She crawled with singular intent toward the darkest of dark corners in front of Merridell Merchandise. She'd hope nobody else fancied the spot.

A second shot came from ahead of her. The muzzle flash lit up a man's face. A third shot followed instantly, somewhere off to the left.

She found a place in the lee of the Merridell stairway, took out her gun, and lay flat. She didn't even think of shooting. Waste of her bullet till she had a good target. Any shadow in the dark could be friend instead of foe.

Scuffling and snarls came from her right, and the horrible sound of a man gagging in pain. *Death over there*, she thought. Knife or strangulation.

Had Peter got away safe? And Raoul? She'd begun to suspect her thief was not wholly a civilian, but that didn't mean he was prepared to fight like this, with guns and knives in the dark. She could only hope those two had found safe corners.

Up above, on a second floor, a window glowed and went bright. The neighborhood was waking up to take an interest. She had them to worry about too.

And down the street, against the backdrop of a distant streetlamp, a man crossed Turnwheel Lane, running.

She took a proper shooter's position, shoulders level, head low, elbows braced in the dirt, and held her fire.

The outline was someone active, slender, and tall. Not Peter, then, and not MacDonald. She tracked the man with her pistol. Probably one of the *emboscados*. But he could be one of the men from the warehouse, running out to help. Or someone from the rooms upstairs, being a gallant idiot.

She had a few seconds. Then the figure was eaten by the dark and her chance to shoot was gone. Her decision had been made, right or wrong. In a little while that one might find her and kill her, in which case she'd made a mistake.

She held her position. The next man to cross that passage of dim light was no innocent. He wore breeches and a big loose shirt. Seaman's clothing. The glint in his hand was a knife. No householder. No warehouse guard.

She didn't hesitate. She chose the right spot in his path. The optimal point. Lowered the muzzle. Held her breath. It wouldn't be an easy shot at this distance with a pistol, but this was why she practiced so often.

He ran into the killing space she'd chosen. She pulled the trigger smoothly, as she'd done so many times. He staggered, twisting, and crumpled, curled limply, to the stones of the street. He didn't move.

She set her gun down, perfectly useless now. She sat up, making no noise about it, and scrunched herself into the corner of the stairs, knife resting across her knees. She let her breath seep out.

A thin scream came out of the dark. Then silence fell with a great finality.

Then some running footsteps. A minute later MacDonald yelled, "Sévie, where are you?" He spoke lower. "Get inside. Get a lantern." That was to somebody else.

She called, "I'm here."

"Are you hurt?"

"No."

"Then come to me."

All the shared experience of fighting and battle were in those shouted words, and it wasn't good news. MacDonald wouldn't call her out of hiding unless he needed help. Someone was hurt so badly that getting her to his side was more important than keeping Séverine de Cabrillac safe.

She staggered toward the sound of MacDonald's voice, shaking with reaction. Almost tripped over a body sprawled in her way. He didn't react when she kicked into him, so he was probably dead. Bluebell and the wagon had stopped there, next to the corpse. Horses do not willingly step on dead people. Just one of many curious facts she'd learned in Spain.

A swinging light arrived—Peter with a lantern—and she could see MacDonald kneeling in the middle of the street. His hands were pressed down against a man's arm.

"He's bleeding," MacDonald said, unnecessarily, when she got close.

Raoul sat on the ground, hunched into himself, red with blood, cursing softly in French.

Thirty-eight

SHE DROPPED HER KNIFE AND FELL TO HER KNEES beside Raoul.

Too much blood. She felt as if she'd been punched in the belly. His coat was soaked in it, shockingly red. How was he sitting up? How was he even alive?

Her second thought was, *He doesn't act like a man who's dying.*

Peter shifted the lantern so she could see better. Raoul had been hit at least twice. One hit somewhere on his upper chest. One hit in his left arm. Blood covered his sleeve and ran down to his shirt cuff. MacDonald had his hand pressed on that wound, tight around the arm, and red seeped between his fingers.

Raoul said, "Are you hurt?"

"I'm fine. You aren't." The wound to his chest had to be a damnably serious one. The whole front of his coat was shiny with blood from his shoulder down his vest. She angled around to his back, waving Peter to bring the lantern there. "Where were you hit?"

"Just the arm. The rest of the blood is—"

"I can't see. Can't find it. I need—"

"Handkerchief," MacDonald said. "Left pocket."

She found it. Pressed it down hard. "I'll cut through his coat."

Before she groped for her own knife, Peter handed down a long, businesslike one, hilt first, across her shoulder. "I found it on the street over there."

Peter was turning out to be useful. "Good work."

A fine knife. Sharp. "We'll take the sleeve off. Ready." MacDonald nodded. She pinched up the wool of the coat and sawed through. She worked as fast as she could and MacDonald kept hold as well as he could. Fresh blood began to drip from Raoul's shirt cuff.

Raoul held still, panting. It was loud when everything else had gotten deathly quiet.

She cut the coat away raggedly. Tore the shirt from the bullet hole outward. Worked the cloth of the coat and shirtsleeve off him. Not hurting him more than she had to. Laid the handkerchief flat on the wound—on two wounds side by side—and pressed it down. Held it with all her strength.

"Two holes, close together," she said. "The bullet's in and out. It didn't get near the bone." Or the vein and artery next to the bone. Six inches to the right and it would have gone into his lung. Ten inches, and it would have hit his heart. "This is what they call a lucky hit. Where's the other one?"

She pushed her free hand under his blood-soaked coat, trying to find where all that blood had come from. They weren't going to be lucky with this other hit.

"It's just the arm." Raoul spoke calmly for someone who'd been shot. "One arm. Nowhere else."

"You're hit in the chest. Or the shoulder. Somewhere."

"If there were other holes in me, I'd notice."

"Men don't always. In battle." Her voice came out thin and breathless. She felt as if something squeezed her chest. "There's too much blood, Raoul."

"Not mine." He touched her right hand, where she held so grimly to his arm. "Sévie, I'm not dead."

"I have to see. I need to get your coat off."

"Undress me later." Impossibly, maddeningly, Raoul

seemed to be laughing at her. "I hurt. I've made some serious mistakes. And there may be more of those men. You have to get yourself off the street."

"I should—"

"We will explore the many shoulds of your life at some time. But later. I have to climb the stairs while I can still walk, and you need to get out of the line of fire. Next time they won't miss."

Right. He was right. She had to get him and everybody else to safety. The warehouse guard had come at a run, holding another lantern that revealed a number of other bodies on the street, all very bloody. She hadn't seen this many deaths in one place since the Spanish battlefields.

"We have company." MacDonald jerked his chin at something behind her.

She turned away from Raoul to see a pair of half-grown children approach. Lazarus's street rats. They avoided the dead with the ease of long practice. A third child flitted from one corpse to another, going through their pockets.

"They're not ours," the oldest child said when she got close. It was a rather pretty girl, about ten. "Scum off a ship at port, killin' without permission. Lazarus'll thank you for dealing with them. Saves 'im the bother."

"Our pleasure," Raoul said softly. "Don't steal anything on that wagon."

The street rats exchanged glances. "Wouldn't touch noffink o' yours, sir."

"Glad to hear it," Raoul said.

Since she had several members of the criminal classes at hand, she might as well put them to use. She said, "Take the horse and wagon into the loading yard. Guard them. I'll pay three and six."

"To each of us." The girl didn't even blink.

Neither did she. "Of course. Tell your friend over there to see if any of those corpses are still breathing. Don't stop them if they are."

That got no response except a wide, innocent stare. Neither of them pursued it.

What did Papa always say? *Stick to the possible.* "The boy here." She indicated Peter with a twitch of her head. "I'm sending him off to run errands. Keep him alive till dawn and it's a pound note."

"A guinea."

She'd always gotten along just fine with Lazarus and the Brotherhood of Thieves. "Done."

She said, "Help me get him up," talking to MacDonald. To Peter, "Get the surgeon, Luke Gentry. You know where he lives. Run. Then go to Meeks Street and tell them I have a street full of corpses and would they like to be part of this. Answer any questions they have."

"Yes, ma'am."

She kept a tight hand on the bleeding arm and steadied Raoul while MacDonald pulled him to his feet. He stood, swaying a little, and he didn't faint. That was a good sign.

Thirty-nine

BETWEEN THEM, SHE AND MACDONALD HELPED Raoul stagger up to her office. A long way to go, but safe at the end.

He was pale and breathing hard when MacDonald unlocked the door. They lowered him to sit on the sofa. MacDonald walked around, lighting lamps.

All the way up the stairs she'd kept her hands clamped tight around the wound on Raoul's left arm, knowing it hurt him and that she had to do it. When he was settled, she stood, still stopping the blood, and he leaned against her. His jawline and the prow of his nose pressed into her belly, warm through her clothes. Coat, waistcoat, and shirt were sticky with blood, thick with it. His right hand and sleeve were soaked in ugly red but there was no bullet hole she could see.

MacDonald lit one lamp after another, starting with the one at the end of the sofa and then working his way around the room.

"I'll cut the coat off," she said. "Find that other hit."

"There isn't one," Raoul said.

"Right." MacDonald fetched scissors and clean handkerchiefs from the desk drawer. He came to take her place holding Raoul's wound. "We'll get you ready for the surgeon either way."

It was easier to untie and unwind the cravat than cut it. She hacked through the collar of his coat, across the shoulders, and down the sleeves. The wool weighed heavy with blood. So much of it. A man leaking this much blood should be dead and Raoul wasn't. Other men's blood, then.

She dropped the coat on the floor. She undid the buttons of his waistcoat and snipped down the silk at the back. MacDonald kept his hand tight around the wound, moving out of her way as she circled Raoul.

Finally, she scissored through the seams of his shirt and ripped it apart and off of him and revealed Raoul's upper body. He was a collection of dirt, smears of blood, and scrapes where he'd left skin on the cobbles. No more bullet holes though.

"Just your arm," she murmured.

"Not so wide as a church door nor so deep as a well, but t'will suffice—"

"Don't you dare quote Shakespeare at me."

"I could swear creatively."

"Then swear. We'll need bandages. Peter—" She remembered Peter wasn't there. "MacDonald . . ."

"I'll get 'em. Let's put him down flat," MacDonald said.

"Not needed," Raoul sat with his eyes closed, taking deep breaths. "And I can keep my own blood inside. It's not bleeding much."

"I'll do this." Carefully, she sat beside him and moved MacDonald's hands away and took over the wound. Raoul's skin was cold to the touch.

He opened his eyes a slit. "Since you insist."

MacDonald took bloody scraps of clothes from the floor and walked out. She called after him, "Bring a blanket. Get one from my bed."

MacDonald answered with a shrug. He had eloquent shrugs.

She found a comfortable position. "Talk to me," she said to Raoul. If he kept talking she'd know he wasn't about to convulse and die from not having enough blood.

"Of course." He wiped his face with his good arm, streaking blood on his forehead. "It's a pleasant evening, Miss de Cabrillac. Warm for so early in the year."

All those years ago in Spain he'd been bloody and half-naked. He was bloody and half-naked now. Then he'd been dark as a peasant with the Spanish sun. The mule boys—he'd been pretending to be a mule driver—stripped down to swim almost naked in the streams or to wrestle among themselves.

He was so perfectly made. Lines of lean muscle ran along his back, lithe and easy-moving under his skin. Ribs in ordered ranks. A flat, hard belly. She'd known a man who was a champion fencer who looked like this. Raoul still wasn't as pale as most Englishmen. Maybe he worked in those vineyards of his. Maybe it was French sun on his skin now.

"You have scars." She would have touched them if her hands hadn't been busy keeping the rest of his blood inside him.

"A few." He sounded more than tired. He sounded hollow.

A collection of scars. Some were hidden by smears of blood. Some were so old they'd become thin white lines, invisible till she looked for them. He healed well. "How many?"

"Seven or eight."

"More than that. This isn't even your first gunshot wound. There's one on your back."

"Two. I get shot running away, by choice. It's my preferred method of dealing with men who point guns at me."

"Mine too."

But most of his scars were knife cuts. Not from bayonet or sabre, but the slices you got from face-to-face knife fights. She'd seen the results of both and she knew the difference.

Another damned dangerous man. She lacked any least trace of good judgment.

His lips were wry with pain and laughter. His pupils, wide and black. She could see tiny lamps in them, the lamp on the table and the far one on her desk. And she saw herself in his eyes. She saw no common sense in him at all.

She'd misplaced her own sanity. Her thoughts had slipped the reins and gone running off. She wanted to find some welcoming spot on him, maybe his jaw, maybe his lips, and set her mouth there and slowly suck at him. Taste him. Eat the texture of him. In the middle of death and madness when she was busy saving his life and he was bleeding, her mind chose to be full of that.

I will have to deal with this, eventually.

MacDonald came down the hall, making noise with his boots so she wouldn't be taken by surprise. He was carrying an assemblage of useful things in his hands and under his arms. "Bandages. Towels. Water. Blankets." He'd brought two thick, rough blankets that belonged to Peter, instead of her good ones. In the larger sense MacDonald took orders, but he took them exactly as he felt inclined.

He laid bandages on the table at her elbow, sorted by size, and stood ready.

She nodded and peeled the handkerchief from Raoul's arm. MacDonald slapped a good thick pad of linen in its place. Now a length of cloth to hold that in place. They circled the bandage around Raoul's arm, pulled it tight, and tied the ends, all with the ease of long practice. Blood wasn't coming through yet. Good.

Raoul sat through this in silence, his head bowed and his eyes unfocused, taking air in distinct, individual breaths.

She pushed hair out of her face with the back of her hand, one of the parts of her that didn't have blood on it yet. "Where the devil is Luke?"

MacDonald said, "Give him time. The man has to roust himself out of bed and get dressed and get here. And Peter might run into something on the way."

"Maybe I shouldn't have sent him."

"He's as safe as you are." MacDonald scouted around the sofa, picking up red cloths from the floor. One of them was his handkerchief. She hoped he hadn't been fond of it. He said, "I'll go load some guns and bring 'em in here."

"Mine's outside in the dirt."

"No place for a good mechanism. I'll tell those thieving rats to bring boxes upstairs. The amount you're paying them, they might as well do some work."

She pulled blankets around Raoul's shoulders and leaned against him. He put his good arm around her. After another minute, she put her cheek on his chest. Her feelings were complicated, but she didn't need to look at them closely right now.

MacDonald stayed at the hearth long enough to get a fire going. When he left the room, he closed the door behind him with an emphatic click.

Forty

AN INVALID WAS ALLOWED SOME INDULGENCES, SO
Raoul held her close. Her hair, rippling and brown, was pulled
tight away from her face into fancy braids and taken into a knot
at the nape of her neck. It was soft as warm wind under his lips.

He loved her hair, the look and the texture of it. He discovered something new every time he got close. He could
smell the herbs she washed it in. Lavender and rosemary.
Single strands worked their way out of the knot and lay dark
on the white skin of her neck.

He'd seen her hair bound in a loose braid, stray wisps float-
ing like a night cloud around her face when he'd climbed to
her window at the inn.

Against his naked chest she said, "You killed them, didn't
you? The rest of the men lying dead out there."

Not the sort of love words a man wished for, but totally char-
acteristic of Séverine. "I was wondering when you'd see that."

"The street rat called you 'sir.' They don't use that word
much. MacDonald brought you two blankets when I only told
him to get one. That's him being respectful. They guessed
about that or they saw you do it."

She'd figured it out. All this going on around her and she still relentlessly unpicked mysteries. Curious, clear-eyed Séverine, with a mind like the sharp edge of glass.

"And you were covered with blood." She leaned soft against him. "It's five or six bodies or so."

"Six." Half a boatload for Charon.

"I got one, I think. Tried to. I don't know whether I killed him or not."

"He wasn't breathing when I went by."

"The rest are yours," she said. It wasn't a question.

"Yes." An hour ago they'd been men. Not good men, but maybe ordinary men in their way. Now they were nothing at all. He should feel something. Remorse? Regret? He felt none of that. *They could have killed her.* With the arm that was still working, he brought her a little closer to him. He'd killed to keep her warm, alive, and breathing. He had no regrets whatsoever. "My small gift for you."

"Thoughtful of you."

"I never know what to give a very rich woman. I hope this worked well."

"A dozen would be too showy. One or two, paltry. Five is the exactly correct number."

She used light words that didn't say what she was thinking. He was doing the same. They leaned on each other and everything important between them went unsaid. If things had gone even a little differently, another body would be a dark mound in the street, empty of Séverine. All she was—the wiry tension and determination, the quick, quick explosions of action, the little gestures, graceful as birds flying—would be gone.

"It's not something I can thank you for easily," she said. "The workshop where they make words doesn't seem to have made the right ones for that."

She stretched with a wriggling movement he felt in his whole body. Sensual, lovely Séverine. She was everything pleasurable and painful, both at once. Temptation beyond measure that he couldn't act on. Madness trapped in a bottle of impossibility.

Beauty wouldn't bring him to his knees, as this woman so undoubtedly did. In the salons of Paris, Madrid, Vienna, beautiful women were common as meadow flowers and just as delightful. He'd written poems to their bright eyes, taken joy in their company, and, he hoped, brought them joy in return.

One did not, he suspected, write poems to Séverine's eyebrows. One slew dragons for her, or stood slightly to the left, holding her spare lance and buckler, while she did the slaying. If he was lucky enough to win her, he foresaw a future of saving the dregs of London from a well-deserved ending on the gallows.

"None of us hurt." She gave the sort of sigh a good housewife gives when the last of the cakes was plucked safe out of the oven. He heard, even if he didn't see, the wry smile in her voice. "Except you."

"A nothing of a nothing." Eventually he'd have to lie down so he'd stop seeing black at the edges of his vision. But that could wait. "I'll recover, if that surgeon you've called doesn't kill me."

"He's the best in London. I send all my gunshot wounds to him." Her dark beautiful eyes were worried. She didn't have to worry about him.

It might be time to get back to seducing her. Dizziness and pain tried to distract him, but she was still bright at the center of his thoughts. He didn't have one square inch of innocence in his head when he was touching Séverine.

He said, "Let's take up where we left off," and he kissed her.

$\mathcal{F}$orty-one

SHE SHOULDN'T BE KISSING AN INJURED MAN. IF she'd possessed a list of activities to avoid when a man had bullet holes in him, passionate kissing would be on it. But he wanted her so much a moderate amount of pain didn't discourage him. If he wanted kisses, kisses he would get. He would . . .

She lost her place in her thoughts. Being kissed by Raoul Deverney was an activity that took all her attention, because he gave it all of his. It was, in its way, like drinking an absolutely excellent wine. You didn't hurry the tasting of it. You didn't let yourself be distracted.

There was no point in discussing the wisdom of this. She wasn't listening.

He kissed her, slowly, appreciatively, sometimes stopping to take deep breaths when he was battling pain out of the way.

Before she heard the first soft sound in the hall, Raoul pulled away and looked toward the door. He continued holding her though. Challenge and declaration from Raoul to whoever was coming.

Hawker walked in. He'd given no warning he was out there,

an impoliteness that showed he was annoyed about something. Raoul, doubtless. He crossed the office with a raised eyebrow and a grim line to his mouth. She glared back to say she didn't want comments on this subject. Much as she loved Hawker, she had no intention of listening to his eyebrows.

He carried one of the crates from the wagon in his arms and took it over to the table under the window. Good enough place, as far as she was concerned. He strolled toward her, settling his cuffs straight in his sleeves as he came, looking amiable. He said, "Sévie." He waited some seconds before he added, "Comte." He could infuse significance into the length of his pauses.

She tried to imagine how Hawker looked to Raoul Deverney. To her, Hawk was the oldest of old good friends. He'd braided her hair when she was too young to do it neatly and he'd tied the sash of her apron behind her when she was in the kitchen learning to peel carrots and bake bread. When she was seven or eight Hawker had started taking her to the docks and tenements of London. Whitechapel, where he was born. Seven Dials. Southwark, across the river. He'd taught her to beg and pick pockets. In return, she'd helped him with the fine points of his French accent.

He was the only person she'd told before she ran away to Spain. She'd never had any doubt he'd trade his life for hers any rainy morning of the year. That was what she saw.

Raoul would look at Hawker and see one of the most powerful men in England, Head of the British Service, a man ruthless in several distinct and unpleasant ways. Raoul wouldn't be fooled by any genial expression Hawk put on.

Hawk said, "I see you've collected dead people on your doorstep again, Sévie. I suppose you expect me to clear them away."

"I'd take it as a kindness." She was sure he was already emptying the wagon to use it for moving corpses. The livery stable would not be pleased if he got blood all over it. "You're prompt."

"I was coming back from Newgate when I met your boy running across Braddy Square. I decided to collect everything you wanted at one time. I brought Luke with me."

But Hawker was looking at Raoul as he spoke. "You're the Comodin," he said. Hawker had apparently decided they'd skip several of the usual steps of getting acquainted.

"That seems to be common knowledge." Raoul slowly and deliberately leaned back on the sofa, his good arm still around her. He had an expression of polite disinterest on his face that matched Hawker's.

"According to MacDonald, you're the man responsible for the corpses," Hawk said politely.

"All but one."

"Still, a good collection. And they say the Comodin doesn't kill."

"One of the disadvantages of depending on rumor. It so often lies."

The two men studied each other, probably not learning anything in the process.

She'd already figured out where Raoul had learned to kill. Maybe she'd been a fool not to see it from the beginning. Maybe Raoul distracted her till she couldn't think when she was around him. But it was obvious to her now. Hawker might be slower coming to the same conclusion because he didn't have her years in Spain.

Hawker said, "I noticed—"

There was a scuffing on the stair, heavy steps and lighter steps, accompanied by voices. She sorted that out as Luke Gentry—the surgeon who treated the agents of Meeks Street—MacDonald, and one of the street rats.

The street rat, a girl, came first, carrying another of the crates. She took her time walking across the room to set it down, her eyes prying, her smooth pretty face innocent while she assessed the pawn value of every object in the room. MacDonald brought two crates, one stacked on the other.

Luke was in his usual mood. Grumpy.

"You're not hurt." He gave her a quick glance up and down. "Good." Without waiting for an answer he stalked past, taking off his coat, criticizing the accommodations for surgery. He pointed out that everybody downstairs was dead as Caesar so he was no use to them. Asked, could they drop the bodies at the hospital for dissection? They didn't usually get corpses this fresh, he informed them. Then he told her to get those bandages off so he could see what some idiot had done to some other idiot. He'd work on the desk as usual. If everybody stopped wasting time he might get back to his bed while it was still warm.

She unwound the bandage and unstuck the pad stopping the bleeding. Bullet holes were never beautiful, but this one looked better than most.

"We seem to have avoided the brachial artery and thus you are still alive. It's shallow." Luke took Raoul's arm with that surprising gentleness, his big ugly hands practiced and mild. "Two holes from one bullet. Don't see that often. I get most of my bullet-hole work from you people, and you shoot better than this."

"We like to think so." Hawker came to look.

Raoul took the bandage from her and covered the bleeding again, assessing Luke under half-closed lids.

Luke walked over to drop his bag on her desk. "Clear this clutter off." Hawker came to do that. "One bullet. No belly wounds, no broken bones, no stabbing and exotic poisons. You didn't have to roust me out of a warm bed for this. Any dolt with a needle and thread could sew the man up."

But, he said, as long as he was there he'd do the job. Get some hot water. Bandages, here. "And I need some damned light."

Hawker swept quills and papers into the top drawer. Leaned the blotter against the bookcase. MacDonald brought small tables and extra lamps from the other rooms. Peter ran down to the pump for water.

"Opium?" she asked. "We have some."

Beside her, Raoul shook his head.

"Then we won't bother with it. Where did I put . . . ?" Luke poked through his medical bag. "Ah. Here it is." He clattered the tools of his trade along the side of the desk. "Don't need it anyway. I'm doing six stitches, for God's sake, not cutting for the stone."

MacDonald handed tea around to everybody, even Lazarus's street rat, who was keeping tactfully to one side.

"No tea for him," Luke said, meaning Raoul. "I don't want him throwing it up on me." He threaded his curved needles with black silk and poked them, one by one, into a pincushion. "You there—George, John, Maurice, whatever—"

"Deverney."

"Can you get yourself over here or are you going to faint like a maiden aunt?"

"My own maiden aunt"—grimly, Raoul stood up—"would have stitched herself up, one-handed."

"Would she?"

"And bit the threads off." Ten stiff-legged steps across the room and Raoul leaned against the desk. "She would have told you to comb your hair neatly, even at three in the morning, and rapped your knuckles for impertinence." He clenched his teeth, loosed his clutch on the wound, and laid his hand flat on the table.

Hawker closed in from the side, sleek and silent as if he were attacking, but actually putting himself within catching distance if Raoul fainted.

Luke finished another needle. "Then she wouldn't have called me out of bed with my wife at three in the morning, would she?"

"No." Muscles flexed under Raoul's skin. In a single smooth effort, one-handed, he lifted himself up onto the desk, turning as he went. Let himself drop down to sitting.

Raoul was strong. The first time she'd seen him he'd just climbed a sheer stone wall, pulling himself up with his fingers and his boots toed into niches in the mortar. She'd watched him leave the inn chamber by the window, casually swinging himself over the sill on the support of curled fingertips.

He'd just killed five men, one after another, in near-total darkness. He was strong, clever, and deadly. Hers.

She went to him, across the room, to where he waited stoically. While Luke finished his full complement of threaded curved needles and set them ready and Hawker folded his arms and prepared to observe matters; while Peter sent the too-observant street girl off to shift more crates upstairs; while MacDonald swirled old tea leaves out into a slop bucket and started a fresh pot, she went to claim Raoul. She got up onto the desk behind him and wrapped herself around his back, kneeling so her thigh supported the arm that would be stitched.

Luke said, "Let go of that so I can see," to Raoul and sponged blood away from the wound, peering at it, muttering, "Clean. And this one is clean. No threads in there. Nothing like getting shot through good material." Red water sluiced down Raoul's arm onto the rug.

Luke took forceps and picked up the first needle. To her he said, "Hold that for me." And she set the edges of Raoul's flesh together and straight while Luke worked.

"Six stitches. That's one." Luke tied off the first knot. "This is a fairly small bullet. Not army issue." A half minute later. "That's two."

Raoul was unmoving as a rock. Silent as one. His expression was distant, almost uninterested, as if he'd done this many times before.

Maybe he had. He was a man of many scars.

She had become rather more acquainted with Raoul tonight. Now she knew what he was. Everything about him told her he'd been a guerrillero, a partisan, fighting for Spain against the French.

That was why he didn't flinch. His scars had been collected where there were no surgeons. No opium. No water to wash the wound. No way to stitch him up as he and the others retreated. Or he'd been alone, with no one to help him at all. He'd be used to pressing a hand over his worst cut and staggering back to some hiding place in the hills. She had spent her own time with the guerrilleros, and she knew.

After a while Luke said, "Six. That's the last one. I'm finished with you. Keep it clean. Keep it dry. Don't poke at it. And it still wasn't worth getting out of bed for."

"Next time, maybe he won't get shot," Hawker murmured. "Or he'll do it more efficiently and save us the trouble of—"

MacDonald said, "He got shot pushing Sévie out of the way of a bullet. More tea?"

Hawker offered his cup. "I do believe I will."

She held a clean pad in place while Luke rolled bandage around the arm. Raoul held his arm out and said nothing. So, along with everything else, Raoul had saved her life and not thought to mention the fact. She had not yet come to the end of Raoul Deverney's craftiness, obviously.

Hawker said, "The sofa, I think. Mr. MacDonald?"

"He'd be more comfortable in Miss Sévie's bed."

"The choice of wounded men everywhere. Nonetheless, we shall put him on the Little Ease of sofas where we can keep an eye on him."

An assenting grunt from MacDonald, a shrug from Luke who was repacking his bag, and they didn't consult Raoul.

Really, this was no one's business but her own. She said, "I'll take him into the bedroom." She picked up the blankets. "I don't need anyone's comment or opinion on this."

Hawker and MacDonald, wisely, said nothing.

Forty-two

HOURS LATER, RAOUL SAT IN ONE OF THE RED CHAIRS at her desk, a pair of clothbound ledgers in front of him and a dozen more to his left, within reach. He'd been quiet for a while, going through them. She hoped he wouldn't be tempted to start carrying boxes around the room. Men had no sense at all, even the best of them. She signaled Peter to bring him cups of tea from time to time so he wouldn't go bounding about the room after tea, either.

Peter had fetched clothes from the expensive hotel Raoul favored, a well-cut suit and a gray-and-silver brocade waistcoat. A clean bandage was wrapped tight around his arm under his sleeve. The bleeding had stopped. There was some mention of being good as new, but this was not true. It was all very well to be manly and kill a few people, but somebody with bullet holes in him should be in bed.

She didn't cross the room and settle a blanket over his shoulders or scold him and put him into bed and bring him thin soup and advise him to sleep. She had the very smallest tendency to care for the people she loved by telling them what to do. She resisted this.

"I'm being robbed," Raoul said mildly. He went from one ledger to the other, comparing entries.

"Ironic," Hawker said, "considering your profession."

"Isn't it?" Raoul agreed. "So much violent crime in the world and I am the victim of a sniveling embezzlement."

"Inferior to the craft of jewel robbery, at which you excel." Hawk lounged at his side of the table with all the noncommittal menace of one of the better breeds of cat.

"Very much so."

Papa sat on his haunches to rummage through a mixed box of spoils. "You found your embezzlement quickly."

"It's poorly done. Money passes from my London business"—Raoul laid his hand flat on the ledger on his right—"through Hayward's books"—that was the ledger on the left—"into Sanchia's accounts." He touched the thin black book in the middle. "The voyage makes everything clear."

Hawker gave the barest nod. That might have been approval for the fraud, or for finding it, or just acknowledgment.

Raoul picked up Sanchia's account book. "She went through a great deal of money. More than I sent."

Hawker said, "You were generous." Looked like he'd done his own investigation of the books while she'd been in the bedroom, washing herself and cleaning blood from Raoul's skin.

"Not much spent on Pilar." Raoul's lips pressed to a long hard line. "Not even what was earmarked for her."

From the other side of the room, Papa said, "There are those who'd say you did more than your duty."

"But you don't say that." Raoul looked as if he'd bitten into something unpleasant. "I never came to look at the accounts. Or the child. What Sanchia did is on my shoulders."

Papa didn't agree or disagree, though there might have been a different quality to his air of placidity. He went back to leaning over the box on the floor, methodically sorting through the bits and bobs gathered up from Sanchia's appartement—quills, pocket handkerchiefs, seals, scissors, a paper bag of scented pastilles . . . and jewelry. Lots and lots of jewelry. An honest man of business would have turned the jewelry over to Sanchia's husband at some point. Hayward hadn't bothered.

Papa brought a double handful of sparklies, all small pieces, brooches and rings and little hair ornaments, over to Raoul.

Who barely glanced at them. "Sanchia's gambling stakes. Rubbish."

There was a sort of woman who wore such cheap things—flawed stones, gilt, colored glass—when she gambled at private tables. She could take off a ring or brooch and fling it on the pile instead of banknotes. There were always men foolish enough to accept them.

"Yours now, I suppose," Papa said.

Raoul just shook his head. Papa dumped the glitter on a side table as comment and decoration. A valediction of sorts. Nobody went to look at it except Peter.

After a while leafing through the black book of Sanchia's accounts, Raoul said, "I shouldn't have left her free in London to wreak havoc. I assumed she'd whore and gamble and take opium, following the custom of her kind. I wasn't expecting blackmail and espionage."

"I'm a spy myself," Hawker said. "Did you know that?"

Raoul presented a blank, polite face. "Why yes, I did."

Hawker said, "Sévie, my very dear, why don't you go see if there's anything to eat beside these muffins Peter keeps offering us. I need a few minutes to carve my initials into the flesh of Monsieur Deverney here. It should only take a moment." Hawk smiled. "He's already wounded."

"That would make it easier," she agreed. "And he's disarmed. I found one knife on his person and he's left it in the bedroom. Do you realize this man walks around weaponless?"

"I had begun to suspect as much," Hawker said. "I can't approve. It strikes at the assumptions that underlie my existence. On the other hand, when armed he kills men by the unconsidered handful."

"Always a problem, folks wandering London, killing people," Papa said.

Papa had showed up an hour ago. "Late to the party," as he put it. "Nothing left but bookkeeping."

Raoul murmured, "I keep finding mistakes in Hayward's arithmetic. He steals from me and doesn't even bother to add it up correctly. I cannot tell you how much that annoys me."

She'd taken a place beside the window, cross-legged in that wide, old leather chair that belonged to Hawker, her skirts tucked about her. Three boxes, the ones that contained most of the intriguing papers, were stacked to the side. It was early dawn. The street shadows were dark as coal dust, the sky white. She'd opened the window to let cold wind blow in her face and keep her awake. Guards from the warehouse were walking up and down around the building, but it never hurt to do some watching of her own.

The cobbles showed brown patches where bodies had been. MacDonald had driven off with a wagonload of the dead. One of the street rats who seemed intrigued with the process had gone off with him. None of this made her nostalgic for the hours after battle, but it was familiar.

She was reading through a packet of Sanchia's love letters to Hayward, the ones he'd kept in that rosewood box in his desk drawer. That struck her as foolish. She'd never understood why people saved this sort of thing. In her spying years she'd received her share of secret letters, clandestine messages, and cryptic words scrawled on a scrap of paper. She couldn't burn them fast enough.

These had been tenderly tied up in a blue ribbon and saved. She took them out, one by one, and spread them open to read. Sanchia was frank but unoriginal. This one called Hayward her Honey Bear Stallion and wrote longingly of his Great Delicious Cock. *I lie in our Love Nest and Moan and stroke my Cunnymuff. My Love Juice flows with Longing for you.*

She'd seen many such letters in Spain when she was snooping for Military Intelligence. Somehow this sort of thing sounded worse in English.

Sanchia's letter ended with a mention of one teeny, tiny, little bill to settle. That was also standard for this sort of thing.

Papa brought her tea. They were all awash in it at the end of a long, hard night. "Useful?" he asked, meaning the letters.

"Love letters from Sanchia to Hayward. Dull stuff."

"Nothing more boring than somebody else's love affairs." That was Hawker, come over to pick a letter from her hand and read it, glancing toward Raoul and being pointed. "Dear me. This is explicit."

She wasn't going to compete with Hawker in outrageousness. She wasn't going to discuss Raoul with him at all. One tiny, very private nightmare nibbling at the edges of her mind was the picture of Raoul and Hawker fighting with knives. That wasn't going to happen.

She said, "Go away and make yourself useful."

She squared Hayward's collection of love letters, put them back in the rosewood box, and laid it in the crate on the floor. This next was a mixed bag of dunning letters. They had been all together in the file in the clerks' room at Hayward's and thus were of no interest to anyone. She went through these quickly and learned that Sanchia spent a great deal of money on clothing and didn't pay her dressmaker. Or the butcher.

She went to the next box. This hadn't been in the open files, but in the safe itself. It was a largish box made of papier-mâché and painted with roses. It was quite full. A mixed box of private letters.

None of these were tied with a sentimental satin ribbon. She started out with a few on top, addressed to Sanchia. A succession of men—Silly Billy, Duffie, Toodles, Snufflekins, and Your Devoted Edward—admired her breasts and her private parts and the ingenuity of her attentions. One had to wonder if Hayward had known how crowded Sanchia's love nest had been.

Under that, she stumbled, abruptly, into new territory.

The first of these new letters was written on expensive paper. The lines of writing, ruler straight, marched down the page like soldiers in formation. *Mistress Deverney*, it read, *I'm not one of the stupid boys you lead around by the nose. I will not be threatened. In the words of my former commander, "Publish and be damned."* It was signed, *W.S.*

That could be read as a threat against Sanchia. Perhaps this, or something very like it, had led to murder. She liked to think the blunt soldier W.S. wasn't guilty.

She read slowly onward, letter by letter. These were no longer love notes. They were the bleating of the blackmailed. None of the rest of Sanchia's unwise lovers had the courage of W.S. They said, *I can't do this for you. I can't*, and *Don't tell my wife*, and *I don't have the money. In the name of God, I don't have it.*

She knew something of blackmailers. A half-dozen times in the last five years she'd tracked down women with such habits and put a stop to it. Nasty stuff, blackmail. She'd seen several practitioners of it off to Australia.

At the bottom of the box she uncovered worse.

Some looked harmless. Here, one man wrote to another about salt beef for the navy, ending with a jocular *a bit rotten*. A woman mentioned the well-timed death of her grandfather with the cryptic comment, *Jeremy did the actual work*. There were so many secret rendezvous it looked like the powerful of the ton did nothing but hop into forbidden beds.

A good many of these papers conveyed nothing sinister. Doubtless they were damning to someone and profitable to Sanchia Gavarre.

The prize here, the great catch, was near the bottom. There were six pages originating in the Foreign Office, two from the Admiralty, and one from Military Intelligence. None of these should be wandering around the world sharing their contents indiscriminately. They dealt with troop movements and campaign strategy. No small matters at all. Documents like these didn't get casually tossed away. These had been bought or stolen or, most likely, blackmailed into Sanchia's hands.

This was the well of poison. Here was death for the soldiers and sailors with their secrets betrayed.

This was probably what had killed Sanchia and caused Pilar's disappearance. Few things in the world were more dangerous than committing treason in wartime. She wouldn't recommend it to anyone.

She finished reading the last of the documents and folded her hands on top of them in her lap. Outside, the sun had warmed the air. Early-morning traffic passed on the street, making its accustomed racket, muted by being two floors below. Already the marks of death and blood were disappearing under the tracks of wagon wheels. The bun seller was in her place on the corner.

She wasn't sure what to do next. They'd have to deal with this. Until they did, they were all in a great deal of danger.

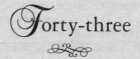

Forty-three

SHE WAS STIFF WHEN SHE STOOD UP. SHE'D BEEN working for hours in this chair, and before that she'd fallen from a wagon and gone crawling around in the dark. She stretched and let her eyes rest on Raoul, who was an excellent man to look upon.

He was absorbed in account books, a deep crease between his eyes. Hawker paced, desk to hearth, bookcase to window, stopping to look over Raoul's shoulder, picking things up and putting them down, frowning. It was his way of thinking, of course, but annoying for anyone in the same room.

She carried the box with roses painted on it, filled with squalid letters, to the desk and set it down.

Raoul scowled at the account books.

She followed his finger as he ran it down the page and said, "Art lessons, dancing lessons, gloves, books in French."

He muttered, "Goddamned flute instruction."

"Everything a child could need."

"But she wasn't getting art lessons. Or riding in the park or being fitted for a new velvet riding habit every six months."

Surprising how much anger could fit into a man's calm voice. "Or any of the rest of these fripperies."

"Provided by her generous father," Hawker murmured.

"I'm not her father. I wish I were. She seems to be a remarkable person." He picked up the cup of tea Peter put down, nodding thanks absently. The boy took away the old cup, cold and half-empty. "You were right. The girl lived like an orphan. All these years I signed the expenses. I thought . . ."

"You thought she was well cared for," she said.

"I didn't think at all." He turned his head to look directly at her. "I'm considered a shrewd man in some circles, but I was a fool about this. I knew what Sanchia was."

"You trusted your agent."

"He and I will discuss that at length."

She wouldn't wish to face Raoul in this mood. Hayward was tucked away at Meeks Street because Newgate prison had turned out poorly for O'Grady. Hayward was whining, according to Papa, and making a thousand excuses.

Hawker said, "If this is the first time you've been betrayed, you've led a singularly unexciting life, Mr. Deverney."

"Unexciting has always been my objective, Mr. Hawkhurst."

"Then you should have stayed in France, harvesting grapes, shouldn't you?" Hawker smiled pleasantly.

"Mildew on the vine, mealy bugs, unreliable weather, and the whims of the wine market. Village harvest festivals. Local feuds between local families. Redigging wells. Repairing every crumbling stone bridge for thirty miles. I find jewel theft relaxing."

"An unusual point of view," Hawker said.

"I cultivate eccentricity. What do you make of these entries, Sévie?" Raoul touched the back of her hand where it rested on his shoulder, just the least tap of his finger, on the way to pointing to lines in the accounts. That was as good as kissing her full on the mouth if he wanted to tell Hawker and Papa they'd made love.

Gauntlets were being flung all over the place, weren't they? When she leaned to look at what Raoul was showing her, she rested her cheek against his hair. Fleetingly. Barely at all. That was throwing down her own gauntlet.

She had no intention of tolerating any of this nonsense.

Raoul understood. The corner of his mouth showed amusement. The wrinkles at the side of his eyes turned up. He smelled like the lavender soap she kept beside the washbasin in back. He smelled like he was hers.

"Look here. This is Sanchia's income from me." He pointed to a sum, not small, and another entry, the same, the next month. "Here's money from another source." It was entered against the initials M.S. "M.S. pays quarterly." He turned pages back. "Here. And here. Other quarterly payments from M.A.C. and from M.V. Then there are a dozen monthly payments from a number of sources. S.L. and B.W. and so on. It's not business," Raoul said. "It's not rental income. There are no expenses. No roof repairs or painting the shutters. No window tax. No land tax. No parish fees. I know what rental accounts look like," Raoul said. "I own properties."

"He's being modest." Hawker considered the page she was looking at. "Your friend Deverney owns a dozen buildings in London. If you wonder what he does with his ill-got gain—"

"I don't," she said.

"He invests it in dull and sober real estate," Hawker said.

"What I own in London is profit from the wine trade." Raoul was meticulously polite. He met Hawker's eyes. "Or grain sales. I don't sell stolen jewels in London."

"I stand corrected."

"I sell jewelry in Geneva where the price is higher and no one asks awkward questions." Raoul turned the ledger toward her. "The outgo is considerably simpler. Gambling losses, some of them matched to the name of the hell. Mrs. Bellows. The Pretty Vixen. Major Clarke."

"Only the best." She went to drag a chair across the room, leaving furrows in the pile of the carpet. If anyone had come to help her she would have sent them about their business, but nobody did. Papa pretended not to notice, as he'd pretended not to notice when she was five and insisted she could climb onto her pony without help. Hawker continued to be sardonic and subtle, every inch the British spymaster.

Raoul said quietly, "That's where the money went. Cards and dice ate up all her income."

Papa came to stand at the fourth side of the desk. Now there were four of them studying Sanchia's life, laid out in paper.

"But the meat of the matter," Raoul went on, "is these few large payments into the account. They're not very often, but they're several hundred pounds apiece. This isn't from Hayward. It doesn't match the petty blackmail that's everywhere else. It's too large to be gambling wins. She's not playing for those stakes. And it's not any business I can easily imagine."

"A business of a sort." She leaned across to close the ledgers and set them aside. She moved the papier-mâché box into the middle, between the four of them, and took the first letters out.

"Blackmail," she said, and set that to the side.

Hawk narrowed his eyes. He knew—they all knew—she had something more coming.

She said, "The important blackmail." She laid down the documents from the Foreign Office, the Admiralty, and Military Intelligence.

Papa took one, frowned at it, and immediately passed it to Hawker. Raoul picked up the next page, looked it over, and dropped it as if it were, say, a snake.

"I didn't see that." He stood up and walked away from the desk.

This was no ancient history. These were recent thefts and significant ones. This would keep the Service busy till next Christmas.

"Here's treason," she said.

Forty-four

AT THE CRACK OF DAWN BART—BARTHOLOMEW Markham, third son of William Doyle who was Viscount Markham when he took his scar off and put his good clothes on—took the kids out of the house before they woke everybody in the place. Betty, who'd been his nanny—nanny to a whole succession of them—was a woman of infinite patience. She stuffed Anson and Anna into coat and hat and didn't try for scarves or mittens. She was a woman who understood the limits of the possible.

"I should put scarves on 'em, I know," she said to him while he looked in the hall mirror and achieved exactly the right jaunty angle to his own hat. "But we'd be arguing about it into next week, and it isn't that cold, really."

He'd been more reasonable when she was his nanny. Or maybe not. He remembered her saying something very similar every year in the spring. About him.

Anna reached as high as she could to turn the key in the lock. It was a solid and deliberately heavy door. Both the little kids were needed to get the knob turned and the door pulled back. Papa said, don't have a door somebody could kick in. He didn't know where Papa picked up that bit of wisdom but it seemed a good idea.

He followed Betty from the house, down the steps, and along the pavement. Anson and Anna were tight in her hold, Muffin the dog at their heels, being protective against all threats, foreign and domestic, his shoulder about level with their heads.

And he? He was just enjoying himself, glad to be free of measles. The sky was pale and hazy with dawn. The wind was fresh. It wasn't raining. He actually looked forward to shepherding the kids to the park in the middle of the square.

Back home, if the weather were this good, he'd take a gun and a dog out to the home farm to hunt rabbits for dinner. He'd even take the kids with him if they promised to stay quiet.

There was a plague of rabbits in Hyde Park, but he wasn't mad enough to take a gun there. A slingshot, though. A David sling. That was tempting to think about. Maybe in the early dawn. Maybe tomorrow he'd sneak out and try that.

"I can too climb trees," Anson said.

Anna responded, "Can't."

"I can climb *tall* trees. I can climb *oaks*. I can climb the oak behind the stables."

Last autumn Anson had fallen out of that particular tree. It was now forbidden.

Anna said, "I can—"

Betty said, "We do not climb trees in the park. Now hold hands so we can cross the street." They ventured out into the little street, utterly empty of traffic, a line of three tightly joined together, followed by the dog.

Papa hadn't come home last night. That wasn't unusual, but it meant there'd been no chance to talk to him about that coach that might or might not have been showing too much interest. No chance to ask Sévie either. Someone else who hadn't come home.

So he was the oldest in the house. He was not exactly in charge but it was another reason to stay close to the kids and keep an eye on them.

The guards, Mr. Tom and Mr. Harry, trailed down the stairs behind them and went left and right. Tom, going ahead to give the park some attention. Harry, lagging behind to inspect the corners and crannies of the houses around the square.

He could have brought a book with him so he wouldn't be bored while the kids ran up and down the paths, jabbering, but he knew he wouldn't get a chance to study. It was an exercise in frustration trying. Besides, Hilary Term was almost over. He wouldn't go back to school till Trinity Term in April. Plenty of time to catch up.

He copied Papa as they crossed the street, taking responsibility for Anna and Anson and Betty, being acutely aware of everything that moved and any changes in the things that stayed still. Being steady. Thinking as he went instead of shuffling along like a cow.

Not a game, this. Or if it was, it was a serious one. There'd been extra men outside the house when he woke up. Extra guards. They all knew what that meant. Papa was worried.

The usual guards, Tom and Harry, were being even more careful than usual, and that was very careful indeed. They'd been infantrymen in the campaigns across France and Spain with a hundred stories to tell. And they had kids of their own at home. Papa always hired guards who had kids of their own.

Tom's children were just young. Six and four. But Harry's second son was on a merchant ship headed for China and his oldest was apprenticed to a surgeon. That was Johnson. Johnny. They already let Johnny sew people up, and once he'd delivered a baby. That had been a sort of accident. He got to watch them cut up dead people. Johnny promised he could come next time. Johnny would sneak him in.

Other boys had all the fun. He didn't want to go to sea or be a surgeon, exactly, but he'd like a life where he didn't have to stay inside with books all day. Something like what Papa did.

Maman said the garden in the middle of the square was widely admired. It was beginning to turn green. The holly bushes along the railings still had a few tail-end-of-winter berries on them. The crocuses were out and the snowdrops and primroses. Back home they'd be everywhere in the woods, and he could do chemical experiments in the potting shed.

Betty unlocked the gate and held it for Mr. Tom to go in first. Harry began to circle the perimeter fence. They had a routine.

No sign of danger. The birds were singing just the way they should be. This wasn't like the country where the birds told you ten dozen things by the way they acted. City birds were stupid, though it was worth listening to the one or two things they did have to say. The crows, especially, were knowing, though mostly what they knew was where the cats were.

The kids slipped under and around Nanny and ran down the gravel paths of the park before Tom had finished the circuit. Muffin waited obediently.

"Barbarian horde," Betty muttered.

In an hour or so, children from other houses around the square would wheedle their decorous nursery maids to take them down so Anson and Anna could lure them into improprieties, like catching beetles. For now that pair had the place to themselves.

"Look! There's a package." Anson ran toward the line of benches under the plane tree. A square box, wrapped in brown paper, sat on the middle of the nearest bench. "It's for me."

"Is not," Anna said.

"Is too. Look. It has my name on it." Anson reached for it. "See. It says Anson."

He yelled, "Don't touch that!" and ran.

He surprised Anson into doing what he was told. He grabbed Anson up against his chest and ran with him to the gate. Tom, the guard, right behind him, carried Anna.

At the gate, he let Anson slide to the ground. Nothing had exploded yet. He'd been in time.

". . . could just *say* you wanted me to leave it alone." Anson continued the comments he'd been making. "I'm not a baby. I wasn't going to—"

"Be quiet." He frowned at the package thirty feet away.

They all looked at it—Anson, Anna, Betty the nanny, both guards, Muffin the dog, and him.

"It's a bomb," Anna said, thrilled.

"A huge bomb," Anson said. "It'll leave a crater in the ground."

"It'll break windows."

It was so completely ordinary. A box wrapped in brown paper sitting on the bench. He said, "It might," and frowned at it.

"I can make a bomb." That was Anson. "Almost."

"I can, too," Anna said. "But mine are better."

"We'll make a small bomb when we get back to Oxfordshire." Maybe that would keep them from constructing one in the nursery. "A stink bomb, with sulfur. I'll show you how." To Betty he said, "Take them back to the house and tell everyone to stay away from the windows."

Anna folded her arms and stuck her chin out. "No."

"No," Anson said.

I should beat them regularly. He had never, never been this difficult as a child. Except for the time he set fire to the nursery. And the incident of the bull.

He went down on one knee. "This is one of those times when you have to follow orders."

Identical mulish expressions emerged.

"This is an Emergency. That means we go by Emergency Rules."

"Papa gets to do that. And Maman," Anna said. "Not you."

"Also me, because I'm the oldest here." He watched them measure him against the parents, not impressed yet. "If there's a bomb in that box, Muffin could get hurt."

"I'll put Muffin in the house and come back," Anna said.

Around the square, curtains twitched back as various inhabitants looked up from their breakfast and noticed odd behavior. They'd be coming out to investigate in a minute. There'd be the devil of a job keeping them back from the park.

That package could be a pound of gunpowder, enough to hurt people all the way to the park railings. Could be set with a friction fuse or one of the chemical fuses Fletcher taught him about. Or it could just go off by itself from sheer inefficiency. Fletcher said bombs were a stupid man's weapon, more likely to kill somebody by accident than not.

He couldn't leave it in place. He couldn't go over and open it up. He couldn't stand here while he waited for help to come. Some idiot would walk right past him and try to take charge of this and get killed.

He said, "Harry, get me some cricket balls. They're in the nursery closet, on the left, in a box. Middle shelf." He felt a moment of shock when Harry turned around and ran for the house without asking questions.

Papa said, "Talk like you know what you're doing. That's all you need."

It wouldn't work on the kids. He looked from Anson to Anna. "What do we do when we hear a rocket?"

"Flat on your face," the kids said in unison.

He thumbed over his shoulder, toward Mrs. Willoughby's staid and respectable town house. "And you take shelter when you can. That's your shelter. Get down the cellar stairs and watch from there. Keep your head down."

They slid eyes toward each other to consult. Made a decision. They ran for the Willoughby stairwell, pursued by Betty and by Muffin, who thoroughly approved of this new game.

The package still sat innocently on its bench. He was going to look like an idiot if that turned out to be a parcel of books left by one of Anson's friends.

He said, "Tom, Old Gillmore's toddling out his front door. Get him back inside."

For the second time a guard took his orders. He wasn't sure why. Maybe it was enough to have a plan.

Harry came from the house, carrying his hat close to his chest. "Three cricket balls." Harry breathed heavily. "I brought the croquet balls, too, in case."

"Good thought." He set the hat on the ground in front of him and took off his coat.

"I should do this part, Mr. Bart," Harry said.

"Play a lot of cricket, do you?"

"Not often. Not since I was a boy."

"Then it better be me." He rolled up his sleeves. "Eton does prepare you for life, they say. You go keep the kids' heads down."

An instant of sharp, narrow-eyed inspection. Then Harry loped across the street to where four heads poked cautiously above the level of the pavement—Anna, Anson, Betty the nanny, and Muffin.

Bart tossed and caught the cricket ball a few times. This would do the job nicely or get somebody killed or accomplish nothing at all. It was an accustomed balance and heft from an old familiar game. Unlike Harry, he played a lot of cricket. He was good at it.

He didn't need to think about it anymore. He drew back. He threw.

Forty-five

RAOUL HELD TWO FINGERS, MARKING THE SPACE of an inch and a half. "That long," he said, "and the thickness of a thumb. Silver. Dull black with tarnish unless somebody's polished it. In the right light you can see designs marked into it. A red stone at the bottom."

Papa was at the little hearth that kept her office warm, feeding coal into the fire with his hands, setting neat, black, shiny pieces in a row on the burning logs. He said, "You had it in your hands, Sévie. Does it look valuable?"

"Not in the dark when you're in a hurry and there's a man in front of you about to get hanged."

Papa said, "An important object? Significant?"

"Nobody would throw it away," she said, because that was what he was asking.

Raoul said, "The top comes off, if you work at it a while. My father let me take it apart once. That's a family secret, by the way, that it's hollow. It's not in any of the books."

"Anything interesting inside?" Hawker asked.

"Empty as a lover's vow," Raoul said. "I recall being disappointed when I was eight."

A selection of street rats had carried crates from the wagon upstairs. Peter was just stacking the last of them in front of the bookcase. He straightened and stood considering it with blank eyes. His skin was pale under the floppy hat he never remembered to take off.

She should send him to bed. It was already morning. This had been a horror of a night, ending with dead men strewn everywhere and bloody surgery on the desk where they were gathered to work. She kept forgetting how young he was.

She was about to tell him to go rest when he left the room, looking as if he had places to go and things to do, his shoulders squared and his step steady. It looked like he was good for a few more hours. They certainly needed the help.

"Any guesses as to where the amulet is now?" Hawker asked it generally to the room, but he meant that for Raoul.

Who answered readily. Almost boredly. "I didn't find it in Sanchia's rooms. She had it six months ago, certainly. She planned to ransom it back to me at great cost. I would have paid it."

"Now you don't have to." Papa wasn't accusing. Just pointing it out.

"If I haven't murdered Sanchia in the last dozen years, I'm not going to do it now." Raoul shrugged. "I'm a peaceable man."

"Who rounds off the night with five men dead," Hawker said amiably. "We're going to run out of criminals."

Papa finished with the fire and came to join the rest of them where they were working. He didn't show up at her office often, always careful about encroaching. He hadn't visited at all since her office had been ransacked. She could see him noticing where things were missing. Being Papa, he was probably wondering how to get replacements for her without being obvious about it.

The bronze Artemis was back on the shelf in its usual place, playing bookend. Papa touched the proud Huntress as he went by, one touch to her shoulder. He had a superstitious relationship with that statue. It was very, very old. "The words 'amulet' and 'de Cabrillac.' They were written by the girl? Are we sure?"

She said, "I wondered the same thing. They were genuine."

"I don't feel good about your name in the middle of this," Papa said.

"Not to mention bullets going in her direction." Hawker had settled into a chair at her desk. Not the big Walsingham chair he was entitled to. He'd left that to her. "If we were keeping score, we'd be losing. I hate it when that happens." He pushed papers aside, put his elbows on the blotter, and tapped his lips with his templed fingers. "I sent Stillwater to the docks to see what ship is missing a handful of able-bodied seamen. They look Neapolitan. Corsican, Sicilian."

"Hard to tell when they're dead," Papa said.

"Neapolitans," Raoul said.

Hawk gave a brisk nod. "I briefed Wellington at dawn. He'll spend the day at the Admiralty Office with strapping Marines on duty. And I stopped at Newgate. There was an attempt to poison O'Grady that failed. He continues remarkably durable."

"Happy news," Papa said, "I'm sending the kids and house staff out of London." Out the window dawn was beginning to show. "I'll send word over when it gets light. I sent more guards to the house."

By tomorrow the kids would be home, back in the country, where every farmer and every villager was a guard for them. Every stranger would be noted and watched.

"You could go with them," Papa said casually, meaning her.

"I'll be careful," she said.

"I know you will. But your doorstep's full of dead men."

"Enough to unsettle any father," Hawker said.

"Intriguing, when you think about it," she said.

"I know you're not going to leave." Papa sounded resigned. "But I don't like the mind behind this. He hired a man to kill his own man."

"Hires them by the dozen," Hawker said.

"Ruthless. Pragmatic," she agreed.

"Fast." Hawker turned papers over, just glancing, setting them aside. They were working their way through the letters out of Hayward's office. "The attempt on Wellington. O'Grady stabbed the next afternoon. Sévie, or possibly Deverney, targeted in the evening. O'Grady again, about midnight. Our murderer keeps busy."

Papa said, "O'Grady knows something."

"They'll bring his food from different cookshops. I am determined he'll live long enough to see Australia." Hawk rejected his way down the pile, letter by letter.

Papa said, "So many murders planned. Wellington, O'Grady, Sanchia Deverney—"

"Sanchia was an accident," she said.

"Premature. Not an accident," Papa said. "O'Grady wouldn't have let her live after she'd seen his face. Then they came after either you or Deverney or both."

"One of them." Hawker set another page aside. "It's too much a coincidence they'd scoop up both the fish they wanted in one net."

Raoul was across from Hawker, occupying one of the hideous chairs from the Meeks Street parlor, going through Sanchia's journals. They were not pleasant reading. She'd looked at them herself. He said, "They were after Séverine. The bullet was aimed at her."

"Six men is rather a lot to send to kill just me." Strange to be talking about her own death like this.

"Wasn't enough, though, was it?" Hawk said.

Papa took away old papers that had been sorted through and brought new ones. He upended the little box of them in the middle of the desk. "Desperation. Stupidity. Recklessness. Madness to try for four or five deliberate deaths in the middle of London."

"Some of us manage it." Hawk gave Raoul a long glance.

"Whoever's doing this doesn't stick at killing women," Papa said. "That's why I want you out of town, Sévie. It's become dangerous for you. If you were one of my agents, I'd tell you the same thing."

She had to smile. "You're the second person who's warned me I'm not safe."

"Who was the other one?" Papa sat, picked up some likely-looking pages, and began to read.

She said, "Carlington."

Raoul said, "He warned you a few hours before you were attacked. Should I be worried?"

"Only if you think him capable of hiring a halfdozen Neapolitan sailors to kill me. It seems beyond him, somehow."

"I could ask him," Hawker said, "while slowly removing his skin."

She didn't look up from what she was doing. "No."

"I may anyway."

"*Much* braver than I am," Raoul murmured. Raoul and Hawker wore almost identical expressions of craftiness. Nobody commented on Robin, which was good because she didn't want to talk about him. They were probably thinking of all the unpleasant things that might happen to him. They wouldn't do anything.

For a good long while they were all silent except for rustling paper and the creak of a chair sometimes. Her own little stack was less promising. She examined and dismissed a dozen letters in a row. Hat shops were not centers of treason and murder. Squabbles over porcelain bonbon dishes did not hold the fate of nations. The next one, though . . .

She said, "I know this handwriting."

"What?" Hawk looked up. They all did.

Life is filled with small correspondence. Dresses to be delivered, a cousin in Paris, books for sale, friends to be met at a confectioner's next Tuesday, and clients asking Miss de Cabrillac to investigate some minor matter.

Sometimes she hired men to do research for her.

She said, "Joseph Smithson."

"Army archivist," Hawker said.

She said, "He does research in army and navy archives for a modest fee. The British Service uses him sometimes. So do I. This"—she passed the letter over—"is his bill for investigating the troops in the vicinity of Cuevas del Valle on May 9, 1809. He charged Sanchia twenty-one pounds, which you'll see she has not paid."

They passed the letter around. Frowned over it. Smithson had rather distinctive handwriting, fortunately.

"We have that report." It was Raoul who'd seen it and re-

membered it. It had been in one of the wood boxes he'd packed
in Hayward's office. A thick document.

Three or four boxes later, they had it. Smithson's report.

Papa spread it flat on the desk. "Let us see what Smithson
has to say." And they all leaned over it.

Papa said, "He gives us every British unit within thirty
miles."

"They were moving into battle." Raoul had gone hard-
eyed. "I was there myself, with the partisans, scouting, working for the English."

"I was not so very far from there myself, with the French,"
she said, "who lost."

"An argument against battles." Hawk ran his finger down
the list. "First Division, Guards, infantry, the Rifles, and the
plucky light artillery. And here we have a list of officers. What
the devil am I looking for?" A glance in her direction. "You've
found something, haven't you? You're looking pleased with
yourself."

She said, "It's near the bottom. The quartermaster corps."

"Carlington," Raoul said.

Hawker looked disgusted. "Is it going to be Carlingtons?
Do I have to believe the Carlingtons are racketing around
London killing people?"

It's not a real connection," she said warily. "It's certainly
not proof. But—"

"It's three times," Hawk said. "Anything that happens three
times stops being a coincidence."

They all heard it and turned to the door, silent. Footsteps
on the stair. In a hurry. Not surreptitious. Lighter than a man's,
but not Peter's feet, either.

The door opened. Bart stood there.

Some effort had been made to straighten him up. His hair
was slicked back. He'd put on clean clothes.

But he was everywhere dusted in flour. His eyebrows and
eyelashes were white. He had flour in every crease of his skin.
And his hair, despite some effort to remove the flour, was still
white from the scalp outward.

He blinked from white-rimmed eyes. He carried the distinct odor of gunpowder.

He held on to the knob and looked from her to Papa. He said, "Nobody's hurt."

That was what Bart always said. The incident of the flying machine. The homemade boat. The trebuchet and the clock tower. The chickens. Oh Lord, the chickens. They'd cleaned up feathers till spring. Fortunately, no chickens were injured. Terrified, of course, and they didn't lay for weeks, but not injured.

She said, "Tell me exactly how nobody was hurt."

Papa took a deep, slow breath.

Eventually Bart wound down to, "It didn't do any actual damage. I mean, flour doesn't do any actual damage. But I had to drag Anson and Anna out of it and they got covered with flour. And all the other kids on the street came out and they got covered with flour."

He looked guilty. "Oh. And the dogs. All the dogs. I think it was a friction fuse. There's a tie-down on the bench."

Papa was calm enough to say, "A friction fuse?"

"I think so," Bart said.

"I'll send Fletcher out to have a look at it. He may be able to tell."

"There are some people angry about the park bench," Bart said. "I mean, they're angry about the whole thing but especially the park bench. They want to talk to you."

"I wouldn't be at all surprised," Papa said.

Eventually Hawker took Bart down to put him back into his hackney and send him to Meeks Street. A phalanx of Service agents would take over guarding the kids till Papa could get them into hiding.

She liked to think she'd looked calm in front of Bart, but she was still shaking. Papa sat heavily in his chair.

"I was slow," he said after a while. "Too slow. I should have taken better care of them."

"Nobody was hurt," she said, just in Bart's way. "It's a warning."

That got an honest smile from Papa. But he said, "I didn't see this coming," and there was no smile when he said it.

"Nobody could have. Papa, if it had been a real bomb, everybody would still have been safe. Safe because you trained Bart from the time he could walk. He made good decisions from beginning to end."

"He did well," Papa said.

Raoul was taking off his sling, trying movement with his arm. "If we're talking about mistakes, I led your daughter into an ambush last night. I almost got her killed."

He hadn't led her anywhere and it wasn't the first time people had tried to kill her. Nothing to do with him, really, except that he saved her life.

He went on, "I should have known. It's the spot I would have chosen."

"It's the spot anyone could choose." Hawker came in. Having been silent up the stairs, he was now silent walking across the room. To Papa he said, "The idea that you're responsible for everything that happens is a particularly boring form of conceit." That sounded like a quote.

Papa looked up from frowning at the rug. "I taught you that. You don't have to toss it back at me."

"I'm passing the wisdom along to Mr. Deverney here. And while I'd like to blame him for getting Sévie shot at, I'm sure she managed that all on her own."

It was always gratifying, the trust and support her family had for her.

She picked up Smithson's report. This was the story of one day in Spain, one exact location, and Carlington was there. What had he done that put him in Sanchia's hands?

Papa and Hawker were at the cupboard to the side of her office, taking out rolled maps. Looking for the Spanish ones. Raoul hung his sling over the back of the chair and bent his arm cautiously, testing it.

A thought had been knocking on the back door of her mind for a while. Finally it made itself heard. She said, "Where's Peter?"

SHE ran down the hall and they followed her. She didn't bother to search the rooms on either side, just went straight to Peter's sleeping place under the stair.

She flung the door open. The mat was neatly spread, the

blankets tight across it. A small, narrow roll of yellowed paper rested on top. Next to that, a scrap of her own notepaper.

She folded herself down cross-legged on the floor beside Peter's mat. The note read,

> *Miss Séverine,*
>
> *I thank you for the sanctuary you provided and for the many interesting things I have learned while in your employ. I leave the contents of the amulet for you. I will return the amulet itself to Monsieur Deverney at some future time.*
>
> *I go to administer justice. Do not worry about me, dear mademoiselle. I can take care of myself.*
>
> > *Pilar Gavarre (Peter)*

Wordlessly, she passed the note to Raoul.

"She didn't use my name," Raoul said.

"No." The girl had signed the note as a bastard signs. Raoul would have to deal with that eventually.

She considered the thin coil of paper.

Here was the cause of several deaths. Sanchia's death. This little paper and what it represented. She began, "I need a—" and Papa had it in her hand before she finished. His quizzing glass. Not a foppish toy, a fine optical lens. She took up a pinch of her skirt and polished it, though Papa kept it polished clean at all times.

Delicately, she set the rolled paper on the floor and crouched over it. It was narrow, less than two inches wide, and long. Crinklingly thin. Tightly rolled. Cracked in places because it was so brittle and Pilar had been in a hurry. She held her breath while she worked with it. Raoul set a lantern, lit to a bright flame, on the floor beside her.

The ink was faded. She read aloud in case the paper was damaged and she would be the last one to see it clearly.

It was written in French, but from the spelling mistake and the little awkwardness, she thought it had been written by an Englishman. *Colonel Carlington speaks French abominably.*

She translated. "They go south May 9 toward Cuevas del Valle by the Calle Real. They should come to the bridge across the Rio Pasaderas about noon. Twenty-two mules and carts with drivers. Arms and munitions. Gold. Seven officers with guns. And then the initial C."

Gently, she let the paper roll up again, which it wanted to do. Papa picked it up and wrapped it carefully in his handkerchief. The Service would want to keep it safe.

Hawker said, "You and Raoul were in that area, Sévie. You'd remember. What happened to that convoy?"

"There were so many convoys lost." She could have named most of them. "But not that one. A convoy that size? I would have heard about it from the French, if not the English."

"They got through safely." Raoul took her arm and helped her up. He saw it at once, faster than she did. The guerrilleros were experts in taking French supply trains. "That was the fish that got away. The amulet was lost before the message was delivered. It was stolen or dropped or the messenger was killed. This convoy lived. The ones before it didn't."

Spain hadn't been Hawker's part of the war, but some things were universal. "It's not the first ambush."

"Too well planned, too smoothly executed," Raoul said. "It's not . . . tentative. They've sent messages like this before."

"Smithson's report gave Sanchia the name of the quartermaster who would have sent this convoy and convoys before this. She blackmailed him."

"Colonel Carlington," Hawker murmured. "My, my, my. What a very evil man you have been. And now you're trying to kill my family. That was a mistake."

"The blackest treason," Raoul said, "is putting supplies and guns into enemy hands before battle. The drivers and the soldiers who guarded those shipments died."

"Wellington would bring this to trial, even after this many years," Papa said.

"Wellington's going to reorganize transport when he becomes Master-General of Ordnance. He said he'd study what was done in Spain and improve on it. Lost convoys, all from the same quartermaster, is exactly the sort of thing he'll uncover. Carlington's doomed."

"How much did Peter . . . Pilar hear of what we said?" Papa asked.

"Everything." So they knew exactly where Pilar was going.

"Damn." Hawker headed for the stairs, just behind Papa.

She stopped to get her gun on the way out, the new one that she'd chosen out of Justine's shop. She wasn't used to it yet, but this wouldn't call for sharpshooting.

A new thought hit her. She ran to the bedroom across the hall and opened the drawer beside the bed. She stood a long moment considering the empty spot.

"She's taken my gun."

Raoul was at her shoulder looking down. "You keep it loaded."

"Every day, with fresh powder."

"Then, whatever she has to face, she's armed." Raoul picked up the second pistol she kept in the drawer. "I'll borrow this if I may, since Pilar didn't make off with it. What a redoubtable girl she is turning out to be."

He followed her down the hall, making acquaintance with the pistol as he walked, handling firearms with the nonchalance of someone who knew exactly what he was about, which did not surprise her in the least.

At the top of the stairs he kissed her, emphatic about it but not lingering. He let her help him down. She wasn't sure whether he needed the help but it was tactful of him to accept it.

At the first-floor landing, she said, "This is to avenge her mother. Everything she's done for the last three months is for that. I hope she doesn't get killed doing it."

"So do I," Raoul said.

Three steps farther on she said, "She could have asked me for help. She could have walked in the door three months ago and told me everything."

"You wouldn't have handed her a gun and sent her off to kill Carlington."

"Of course not."

"Then you wouldn't have given her what she wanted. Revenge." Raoul kept a hand on the bannister. His face held the calm of men going into battle. He was stripped to essentials. Single-minded. "I understand her."

"And I don't?"

"You're not a Deverney." They'd reached the ground floor. Clerks in the offices watched them pass, curious. He was serious again when he said, "You wish she'd come to you. Think how much more I wish she'd come to me when I arrived in London. It's my fault she didn't." He opened the front door for her. "Now she's alone, twelve years old, with a stolen gun, going to face her enemy. It's magnificent."

"It's madness."

"I would do the same," he said.

WILLIAM Doyle whistled for the Service hackney. His greatcoat was on the seat, a pistol in the right pocket. He took half a minute to check that the powder was dry in the pan.

"Don't carve your initials in this one," he said, meaning Raoul. "I think Sévie's going to keep him."

"It looks that way," Hawker said.

"He has a sense of humor. He's competent with a killing knife. He makes wine."

"I'll leave him alive, then. God knows how long it'd take her to find somebody else." Hawker frowned. "Why doesn't she have more guns about the place?"

Doyle closed the pan and slid the gun into its accustomed place in his pocket. "She tells me her work is peaceful as a lending library."

"All books and tea cakes." Hawker grinned a nice, feral, born-in-the-rookeries-of-London grin. "Let's go kill the man who set a bomb for the kids, shall we?"

Forty-six

THE HACKNEY CLATTERED WILDLY OVER THE STONES and jostled them all together at every turn. Raoul braced himself against the side of the coach, using his good arm. Hawker remained unfazed by a little shaking. Papa, arms folded, in the corner, let himself be jounced about. All of them watched the street, looking for Peter.

Fletcher was on the box, unconcerned with the safety of pedestrians and other traffic on the road. British Service coach horses were chosen for their ability to round a corner at speed. Luckily most folks on the street at this hour were honest working people, spry enough and wise enough to get themselves out of the way of a hurtling coach. The leisurely and self-absorbed were still in bed.

Peter—Pilar—couldn't be far ahead of them.

"Maybe the colonel left town last night," she said. "I would. Maybe he's halfway to Dover and we'll catch him up in Canterbury."

"I think not," Raoul said.

When they got to Carlington House, the street dozed, empty

of traffic and pedestrians. Behind each curtained window, housemaids and footmen scrubbed and polished, lit fires, dusted, and generally got on with their work in hushed quiet.

Except for one household. A traveling coach and four horses stood at the door. Piled luggage on the pavement said somebody was leaving for an extended journey.

Fletcher pulled up the hackney with a jerk, there in the middle of the road. She grabbed the door as it swung open, rode with it, and dropped to the street. Raoul was behind her, so close she felt him breathing.

On the pavement ahead, drama unfolded. Pilar faced Colonel Carlington over the barrel of a pistol.

She slowed. Any word, any incautious movement, any threat might send this scene spilling into violence. The trigger on that pistol was so sensitive a sharp intake of breath might set it off and Pilar would commit murder.

Raoul was at her side, easy and unruffled as if he escorted her onto a dance floor. As if the possibility of gunfire and death did not exist, never had existed, never would exist. At a greater distance, inconspicuously, Hawker circled the Carlington coach and took a position blocking the colonel's escape. Fletcher stayed up on the seat of the coach where he could see everything, his gun pointed in a useful direction.

And Papa walked through the stunned Carlington house servants, being authoritative and reassuring, sending them inside, out of the way. They trickled off in twos and threes, reluctantly, taking their comment and confusion with them. Papa, who could be a bear of a commander, chivvied the stragglers onward with a formidable glare.

Robin Carlington was left behind when the servants departed, backed against the palings of the fence, apprehensive as hell. At least he was silent.

The air had the transparent clarity that meant a lovely day was coming. The breeze kicked up little eddies of swirling bits of paper and broken leaves. It was quiet in the houses up and down the street because nobody had shot anybody yet.

Peter faced Colonel Carlington. No. Pilar. In some indefinable way she had become female. She still wore the same ragged, oversized clothing she'd worn all these weeks. The floppy hat. The man's coat that was too long for her. The sagging trousers. But it was a woman inside those clothes now.

Pilar didn't turn to look at the new arrivals. She said, "You shouldn't have come, but I'm glad you did. This act requires witnesses."

The gun Pilar had taken from the bedside table pointed unwaveringly at Colonel Carlington. Fortunately, she had a few things to say before she killed the colonel, which gave everyone time to deal with the situation.

The colonel did not acquit himself well for a military man. He was extensively groomed, freshly shaved, hair neatly arranged, cravat tied in a neat, grave knot. His clothing was spotless. His boots, highly polished. He could have been leaving to attend church if not for the pile of luggage and the gun pointing at him.

And his fear. He was quite terrified. His ruddy face had gone white. The flapping tongue that had wrapped around so many foolish words stumbled and fumbled. "I'm not— I have never—"

"Committed murder?" Pilar said quietly. "But you did."

"Never. I don't know what you're talking about. This is a dreadful mistake. Miss de Cabrillac, I beg you to put a stop to this. I promise you—"

He'd retreated till he was against the big rear wheel. He edged sideways as if he could scuttle aside and disappear behind the coach. The gun followed him hungrily and he changed his mind.

"I wasn't sure I had the right man till I heard you speak." Pilar supported the gun upon her other forearm. Guns were heavy if you weren't used to them.

"I'm not—"

"I recognized you then," Pilar went on. "I knew your voice. You were one of the men in the front room, killing my mother. I heard you and the other man threaten her and hit her. When she was choking and gasping and begging, I heard you tell her to answer your questions or you would hurt her more."

"My dear young woman—"

"I am not your dear young woman." Pilar's chin lifted. "I

am the daughter of Maria Sanchia Adelita Fidelia Gavarre y Vega, the woman you killed. I am your death."

A calm voice. One believed her entirely.

Papa's hand was casually in his greatcoat pocket, holding something. In this case, a gun. His intention was obvious to anyone who knew him. If Pilar fired, Papa would too. No one would ever figure out which shot had come first and who had killed the colonel.

Hawker, in his chosen spot, showed no inclination to interfere with events, possibly because all the guns were on his side and he wanted the colonel dead anyway.

As for her . . . In spite of the growing consensus in favor of it, she disapproved of letting a twelve-year-old do murder. She cleared her throat and entered the conversation. "Pilar, have you considered not killing this man? The entire British legal system is at your disposal."

"My mother would wish it," Pilar said in a dangerously calm voice. "She would demand his blood."

"But then, Sanchia was not always wise, was she?" Raoul took six leisurely steps to the right so Pilar could see him without taking her eyes away from the colonel.

Pilar said, "She was not very wise, but she was my mother."

Pilar wore the Deverney Amulet openly on her chest where the folds of her oversized coat hung open. The colonel had his eyes on it, and every malevolent emotion churned in his gaze. Anger, hatred, despair, greed.

The colonel, all this time, continued to babble claims of innocence. Raoul looked upon him dispassionately, then back to Pilar. He said, "If you wish to avenge your mother, there are better ways."

"I do not believe so." Pilar, too, could be dispassionate. Her variety was like a cold sea filled with toothed monsters. "The law will not touch this man for what he did to my mother. I heard you and Miss Séverine talk about it."

"I've said a great many things in your hearing, Pilar, that I wish I could take back."

"She choked for air and they did nothing. She could not breathe and they laughed, monsieur. That was the last sound she heard. Their laughter. So I will laugh as this colonel dies and hope he appreciates the humor of it."

Raoul took a long step toward her. Not within grabbing distance of the gun, but close enough that he and Pilar talked face-to-face instead of across a distance. "Pilar, I offer you a better vengeance. One infinitely more satisfying. He's committed treason against England. We have the proof of this."

She looked suspicious.

"The paper from the amulet," Raoul said. "It gives us his name. It's proof of treason. He'll hang."

Pilar shrugged. "They don't hang the son of a baron."

"For treason, they do. Wellington won't let this pass. Even if Wellington weren't the honorable officer he is, some of the men this creeping slug sent to die in ambush belonged to powerful families. For that alone, he'll hang."

"I have vowed to send him to hell."

"You will. Send him there by way of a trial that even the shepherds in the fields will know about. His name will be spat upon. His family will slink away in shame, ruined and bankrupt. The ghosts of the men he sent to death will visit him in his prison cell and walk beside him to his execution."

Pilar considered this.

Raoul said, "If you'll set aside killing him with your own hands, you can destroy him utterly. Don't give him a quick, honorable death. Let him die like the dog he is."

"And if he escapes British justice?"

"Then we'll hunt him down together, you and I, wherever he tries to hide. I'll help you kill him any way you choose. My promise on it."

The barrel of the gun did not waver away from the colonel's chest.

"Pilar," Raoul said. "I do not wish my daughter to commit murder before her thirteenth birthday. It does not reflect well upon me as a father. It's not in the tradition of the Deverneys to send our children to take vengeance when there are still adults to do it."

Pilar turned toward him, fiercely, suddenly. It simplified matters that she'd taken her finger off the trigger and pointed the muzzle to the ground. "I am not your daughter."

"You are."

It was Peter who faced Raoul from under the great flopping brim of his hat, and also Pilar. Whichever one she might be, she was heartbreakingly young. Her voice was unsteady. "I am your wife's bastard. You said so."

"I was wrong," Raoul said.

After a while he continued, "A man makes huge mistakes sometimes. This was mine. Enough mistake for a lifetime."

She didn't answer. When he reached his hand out slowly for the gun, she didn't back away. She let him gently take it from her and put it up on the box of the Carlington coach, out of the way. Then he stood squarely before her, shutting Colonel Carlington out of sight and out of their attention.

Slowly, emphatically, Raoul said, "Pilar, you are Deverney, mind and spirit. You act as a Deverney does. You have the Deverney courage. I should have seen it at once, whatever disguise you wore. I ask your forgiveness for what has gone before."

Pilar was very still, as if the slightest movement would break this moment. As if the world were glass.

"Will you be my daughter?" Raoul offered his open hand to her. "I'm proud of you beyond words. I will be honored to care for you and protect you as a father does."

Pilar blinked a few times. "You never came. In all those years when I needed you, you never came for me."

"I'm here now. I will be here in the future."

Pilar had become a little acquainted with him in the past days. The dozen simple words seemed to convince her more than a long speech and six or seven promises would have. She slid a leather cord with the amulet out from under her coat and lifted it to go over her head. "I said I would return this to you when I was finished with the vow to—"

"Keep it." Raoul took the amulet in his hand and looked down at it. "It's been worn by the Deverney heir for many years. We'll let it pass in the female line for a while. It's made a choice."

"I am a Deverney," she said slowly.

"You are Pilar Deverney, latest in a long line of Deverneys. My daughter. You will add luster to the reputation of our house. Never doubt it."

Pilar took the amulet back and for an instant her fingers closed around Raoul's. The significance of the moment rang like a bell.

"We've been a colorful collection down through the years," Raoul said. "I'll tell you the stories. You have a lot to catch up on." The colonel had been providing an annoying background noise, trying to get past Papa toward Carlington House where he would—she didn't know what—hide in his study? He was going to be a difficulty and an embarrassment to everybody. There'd be more treason and murder to uncover before this was done. Did the son of a baron get sent to the Tower or to Newgate to keep O'Grady company? She'd never thought much about it.

"The child's a lunatic," the colonel barked. "Dressed like that, of course she's mad. You can't believe anything she says. The Spanish woman was mad too. Nothing to do with me." He didn't meet anybody's eyes. "I have important people to talk to. I have to go. I—"

Gunshot cracked. Very close. She ducked and spun around. Nothing out of place. Raoul snapped Pilar against his chest and looked for the shooter's direction. Papa and Hawker didn't move at all.

The deafening noise carved a silence around it. The colonel stopped in mid-harangue. He had not yet fallen, but he was dead. He touched the jagged red tear in the middle of his chest, looked confused, and crumpled to the ground.

Into the silence the coachman said, "Oh damn."

Hawker muttered distinctly, "Another corpse. What is it about today?"

Robin backed away from the colonel's body, the emptied gun slowly lowering in his hold. Softly, clumsily, he sank to the curb. He laid the gun down carefully next to him. He put his head in his hands. Every time he lifted his head he saw the colonel sprawled out on the pavement and looked sick.

Raoul turned Pilar so she wasn't looking at the body and began talking to her, quickly, in a low voice. ". . . as dead as anyone could wish. And by the hand of his nephew. It is fitting."

She could count the seconds before housemaids would come

running out to take part in this event. Daylight murder was usually well attended. She walked to put a hand on Raoul's shoulder and on Pilar's. She said, "We must leave. Pilar, you should not become part of this. Do you want to see his body? The colonel's body? Or I can take you away from this altogether."

"I will look at him," Pilar said in a small voice, very stiff and determined.

Raoul put his arm around Pilar and took her to view her vengeance. The two of them contemplated this outcome, side by side, becoming father and daughter.

In architectural crannies up and down the street the sound of birds started again. Hawker and Papa stood over the body, heads together, conferring on technical details. Then Hawker glanced up at the Carlington coachman. He said, "You're . . . ?"

"Jeffers, sir."

"Did you see anything?"

That was when Jeffers exhibited the sense of wily self-preservation that is the birthright of every freeborn Englishman. "Not a thing, sir."

"Excellent. You keep doing that. In case anyone asks, Colonel Carlington was putting the coach pistol into the coach before his journey. It went off and shot him straight through the heart."

"That it did. A turrible h'accident, sir. Very sad."

"Very."

In his place on the curb Robin had begun speaking in a random, disjointed way. She wasn't speaking to her or answering a question. It was only words coming out. "I had no choice. He would have destroyed us all. He wouldn't leave England. He would have gone to trial and lied and everything would have come out." Robin's mouth twisted in a sort of smile. "At least he doesn't have to go live among foreigners. He would have hated that."

It seemed a suitable epitaph for Colonel Carlington.

Hawker left the colonel's body in Papa's charge and joined them. He knelt in the street so his eyes were level with Robin's. "The colonel was a fool to come after Séverine. Why did he do that, by the way?"

"She knew about the amulet." Robin's eyes shifted. Pilar was wearing the Deverney heirloom. "Ugly thing, isn't it?"

"It is," Hawker agreed.

"That's the heart of it all. My uncle was a fool. And O'Grady was a lumpish, violent fool."

"Tell me about it." Hawker sat more comfortably.

"You know about the treason," Robin said dully.

"Oh, yes."

"I thought you did. You wouldn't be here if you didn't know everything."

"We try."

Servants were dribbling back out of the house into the street to gather around the colonel's dead body, making a great deal of noise and waiting for somebody to give orders. Papa obliged. He told them to stand back and keep out of everybody's way.

"O'Grady was the colonel's sergeant in Spain? Right?" Hawker sounded only mildly curious.

"It was O'Grady from the beginning. He found the French spies. He used the amulet to carry the location of the next arms shipment to the French and to carry the payment back. This is his fault."

"It does sound like that. Then he misplaced the amulet. How?" Hawker prompted.

"He got his pocket picked. Knowing what I do of O'Grady, it was probably in a brothel. That was when my uncle realized the amulet could be traced to him."

"That's when my Sévie gets involved. Between a pickpocket and a brothel. Here. Use this." Hawker shook out a handkerchief and gave it to Robin. Tiny specks of blood had hit Robin's hand from when he fired.

Robin wiped the red speckling off with a sort of blank distaste, as if he couldn't imagine how it got there. "One person knew. It was 'your Sévie,' as you call her. She must have been very young. She was working for Military Intelligence in Spain. She saw the amulet in some army camp and sent it to the quartermaster. To my uncle. She was the only person who could tie the amulet to him."

She didn't want to interrupt Hawker when he was getting

information out of Robin, but that was wrong. "A dozen men were there that night. They saw better than I did."

"I think they're dead." Robin wiped his hands again on the linen square and let it drop to the cobbles. "I think my uncle sent them as guards with convoys that were ambushed. I suppose you could say he murdered them."

"I'd call it that," Hawker murmured. "The army takes a dim view of that sort of thing."

She faced a scene in the street with a sprawled, bloody figure in the foreground. Years of war and the casual violence of the rookeries had not dulled the edge of her dislike of such things. But that man, that colonel who lived in this expensive mansion and wanted for nothing, had killed so many men. So coldly. *It's a just ending. More merciful than he deserves.*

Robin plodded painfully on. "My uncle didn't find his woman spy for years. When he finally found out who she was, the war was long over. And the amulet had never turned up. Gone forever, he thought. He didn't go after her."

"A lucky escape for Séverine," Hawker said.

None of her unfinished business from Spain had come hunting her with guns. She should be grateful, she supposed.

Pilar, having looked well and long at the colonel's dead body, came to listen to what the living Carlington had to say. Sometimes she murmured a word to Raoul. The overlarge boys' clothing she wore hung in folds around her like some ceremonial costume. It was because she stood very straight.

Robin didn't pick up Hawker's handkerchief from the ground. He hunted one out of a pocket in his coat. "Then, about six months ago, that Spanish whore found him." His hands trembled when he wiped his nose. "And blackmailed him."

"My mother," Pilar murmured dangerously.

Hawker said, "The colonel and O'Grady killed Sanchia Deverney?"

"They went there to talk to her. Just talk. I don't know how she died. An accident. I don't know." Robin licked his lips. "I didn't know about any of this."

"You lie," Pilar said.

"Comprehensively," Hawker said. "But he wasn't there when they did it. Think about his voice. Did you hear him?"

Reluctantly, "No."

"Then we must remove that from the list of charges."

A shrug from Pilar. "As you say."

"They sent me to Séverine."

The *they* he spoke of must be the Carlington family. Robin was not the only one involved in this.

Robin spoke without any animation in his voice. He still hadn't looked at her. "They told me to get you out of England. 'Marry her,' they said. 'She's rich. Take her and go live on the Continent.' They said, 'If that doesn't work, ruin her and she'll leave on her own.' We both know what came of that."

Raoul looked like a man pondering carefully nuanced reprisals.

Hawker did, too, though he was less obvious about it. "As you have discovered, all the king's horses and all the king's men cannot make Sévie do what she doesn't wish to. Tell me about Wellington."

"I didn't know what they were planning. I had nothing to do with it."

Hawker said, "Wellington's studying army transport records from the Peninsula. He's going to expose some fools."

"Somebody wanted Sévie dead last night," Raoul said. "Is that something else you had nothing to do with?"

"None of this is my fault. I did what I could. I warned her." Robin wiped his mouth with the back of his hand. "O'Grady made a bomb. He was going to leave it in her office.

"I poured out most of the gunpowder and packed it with flour. I figured it'd scare you out of London." Abruptly, Robin ran out of things to say. He lowered his head into his hands and hunched up tight.

PAPA had already left, on his way to give the newspapers the information they needed and deserved. Hawker grabbed the nearest of the milling servants, who turned out to be the butler. "You. Yes, you." Hawker snapped his fingers. "Look at me. That's right. Now, I'm leaving. This is your problem. Get the body off the street. Send to the magistrate and tell him the colonel shot himself accidentally as he was getting into the carriage.

And take that"—he indicated Robin, who was rocking himself back and forth—"inside and put him to bed. Don't let him talk to anybody. Don't let the magistrate question him. He's taken some strange notions into his head about this accident. Find the baron and tell him to be quiet too. That's it. You understand?"

She walked off with Hawker, leaving the butler doing none of those sensible things but just standing and staring around.

Hawker said, "This ties everything up nicely. I like that."

"I'm fond of neat endings," she said, "though not of dead men on the pavement."

"I don't know what it is about you, Sévie. Kingdoms have changed hands with less bloodshed than I'm encountering lately."

She resisted an impulse to say, *None of this was my fault*, since she'd heard that rather too often lately. So she just said, "I've accomplished more or less what I set out to do, so my investigation is closed. To lessen the chance of further bloodshed, I will depart."

"Excellent. Take your jewel thief and his intrepid daughter with you. I will spend the rest of the day explaining events to Wellington and Liverpool, trying very hard not to incriminate anyone I don't want to. I'll see you when I can."

He walked off toward Whitehall. She was pretty sure he was whistling by the time he reached the corner.

Pilar and Raoul were speaking carefully to one another beside the coach. She put Pilar up on the box with Fletcher, who would doubtless entertain her with gentle conversation about bomb making.

She climbed inside the coach with Raoul.

Forty-seven

SHE SETTLED INTO THE COACH, UNDER THE ARM
Raoul had waiting for her and tight against his side. He didn't
seem feverish, just very tired. He'd do well enough once she
got him to bed and climbed in next to him. They'd be naked
and she'd know immediately if he developed a fever or started
bleeding again.

She had taken her place on his right side so she wouldn't
hurt him. Did most people keep track of their lover's wounds
so they didn't knock into them by accident? Was it only spies?

The wives of acrobats would be wary. The wives of soldiers. Women who were married to criminals. Raoul had been
a soldier of a sort and he was a criminal. Perhaps he had also
been an acrobat. She had a feeling he had done a number of
things he had not yet been open about.

"Where are we going?" Raoul didn't seem particularly
concerned. He wasn't even watching the houses outside the
window to see where they were going. She could have been
kidnapping him to Siberia for all he knew.

"To my office. To my bed."

"That's good." Raoul pulled her in close and they kissed for a while. She lay in the crook of his elbow and he was in no hurry at all. He was scratchy with beard, but that was also something she liked. At last he said, "What about Pilar?"

"She can sleep in her usual place for a while. It's not elegant but it's not horrible, either. If you want to find someone niffy-naffy about sleeping arrangements, don't ask those who spied in Spain in wartime."

"I won't."

He tasted of the truly excellent tea she served in her office. It came through Russia and was sent to her by a good friend. She sucked it off his lips and imagined a future where she would be able to do this regularly. She said, "I'll take Pilar to buy clothes tomorrow. If you will be a father, you must accustom yourself to spending large sums on clothing."

"I am accustomed," he said dryly.

"Clothing that is actually delivered."

"Ah. That." And in a while he added, "I have no idea what to do with a young daughter. With any kind of daughter." It was not a complaint. It was more the voice of a man beginning an interesting project.

"Is she yours?"

"Yes." That came back instantly. "I say she is. I decree it, and I'm the one who can." He spoke softly and swiftly. Then, more slowly, "She might be. Sanchia could have lied about the date of Pilar's birth for any of a dozen reasons, including simple malice." He lined up words, one by one, and looked them over carefully before he said them. "And it doesn't matter. You've been right all along, Sévie. I won't let an accident of blood keep me from claiming that remarkable child." He'd relaxed. The choice was made and spoken. It was binding so far as a man like Raoul was concerned. "She's mine. Now I have to figure out what to do with her."

"Ask her," she said. "I imagine she has opinions."

"I hope they don't include killing people. Or at least, not many people." He thought for a while. "Do you suppose she'd like to learn to make wine?"

"It's possible."

"Or investigate crimes in London. That would combine shooting people with the delicacy and social poise a father wants to see in his daughter."

"I find it rewarding."

He'd closed his eyes in a peaceful fashion. He simply held her. He wasn't going to sleep because he was greatly aroused.

He was, she thought, circling around a topic. Approaching slowly.

He said, "Will you marry me?"

She'd thought about this, of course. "I don't know. Perhaps I will just live with you forever."

Raoul leaned back, being sleepy and at ease. She did not believe him in the least. She looked out at London. She had no idea what to say to him.

"Marriage is a great uncertainty," he said. "I could fall down the steps one night, coming home drunk, though I'm really remarkably hard to kill. Determined people have tried, and I once slipped in a very large bathtub in a whorehouse in Munich. I would have drowned if the madame hadn't noticed I was missing."

"I suspect you hadn't paid the reckoning yet."

"I had not, now that you mention it. Or I might betray you with a tavern wench. You don't know me very well. I might have an unseemly taste for tavern wenches."

"You would not exercise it twice," she said.

"I see. One problem solved, then. Are you afraid I'll bore you with rambling, pointless stories? I suspect I could be discouraged from the practice."

"I like your stories." She would never be bored with him.

"Do you think I'll try to bully you?" He'd roused himself sufficiently to turn on the seat and face her directly. "If you can keep your father and your brother-in-law and God knows how many other men from telling you what to do, you can keep me in line too."

The image was ridiculous. She had to smile.

She said, "Yes."

"Yes what?"

"Yes. I will marry you."

He breathed out, as if he'd been worried about that. Foolishness on his part. He was very much exactly what she wanted. She would devote time and thought to making him realize it.

He was wounded and they were in a coach in the middle of London with a twelve-year-old a few feet away. They could not remove their clothing. They could kiss, though, and she started right on the tip of his nose. Then she went along the curve of each eyebrow. His were rather straight but that was not a problem. She was not surprised to be grabbed strongly and pulled toward him to kiss, mouth to mouth, deeply.

They ended, breathing raggedly at one another. Her eyes were closed and she very much wanted him. She calculated how long it would be before they could get into bed.

She was inelegantly sprawled upon him so she threw herself back onto the seat cushions and became respectable again, in case anyone happened to be looking into the carriage. They sat, side by side, holding hands. He said, "I never did finish my story about the hero who went on a quest for his family's lost treasure."

"I believe you didn't."

"Our hero had many adventures, dashing escapades, and daring escapes. But one day when he was somewhat older and wiser he met a heroine who set upon quests of a different sort. She saved maidens from ogres and rescued poor miserable fellows from being hanged. Our hero introduced himself and gave her his knife as a token of esteem."

"It was a kitchen knife you stole downstairs. Also, you broke in."

"I was maladroit. In any case, our hero decided this woman was more important than any number of family heirlooms. He settled down to become a somewhat dull merchant. Perhaps he developed a potbelly. And soon everyone wondered what she saw in such a bore."

"But he didn't get hanged as a thief, which is a good thing."

"Jewel theft is all very well in its way, but it's not a good example to set a growing girl."

"Still, it's a valuable talent. I'll find places for you to break into when you're not importing wine. I'm never short of useful work."

"Sounds intriguing," he said, and kissed her some more.

Joanna Bourne is the award-winning author of *Rogue Spy*, *The Black Hawk*, *The Forbidden Rose*, *My Lord and Spymaster*, and *The Spymaster's Lady*. She has always loved reading and writing romance. She's drawn to Revolutionary and Napoleonic France and Regency England because, as she puts it, "It was a time of love and sacrifice, daring deeds, clashing ideals, and really cool clothing." She's lived in seven different countries, including England and France, the settings of the Spymaster series.

Joanna lives on a mountaintop in the Appalachians with her family, a peculiar cat, and an old brown country dog. Visit her online at joannabourne.com and twitter.com/jobourne.

Ready to find
your next great read?

Let us help.

Visit prh.com/nextread

Penguin
Random
House